AFTER EGYPT:
ISADORA DUNCAN
& MARY CASSATT

OTHER BOOKS BY MILLICENT DILLON

FICTION

Baby Perpetua and Other Stories
The One in the Back Is Medea (novel)

NONFICTION

A Little Original Sin: The Life and Work of Jane Bowles
Out in the World: The Selected Letters of Jane Bowles
(editor)

MILLICENT DILLON

AFTER EGYPT:
ISADORA DUNCAN
& MARY CASSATT

A WILLIAM ABRAHAMS BOOK
DUTTON   NEW YORK

DUTTON
Published by the Penguin Group
Penguin Books USA Inc., 375 Hudson Street,
New York, New York, 10014, U.S.A.
Penguin Books Ltd, 27 Wrights Lane,
London W8 5TZ, England
Penguin Books Australia Ltd, Ringwood,
Victoria, Australia
Penguin Books Canada Ltd, 2801 John Street,
Markham, Ontario, Canada L3R 1B4
Penguin Books (N.Z.) Ltd, 182–190 Wairau Road,
Auckland 10, New Zealand

Penguin Books Ltd, Registered Offices:
Harmondsworth, Middlesex, England

First published by Dutton, an imprint of Penguin Books USA Inc.
Published simultaneously in Canada by Fitzhenry & Whiteside, Limited.

First printing, May, 1990
1 3 5 7 9 10 8 6 4 2

Library of Congress Cataloging-in-Publication Data
Dillon, Millicent.
After Egypt: Isadora Duncan and Mary Cassatt / Millicent Dillon.
— 1st ed.
p. cm.
"A William Abrahams book."
Includes bibliographical references.
ISBN 0-525-24846-3
1. Duncan, Isadora, 1877–1927. 2. Dancers—United States—
Biography. 3. Cassatt, Mary, 1844–1926. 4. Painters—United
States—Biography. I. Title.
GV1785.D8D46 1990
792.8'092—dc20
[B]   89-23637
CIP

Printed in the United States of America
Set in Century Expanded
Designed by Steven N. Stathakis

for Billy

What the plant-world demonstrates so beautifully—that it makes no secret of its secrets as though knowing they would always be safeguarded—is exactly what I felt when standing before the sculptures in Egypt, and what I have always felt since then with all things Egyptian: this laying bare of the secret that is a secret through and through, on every spot, so that there is no need to hide it.

—RAINER MARIA RILKE

CONTENTS

Illustrations follow pages 20, 84, 180, and 340.

INTRODUCTION

Biography as we have come to know it is the telling of a life in time. He or she was born, grew up, got married or didn't get married, became middle-aged . . . Sometimes the larger sequences are called upon, sometimes the smaller details of daily life. But all eventually ends at the expected ending in time—death.

At the end of this telling or even in the midst of it a small disappointment nags at the reader as well as the writer. It seems accumulation of fact is insufficient. More than that, the more we find out—as readers and writers—the less we seem to know. We are carried forward relentlessly through fact, into fact, by fact, even as we tamp down the disappointment, searching all the more obsessively for that information which, when ringed around with explanation, will let us know—what?—about these lives, these beings: who they were, what they were, why they were, how they were, if they were like us or different. We hope to know, we think we are coming to know, but something has evaded us in this way of telling of a life in time, as if we've lost access to the life in the telling.

This book will attempt a telling of another kind. Awkwardly, one step forward and two steps back, it will go in pursuit of a different kind of knowing, to search for explanation that proves the limitation of explanation, to break sequence to establish another kind of sequence through odd juxtapositions, abrupt branching out and obsessive tunneling, through heavy-handed intrusion and even purposeful turning away.

Fact is not discarded but is called upon for effect. It is not fact that thwarts our understanding in the ordinary way of telling. It is fact seen as fixed, placed in time as if into a jigsaw puzzle. There, the biographer thinks, placing it, now I know that, really know it, can take a breather, and then go on in sureness. Fact, once placed, seems to place us, the writer as well as the reader. And if there is a rigidity in the end result, well, at least it is preferable to the relentless motion of uncertainty.

The oppressiveness of biography arises out of this rigid placement of fact in time that calls itself the rendering of a life, with a proper beginning and middle and end, as if life were a story lived on a line, in line, in a line in time. But time's ordering of life is only one of mind's ways; it is rarely feeling's way.

The telling of this book is not "in line." It is continually being broken, fomented, and revised. It returns again and again, by allusion, by inference, by echoing, to first episode, first incident. Yet it also holds to the recognition of that which is steady and ongoing, unchanging within an individual life, no matter what time indicates, whether we reside in a body just beginning to move and to see, or in an aged body, relinquishing movement and last sight.

My model is memory, which in its vagaries relies upon multiple tellings and single tellings, old stories as they evoke newer stories, repetitions that make out of many events one event, even, especially, the most ordinary daily narrative as it circles about itself and comes back again to starting episode.

It seems clear that each starting point, each initial episode used in the telling of a life, brings about a different ordering of that life. Episode is more than a beginning. It is a locus, it is itself a black hole, into which everything before and after can be swallowed up, and then, exploding outward again, falls into what follows, with a new meaning of *after*.

This, then, is a story called *After Egypt*. And the word

after, relying on the dictionary definition, means "moving toward from behind," "flowing in the course of," "in search of," "in pursuit of." It also means "in relation to" as well as "later in time than."

I believe, however, that beginning with an event creates sequence. It is the very notion of story.

This is a story of two women who went to Egypt, two women who never met. It alternates between them, places them side by side; it layers the two lives. Out of this telling of two stories that mesh together, a third seems to appear, found as much in the shape of its telling as in what is told.

PART
ONE

On New Year's Day 1911 Mary Cassatt came to Egypt. With her brother Gardner and his wife and children, she landed in Alexandria at four in the afternoon. At nine-thirty in the evening they reached Cairo, where they boarded a luxurious dahabeah, a houseboat that would take them up the Nile.

All this is told by the sixty-six-year-old painter as she sits aboard the dahabeah on the fourth of January, writing a letter to her friend Louisine Havemeyer in which precise fact follows upon opinion, which follows upon fact. They have been taken to the Pyramids, then to see the tree the Virgin Mary rested under when she fled to Egypt, then to drink from the well the Virgin drank from. As for Egypt itself: "My impressions here are very mixed."

Among all the sentences that pile upon each other fast, of questions about Louisine's family, of statements about art matters, of opinions on the buying of certain art objects, of comments on acquaintances and on a "Psychic lot" of Americans she came across in Constantinople, she writes one that shows that here at the beginning she is thinking of the end of the journey, as if what is before her is something to be gotten through. "I really must be back in the beginning of March."

To be back—back in Paris where she has lived for thirty-three years, where she has established a daily life and a career, where she lives alone and works, propelled by a Puritan ethic that repudiates neither comfort nor decoration.

She has not really wanted to come here. In fact, she has looked forward to the journey with fear and trembling. Any sea journey frightens her, any sea, even the Mediterranean—so ill does it make her. But she has risked it this time for the chance to be with her brother, she and he the last surviving members of their first (and her only) family.

They traveled up the Nile in the dahabeah called *Hope.* On January 17 she writes to Louisine from a point above Luxor, on the way to Aswan. Their passage has been delayed as her brother has been ill with a case of hives so severe two doctors were brought on board, one an Egyptian, the other a visiting American. But now once again the dahabeah is moving.

"We are distinctly disappointed in the climate—to tell the truth thus far in what we have seen. This morning the temple of Luxor, fine of course, last night Karnak by moonlight. I was so provoked at seeing the ruins first by moonlight . . ."

With asperity she goes on: "We know Egyptian art without coming here and the Temples can teach us little more."

Still, not one to fall easily into complaint, she pulls herself up. "We are very comfortable and very well in this boat . . ." Yet she must add another's words, if not her own, about the enforced containment of life on the boat: "My sister in law declared that were she forced to spend three months on the Nile she would grow melancholy."

It is as if each sentence in this plain awkward prose carries its contradiction in the one following. Thoughts of health and of getting better alternate with thoughts of the grave illness of a friend. Saying that she is feeling well is almost immediately followed by ruefulness that she has not grown fatter, as she had hoped. "I am beginning to dry up, as the Empress Eugénie says she is, only she is 85."

Once more she refers to the end of the trip and her fear of the return voyage: "I *do* dread the sea journey, it pulls me down dreadfully." But she resists being pulled down, she fights against the sense of being contained, of making little headway, she who dashed off boldly to Europe as a young girl to seek what mattered to her. And she fights against containment of the young. So one day, as they are cruising on the Nile, the dahabeah strikes a sandbar. Her two nieces, Ellen Mary and Eugenia, want to jump in for a swim but their parents refuse. "Nonsense," says Mary. "There are no crocodiles here. Let them."

2

Isadora Duncan came to Egypt in 1910.

In a party that included her lover Paris Singer, Deirdre, her daughter by Gordon Craig, her brother Augustin and his daughter Temple, she traveled on Singer's yacht, *Isis*—renamed for her—and reached Alexandria in early January.

On January 25 she writes to a friend from the dahabeah *Horus,* which has taken them up the Nile to the Luxor Winter Palace: "It is all so Heavenly and Wonderful . . . It is beyond any thing that I have ever dreampt or read or imagined—We have sailed up the Nile as far as Aswan seeing all the wonders and Glories on the way and now we return to Cairo . . . I feel so lazy but in this boat the days and the banks of the Nile glide by like a dream—and the great Temples and Monuments also seem like the conjuring of some Geni and not at all real . . . this experience is too lovely to end, this year—we will surely come again."

In a similarly ornate prose, in which everything she sees is translated into its transcendent meaning, Isadora relates the story of this journey in her autobiography, *My Life.* "As the dahabeah voyages slowly up the Nile the soul travels back a thousand—two thousand—five thousand years; back, through the mists of the Past to the Gates of Eternity.

"How calm and beautiful was this voyage to me at that time . . . Temples that spoke of Ancient Kings of Egypt penetrating through the golden desert sands, down to the profound mysteries of the Tombs of the Pharaohs . . . The purple sunrise, the scarlet sunset, the golden sands of the desert . . . The sunny days spent in the courtyard of a temple dreaming of the life of the Pharaohs—dreaming of my baby to come . . ."

"I am called Isadora," she had written earlier. "That means Child of Isis—or *Gift* of Isis. Isis is the Goddess of Birth—Isis will always protect me because I have her name."

But here in the land of Isis, the thirty-two-year-old dancer, pregnant with Singer's child, did not find the protection of the goddess absolute: "It would have been a dream of happiness— it almost was—if it had not been for that same monster Neurasthenia, which appeared from time to time like a black hand covering the sun . . .

"The little life within me seemed to vaguely surmise this journey to the land of darkness and death. One moonlight night, in the Temple of Denderah, it seemed to me that all the eyes in the battered faces of the Goddess Hathor, the Egyptian Aphrodite . . . were turned toward my unborn child."

Yet in her telling she moves away from darkness to the light, to watching, not being watched. "The dahabeah moved slowly to the singing of the sailors as their bronzed bodies rose and fell with the oars, we watching idly and enjoying all this as spectators."

She shapes her story as she shapes her dances, to end with a willed affirmation that resists being pulled down into darkness. At Wadi Halfa, "the men of the party left to go on to Khartoum, and I remained alone on the dahabeah with Deirdre and spent the most peaceful time of my life, for two weeks, in that marvellous country where worry and trouble seem quite futile. Our boat seemed to be rocked by the rhythm of the ages."

3

On January 20, from Aswan aboard the dahabeah *Hope*, Mary Cassatt wrote to Louisine Havemeyer: "We are glad to be here and hope now really to see something. Today was my first impression [of] Kom Ombo it is very Greek but of course heavier, still it does not bowl you over like the Concordia. Tomorrow the Tombs, and Philae on Sunday. We are hesitating about going above to see the rock Temple. We have so much to see we may give that up—Life on the boat is something like prison life, when we tie up we rush out for a walk even when it is dark . . . My brother isn't very well, only an outward affliction, *hives*, but not pleasant. The weather's cold and grey, and very unusual on the Nile . . ."

On January 28, from Luxor, she writes in great agitation about a visit she has just made to a Mr. D. and a Mrs. A. "Oh Louie would that I could talk to you . . . My dear never did I see such a bare faced situation, that old woman fairly boasts of it. Do you know the story? I hear no one at Newport visits them, that woman pirate has made the wife walk the plank and brazenfacedly takes her place. She looks seventy-five, older than he does . . . there is no life in her and such cold eyes, and taking me to see the boat and showing me her luxurious room at the end, and that she is the *mistress* in every sense of the word, such an unnecessary proceeding. I never could have dreamed of such a situation and he telling he has given her $100,000 string of pearls . . . Oh the dignity of work, give me the chance of earning my own living, five francs a day and self respect. If there had been a great love, and she entirely disinterested one might have felt a certain pity, even if they had gone off the track, not for jewels and dresses and all that at that age, and she could not have been young when it began. Oh those women pirates . . .

"Well enough of them"—she calms herself—"I am writing to you with fingers covered with old Egyptian rings; one terra cotta and gold, I cannot resist these things and cloudy amethyst necklaces . . ."

But soon in a note of worry with a frantic edge, as if it was the shadow behind the earlier outburst, come the words "It is very cold and my brother again ill, he . . . is *so* imprudent, changes his underclothes everyday it seems to me, and in this changeable climate it is so much better to stick to one kind of underclothing. We have had no luck here with this cold wind. Tomorrow we go to the tombs . . . but my brother is in bed and we have just had a doctor the fourth since we started!"

On February 11 her letter to Louisine circles about the subject of death, even as she keeps pulling back away from it. She tells of having heard of the death of her friend in Paris, Moise Dreyfus. Of his widow she writes, "Now she is all alone no child, what a misery life is; as long as one can stir up ideas as the French say it has an interest and when one can work. I do pity those who cannot work any more, may I go before I must sit with idle hands."

Without transition she hurries on: "No my dear we are not enjoying ourselves, my brother saw his *sixth* Doctor today! . . . he has Nile fever very slight but he is miserable, and in bed most of the time. Such a day yesterday! We could not move, had to anchor, blowing the river into white caps, *cold! oh how cold,* and grey with a white sun, and such a flying of sand like a mist . . . we have a tug to take us down to Cairo and may go direct without stopping at Beni Hasan . . . I am thoroughly disappointed the Tombs don't seem so very interesting to me. I am looking for Art not Archaeology . . ."

A doctor has told them of an American who fell getting on a donkey and ended up in an Egyptian hospital. He is "delirious and will probably die! . . . Fancy dying in this strange place. Why do people so love to wander? I think the civilized parts of the world will suffice for me in future."

She rushes on, no transition, no new paragraph, to the thought of that in life which can stave off misery and darkness: "I am pining to get back to work, there are things I am dying to do, it will be so good to do them if I can . . ."

On a more even keel now, she falls into talk of acquaintances and of her pleasure at the thought of Louisine's new grandchild. "I am glad you have the baby in the house you must enjoy that. I like having my young ones here, and they are such natural and really good children, never a complaint yet it isn't particularly gay for them. I wish we were all once more in Europe."

On March 8 she writes to Louisine from Cairo that she has not "had the heart" to write earlier, so worried has she been about her brother. But now she hopes that all will be well and that he and his family can sail for Marseilles in a week, though "I hardly dare write it. I leave tomorrow for Naples and Paris direct. I stayed, though I was entirely useless, till I was sure that he was convalescent. To me it has been a *dreadful* time. I haven't slept *one* night properly and some nights I have not closed my eyes—Just think—we saw *seven* doctors along the Nile, not one had the sense to tell us to stop and go back to Cairo though I begged my brother to and follow a treatment! . . . Poor Jennie [Gardner's wife] I do pity her she is very devoted but believes in doctors. I don't—I feel so utterly helpless and I am, yet I fought for my mother's life, and I did nurse my sister, I feel so done for—This modern way of sending for a nurse to make a poultice humiliates me—Really Louie if I look at the women here we do seem useless creatures."

And then, without preparation, without warning, words that reveal a recognition that has been forced upon her of a power here she did not foresee and did not want to see: "Then this country, its Art how overpowering, fancy going back to babies and women, to paint. I am glad Mr. Stillman [American banker James Stillman] will pose for me, he wanted me to paint him last year. I did not feel I was equal to a man's portrait but now I must to work off if possible this overpowering impression—I am crushed by the strength of this art—I wonder though if ever I can paint again . . ."

4.

After Egypt, Isadora and Singer went to the south of France, to Beaulieu, where he rented a luxurious villa, and where Isadora awaited the birth of her child. In *My Life* Isadora says that there Singer was "obsessed by an abnormal restlessness," which led him to rush off to Cap Ferrat to buy land or to continually make trips to Paris. She says of herself that she "remained calmly in the garden by the blue sea, pondering on the strange difference which divides life from Art, and often wondering if a woman can ever really be an artist, since Art is a hard task-master who demands everything, whereas a woman who loves gives up everything to life."

Following Patrick's birth on the first of May, she and Singer and the children moved to the Trianon Palace Hotel in Versailles, where she lived an increasingly luxurious and social existence. In July Singer became ill in England, apparently having suffered a small stroke. Isadora joined him there and together they went to Singer's estate, Paignton, in Devon. There she agreed to his suggestion that they try out a daily existence together, and if she liked it, she and Singer would marry. (Singer, though separated from his wife, was still married at the time.)

It was at Paignton that an equally "abnormal" restlessness took hold of Isadora. Describing the atmosphere there, she takes on the voice of a childlike observer, innocently commenting on the dreary climate and the dull daily routine. "The English people do not seem to mind it at all. They rise and have an early breakfast of eggs and bacon, and ham and kidneys and porridge. Then they don mackintoshes and go forth into the humid country till lunch, when they eat many courses, ending with Devonshire cream.

"From lunch to five o'clock they are supposed to be busy with their correspondence, though I believe they really go to sleep. At five they descend to their tea, consisting of many kinds of cakes and bread and butter and tea and jam. After that they make a pretence of playing bridge, until it is time to proceed to the really important business of the day—dressing for dinner . . ."

Her tone shifts to ridicule as she speaks of Singer's behavior in response to his stroke (although here Isadora casts doubt upon the nature of his illness by using the words "what he always considered to have been a stroke"). Once she had been "placed" in a room far away from Singer by the attendant physician, and told not to disturb him, he spent "hours every day in his room on a diet of rice, macaroni, and water, and every hour the doctor came to take his blood pressure. At certain times L. [Lohengrin was her name for Singer in *My Life*] was led down to a sort of cage which had been brought over from Paris, in which he sat while thousands of volts of electricity were turned on him, and he would sit there looking extremely pathetic and saying:

" 'I hope this will do me good.'

"All this added considerably to my condition of restlessness . . ."

Apparently aware of her dissatisfaction, Singer suggested that she send for her carpets and drapes and set up a studio in the ballroom so that she could work. He also urged her to send for a pianist, to work with her. Soon André Capelet arrived, a musician Isadora had met before, whose physical appearance was totally repugnant to her. "To drown my ennui and dissipate my annoyance, I began to work with X. [Capelet], much as I disliked him, but whenever he played for me I placed a screen around him, saying:

" 'You are so unspeakably offensive to me that I cannot bear to look at you.' "

Within a few days Capelet, who had been so unappealing to her, became the object of her obsessive desire. "How had I not seen it before? His face was perfectly beautiful, and in his eyes there was a smothered flame of genius." Passion seized her and she pursued it and him flagrantly. The expected end occurred. Singer found out about the affair and broke with her.

"This episode proved to me that I certainly was not suited to domestic life . . . ," Isadora writes.

She returned to Paris and in January 1911 performed at the Châtelet Theater. There, for the first time, she presented her two *Dances of the Furies*, choreographed to the music of Gluck's *Orfeo*. (To the ancient Greeks, with whom Isadora frequently identified, the Furies, the Erinyes, were avenging spirits who took retribution on those who violated natural laws. They were also thought of as snake-haired women, who in pursuit of their victims drove them to madness.) These *Dances of the Furies* were a startling departure from Isadora's usual lyrical style. Instead of a constant upward movement in the body, there was a heavy downward movement. Instead of a continual flowing motion, there was recurring sharpness, even percussiveness. These dances have been described as an expression of "tremendous force under constraint." But they can also be seen as a struggle, a split between two aspects of one being, the one acted upon, the other acting, the one moving, the other moved.

In February Isadora went to the United States to perform. While there she appealed to her audiences for help in reestablishing her school and also for money for a "great Amphitheatre, the only democratic form of theatre . . .

"Fine art comes from the Human Spirit and needs no externals. In our School we have no costumes, no ornaments—just the beauty that flows from the inspired human soul, and the body that is its symbol, and if my Art has taught you anything here, I hope it has taught you that."

Her public words were, as always, an expression of her commitment to the "Ideal" in "Art." At the same time, however—and Isadora seems not to have considered it in any way a contradiction—a shift, one could almost say a split, took place in her private life, away from another "Ideal." She had previously thought of "Love" as the merging of genius with genius. Of her love for Gordon Craig, she had felt that "in him I had met the flesh of my flesh, the blood of my blood . . . This was not a young man making love to a girl. This was the meeting of twin souls. The light covering of flesh was so transmuted with ecstasy that earthly passion became a heavenly embrace of white, fiery flame."

But in the United States she found the joys of " 'Pagan Love' . . . now that I had discovered that Love might be a pastime as well as a tragedy, I gave myself to it with pagan innocence. Men seemed so hungry for Beauty, hungry for that love which refreshes and inspires without fear or responsibility. After a performance, in my tunic, with my hair crowned with roses, I was so lovely. Why should not this loveliness be enjoyed? . . . Now it seemed to me more natural to sip champagne and have some charming person tell me how beautiful I was. The divine pagan body, the passionate lips, the clinging arms, the sweet refreshing sleep on the shoulder of some loved one—these were joys which seemed to me both innocent and delightful."

In the spring she returned to Paris and to a reconciliation with Singer, but one that became increasingly volatile.

In a letter to his sister Gertrude in the late spring or early summer of that year, 1911, Leo Stein gave her news about Isadora and Singer. (The Steins had grown up in Oakland, California, as had the Duncans, though their only meeting at that time had been when Leo Stein, as a young student, had studied ballroom dancing with Isadora and her sister Elizabeth. Later, in her early years in Paris, Gertrude Stein had become acquainted with Isadora through her brother Raymond Duncan.)

"Isadora has not danced and is not in Paris. At present she is at Nice and is then going on to Venice. S. [Singer] said that she is thinking of giving up dancing on the stage, that she wants to buy a chateau somewhere out St. Cloud way for 2,000,-000 francs, I believe. S.'s millions, I suppose and after that I don't know what comes . . ."

Leo Stein had fallen in love with Nina Auxias and he mentioned now that Singer was also in love with her. "I know last winter that he was interested in Nina . . . But it was news to me that with Nina he was not interested but madly in love. I saw a couple of his letters—he writes to her every day . . . He can't live except in the light of her eyes. If she will only take him he will have a real inspiration and write the music of the future . . . he longs for her every minute; and if she will only say the word he will break at once with Isadora and come home on the wings of love and the wheels of an express train . . ."

On August 22, 1911, Leo wrote to Gertrude Stein again: "I saw S. who has finished with Isadora—he is looking very badly. Nina is looking very well. Their present plans look to permanence."

But the permanence between Singer and Nina Auxias was only looked toward, never achieved. (Nina Auxias later became Leo Stein's wife.) Singer once again reconciled with Isadora and at the beginning of 1912 they returned to Egypt.

Isadora does not mention her second journey to Egypt in *My Life*. But in 1965 her former pupil and "daughter" Irma published an account of it in her autobiography, *Duncan Dancer*.

She relates that one day soon after the new year, Elizabeth, Isadora's sister, who ran the Duncan school in Germany, rushed with her to Trieste, where they were to meet Paris Singer and Isadora and the rest of the party that was to sail to Alexandria and "the fabled land of the pharaohs." Irma trembled with anticipation at the thought of being in Egypt and of being once again with her idol, Isadora.

This trip was, if anything, even more lavish than the earlier one. Singer had arranged for Isadora's new pianist, Hener Skene, to come with his grand piano, so that he could play Beethoven and Bach for their many guests.

"Between Luxor and Aswan, our most southern stop before turning back, we passed through the narrow gorge of Silsileh, reaching Kom Ombo after dark," writes Irma. "A full moon illuminated the temple, splendidly situated on a bluff directly above the river. It stood so close to the river that the propylaea had been washed away, but the building was protected by a high wall, and was the only ancient edifice erected directly on the banks of the Nile. Its other peculiarity was that

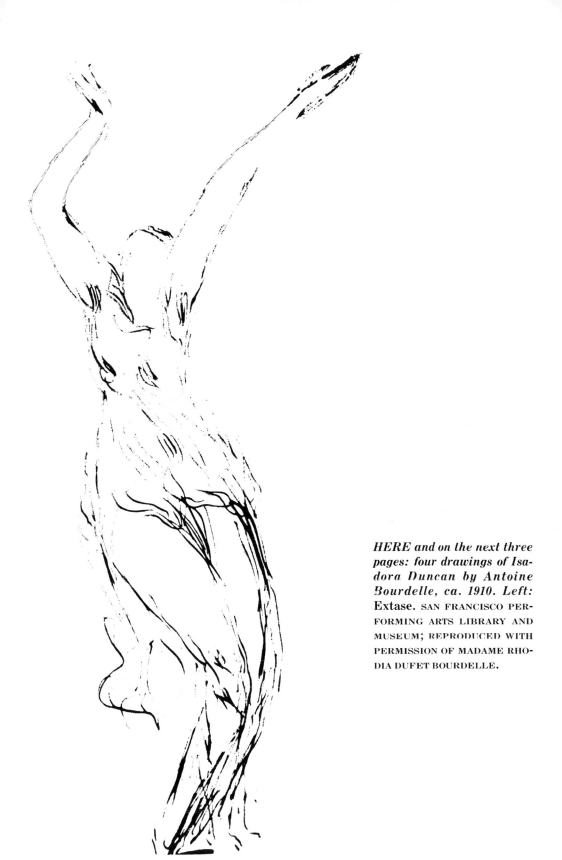

HERE and on the next three pages: four drawings of Isadora Duncan by Antoine Bourdelle, ca. 1910. Left: Extase. SAN FRANCISCO PERFORMING ARTS LIBRARY AND MUSEUM; REPRODUCED WITH PERMISSION OF MADAME RHODIA DUFET BOURDELLE.

Jeu de Voile.

Tempête.

Danse des Scythes.

HERE and on the next three pages: four drawings of Isadora Duncan by Abraham Walkowitz, ca. 1915–1918. PERFORMING ARTS RESEARCH CENTER, THE NEW YORK PUBLIC LIBRARY AT LINCOLN CENTER.

it was dedicated to twin deities—Horus and Sobk—spirits of good and evil."

Isadora requested that Irma dance before the company in the temple. Frightened and uneasy, Irma at first refused, but Elizabeth insisted. " 'Ah, here she is,' I heard Isadora say as I entered the forecourt where the whole party sat on broken columns and other bits of ruins strewn about . . . 'I don't know what to dance,' I murmured sullenly, 'without music and everything . . .'

" 'On such a wonderful moonlight night,' Isadora enthused, 'in this beautiful temple surely inspiration should not be lacking. Dance anything you fancy, whatever comes to mind.' "

Stumbling over the broken masonry and rubble, Irma danced until "my sense of the utter inadequacy of the whole performance struck me dead in my tracks." No one moved or clapped. Slowly Isadora rose from her seat and said, " 'Have you noticed how entirely unrelated her dance movements were to these extraordinary surroundings? She seemed to be completely unaware of them. What she just did consisted of some pretty little dance gestures she has learned—very nice, very light-hearted, but not in the slightest degree in harmony with the almost awesome sense of mystery that pervades this place . . .

" 'Any dance movement executed in a place like this'—and she swept the vast enclosure with a majestic gesture of her right arm—'must be in close rapport with the mystical vibrations these temple ruins generate.' "

Then Isadora herself began to dance. "Adjusting her flowing white shawl, she strode across the court and disappeared into the shadows in the background . . . Presently . . . we saw her emerge from the deep shadows cast by a peristyle of such massive proportions that it dwarfed her white-clad figure. But as soon as she started to move in and out of the tall lotus columns she seemed to grow in stature. The long shadows cast by the columns on the floor formed a symmetrical pattern. And each time she stepped in her stately dance from the shadows into the strip of bright moonlight in between, there was a sudden flash created by her appearance . . ."

5

On March 17, 1911, from her apartment at 10 rue de Marignan in Paris, to which she has just returned, Mary Cassatt writes to Louisine Havemeyer: "All that Egypt has left of me arrived this morning. What an experience. I fought against it but it conquered, it is surely the greatest Art the past has left us. All strength, no room in that first empire for grace, for charm, for children, none, only intellect and strength—how are my feeble hands to ever paint the effect on me. I am so weak now I could not do anything. I am so glad I did not see Greece I don't want to weaken the impression. We had the smoothest crossing to Naples, still I had to stay two days there to recuperate and I did go to the Museum. I wanted to see the Titian, but the sculptures even the Greek did not interest me and as for the Romans, what pretentious poseurs— Going from Rome to Florence I met Nicol in the restaurant of the train, he exclaimed at my appearance. I am sure I have lost twenty pounds. I will say he understood at once and said the impression had been too strong for me. The French do understand what art is . . . I have a cable from Jennie they sail next

Wednesday or Thursday, what our experience there has been I cannot write about, if only all turns out well in the end, but I am afraid my brother has long convalescence before him, and he may not be ever so well again, nor may I, only if I can paint something of what I have learnt, but I doubt it—"

On March 24 she writes again to Louisine. She does not mention "Egypt" and, in fact, will not mention it again except for a few seemingly casual lines in the next two years. The first part of this letter is like many letters Mary wrote to Louisine before her voyage. She speaks of what she knows and has known, has opinions that are opinions she has held before. She has fallen or, rather, is attempting to fall into her daily life.

"I have [received] the photos of the Saint [a statue Mary had arranged for Louisine to buy] and your daughter-in-law and the lovely one of 'wee' Electra and her mother [also Electra]. She certainly is a remarkable baby." She goes on to talk of babies and weddings, then responds to a statement that Louisine has shown the "Saint" to the American painter Cecilia Beaux, of whom Mary has often been critical. "I am glad Miss Beaux liked the Saint but how then can she continue to think so much of Sargent [of whom Mary also disapproved] . . . ?"

Thoughts of illness and death, however, break in once again. "I saw poor dear Mrs. Dreyfus and told her how much you felt for her and she was so much touched and begged me to thank you. She is of course very sad, but if it [her husband's illness] had gone on much longer she would have succumbed, and now there is a chance of her having a few quiet years. Many perhaps, before she is called herself . . .

"If only we could eliminate disease!" she cries out a few lines later, before ending with an anxious note about her brother, who is coming by boat to Paris, where he will recuperate for four weeks before returning to New York. "I wish he was safely in America."

On March 31, from rue de Marignan, she writes Louisine in haste. Her brother arrived three days earlier, seriously ill. "I met them at the station with Dr. Whittman and an ambulance he had two nurses travelling with him and took him to the Crillon where they had reserved rooms, little thinking of his state . . . all I can hope for is that there is a chance . . . The girls are with me, and everything he can take is made here and they are feeding him . . ." She lashes out at those whom she accuses of having mistreated her brother: "They kept or rather the English doctors in Cairo kept him until he was in this state, my dear they are murderers! Here I can do something but I am dreadfully down—"

On April 12 (the intervening correspondence has been lost) Mary sends a cablegram: "Doctors order rest and to be alone so grateful dear Louie come later when I am well love Mary."

(Gardner has died on April 5.)

She is a woman practiced at grieving. In 1882 she lost her sister, Lydia, in 1891 her father, in 1895 her mother, in 1906 her older brother Aleck. And now Gardner, the last one besides herself, was gone.

Alone, after her mother's death, she had cried until she thought she "could never weep again." After a time she had sought hope in spiritualism, in the belief that the dead lived on, that communication with them was still possible. Of F. W. H. Myers's book *Human Personality and Its Survival of Bodily Death,* she wrote in 1903 to Theodate Pope, the friend who had given it to her, "What a book! I simply am overcome." In the evening when she sat alone in her château at Beaufresne, she read the Myers book. "The more I read the more I admire, and the more I hope . . .

"Oh! we must not lose faith, the faith that life is going on though we cannot see it, you may some time have a convincing proof . . . What a consolation for those who have had it."

She attended a number of séances, including one in which she saw a table rise four feet off the floor twice. In a letter of 1909 to Louisine's daughter Electra, she told of hearing of some friends' experiences with spiritualism and finding them "thrilling."

"They think the religion of the Egyptians and Greeks was founded on certain things of this kind and now we are rediscovering them through a scientific road. Oh! You young ones may see things we never dreamed of . . . we are on this planet to learn. I think it very stimulating to believe that here is only one step in our progress."

But, after Egypt, all hope of such communication and such help seemed to have faded. Ill and grieving, something fundamental in her having given way, she sought relief in willed solitude in her apartment in Paris or at Beaufresne, attended only by her servants.

But after all, she was a realist, as she often proclaimed, as her actions show, as her paintings seem to show. If she chose solitude it was not to dwell in the past, but to find her way back to order and to the control of her own life in the present. To leach out through the daily contact with the real the effects of death and the effects of Egypt, now melded together as if they were one.

Those images of Egypt that were such a blow to her must be, if not erased, diminished. At the same time, the images of her lost family must be held to, must not be allowed to vanish. But these latter images exist in a convoluted way, not only through her memory of actual events, but also as the memory of those images that as an artist she herself created. These paintings, these drawings of her mother, her sister, her brothers, her father, have a place and function in memory of another order, arising out of the intense concentration of working hour after hour to catch the pose, the light, the shadow, the form that will illumine the individual life. These memories, images of images, that she herself had created, did they come to rival, did they come to erase, those other remembered images? Did they become one?

6

In 1871, at home in Philadelphia, having been forced to return to the United States from France because of the Franco-Prussian War, Mary Cassatt began to work on a portrait. "I commenced a study of our mulatto servant girl but just as I had the mask painted in she gave warning [notice]," she wrote to a friend.

Discovered years later by an art-student lodger in the attic of Mrs. Currey, the former servant, the unfinished canvas is a double image. Beneath the initial portrait, the head and powerful shoulders of a dark young girl wearing a white cap, is a sketched-in portrait, upside down, of Robert Simpson Cassatt, Mary's father. The effect is startling: the bust of the dark, strong feminine image, and growing out of it, out of those powerful shoulders, like a mirror image, the sharply sloping fragile-looking shoulders of a man with white hair and a white beard, serious, worried, indeterminate, unclear.

(There exists a description of Robert Cassatt in the early seventies by a distant objective observer, J. W. Townsend, the author of *The Old Main Line:* "The elder Mr. Cassatt was a 'gentleman of the old school,' tall and dignified, dressed in summer in an immaculately clean white linen suit.")

As an adult in his early and middle years, Robert Simpson Cassatt was afflicted with restlessness, geographically and financially. He was a man who would buy a house for his family, then sell it soon after to buy another, only to rent or buy another and then move from that one soon after, making his way eastward in Pennsylvania. The Cassatt scholar Frederick A. Sweet laconically observes, "Robert Cassatt's constant shifts in real-estate holdings indicate his lack of decision regarding what he wanted to do." Yet he was a man who made his decisions arbitrarily. His wife, Katharine Kelso Johnston, although apparently not happy about the frequent moving, was obedient to his wishes.

In 1847 Robert moved the family from Allegheny City, where he had been elected mayor, to Pittsburgh. Later that year they moved again, farther east, near Lancaster, to a house they called Hardwick. In 1849, while maintaining Hardwick as a country house, he moved his wife and five children to a rented house in Philadelphia. Besides Mary, born May 22, 1844, there was Lydia, born in 1837, Alexander, born in 1839, Robert (Robbie), born in 1842, and Joseph Gardner, born in 1849.

In Philadelphia Robert Cassatt maintained a brokerage office, though, says Sweet, "he was never a very successful businessman." Nevertheless, he managed to provide a very comfortable, if not luxurious, existence for his family with many servants, in part helped by a small legacy he had received on the death of his uncle.

In the country he fancied himself a gentleman farmer. He loved to ride. He taught Mary to ride. To all appearances Mary, as a child and long into her adulthood, idolized her father. He was, as one in-law later observed, "the only being she seem[ed] to think of."

He was a man addicted to rectitude—or at least to the outward display of rectitude: stubborn, irascible, insistent upon his authority in the family, and sure of the rightness of his decisions, which seemed to him to be based entirely on practicality. His attitude toward money was paradoxical. He prided himself on being a businessman, though many of his projects were short-lived and impractical. According to Sweet, he was a man who "had really no great interest in business or any activities associated with earning a living." (His own father, a man of "good family," had died penniless as a result of poor real estate investments when Robert was a young boy.)

In the fall of 1851 Robert Cassatt decided that the family would set off for Europe for an extended stay. (According to Cassatt's biographer Nancy Hale, the Cassatts, like many newcomers in Philadelphia, had not been accorded either prominent social position or acceptance in the community. Hale believes that this sense of rejection, while not openly acknowledged in the family, was to color Mary Cassatt's vision of Philadelphia ever after.) Katharine was not too pleased by the thought of yet another move—and this time an extended journey—but on Robert's insistence, she of course acquiesced. Perhaps one of his justifications was that Robbie had a knee-joint disease and better medical treatment could be obtained in Europe.

On the Continent, where they stayed for five years, they moved several times. First in Paris they took a furnished apartment on the rue Monceau, then one on the avenue Marbeuf. After some months Robert Cassatt decided it was time to move again, to Heidelberg.

There an artist, Peter Baumgaertner, was commissioned to paint a portrait of the family. Absent from the portrait is Aleck—presumably away at boarding school—and Mrs. Cassatt and Lydia. In the engraving, the other four members of the family are grouped around a table, upon which several objects are prominently displayed: a paisley shawl, an elevated chessboard, a cup and saucer, a number of toy soldiers. Mr. Cassatt and Robbie are playing chess. Mr. Cassatt leans slightly forward on his elbows. Robbie, aged twelve, sits opposite him, much lower at the table, leaning on his left elbow, his face delicate and thoughtful. In front of Robbie, partly obscuring him, stands Gardner, aged five, wearing a tartan dress and lace collar, looking straight ahead, he too leaning on the table. In the background, between Mr. Cassatt and Robbie, stands Mary, not yet ten, her body leaning toward Robbie, her head upright.

No one seems to be paying attention to anybody else: Robert is looking at the chessboard, as is Robbie. Gardner seems to be looking out at the artist. Mary is looking slightly down and to the side—neither out nor in. Though they do not look at each other, there is in the placement of their bodies a sense of a leaning into each other, reinforced by the strong family resemblance the artist saw, as if each face was a variation on the same theme.

There are certain things about this family that can be surmised. They created among themselves an intensely tight unit, then and later, as if the family was a community, a self in itself. We know something of the rules of the family, its attitude toward obligation, obligation to each other, and to the external world: proper behavior—rectitude before others as well as for oneself. There is in this family the sense of others as outsiders, and at the same time as watchers outside. The family is refuge and protection as well as containment. There is in the family the sense of form as primary, of individuals within a group inextricably tied together by the forms of daily life.

Though the family had come to Europe, and stayed away five years, under Robert's leadership they maintained the previously established forms assiduously. If they were strangers in a strange land, as exiles (then and later) they lived as if they were still in the city and country of their origin. One goes away but one does not discard the forms. To forfeit obedience to the forms would be regarded as betrayal—just as to acknowledge that Robert Cassatt, the head of the family, is indecisive, is difficult, is changeable, is even erratic at times, would be betrayal.

After a short time in Heidelberg, Robert Cassatt moved the family once again, to Darmstadt, apparently so that Aleck could attend the technical university there. One fact is known of that time in Darmstadt. It was there that Robbie died on May 25 (three days after Mary's eleventh birthday), according to an entry by Robert Cassatt in the notebook he kept for family records: "Robert Kelso Cassatt died at Darmstadt the capital of the Grand Duchy of Hesse Darmstadt in Germany on Friday the twenty-fifth of May A.D. 1855 at 5 o'clock P.M. He is interred in the Cemetery belonging to the corporation of Darmstadt in lot No. [blank space] —"

The detail of the death, the occasion for the family's grief, is told in formal precise terms, appropriate for the time, and to the occasion. But then the words slip in to comment on Robert Cassatt's own part in the proceedings:

"—purchased for the purpose by his father—It being the intention of his parents to have his remains brought to the United States as soon as practicable, a simple gravestone is placed over his grave in Darmstadt merely recording his name and country."

But then changing from a formal tone to one of more personal grief, he writes, "For almost five years previous to his death Robert had been afflicted with disease of [the] knee joint. He suffered very severely at times. He was a model of fortitude and patience. Dear, dear Boy! how gentle and good he was!"

A death in a strange land. A child, a brother left alone—his body left alone—after that death in a strange land. ("Fancy dying in this strange place. Why do people so love to wander?" Echoing words, fifty-six years later.)

There had been one other death in the family in Mary Cassatt's lifetime before this: George Johnston Cassatt, born January 22, 1846 (when Mary was not yet two), died a few weeks later, on February 17. Did that first death even exist in her consciousness? Or was there another thought that might come to her in retrospect? That the child just younger than she, a boy, had died. And now the child just older than she, a boy, had died. Yet she, a girl, had survived.

The death of a child in Victorian families was a frequent occurrence, we are told. But the fact of frequency does not tell us how this particular family dealt with such a death. All families—happy or unhappy—are not alike. We do know that the Cassatt family was not conventionally religious, or at least they were not regular churchgoers. We know from later evidence— for example, the fact that they used black-bordered stationery for two years after a family death—that their mourning for a member of the family was long-lasting, in form as well as in substance.

Many years later, in the summer of 1883, when he was a frail, elderly man, Robert Cassatt set out on a railroad journey to bring back Robbie's body. He never did get to Darmstadt; he simply abandoned his quest.

To his son Aleck, on his return home to Paris, he wrote, "I did think of going on from Antwerp to Darmstadt for the pur- pose of having Robbie's remains deposited at Marly, & actually started Saturday PM for Cologne via Malines which they told me was the shortest and quickest rout[e] but when we arrived at Malines the express had passed & they told me I should have to wait there seven hours or go on to Bruxelles. So I chose the latter & on my arrival there found myself so worried and fatigued that I concluded to forfeit my Cologne ticket & get back home. Stayed all night at Bruxelles & until 1:20 P.M. Sunday & then home for dinner only 5 hours [and] 33 [minutes] en route! Do not suppose that I have given up the idea of disinterring Robbie's remains & reinterring them with his sister's [Lydia's]—No, it is only a postponement, and as soon as I am a little rested I will set out again with that object alone in view & hope to be able to accomplish it before I am called upon to take my rest beside them . . ."

It remained to Mary Cassatt, some years after Robert Cassatt's death, to go to Darmstadt and bring back Robbie's remains, as part of her baggage. He was buried in the family burial place at Beaufresne, united with the family in death as he had once been in life.

7

Ever since her liaison with the man who could provide her with luxury and every mundane distraction money could buy, Isadora's career had been neglected. But suddenly, upon her return from Egypt, she experienced an upsurge of her creative impulse . . . [She] set herself to work with renewed vigor, composing a whole program of new dances," writes Irma Duncan.

But in fact there is no indication that Isadora, after Egypt, did set to work. There is no record of any performance by her that year and in a letter to Singer sometime that summer, she wrote, "I am working trying to get in Condition but as I am very tired it will probably work better when I have a rest."

She was living separately from Singer on property that she owned in Neuilly, purchased in 1909 before meeting him. It contained two buildings, one a three-story chapellike studio, which had a private apartment on the balcony, exotically decorated for her by the famous designer Paul Poiret. A second, separate building housed the two children and their nurse and the servants.

That summer of 1912 Singer was engaged in a project to build a theater for Isadora on land near the Champs-Elysées that he had purchased before their trip to Egypt. It was not only to be a theater for her school but also a theater that she wanted to be a "meeting place and a haven for all the great Artists of the world."

In her letters to him at the time, there is a tone of diffidence, of uneasiness. She seems to tread lightly in what she says. She is often tentative and even self-justifying, making requests as if she doubts that they will be fulfilled. She asks him about plans for the theater, she asks him to persuade his sister, the Princess de Polignac, to use her influence to get the plans for the theater approved, she asks him to approve the spending of money to rent an office before the theater is built, she asks him to go to Bayreuth with her to see the production of *Parsifal,* she asks him to accompany her on a vacation trip. "I will leave next Wednesday for Plombières but if there is any chance of your coming to see me I would go any place you suggest."

In response to a letter from him questioning her about some bills and the way she has handled some negotiations, she writes, "Dearest I wonder if you know that when I receive a kind letter from you I feel strong and happy and can *work* and when you write me unkindly I am so depressed I feel heavy & can not think of work—you probably do not know that you have this power—or you would not too often use it so ruthlessly . . ."

Singer responds to her complaint, addressing her as Isis. He writes that he is sorry that she is hurt but it is only his keen desire to be of help to her with the theater that makes him speak as he does. He seems in his letters thoughtful, caring, but distant—wary, perhaps self-protective.

She has suggested that her former lover Gordon Craig be involved in the design and eventual use of the theater, but Craig, as usual, has been fractious in any situation that demands that he work with someone else. Writing to Singer, Isadora defends Craig against Singer's accusation that he is interfering: "The misunderstanding on Craig's part was simply that he *does not understand French.*"

The tone of her letters has a sense of "it" not being enough: whatever Singer is doing for her, including planning

for the creation of what she calls her dearest dream, is somehow insufficient. She gives the sense that she is pressing him
for more, even as she tries to placate him, to appease him.

He writes to her carefully, methodically, breaking things
down into what he calls "schemes," as he discusses handling
the practical management of the theater. Interested as he is in
architecture, he gets caught up in the specific detail of the
structure. He has made specific alterations in the drawings, but
none of his changes, he assures her, affect the stage or audito-
rium. They only have to do with sanitary facilities, safety appli-
ances, and fire exits. However, he does add, he is beginning to
think that it is not a good idea to have the boxes (for the
"overfed rich") where they have been placed, or indeed to have
boxes at all.

She in turn writes, "Your idea of the cheaper places being
near the stage is good but I am rather afraid of it—as I think
the masses should be at the *extremity* of the circle and work
down to less—on account of the rays of magnetism being necessary for them to *increase* as they travel outwards . . ."

There is one other letter, undated, written by Isadora to
Singer, which Francis Steegmuller suggests was written in the
summer of that year.

"Please, if I really bore you as you say if you are tired of
me or if there is any one else that you would rather take to
Greece Please dear tell me *now*— I am far too proud to care
to stay with you if you do not want me—I love and adore you
and I love little Patrick— . . . Please tell me the *truth* if you
do not care for me any longer—if there is anyone else—it would
be much *kinder* to say so—I find it too humiliating to take
every thing from you and have you say that in return I only
annoy you—If I am no longer any pleasure to you—tell me now
. . . The idea that you may continue to see me from a sense of
duty and not from love of me makes me quite sick & desperate.
You know I never accepted anything from any one before I met
you—and I cannot *bear* the idea of taking things from you
unless you love me—

"Answer me the *truth*."

In November of that year, Isadora made another move. It
was not so sudden or so violent or so reckless or so seemingly

eccentric as was the move with Capelet. Rather it was provocative, an ostensibly passive act, but it resulted in a similar outcome.

In his autobiography, *King of Fashion,* Paul Poiret tells of going to a party given by Singer at Isadora's studio. When the guests assembled at the table for dinner, Isadora chose Poiret to sit next to her. Angered by her choice, Singer walked out but he returned to the party shortly, only to be told that Isadora, who was not present, had gone to her bedroom to rest. Singer went upstairs to her private apartment and found Isadora in what Poiret calls an "intimate conversation" with a guest, playwright Henri Bataille. Another report said that Singer, upon entering her room, saw Bataille kissing her foot. No matter what the exact position was, Singer flew into a jealous rage and publicly broke with her, announcing that he was not going to finance her theater anymore.

In Isadora's version of this event in *My Life* she proclaims her innocence, even as she suggests, as she did of the incident with Capelet, that there were external forces at work. The seductivity, she says, was not anything purposeful on her part but was the result of the sensual atmosphere produced by the apartment Poiret had designed for her.

> My studio was like a chapel . . . But there was a little apartment on the high balcony which had been transformed by the art of Poiret into a veritable domain of Circe. Sable black velvet curtains were reflected on the walls in golden mirrors; a black carpet, and a divan with cushions of Oriental textures, completed this apartment, the windows of which had been sealed up and the doors of which were strange, Etruscan tomb-like apertures. As Poiret himself said on its completion, "Voilà des lieux où on ferait bien d'autres actes et on dirait bien d'autres choses que dans des lieux ordinaires."
>
> This was true. The little room was beautiful, fascinating and, at the same time, dangerous. Might there not be some character in furniture which makes all the difference between virtuous beds and criminal couches, respectable chairs and sinful divans? At any rate, what Poiret had said was right. In that apartment one

felt differently and spoke differently than was the case in my chapel-like studio.

On this particular evening the champagne flowed as freely as it always did when L. gave a fête. At two o'clock in the morning I found myself sitting on a divan in the Poiret room with Henri Bataille and, although he had always been to me as a brother, this evening, filled with the fascination of the place, he spoke and acted differently. And then, who should appear but L. When he saw Henri Bataille and me on the golden divan reflected in the endless mirrors, he flew to the studio, began to apostrophise the guests about me, and said that he was going away, never to return.

This had a somewhat damping effect upon the guests, but in a moment turned my mood from comedy to tragedy.

"Quick," I said to Skene, "play the Death of Iseult, or the evening will be spoilt."

Rapidly I discarded my embroidered tunic and changed into a white robe, while Skene at the piano played even more marvellously than usual, and then I danced until dawn.

She finishes her story by saying that she pleaded with Singer in vain to realize that she was innocent, and that finally he agreed to see her, but only in his automobile. When they met, she says, he began by cursing her. "Suddenly he stopped cursing, and opening the door of the auto, pushed me into the night. Alone I walked along the street for hours in a daze. Strange men made grimaces at me and murmured equivocal propositions. The world seemed suddenly transformed to an obscene Hell."

Two days later she heard that Singer had left for Egypt with another woman.

In January 1913 Isadora set out with her pianist Skene for a performing tour of Russia.

From St. Petersburg she wrote a letter to Louis Sue, the architect, who had been involved with the aborted plan for the theater. "Here I'm living like a monk and except for the moments of exaltation and extasy it's very depressing. Paris in Egypt *doesn't answer* my letters . . . it's very cold here—not the slightest warmth, nor perfume, nor Love   I am desolate— When will spring come again? My soul is drying up."

8

Yes I *am* better but not well yet—and of course the treatment tires me and takes much of my time," writes Mary Cassatt to Louisine Havemeyer from rue de Marignan on December 1, 1911. The medical treatment she is undergoing is the inhalation of radium, thought to be beneficial because of its mysterious radiation. "When I get back here after an hour and a half I sleep for an hour wake up and take a soup and off until morning with intervals with all this sleep. Two hours in the day beside . . . I haven't any more those frequent feelings of exhaustion, and walk more . . ."

Despite her pain she is making headway, returning to her daily life and the Parisian art world. "Degas is almost out of his mind for he has to move and he hasn't even dusted his pictures for years. His temper is dreadfully upset." And then without a break in her telling, she writes about the scandal of Madame Curie. "I send you the account of the Curie business [the accusation that Madame Curie had an affair with Paul Langevin, professor of physics at the Collège de France] . . . We Louie are living on the morals of our forefathers but people

who hadn't any forefathers! . . . after Madame Curie, what can
we count on?"

On December 14 she writes from the doctor's office where
she is having the radium treatment. "This is the 8th day and I
am suffering very much, which it seems would prove that it is
doing me good, that it will be a success, provided I can stand
it. We are a party, an old Englishwoman . . . and a French
comtesse an Italian princess, and Miss Hallowell. I would find
it easier were there fewer persons, and if we were not forced
to talk."

To be forced to talk when all that she wants is to undergo
the treatment and be able to get back to her daily life. But now
body and thoughts of body rule (replace) her daily life. Now
body contains her, limits her in illness, as it never has, holds her
to the concentration on what she feels in her nerves, in her
muscles, in her joints, holds her to the observation of the smallest shifts. When pain narrows life down to the observation of
and care of and feeling of body, or trying not to feel, there is
no way to outwardness, no way to work. Pain itself is an outward explosion, blocked, as attention is relentlessly reined in.
Pain is in fact a new form of containment for her, reinforcing
all that has contained her up to now, though she struggles
against it, just as she has struggled against (and obeyed many
of) the containments in her life.

On December 29, having ended the radium treatment, she
writes of her plans to travel through the south of France for
an "auto cure," prescribed by her doctors. In the automobile,
given to her by Louisine, she will go to Tours and Bordeaux and
Biarritz, and then Cannes. James Stillman, with three traveling companions, will take the same route and she and they will
meet up frequently. "He seems very pleased with the plans
and of course I am, but I won't allow him to have me on his
mind . . ."

On her mind for the moment, still and again, is Madame
Curie. "Did you know that Columbia College has become a
college for Jews? Mr. Stillman tells me that Doctor [Nicholas
Murray] Butler told him that these young Jews have absolutely
no sense of right and wrong. Now my dear Madame Curie is
a Polish Jewess! So I have been assured and it is only too
evident that she has no sense of right and wrong. That comes
of centuries of oppression. Professor Langevin is a genius, it is

said, and he helped Mme. Curie in her lectures she isn't capable
by herself of doing anything like that, but must always have
someone to help her . . ."

The radium treatment has not eased Mary's pain. "Louie
I am still suffering and that after all this cure, the Doctor was
horribly upset at this return of pain, but thinks it may be too
strong hypodermics which he has very lately given me, of
course I am stronger and look better though not one bit fatter,
but suffering and since these last few days not sleeping so well,
before that I slept nine and ten hours."

Nevertheless, in pain or out of pain, she does what she
must do, she obeys the injunction of how one must behave, she
invokes judgment on those who transgress. The judgment of
Madame Curie is of course a judgment for having fallen sexually, but it is also a condemnation because of its betrayal of
others, as if all suffer from the "falling" of one. ("After
Madame Curie, what can we count on?") The judgment of the
Jews is a judgment on outsiders, without "forefathers," who
are improper in their behavior. It is a judgment shared by many
of her "set," her class, and her time, a judgment that reaffirms
one's place, one's class, through the separation from those who
are not in it. (It is a judgment with which she has not always
aligned herself. Almost twenty years earlier, in 1894, she was
an ardent defender of the innocence of Dreyfus, a stance in
opposition to many of those in her "set.")

Even in the mention of the memorial service that has been
held for her brother at the English church, judgment is invoked.
"I was there but did not stay until the end . . . there was an
account in The Herald which was I think in bad taste . . ." Again
the question of proper behavior, of what must be done, of what
isn't done by others, of those who merit praise, and of those
who merit blame, whether as a group or as individuals. There
is no mention of Egypt. The intensity of that experience, unresolved, never "painted" (as she feared she would never be
able to paint it), has been replaced by two intense preoccupa-
tions—a consuming focus on her illness and, second, on the one
thing in the world that guarantees stability and ultimately protection: proper behavior.

The weighted words "I feel so utterly helpless" . . . "I
fought for my mother's life" . . . "this overpowering impression" . . . "I am crushed by the strength of this art" . . . "All

strength" . . . "only intellect and strength" . . . "my feeble hands" have given way to words that adhere to the detail of daily experience, to the detail of her sense of her body and its treatment, to words that reinforce the existing, real, visible world, to words that speak about the necessity of the adherence to what is—as if, were these things to give way, everything solid and visible and reliable would crumble. Moments come when she is seized by the necessity to attack—the Jews, Madame Curie, others in her "set" who do not behave as they should. It is all about containment and survival in containment, her story, even—especially—in her lashing out.

In Biarritz, encountering damp weather, she once again feels very weak. "I confess to feeling very blue," she writes to Louisine. But then, as if she will not allow herself to be cast down, she goes on to enumerate the works she has just seen at the Bonnat Museum that afternoon, several paintings by Degas, some drawings by Ingres, and a Rembrandt sketch. She asserts insistently the difficulty of figure painting as compared with landscape painting. (She is a figure painter, not a land-scape painter.) And she speaks of what American artists have not yet done, of how they are "behind."

On January 16 from Cannes, she writes of the death of the painter Henri Rouart and mentions that two of her own works in his collection will now be for sale. One is "of two women with a silver tea set in the foreground, and a pastel of mine which I don't think as good. I so long to be well and at work again, but I am still too weak to work . . ." There is the desire to work, there is the thought of past work—evaluated, not praised too highly, but thought well of. All that work implies is for the moment beyond her, though there is still open to her the use of her critical faculty in judging works of art—as well as behavior in the world.

Ten days later—was it nerves or muscles or joints or some illness she picked up on the Nile (that too a possibility), or was it something new now, a response to the radium treatment?— whatever it was that afflicted her, her suffering returned with a vengeance.

"I have had a relapse and have suffered much and been very depressed," she writes from the Hôtel de Californie in Cannes. "I broke down when the weather turned fine; and finally saw a Doctor here. He thinks I got far too much treatment in Paris, and gives me only a *little* electricity . . . [He] thinks I may be as well as I ever was, I feel not . . ."

And then in a new paragraph, at last, a mention of Egypt: "A lady has been telling me of the weird stories about the dreadful things that have happened to people owning Egyptian mummies, one it seems in the British Museum is never shown to anyone such dreadful things happen. I have necklaces coming from the tombs and so have you."

9

Now, after Egypt, after the fight with Singer, Isadora, adhering to her sequence, tells in *My Life* of that tragedy which, she says, was "to end all hopes of any natural, joyous life for me—for ever after . . . I can only say that those last few days of my life, before the blow fell, were actually the last days of my spiritual life."

She begins by telling of her visions in Russia. (Even the telling of this most awful event must be shaped. It is not possible for her to do otherwise, just as it is not possible for her to refrain in any telling from proving the existence of forces beyond the real, the overdetermining of incident, as in a dream.)

In Kiev, riding in a sleigh to the hotel, she saw on either side of the road two rows of coffins of children. In terror, she pointed them out to Skene. " 'Look . . . all the children are dead!'

" 'There is nothing but the snow,' " Skene said, and tried to reassure her by telling her she was only suffering from fatigue.

Later that day she went to the Russian baths, was overcome by the heat, and fell on the marble floor from an elevated shelf. That night, despite being warned that she had had a slight concussion, she insisted on performing. At the end of the program she suddenly told Skene to play the Chopin "Funeral March."

" 'But why?' he asked. 'You have never danced it.'

" 'I don't know—play it.'

". . . I danced a creature who carries in her arms her dead, with slow, hesitating steps, towards the last resting place. I danced the descent into the grave and finally the spirit escaping from the imprisoning flesh and rising, rising towards the Light—the Resurrection."

When she finished, she says, Skene was "deathly pale and trembling . . ."

" 'I experienced death itself,' " he said to her, " ' . . . and I saw coffins of children—' " She concludes that "some spirit gave us that night a singular premonition of what was to come."

She returned to Paris, to her life with her children, described in idyllic terms. "Living there at Neuilly, working in the studio, reading for hours in my library, playing in the garden with my children or teaching them to dance, I was quite happy, and dreaded any more tours which would separate me from the children . . .

"Not only was I allied to these two adorable children by the poignant tie of flesh and blood, but I also had with them a higher bond to an almost superhuman degree, the tie of Art."

Isadora dreamed that Deirdre would "carry on my School as I imagined it," and that Patrick would become a "great Artist . . . who would combine the two gifts of creating music and dance simultaneously . . . who would create the new dance born from the new music."

But in spite of the fact that she should have been happy with her life, says Isadora, she suffered from the strange oppression that had begun in Russia. She was performing alternately at the Châtelet and the Trocadéro, and one night at the Trocadéro she danced the "Funeral March" again and felt an "icy breath" on her forehead and smelled the "strong scent of white tuberoses and funeral flowers."

Another night, shortly afterward, when she was in bed after the performance, she saw a moving figure draped in black emerge from one of the double black crosses Poiret had put on each of the golden doors of her apartment. The figure "approached the foot of the bed and gazed at me with pitiful eyes. For some moments I was transfixed with horror, then I turned on the lights full, and the figure vanished; but this curious hallucination—the first of the kind that I had ever had—occurred again and then again, at intervals."

Troubled by her visions, she went to a doctor, who told her she was suffering from nerve strain and suggested she go to the country. But as she had a contract to perform, she decided instead to go with the children to stay at the Trianon Hotel in Versailles, and drive into the city for her concerts.

The day after her move she felt that the oppression had lifted and that night she danced "as never before. I was no longer a woman, but a flame of joy—a fire—the sparks that rose, the smoke whirling from the hearts of the public . . . and as I danced it seemed to me that something sang within my heart, 'Life and Love—the Highest Ecstasy—and all are mine to give to those who need them.' "

After the performance Singer, whom she had not seen since his departure for Egypt, came to see her, and seemed, she says, deeply affected by her dancing and their meeting. She invited him to join her at her brother Augustin's apartment for supper and he apparently agreed. At Augustin's Isadora waited for him but he did not appear. "Moments passed—an hour passed—he did not come. This attitude threw me into a state of cruel nervousness. In spite of the fact that I knew he had not taken that Egyptian trip alone, I had been deeply glad to see him, for I loved him always and longed to show him his own son . . . But when three o'clock came and he had not arrived, bitterly disappointed I left to rejoin the children at Versailles."

The next morning, she writes, she reached out her hand to the night table on which was a copy of the work of Barbey d'Aurevilly. She picked up the book and opened it to find the name Niobe, the Greek mythical figure whose children were destroyed by the gods because, in her pride as a mother, she had compared herself favorably to them.

"And the direct thought came to me—How empty and dark would life be without them, for more than my Art and a thousand times more than the love of any man, they had filled and crowded my life with happiness."

Reading further, she came upon the revenge taken upon

Niobe by the gods. "The arrow of the gods is held back and plays with you.

"You wait thus, your entire life, in quiet desperation and dark restraint . . . You become inert . . . changed into stone . . ."

Suddenly, she says, the telephone rang. It was Singer calling, asking Isadora to come to town to meet him for lunch and to bring the children. The nurse, worried about rain, suggested Isadora leave the children at home, but she thought the meeting with Singer would be much "simpler" if they were present. "I knew that when L. saw Patrick he would forget all his personal feelings against me . . ." In the taxi with the children Isadora thought of Singer and dreamed that "our Love might go on to create some really great purpose." Her heart was "light with great hopes of Art."

After an idyllic lunch, at which Singer once again offered to finance her theater, she left with the children for her studio, where she planned to rehearse. She told the nurse to take the children back to Versailles in the car. Just as the car was leaving, Isadora relates, Deirdre put her lips on the window for a good-bye kiss and Isadora, kissing her through the glass, felt "an uncanny impression."

Entering the studio, she decided to rest before the rehearsal. As she reclined on a couch in her apartment, eating bonbons sent to her by an admirer, she thought, " 'Surely, after all, I am very happy—perhaps the happiest woman in the world. My Art, success, fortune, love, but, above all, my beautiful children.'

"I was thus lazily eating sweets and smiling to myself, thinking, 'L. has returned, all will be well,' when there came to my ears a strange, unearthly cry.

"I turned my head. L. was there, staggering like a drunken man. His knees gave way—he fell before me—and from his lips came these words:

" 'The children—the children—are dead!' "

10

Her words, her telling, even as they seem to be confessional, act as a barrier. They surround her and encapsulate her. She herself remains impenetrable, half in and half out of the aura of performance. It is hard to place oneself inside Isadora's life, as she describes it, to feel what she is feeling at this most terrible moment of her life. The result is tragedy at many removes.

Is it some effect of our time I am responding to, that in the more than sixty years since she wrote her book, there have been so many public cries of grief that in self-protection one becomes inured to them? For there is something "public" in her telling, as if she, after the many repetitions of the telling—for this was written twelve years or so after the event and she had spoken of it often—was watching herself, rehearing herself tell it to others.

Or is it that her words are too extravagant, too grandiloquent, her framing of episode too shaped? (Our time has taught us to be suspicious of grandiloquence and of extravagant words, of too carefully shaped telling, to expect sooner or later that they will be betrayed.) It feels as if intention and meaning do not merge accurately here. Hints of other things are carried in the words, of things known and not known, of things held back.

Or is it that she has used weighted words like *desperate* so often before in her telling that they have lost their power to move, that she has defused their impact with overuse?

Or is it that it seems there is too much manipulation in her insistence on her prescience, on her visions beforehand, presented so as to make the deaths seem fated as in Greek tragedy? (In her story she compares herself to Oedipus as well as to Niobe.)

And what of the visions? Did she indeed have them? (Who is to say no? How can such things be proved?)

Or is it that what she says about the absolute break in her life, before and after the event—that before was an idyllic life and afterward a life of total desperation—does not ring true, because of what she herself has told us? She seems to have forgotten those other blacknesses in her life, that "Neurasthenia" which came to her so often (even, especially, in Egypt). It is as if all blacknesses, all sorrows, have been absorbed into this one sorrow.

She has forgotten that from St. Petersburg she wrote, "My soul is drying up." What did she mean by it? Was it only a manner of speaking, her style? (But does not style have meaning?) Did she mean that her soul was drying up because of the fight with Singer? Or did she mean that she had fought with Singer because her soul was drying up? Listening to her words, one cannot be certain what she meant, since she herself did not seem to know in the way in which we ordinarily speak of knowing. Cause and effect, outside force and inside choice, appear to have been indistinguishable for her.

There is always fact; it is time to be grateful for fact. Here is the account of the tragedy from the *San Francisco Examiner*, Monday, April 21, 1913:

> Paris, April 20. . . . Mme. Duncan had intended to leave her villa in the rue Chauveau for the Trianon Palace Hotel at Versailles after dancing . . . at the Châtelet last night . . .

At 3:30 Mme. Duncan had sent off her two children, Patrick and Deirdre, with Annie Sine [Sim], their English nurse, to precede her. The children had just entered their mother's limousine and were being driven down the rue Chauveau toward the Seine, when, to avoid collision with a passing taxi, their chauffeur, Paul Morverant [Morverand], stopped the Duncan car. The chauffeur had alighted and cranked the engine of his own car and was about to take his seat when, to his horror, the car suddenly leaped forward, descending the steep bank and sank in the river.

The chauffeur was crazed with fear and for the moment unable to do anything except shriek and wring his hands. When he realized that he was powerless to rescue the three victims he rushed to the Neuilly police station and surrendered.

When the news of what had happened within fifty yards of her peaceful little villa was broken to her, Mme. Duncan swooned. Her grief is heartrending. All night she watched and wept beside the bodies of her pretty babies, which had been taken home at about 10 o'clock after lying for a time in the neighboring American hospital. Drawing a veil about her face, she knelt beside the bodies and sobbed and refused to be comforted . . .

Since this morning visitors by the hundreds have been streaming into Neuilly to leave flowers and offer sympathy and condolence to the bereaved mother.

The only witness to the accident except Morverant was Sophie Reindyck, a school girl.

There is in Isadora's life another telling of a drowning in the Seine, of a death that was not a true death, but an imagined death. It is in a story written by Joseph Charles Duncan, Isadora's father, in 1841, when he was twenty-two and living in Charleston, having made his way south from his birthplace in Philadelphia. This story, "The Tri-color," was published in the first edition of his literary journal, *The Prairie Flower.*

What is known of Joseph Charles Duncan is known mainly from his later years, after his arrival in California, where he made a name both infamous and famous. A handsome, charming, charismatic man, persuasive to both men and women alike, he married three times. (Isadora's mother, Dora Gray, was his second wife.) He was a man continually creating new and different schemes, in finance, in journalism, and in the selling of art objects. He ran a lottery and failed, he published at least three different newspapers, he started an auction firm, the Chinese Salesrooms, which sold Chinese shawls and art objects. He opened a gallery and sold paintings he purchased on trips to Europe. He founded the San Francisco Art Association, he wrote poetry, he started several banks, he founded a safe deposit company. When an editor of a rival paper criticized his ethics, Joseph Duncan challenged him to a duel in the pages of his own paper. Everything he did involved risk. When one risk failed, he simply went on to the next. In San Francisco he made and lost three fortunes. He was described as "a man of sanguine temperament, great energy, full of push and pluck." With each new moneymaking scheme, he managed to convince others to become involved with him, including his son-in-law and his wife's father.

Shortly after Isadora's birth, his bank and safe deposit companies went broke, having been founded upon assets that did not exist. The story of his flight from his creditors—and depositors—and his subsequent arrest and trial was told in great detail in the San Francisco newspapers. Tried four times but not convicted, he subsequently ran off with another woman and Isadora's mother divorced him. In Los Angeles, where he remarried, he made and lost yet another fortune.

But this story of a drowning in the Seine was written long before any of these events, when he was a young man, just starting out, naïvely proud of his literary talents.

The story is set in Paris (to which Duncan had not been at the time) on July 27, 1830, the beginning, says the author, of "the struggle of the people against the minions of Charles the tenth . . . Frenchmen had arisen in their strength, spurned the decree of the Tyrant . . . The glorious picture of American liberation was before them—Lafayette, the adopted brother of Washington, in their midst—and freedom and independance [sic] in their grasp."

The hero, twenty-year-old Eugene, because of his "courage and boldness . . . [and] enthusiasm in the cause," has been chosen to be one of the leaders of the attack that is to take place the following day. "The youth referred to held his solitary way down a narrow street to a part of Paris far from the scene of strife. 'Tis said that Glory and Love should go together.—To the former he was aspiring—in the latter he was far, far, gone . . ."

He visits his betrothed, his beloved Marie, and "when he disclosed the struggles that would take place in a few hours and slightly touched on the part he was expected to bear in the fearful drama, a dark foreboding of evil, a shadow of the coming event came over her buoyant spirits, she struggled in vain to assume a cheerful look . . ."

They part but the next morning Marie places "a small flag in his hands—'Freedom's bright rainbow'—the tricolor—and lifting up her full dark eyes suffused in tears—breathed an inward prayer to the DEITY for his safety; then hurriedly sought her chamber to give vent to all a woman's feelings—too sacred for intrusion."

In the attack hundreds of the revolutionaries are killed by the "murderous fire of the artillery . . . and many would have given up the attempt as hopeless—but for one—*that one* was Eugene—dashing through the crowd 'onward' he cried—'for liberty and those we love' and, bearing aloft the tricolor, he rushed on the bridge, gained the pillar next to the enemy— mounted to its summit—and there planted the white, red and blue, the flag of the French—the gift of Marie—a hundred bullets whistled around—his hands relaxed their hold—a low moan escaped—and with a . . . struggle the body of the noble youth fell heavily in the dark water below." But spurred on by Eugene's action, the revolutionaries rush to the attack and Eugene is "avenged."

When the news of Eugene's fate is brought to Marie, "she could not weep—'for there is a dignity in cureless sorrow that disdains complaint'—unheeded were the entreaties of friends for her to seek repose; time passed by—and she was alone—left to that solitude, so dear to those broken and crushed in spirit . . ." The next morning, however, a "fragment of paper on which was traced a single line" is brought to Marie. On it are the words " 'Come to me Marie.' " She faints, but when restored to consciousness, she is told that Eugene is not dead, after all. ". . . The instant he fell into the Seine numbers leaped to his rescue his insensible form was borne ashore to a . . . hospital

. . . there by the unremitted exertions of those who had wit-
nessed his herioc [sic] conduct, he recovered."

But they, Isadora's children, were not saved. Nor had her
father himself been saved. According to the *San Francisco
Examiner* of November 13, 1898, he was drowned the month
before in a shipwreck, returning from England to the United
States with his third wife and child. "Joseph Charles Duncan,
his wife and their twelve year old daughter, were passengers
on the unlucky ship, and a few hours after the wreck, the
waves, with strange caprice, laid their bodies one after the
other on the . . . beach . . . so that the three who were bound
together in life might lie together in death, and so it came about
that with what seems like retributive justice, the wrecker of
lives in San Francisco fell victim to wreck himself."

11

 longer "a mother," Isadora became in the eyes of others "The Mother."

On the day of the children's death, "the sculptor Antoine Bourdelle, with streaming eyes, threw himself on his knees before Isadora and put his head in her lap: 'She looked at him as the Mother of God might have looked,' " wrote one observer.

Another wrote, "The mourning mother, in her frozen suffering for all eternity, remained in her room. She seemed to belong to that other world to which her children had gone. Later, she passed before us like a shadow on the way to the room that held the coffins . . . Never was there a more moving ceremony . . . Alone, Isadora walked at the head of the endless cortege. She resembled a mourner of the ancient times . . . I wanted to kiss her naked feet in their sandals."

No longer "Child of Isis—or Gift of Isis," no longer "protected" by Isis, but still bearing her name, she began to take on, through some transformation in her grief, and through the reflection in the eyes of others, an identification with the mother goddess, as if with Isis herself. So in a letter she published in newspapers in Paris and in New York, in response to the many letters of condolence she had received, she said, "All men are my brothers, all women are my sisters and all little children on earth are my children."

(One man, it is recorded, took exception to this statement. In his journal Count Robert de Montesquiou, who was the model for Proust's Baron Charlus, wrote, "Today Europe and the world mourn the illegitimate children of Miss Duncan . . . The celebrated dancer and unfortunate mother has published an ostentatious and naïve letter, in which she states that, 'all men are her brothers, all women, her sisters, all children, her children.' Evidently, all men are her brothers; for not one is her *husband*. But all women wouldn't want to be the sister of a courtesan, nor all children, her bastards.")

It is true that in her dance Isadora had always been seen—and had a sense of herself—as godlike. From the time that she had been a young woman, she had spoken in transcendent terms about the expression of her soul, about her aspiration to convey to the world her "mission." She wrote of spending "long days and nights in the studio seeking that dance which might be the divine expression of the human spirit . . . I sought the source of the spiritual expression to flow into the channels of the body filling it with vibrating light . . ."

She had regarded herself not as a performer but as the priestess of a new religion, in contact with the gods, in the service of the gods. And when she danced, many people in her audience had responded to her as if she was "godlike." In reviews of her work, from the time of her first triumphs in Europe, the words *divine* and *eternal* appear frequently.

In Berlin in 1904, she herself noted, "My popularity . . . was almost unbelievable. They called me the Göttliche [Divine] Isadora. It was even bruited about that when sick people were brought into my theatre they became well. And every matinée one could see the strange sight of sick people being brought in on litters. I had never worn any other dress than the little white tunic, bare feet and sandals. And my audience came to my performances with an absolutely religious ecstasy."

Still, though imbued with this sense of herself as conveying the eternal and divine in dance, she had made (and sometimes lamented) the distinction between that self who created her Art and that self who lived her life. Pregnant with Patrick, she had pondered on "the strange difference which divides life from Art" and she had even wondered "if a woman can ever really be an artist."

But now with the death of her children, she began to be seen—and to see herself—in an isolation of myth, the victim-goddess who is simultaneously the incarnation of a terrible Fate and of divinity. It was daily life that now grew shadowy for her. "All life [since the death of Deirdre and Patrick] has been to me but as a phantom ship upon a phantom ocean."

After the funeral Isadora returned to the Neuilly studio, where, she says, "I had some definite plan to end my own life . . . If a great love had then enveloped me and carried me away—but L. [Singer] did not respond to my call."

With her sister Elizabeth and her brother Augustin she went to the island of Corfu, but there she felt she had "entered a dreary land of greyness where no will to live or move existed."

Prostrate on her bed, her hands clasped on her breast, she repeated over and over a message to Singer, who was then in London: " 'Come to me. I need you. I am dying.' " Miraculously, she says, Singer appeared. Convinced that he had received her words telepathically, she hoped that "by a spontaneous love gesture the unhappiness of the past might be redeemed." But a great love did not "envelop" her. Once again what Singer gave her was not enough. Her lamentation was too much for him to bear, the expression of it—in all its power—was too unrelieved. She, who projected feeling so intensely in her dance that many in her audience were moved to frenzy, now was projecting, in life, feeling without limit, without containment, and in its hugeness no one, least of all Singer, could take it. "My intense yearning—my sorrow—were too strong for L. to stand. One morning he left abruptly, without warning."

Her brother Raymond persuaded her to go with him to Albania, to the settlement at Santi Quaranta, where he was going to work among the refugees from the Turkish-Balkan War. In a letter to Gordon Craig from Corfu in May she wrote that she had gone with Raymond the week before to Epirus, where they had bought tents and provisions, and that they were soon going back to erect shelters for the children. She asked

Craig, "Do you remember I sent you a little picture of Deirdre sitting on the Great Temple at Karnak—looking up so calmly and sweetly. That is how she was—more and more bright and sweet and gay—She would never have agonized through life as I have—when I looked at her I always thought—mine is all broken pieces and disaster—hers will be beautiful and Complete . . ."

12

On February 18, 1912, Mary Cassatt writes to Louisine Havemeyer from Cannes: "Yesterday we [she and James Stillman] made the most wonderful excursion, I never was in a colder or more desolate place . . . I slept well after that . . . Oh! but it is long to get back one's strength, if ever. I am *so* weak on my legs but if only the pain is less I won't mind."

She mentions a Courbet painting that she admired but that Stillman showed no interest in buying, then immediately returns to a statement about her medical treatment. "See how often I come back to my ailments!" she adds ruefully.

Back in Paris early in March, she thanks Louisine again for her sympathy. "I often think how patiently you used to stroke my aching legs [Louisine had visited her the summer before] and those long sleepless nights, now I hope and pray they are a thing of the past." She is once more attending events in the Paris art world. "There is an exhibition of Rouart's pictures and watercolors, the latter best, very correct like an engineer's drawings, but just lacking to be Art. But three portraits of him by Degas fine. I saw Degas there looking very old, but well, he surely must miss his old friends most of them now are gone, all of them I used to know, this is a shifting scene." (Others age, others suffer, not only she, it is part of existence. So she seems to be trying to persuade herself.)

On March 12 she writes that she has been told that it will be a year before she is well. "That is a sad prospect but I must have patience . . . If only I could get rid of the pains."

Stillman had impressed upon her the "absolute need for quiet" when they were driving. "No more talking, we sat in his auto for hours at a time without opening our lips, he thinks if only I won't exert myself I will come out all right."

She is determined to "come out all right." She reminds Louisine and herself of her own "toughness." Of one of the doctors whom she has seen, she says that if he did not "kill me it is because I am tough." But thoughts of toughness seem to slide away from her. There is the need for kindness and for being cared for, there is the sense of herself as being old and ill. She says of Stillman that he looks so well and so young. "He was kindness itself; but I think he must be glad to be rid of this sick old woman. I think I would be in his place." And once again, pulling herself up, without transition she goes on to the buying of art works, of how Stillman still thinks pictures are going to fall in price, but "there are only a limited number of fine pictures, and all the world wants them." She tries to abide in the sureness of her own judgment, in the reality of her assessment of the world and its wants, objectified through purchasing.

She wants to work, she needs to work, but the pains still prevent her. She writes on March 23 that she has promised a friend that she will do a study of his wife and their little girl, "if I am well again ever, and can work." On March 29 she writes that she is a "living barometer . . . Yesterday I went to Beaufresne and there was wind and the weather changeable and I came home so wretched I cried myself to sleep, and today after a sunbath I am feeling quite well for me."

She tells Louisine that everyone in Paris is buying revolvers because of what she calls "desperadoes," and she herself has bought a revolver for her chauffeur to carry. Protection and yet more protection, as if there were not enough in the world to defend her from what she must be defended against.

The news of the sinking of the *Titanic* comes as another

blow to her view of the world; everyone, she says, was told that it could never sink.

And then on August 1, 1912, in an outcry against others who would make her do what she can no longer do, come the words "All my doctors want me to work! How is it possible, they don't know what it is to paint . . ."

13

Unable to bear the suffering she saw at Santi Quaranta, Isadora went with Penelope, Raymond's wife, to Constantinople. Wandering in the old streets of the city, they came to a dark narrow lane, and entered the house of an old woman who was a fortune teller. Isadora reports that she asked what her future would be and the woman responded, in further confirmation of her godliness, "You have been sent on earth to give great joy to all people. From this joy will be founded a religion. After many wanderings, at the end of your life, you will build temples all over the world . . . All these temples will be dedicated to Beauty and Joy because you are the daughter of the Sun."

Unable to move—in her work—and yet unable not to move, Isadora kept rushing from one place to another. She returned to Santi Quaranta with Penelope, then left by steamer for Trieste. In Trieste she sent for her car and chauffeur and traveled north, first to Switzerland and then, "following an irresistible impulse," into France and back to Paris.

In her studio she tried to work again but when Skene came to play for her, she could not proceed; "the sound of the familiar music only had the effect of throwing me into fits of weeping." In a hallucination she heard the children's voices in the garden. And when she entered the separate house where they had lived, and saw their clothes and toys scattered about, she "broke down completely" and moved on again.

She drove back over the Alps and south into Italy, continuing on to Venice, to Rimini, and to Florence, where Gordon Craig was living. She says she thought of seeing him but did not see him. Instead, when she received a telegram from her friend the great Italian actress Eleanora Duse, asking her to come to her, she went at once to Viareggio. There, Isadora writes, Duse "took me in her arms and her wonderful eyes beamed upon me such love and tenderness that I felt just as Dante must have felt when, in the 'Paradiso,' he encounters the Divine Beatrice.

"From then on I lived at Viareggio, finding courage from the radiance of Eleanora's eyes. She used to rock me in her arms, consoling my pain, but not only consoling, for she seemed to take my sorrow to her own breast . . ."

One day, says Isadora, Duse said to her in a choking voice, " 'You have on your brow the mark of the great unhappy ones of the earth. What has happened to you is but the Prologue. Do not tempt Fate again.' "

Duse urged Isadora not to seek happiness in her personal life but to return to her Art. " 'If you knew how short life is and how there can be long years of ennui, ennui—nothing but ennui! Escape from the sorrow and ennui—escape!' "

But, says Isadora, "my heart was too heavy. I could make some gestures before Eleanora, but to go again before a public seemed to me impossible."

14.

A dancer's body is her instrument and the memory of that instrument's past—in rhythm, in pattern, in dynamic, in shape, in direction, in level, in the use of breath, in the response to music and to silence—does not fade. To an audience dance may be a transient art, but to the dancer the art is rooted in the memory—in the muscles and tendons, in the nerves—through the acutely developed kinesthetic sense.

But there is also in the dancer's body the memory of every-day existence, the memory of motions executed in daily life. So one has lifted a child or held out one's arms, or pushed someone away, or waved good-bye. The same muscles and tendons and joints and bones are called upon in dance as in life, even though the ultimate purpose of motion is not the same. In dance all motion, every single gesture, is heightened through the most intense concentration.

For those dancers whose discipline is a highly stylized dance form like ballet, there is a built-in separateness between its heightened movement and the movement of everyday life, though both call on the same bodily instrument. (The extreme turnout of the leg at the hip, the dancing on toe in the interest of an elevated line are only two examples of a strict departure from daily, "natural" movement.)

But Isadora's technique was based, from the beginning, on the body's natural motion. (No toe shoes, no extreme turnout, flexibility in the entire body, much use of daily movements like running and skipping and walking.) Her stated intention was the elimination, in the service of spiritual expression, of all that she felt was unnatural and falsely stylized. And in that expression the border between motion in dance and motion in life was not a rigorous one.

She had looked for and discovered "the central spring of all movement, the crater of motor power, the unity from which all diversions of movements are born . . ." Through a following of the sensations that "streamed" in her body she had found her "Spiritual Vision." But now the sensations streaming in her body were ruled by grief and loss. The more she sought transcendence, the more she was ruled by the body's grief.

In her dance, through her imagination, she had sought to transcend the "real" world, even to transcend the body. Through her great gifts, she had been able to create the illusion of another kind of world for others to visualize. But now the real world had overwhelmed her. Trusting to movement as continuity, as continuing wavelike forms—even *The Dances of the Furies* has that sense of continuity, of sharpness delimited by wavelike forms—now in life she had been subjected to the greatest abruptness of all.

To Gordon Craig she wrote, "This so called *real* world is the refinement of Torture—and if it weren't for the escape the Imagination offers it would be Hell indeed . . . Water cannot drown people . . . —neither are they born or do they die—*All is*—and the Eternal Truth is only seen in precious moments by such spirits as Phidias, Michelangelo—Rembrandt—Bach—Beethoven—others—and Yourself . . . all the rest is semblances, illusions—veils—, I know that, but what will you—at present my poor Body cries out and my mind is clouded . . ."

15

At night in the lonely villa she had rented near Viareggio, she would get up and go out into the sea. "I thought I would swim so far that I should be unable to return, but always my body of itself turned landward—such is the force of life in a young body."

She continued to think, dream, feel that her children were still alive, or alternatively, she thought, felt, dreamed that she was dead and with them. "One grey, autumn afternoon, I was walking alone along the sands when, suddenly, I saw going just ahead of me the figures of my children Deirdre and Patrick, hand in hand. I called to them but they ran laughing ahead of me just out of reach. I ran after them—followed —called—and suddenly they disappeared in the mist of the sea-spray . . ."

As a solo dancer, Isadora had the remarkable capability of being able to evoke for the audience the presence of others onstage with her, as if she was a being of multiple personalities, with all the personalities visible simultaneously. What she imagined, she saw; and she persuaded others to see. But now that talent for imagining, for seeing, for evoking, was express- ing itself spontaneously in life, not in Art.

At the same time it is odd—or is it?—that the physical action she envisaged, the children appearing and then leaving her, is an uncanny reflection of her physical relationship to them as it had been in life, marked by frequent disappearances, by sudden comings and goings. For example, in 1908, she had gone to the United States, leaving Deirdre, not quite two, be- hind in France, and had not returned for six months. These absences had been repeated many times during the short lives of both children.

In Viareggio, Isadora made—was moved to make—an- other crucial move. Lying upon the sand, grieving, suddenly she felt "a pitying hand" on her head. She looked up and saw a handsome young man, who resembled one of the figures in the Sistine Chapel. "He stood there, just come from the sea, and said:

" 'Why are you always weeping? Is there nothing I can do for you—to help you?'

"I looked up.

" 'Yes,' I replied. 'Save me—save more than my life—my reason. Give me a child.' ... And when I felt his strong youthful arms about me and his lips on mine, when all his Italian passion descended on me, I felt that I was rescued from grief and death, brought back to light—to love again."

The next morning she told Eleanora Duse what she had done, and Duse "did not seem at all astonished." Being an Artist, says Isadora, Duse thought it natural ("Artists live so continually in a land of Legend and Fantasy . . ."), and she "graciously consented" to meet Isadora's new young lover, a sculptor, a "second Michelangelo."

Isadora's solution to her grief, escape into the consolation of love, did not, however, last long. The young man wrote her a farewell note, saying that he had neglected to mention he was engaged to be married. "But I was not at all angry with him," Isadora writes. "I felt he had saved my reason, and then I knew I was no longer alone; and from this moment I entered into a phase of intense mysticism. I felt that my children's spirits hovered near me—that they would return to console me on earth."

There are, it seems, discrepancies in Isadora's story of what happened following the death of her children. There are, not surprisingly, other tellings, other facts.

It seems that Isadora, after returning to Paris, did not go to Italy but to England, where she visited Craig's mother, the great actress Ellen Terry. To Craig she wrote, "I am half mad with grief and pain and I wanted to feel your Mother's arms about me—as I used to dream they were before Deirdre was born—and to feel that dear pity and love that *she* gives that no one else has known how to give since their death . . ."

It seems that Duse did not send for Isadora but that it was Isadora who sought Duse out. Irma Duncan cites a note dated September 13 from Duse to Isadora on her arrival in Viareggio. "I embrace you and thank you . . . for having come and searched me out at this moment which is without life, without art for you."

It seems that the beautiful young sculptor, who appeared from the waves to Isadora in her desperation, was in fact not unknown to her. According to William Weaver, Duse's biographer, he was "a sculptor named Romano Romanelli, to whom Duse introduced Isadora. He made a bust of her, and she deliberately arranged to conceive a child by him."

It seems that Duse did not find Isadora's actions with the young sculptor "natural." Shortly after Isadora's brief affair Duse wrote to a friend: "Nothing of that which is irreparable is understood by this magnificent and dangerous creature! Her generosity is quite as great as her error of imagination.

"The 'irreparable' which nevertheless exalts the tone of life—no—she does not even see it and she wishes to throw herself back into life, bleeding life . . . and see again . . . What?—the smile of her dead child *in another* smile of another child that will be hers!

"Be sorry, my friend, for my littleness, for I understand nothing of *that will,* of that folly, of that supreme wisdom.

"Isadora Duncan has on her side the Supreme Strength— greater than life itself . . ."

It seems that Isadora was very upset by Duse's immediate reaction to her affair with the young sculptor. According to the playwright Mercedes de Acosta, who knew Isadora intimately in 1926 and 1927, Isadora told her that when she went to Duse's house and recounted her meeting with the "Greek god," Duse, "far from entering into the spirit of this adventure, was scandalized. Her disgust and disappointment in Isadora were so profound that there was nothing further for Isadora to do but leave her house. Duse never forgave this act of what she considered promiscuity, nor could she forgive the fact that while Isadora was grieving for her children she could, at the same time, have a sexual adventure. Isadora claimed it was not a 'sexual adventure,' but only a means toward an end in having another child.

"Isadora and Duse met years later but they were never again real friends. Isadora spoke to me many times about this incident and, although it had occurred many years in the past, it seemed to be often in her mind . . . Being such a complex person, she was rather puritanical at heart despite her outward behavior, and regardless of what she said about Duse, I believe she felt a deep guilt about the matter. She said, 'I never could have imagined that such a supreme artist as Duse could be so narrow-minded.' "

Did Isadora simply not remember in 1926, when she was writing her book, that she had visited Ellen Terry in 1913? Or was it too difficult for her to say that she (to others "The Mother") had sought out Ellen Terry as a "mother," just as it may have been difficult to say she was the one who had sought out Duse? Or had she forgotten that too? And in her telling of the young man and his appearing from the sea, did Isadora forget that she had known the young man and did she come to believe—because it was central to her sense of her self—that he had appeared from the waves, given by the gods?

16

One day in June 1912—when Mary Cassatt could not "draw a line nor think of work," a writer came to her with the intention of writing her biography. Years before Mary had said: "One would like to leave behind one superior art and a hidden Personality." But now she agreed to the project, in which she was assured there would be little written about her personal life. She also retained the right to make corrections in the manuscript, which was published the following year as *Mary Cassatt: Un peintre des enfants et des mères.*

The author, Achille Ségard, describes Mary in his first paragraph: "A very aristocratic woman with a tall and slender figure, dressed in black, leaning on a cane, and advancing cautiously on the sandy paths of her park with its magnificent trees: Thus Miss Mary Cassatt appeared to me the day when I visited her for the first time in her beautiful hermitage, Château Beaufresne, in Mesnil-Théribus, Oise. I helped her to climb the front steps. A smile of extreme kindness lit up her serious face and under curls threaded with gold, grey blue eyes, the color of still water, animated the strongly marked planes of her face. She held out an energetic fine hand, long, thin, hardworking and vital, vibrating with sensibility. We talked. On the walls of her windowed galleries Japanese prints . . . created an atmosphere of art. Through a half open door, one could see the sketch for a portrait of a child in a spring hat . . . sitting by a young mother . . . The trees of the park were still. The silences between our words were solemn."

A tone of intense admiration, if not adulation, permeates Ségard's language throughout the book. In part it is the tone of a writer working with a living subject, wanting to please, needing to please, knowing the subject will read and have the right to correct his work. It is the tone of a writer trying to say what is expected.

But one hears, if one listens, something else in Ségard's tone. It is hard to pinpoint exactly—and certainly it is made harder by the almost eighty years that separate us from his writing—but there is in the words about Mary Cassatt a hint of a twinning that has occurred between projected images— that of the biographer and that of the subject.

Just as he praises her, he praises himself; his values have become her values, her courage has become his courage, her independence, his independence. The image that is created is not her, not him, but something vibrating between the two of them, made up of desires and envies and hopes and, yes, practical needs—after all, he must also please his audience and his publisher.

On his part, gained in this twinning is a certain reflected glory from the praise of his subject. On her part there is the satisfaction—even if she participates reluctantly—of a need to have others see herself and her work as she wants them seen. And these two impulses entwine and reinforce each other. So reading this work, one feels as if one is trying to solve a single equation with two unknowns—two unknowns that keep shifting. But of course this is no equation, and solution is not the point.

If it seems at first that Ségard is overwhelmed by the strength of Mary's personality, that she is the one who is leading him on, it is also clear that he too has his own measure of control. He begins his report on her personal history with a statement by Mary that though she has long been a resident of

France, she remains irrevocably an American. Still she—and he—soon emphasize the influence of France upon her: the fact that one of her ancestors on her father's side was born in France, the fact that Mary's mother as a girl had learned to speak French well and had a general knowledge of French literature.

Ségard quotes Mary as describing her father as "a banker in Pittsburgh but he didn't have the soul of a man of affairs. He was imbued with many French ideas and devoted himself to our education." Ségard reports her telling of her first trip to France as a child of five or six and of the family staying five years before returning to Philadelphia.

" 'In about 1868,' " he quotes her, " 'I decided to become a painter. I decided at the same time to leave for Europe." The decision to make this departure, says Ségard in a footnote, was not without difficulty. "Miss Cassatt's father . . . frightened at the voyage . . . said 'I would rather see you dead.' "

After briefly noting Mary's studies in Italy and France and the influence of Correggio and of Rubens upon her work, Ségard arrives at the crucial episode of her career. In 1877, her work having been refused at the Salon, Mary was invited by Degas to exhibit with the Impressionists. Ségard quotes her as saying, " 'I accepted with joy . . . I had already recognized who were my true masters. I admired Manet, Courbet and Degas. I despised conventional art. I began to live . . .' "

His praise for her independence now erupts in rhetorical phrases. "How could a young American who came to France almost by chance, so young, still unacquainted with Paris have made such a remarkable choice? . . . Other women are pulled toward pretty art and elegance . . . She was drawn to the original and the strong . . . One could understand such a choice in Berthe Morisot or Eva Gonzales . . ." After all, says Ségard, they were ruled by personal considerations, in particular their relationship to the Manet family. And isn't it usual, he insists, in feminine psychology to be so affected by such considerations?

But Mary Cassatt's decision was not, he or she (he and she?) insists, of this order. Hers was a personal, independent decision. It was through an act of "free will, of spontaneous choice," that she separated herself from "the ordinary painters of her time." For a young girl to have done this was an indication that she was a singular personality, of an "élite" nature, who undoubtedly derived strength from her "forefathers." (Again, those "forefathers.")

"I imagine that a Whistler or a Mary Cassatt, rare in any country, is still more rare in England or in America than in France. They are . . . people . . . of exceptional character . . . One could say that the intelligence and sensibility . . . in the masses of these great nations are polarized in a small number of individuals, in whose characteristic types one finds . . . the subtleties of European culture . . . The intellectual Parisian milieu is often necessary to these exceptional natures in the same way that the temperature of a hot house is essential to certain rare plants . . ."

Yet, says Ségard, though Mary had joined with the Impressionists, she refused to sacrifice her own independence. The Impressionists, in their preoccupation with light and with air and with the exploration of a new palette, remained primarily landscape painters. Enchanted as they were with atmosphere, they looked at nature in a purely visual way. They were strangers to painting "the human soul." But in this aspect, he insists, "Mary Cassatt was an exception. Precisely what mattered to her was the individual expression of the human soul."

In her art she was "led little by little to restrict her search to . . . [the] primordial feeling [of youth in its flowering]. She wanted to understand it differently and more intimately . . . She wanted to draw from it entirely new variations in form, in movement and color . . ." So "by a sort of predestination" she eventually became a painter of mothers and children. Yet always, Ségard stresses, what mattered to her was reality, the reality on the canvas, without making use of any "enticement."

Once again he speaks of her independence: "Mary Cassatt is a rebel against all constraint . . ." Even though she admired Degas's work enormously—his incisiveness, his sureness, the ease of his rigorous design, the novelty of feeling that he evoked, the exactness of the movement of his subjects that he captured in his portraits, the way he seized the characteristic gesture—she was not and would not be his disciple. Clearly, says Ségard, Degas's terrible lucidity, his judgment on mankind, the cruelty of his observation, the piercing quality of his work, and his bitter irony, all of which set him apart from the other Impressionists, show an "order of feeling that had noth-

ing in common with Mary Cassatt," who, Ségard insists, was
more intellectual, more intellectually refined than any of her
"Impressionist comrades."

"I like to think to myself of Mary Cassatt's beginnings in
Paris," Ségard allows himself to say. "She ignored everything
that wasn't essential. She loved painting and she had no ambition. Instinct led her on . . . Precisely because she was a woman
and naturally pulled to the beautiful and gracious, she bridled
her temperament, reined it in to avoid the easy and the superfi-
cial . . . She submitted herself to a reality devoid of any attempt
at seduction or charm or grace . . . She wanted to do what was
true, simple and vigorous . . ."

He charts the development of her work from her early
admiration of Courbet, Manet, and Degas and a preoccupation
with realism, to a period beyond realism in which she studied
the Japanese masters and incorporated their simplicity and elegance into her own work, to the next period, when she returned
to realism, and finally, "in the last years," her progression to
a "tender and gracious art." It is the work of this late period,
almost exclusively studies of mothers and children, that Ségard
(and Mary?) judges her best, finding in it the most clear expression of the human "soul." (It is the work of the last years of
Mary Cassatt that modern critics, however, tend to view as
least impressive, repetitive and without force.)

Of one of the pastels of the late period, *Leaving the Bath*,
he says that it could as easily be titled *The Adoration*. In the
pastel two women are standing, a mother and perhaps her
sister, surrounding and holding a very young boy, unclothed,
just coming from his bath. The two women "lean toward the
infant-king . . . This baby is joyous. He laughs and raises his
little left hand to his mother, which she takes and brings devot-
edly to her mouth. The leaning of these two women toward the
little boy expresses love without limit, devotion without boundary, life entirely concentrated toward one end: the renunciation
of all that is personal for the eventual accomplishment of a
perfectly happy destiny. In their leaning toward the future,
they sacrifice to him the present. He is 'youth,' that is to say,
radiant innocence and perhaps also unknowing cruelty . . . He
is the little prince, the young all-powerful one, the idol who finds
it only natural that the whole world is at his feet."

But now, in a rare personal aside, Ségard allows himself a

departure from their unified vision. "It's possible that Miss Mary Cassatt, having had only the children of others to love, exaggerates, in a certain measure, the role of parents with regard to their children." But immediately he attributes to her a higher purpose for this exaggeration. "I sense that she understands only absolute sacrifice . . . without doubt this conception of family life is only the consequence of a yet more general opinion (perhaps unconscious) about the visible and invisible universe: nothing is of value but love and love is only of value through the sacrifices it demands.

"Do not look," he says, "in her work for the suffering, the miserable," for those who carry "hereditary stigmata or taints . . . Do not look for illness or degeneration of any sort . . . Not one infant who suffers. Not one child who cries or has a temper tantrum. Not one evil face. Unhappy childhood breaks her heart.

"It seems the Anglo-Saxon idealism and the need for justice of Miss Cassatt cause her to avoid this misery. She is too sensible and too much in the grip of fierce tenderness to bear that pain . . .

"Miss Mary Cassatt is devoted to art as if it were a religion. She has the eyes of a painter and to a certain extent the mentality of a sister of charity . . ."

In retrospect, he summarizes, "These works assure her in the history of art of this period an important place . . . [They are] a contribution to the glorification of the great impulses of the human soul and more particularly of maternal feeling."

She is an artist, he concludes, who does not pretend to be more than she is. She is not a technical innovator; innovation she learned from Degas and from Manet. But she has a great talent for design and color. "She has preferred to live in her place, which is not the first [among artists] but very close to the first . . . In her life and in her work she has been delicate, energetic and scrupulous." Her work will give to her compatriots the example of an "aristocratic art, which is clearly opposed to the brutal tendencies of certain schools that one could call democratic."

This harmonious vision of Mary Cassatt and her work—the painter of mothers and children, independent, sensitive, bound to reality but "opposed to tumult," an idealist too tender-hearted to allow misery to enter her work, a sister of charity

opposed to the "brutal tendencies" of certain modern schools—
is presented, is created, only a little more than a year after that
powerful event in her life, to which she has responded with the
words "fancy going back to babies and women, to paint." And
it is presented, created, at a time when not only was she suffering physically, but she was unable to work, mired in her body,
through her body. Yet, of course, nothing of this appears in
Ségard's work. Rectitude before others is still maintained.

There is only one small exception to this presented harmony, the telling of an episode in which tears are mentioned.
In a footnote Ségard records a memory of Mary's from 1891:
At that time her fellow artists had just formed the Société des
Peintres-Graveurs Français and had instituted a rule that for-
eign-born artists could not exhibit with them. Mary and Pissarro, who was born in the West Indies, finding themselves
excluded from the first exhibition of the new society, arranged
to have a simultaneous exhibit of their own work at Durand-
Ruel's Gallery. The night before the opening the members of
the Peintres-Graveurs held a dinner party to which Mary was
invited, and she agreed to go. In the course of the evening, the
other guests, members of the society, "teased her so merci-
lessly" that she left the dinner totally upset and practically
in tears.

There is also one glancing reference to Egypt in *Mary
Cassatt: Un peintre des enfants et des mères.* "Let us add that
during the greater part of her career Miss Mary Cassatt has not
been a traveler. Her point of attachment has always been Paris
. . . Miss Mary Cassatt has loved Paris. She loves it still. She has
never really left it. When she did go away to Egypt or to revisit
Italy or Spain or to visit the provinces of France, these trips
were for her only for rest or diversion."

On June 7, 1912, having seen Sé-
gard the day before for the first time, Mary writes to Louisine:
"After he left I was *exhausted*. I cannot talk or listen to much
talk, silence and solitude are best for my state . . ."

As the days pass she finds her own "uselessness" unbearable. "I am no use to anyone Louie dear and no one can be any
use to me until, if ever, I am rid of these pains. All my doctors
want me to work! How is it possible, they don't know what it
is to paint, they say only ten *minutes* a day . . ."

But by fall she is beginning to feel a little better. Though
she still has pain, she has found the determination to fight
against her own invalidism and weakness. She starts to assert
herself in the world through anger. It is a way she knows and
has known well.

"I am sick of the doctors," she writes on September 6. And
on September 26: "I must tell you . . . about Carnap [a man who
has not paid her some money he owes her]. I do feel glad I got
even with him . . . Such an insolent letter as he wrote to me,
laughing at me he laughed on the other side after the seizure

[impounding of goods], or after the threat of seizure . . .

". . . I am having some fun with Boignard [her doctor], he wanted to begin again like last year and talk Art and books. I brought him up short and insisted on medical talk, he does not like it, and really I don't need him he has done absolutely nothing for me, my dear Louie one must use one's own wits and then luck has something to do with it . . ."

By October 2 she is sleeping well at night. Only one night recently has she not slept and that was when Dr. Boignard came to see her while she was eating her dinner, "if you can call it dinner, which consists of soup, tapioca, which he at once forbade because tapioca is made of flour, and a roast potato, and an artichoke. Now I ought to see *no one* after five, and as much as possible no one before . . . Last year I was still using up my nervous force now I am in a reactive state . . ."

Once again and with confidence she speaks of "Art Matters." "As to the Rouart sale I cannot advise you, you will see for yourself when you get the catalogue. Of course I know you are able to buy anything you want without selling your Cézannes still I strongly advise you to sell, Mrs. Sears was offered 12500 francs for that nature morte, a bottle and an apple, I think very sketchy . . . The whole boom is madness and must fall."

On November 1 she mentions the visit of a "beautiful child" to her house. "What sunshine little children are in a house, you who are such a lover of babies you ought to have seen here the other day such a specimen as I have rarely if ever seen—a perfect type of the genus, blonde such as dolls are modeled on with a lovely expression nine months old . . ."

As winter approaches, she finds herself longing for the sun. She is planning to go by train to the south of France with her housekeeper, Mathilde Vallet, but she is worried by troublesome events in the world outside, "the Balkan business . . ." By November 15 she says, "The war cloud seems moving away, it was a dreadful prospect . . ."

She speaks again of her anger at Dr. Boignard and suggests that all he is interested in is getting money from her. "Now for Art matters," she goes on, suggesting to Louisine the proper purchase price for a Degas oil, *Danseuse à la barre*, that is for sale. Two hundred thousand francs or more isn't too much to pay for it, she writes. In the same sale someone has bought two of her own pastels, and her *Mother and Child* is expected to bring ten thousand francs. "I sold it for 600 and the 'Thé' [*Cup of Tea,* 1880] for 1000, together they may bring 25 to 30000 and I used to be afraid my pictures were not a good investment."

By the end of November she has moved into the Villa Angeletto in Grasse, in southern France. With her in the household are Mathilde Vallet, her chauffeur, the maids, and her two dogs—all those who help her to maintain her daily life, its necessities, its small and large realities.

On November 30 she writes with obvious pride that she has received a letter from a friend who was in Paris with "the Crown Prince and Princess of Sweden who are there incognito and wanted me to dine with them tomorrow, I of course telegraphed I am here . . ."

By now she thinks less and less of her illness and her pains; she is getting out in the world, though she still goes to bed every night right after dinner. She complains to Louisine, who is an ardent suffragette, about the attitude of her sister-in-law Jennie toward women. "I feel distinctly upset, the Herald of yesterday reproduced Jennie's remarks as to spanking the militant suffragette! Fancy any woman let alone a lady saying such a thing, proposing such a thing about other women. One can see that my brother is no longer there to keep her in order. The insolence of a woman in her position, never having known anything of the struggles of life judging other women . . .

"I must not think of it too much or I should let myself go telling her what I think of such *vulgarity.*"

But one day at the end of that year, she does "let go." A feeling explodes in her; containment does not hold. It has to do with an image of herself. And it has to do, in some way, with what Art is and is not to her.

In the early 1880s Degas painted a portrait of Mary, which still remains in her possession. He had done other paintings and etchings of her, but in those her back was turned to the viewer. In this portrait she faces the viewer. She is shown sitting, leaning forward. She is wearing a hat. Her shoulders are slightly hunched, her arms held close to her torso, her weight

leaning slightly on her arms. Her body, except for the attitude
of leaning, covered as it is by a black dress, is essentially indeterminate in its expression. In her hands she is holding some
cards or illustrations. They do not command her attention.
Though she is looking down, it is not the cards she is seeing.
There is the suggestion in this woman, in the leaning, in the
gaze, of something undecided, perhaps of something vulnerable but unrevealed. The face and the hands, the wrists sharply
demarcated by white cuffs, are linked by their placement in the
forward plane of the picture. Sitting in the chair, which is only
sketched in, the background indeterminate though intensely
light behind her head, she seems isolated in an unresolved
space.

Now suddenly—in late December 1912—she writes to the
dealer Joseph Durand-Ruel, telling him she wants the painting
sold. She does not want it left to her family as a portrait of
herself. "It has qualities of art, but is so distressing and shows
me as a person so repugnant that I would not want anyone to
know that I posed for it . . . If you believe my portrait to be
saleable, I would like it to be sold to a stranger and especially
that my name should not be attached to it." And in a postscript
she adds, "As for the price of the picture, I leave that to you.
I cannot make an estimate of its value—that is a distressing but
a very strong feeling. It seems to me a true Degas."

A true Degas. And yet it must be gotten rid of.

Whatever this image has been to her, an image of herself
as she was almost thirty years before, it is having its effect
upon her in the present and threatens to affect the future. It is
not as she wants herself to be seen, to be remembered . . .

What was in the painting that she found so repugnant?
Was it the body, the face, the hint of sadness, the unguarded-
ness, the letting go into being seen? What had Ségard (and
Mary?) said about Degas? His "terrible lucidity," his "judgment on mankind," the "cruelty of his observation," the "piercing quality of his work," his "bitter irony." Did she see these
qualities in the portrait now? Had she not seen them before?

Or was there in her that almost indefinable reaction that
women sometimes feel when they look in the mirror and see the
contour, the shape, the line, the color, the weight of the image facing them, as if the physical itself has been translated
into fate, and all possibility of modification—by dress or by

makeup—annulled? A sense of repugnance in which others' eyes are invoked as judge of oneself.

Perhaps.

But she is a painter. Above all else, it is what she sees that matters to her. She does not want to see—in life, in a painting (how are they connected for her?)—what she has seen in this portrait of herself.

There is a photograph of Mary, taken that year—or the next—in the cloisters of St.-Trophime in Arles. It shows Mary standing—in profile—in a garden, beside a bed of flowers or ground cover. Behind her are two columns, topped with elaborate capitals, beneath a stone arch. She faces to the right. She is wearing a hat with a wide brim and a high crown, surmounted by what looks like a plume. The hat almost completely shadows her face, except for a small shaft of light on her chin. Wearing a long-skirted suit with severe, though elegant lines, she stands stiffly erect. She holds an umbrella in her right hand, its tip on the ground, but there is no weight upon it, there is no leaning here. Standing among the flowers, she looks stony, as if she were carved, still.

In *The Burden of Egypt* the noted Egyptian scholar John A. Wilson writes of Egyptian sculpture, in the round and in relief, and of Egyptian painting: "The essential cubism of Egyptian statuary produced that squared, static, and solid flat figure which covers the walls of Egyptian tombs and temples. The flat planes of statuary appeared here skilfully twisted, with eye and shoulders in full frontal view, the rest of the body in profile. For its purpose, this figure was wonderfully successful. Like the statue, it was designed for eternity. Each figure claimed eternal life by solidity and stolidity; by avoiding the appearance of flexibility, momentary action, or passing emotion; and by standing massive and motionless, sublimely freed from a single location in space or a single moment in time."

PART
TWO

18

Mary Cassatt painted two self-portraits. The first is dated 1878, when she was thirty-four, recently settled in Paris. She is shown wearing an elegant dress and bonnet, sitting on a striped couch, leaning on her lower right arm, which in turn rests upon a striped cushion. Under the decorative bonnet, which is tied below her chin with a long bow, the face is intent, the mouth set willfully (almost on the edge of rancor). The use of color in the portrait is very subtle and highly organized. The background is green and yellow, with a small amount of red, colors repeated in the striped couch and pillow. The dress is luminously white, alizarin crimson in the shadows, frilly, light. The body underneath, as suggested by the drapery of the dress, is not clear, its position contradictory in its turning. The upper part of the body, facing front, is held still, idealized with its thin waist, and the faint suggestion of the breasts. The lower part of the body, sketched in, shows the sitter's left hip raised, but the leg coming out of the hip on the diagonal is misplaced. The body in its laxity and stillness is floating, filmy, unfelt. It is an idealized feminine form, without weight or vigor or intention, covered over, hidden beneath a surface whose principal function is to reflect light. In contrast, the head and face are strongly rooted in the canvas space, thrust forward by the darkness of the bonnet and the enclosing ribbon. The solidity of the head and face are balanced by the solidity of the striped cushion on which she leans. The face, despite the bonnet, despite the ribbon, despite the one earring shown, could be, if not masculine, a neuter face.

The second self-portrait dates from around 1880. It is one of the few watercolors that Mary did. She sits in a chair, wearing a dark dress of a color that seems to be prussian blue mixed with black. A bonnet (of violet and raw sienna), hastily sketched in, ties under her chin. The position of her hands, also vaguely sketched, suggests that she may be at an easel. The body is upright, one might almost say stiff. Yet the delicacy of the rendering contradicts that suggestion.

Despite the sketchiness and vagueness of this portrait, mystery is resolutely refused, as if it had been withdrawn, retracted, dissolved away in the watery medium, robbed of strength. (The only shadow, from the bonnet, is on the upper part of the face.) The expression of the face is neither meditative nor focused. Body and face and head are suffused with an idealized softness, with ''prettiness''—I can find no better word than that. It is like a portrait of a young woman who paints for pleasure. There is something of that lack of seriousness in it.

A self-portrait. How is it for the one who paints it? Of course, she—the artist—looks at it, as at any painting, as a composition of balancing and opposing forces, of color, of line, of contour, of shape, of volume, of depth, of tension, of negative and positive space. And yet there are other less abstract considerations involved since it is a portrait of the self: the personal, the historical, the emotional, the anecdotal, the accidental. The abstract and the specific, the formal and informal, the impersonal and the personal—in a self-portrait they lie together, enmeshed.

She—the artist—looks at herself in a mirror, yet she sees the image as if it is another. She is creating an image of how others will, someday, see her. (It is a kind of performance, this presentation of the self.)

The function of mirroring in self-portraiture is intricate

Mary Cassatt, Portrait of the Artist (Self-Portrait); *gouache on paper (1878)*. THE METROPOLITAN MUSEUM OF ART, BEQUEST OF EDITH H. PROSKAUER, 1975.

ABOVE: Mary Cassatt, The Boating Party; *oil on canvas (1893–94).* NATIONAL GALLERY OF ART, WASHINGTON, D.C.; CHESTER DALE COLLECTION.

OPPOSITE: Mary Cassatt, The Woman with the Red Zinnia; *oil on canvas (1891).* NATIONAL GALLERY OF ART, WASHINGTON, D.C.; CHESTER DALE COLLECTION.

Mary Cassatt, The Coiffure; *drypoint and soft-ground etching in color (ca. 1891).* NATIONAL GALLERY OF ART, WASHINGTON, D.C.; ROSENWALD COLLECTION.

Mary Cassatt, Woman Bathing; *drypoint and soft-ground etching in color (ca. 1891).* NATIONAL GALLERY OF ART, WASHINGTON, D.C.; ROSENWALD COLLECTION.

OPPOSITE: Mary Cassatt, Mrs. Robert S. Cassatt, The Artist's Mother; *oil on canvas (ca. 1889).* THE FINE ARTS MUSEUMS OF SAN FRANCISCO, MUSEUM PURCHASE, WILLIAM H. NOBLE BEQUEST FUND.

ABOVE: Mary Cassatt, Lydia Leaning on Her Arms, Seated in a Loge; *pastel (1879).* THE NELSON-ATKINS MUSEUM OF ART, KANSAS CITY, MISSOURI; NELSON FUND.

Edgar Degas, Mary Cassatt; *oil on canvas (ca. 1880–1884).*
NATIONAL PORTRAIT GALLERY, SMITHSONIAN INSTITUTION;
GIFT OF THE MORRIS AND GWENDOLYN CAFRITZ FOUNDATION
AND THE REGENTS' MAJOR ACQUISITIONS FUND, SMITHSONIAN
INSTITUTION.

and dense, as if mirrors are reflecting other mirrors endlessly. The painter has looked into a mirror—a virtual, not a real space—made by the eye following lines of sight reflected off the glass, as if there is a depth, but there is no depth. (That the image is reversed is accepted.) The painter, accepting that mirroring, translates that mirroring into a new—actual—image.

There is above all for a woman in self-portraiture the consciousness of being judged in relation to other women, as more beautiful or less beautiful. It is a consciousness that never faded in Mary Cassatt. In a letter of November 29, 1907, to Louisine she wrote, "You are the only Mother I have known who had not a marked preference for her boys over her girls, my Mother's pride was in her boys. I think sometimes a girl's first duty is to be handsome and parents feel it when she isn't. I am sure my Father did, it wasn't my fault though . . ."

19

In late November or early December 1913, Isadora left Viareggio and went to Florence with Hener Skene. There she wrote to Gordon Craig: "I am passing through Florence—If you would *like* to see me come tomorrow afternoon about 6—But if it would give you too much pain—*don't*—Let me know in the morning—Myself I am in a strange state beyond anything human I think—I am on my way to Rome—and then perhaps to Egypt—to Karnak to rest in that Great Temple that I sent you once a picture of with little Deirdre sitting there looking up so calm and sweet."

After seeing Craig briefly, she continued on to Rome with Skene. She may have thought of going on to Egypt but she did not go. When she received a telegram from Singer "beseeching" her to return to Paris, "in the name of [her] art," she journeyed north instead.

Upon her arrival she found that Singer had reserved for her a "magnificent suite of rooms" at the Crillon, which he had filled with flowers. When they met she told him of her "Viareggio experience" and of her "mystic dream of the children's reincarnation and return to earth." (By now she knew that she was, once again, pregnant.)

Singer's response, according to Isadora, was first to hide his face in his hands, and then, "after what seemed a struggle," to urge that he and she put personal considerations aside to create the school she had always wanted. He had purchased the former Paillard Palace Hotel at Bellevue, outside of Paris, with its extensive gardens, and he now offered it to Isadora along with the assurance of the necessary funds to maintain it. Further he had decided that the theater he had once promised to her should be built on the property at Bellevue.

"Seeing what a tangled mesh of sorrow and catastrophe this life had brought me, in which only my Idea [for the school] always shone bright and untarnished above it all, I consented," writes Isadora. Under her direction decorators and carpenters transformed "this rather banal hotel to a Temple of the Dance of the Future."

Fifty children were chosen to be the first pupils, to be housed, fed, and clothed by Singer. "I bought for the children many-coloured capes and when they left the School to walk in the woods, as they danced and ran, they resembled a flock of beautiful birds." She saw in them a "new movement in humanity . . . the gestures of the Vision of Nietzsche:

" 'Zarathustra the dancer, Zarathustra the light one . . . ready for flight, beckoning unto all birds, ready and prepared, a blissfully light-spirited one.' "

Of her work at the school, Isadora writes, "I spent hours every day teaching my pupils, and when I was too tired to stand, I reclined on a couch and taught them by the movements of my hands and arms. My powers of teaching seemed indeed to border on the marvellous. I had only to hold out my hands towards the children and they danced. It was not even as though I taught them to dance, but rather as if I opened a way by which the Spirit of the Dance flowed over them."

An undated photograph of Isadora with her pupils, taken in Paris, shows Isadora sitting, her face in profile, her upper body half turned to the front. She sits easily and erect, her left arm resting on the high back of a chair, over which is draped one of her elegant shawls. Her lower right arm rests on her right knee. Her right wrist and hand are extended toward the girls, who sit and stand before her, reverently gazing at her.

Her right index finger points to and indicates a diagonal above their heads. She and the girls are in light, the background is black. She is, as always, totally at ease before the camera, with any and all eyes upon her. Though she is still, in her stillness she is about to move, about to induce motion in the others leaning toward her. She is summoning them to motion, and they, like aspects of herself, on a living Greek frieze, are about to respond.

Toward the end of *My Life* Isadora quotes Nietzsche once again. "Nietzsche says, 'Woman is a mirror,' and I have only reflected and reacted to the people and forces that have seized me and, like the heroines of the 'Metamorphoses' of Ovid, have changed form and character according to the decree of the immortal gods."

20

There was a Mary who was a witness to the birth of Isadora's third child, Mary Desti, an American, who, as Mary Sturges, had met Isadora in Paris in 1901. Having just arrived in Paris with her baby, Preston (later to become a famous Hollywood director), Mary Desti stumbled on the Duncans by chance, when she was looking for a place to live.

In her biography of Isadora, *The Untold Story*, she tells of their first meeting: "How describe Isadora? Had I been ushered into Paradise and given over to my guardian angel, I could not have been more uplifted. Isadora was in her little dancing tunic, a colorless gauze of some sort, draped softly about her slender ethereal form; her exquisite little head poised on her swan-like throat and tilted to one side like a bird, as though the weight of her auburn curls caused it to droop; a little retroussé nose that gave just the slightest human touch, otherwise I should have thrown myself on my knees before her, believing I was worshipping a celestial being."

Mary Desti was to see that "celestial being" frequently

over the next years. Though much of the time she lived in the United States, where she married a third and then a fourth husband, she always seemed to be present at the crucial happenings in Isadora's life. She was in Paris with Isadora at the funeral of Deirdre and Patrick; she was with her at the birth of her third child; she was with Isadora in France and Germany in 1923; she was with Isadora the day of her death.

Victor Seroff has attacked Mary Desti and her story in *The Real Isadora,* his own biography of the dancer. But it must be remembered that Seroff, a rather bad-tempered biographer (and who can blame a biographer for being bad-tempered?) was Isadora's lover in her last years and disliked anyone else who, having known Isadora, wrote about her. In particular he disliked Mary Desti, of whom he writes, "She was about Isadora's age, a robust woman with a liberal amount of unspent energy, bringing with her wherever she went more noise and disorder than harmony and peace. In her approach to life, she thought everything 'terribly funny . . .' "

As his book progresses, Seroff becomes more and more enraged at Desti. He calls her "This obese, loud-mouthed, middle-aged woman" (though in fact Mary Desti was about the same weight and size and age as Isadora) and "an illiterate megalomaniac." (His words testify, more than anything else, to the complexity of feelings Isadora, rather than Mary Desti, evoked in others.)

It is certainly true that there is a good deal of naïve self-praise in Mary Desti's book. Often she assigns herself a major role, secondary only to Isadora. And it is also true that there is something strangely amusing in her description of events when the events are indeed not amusing events, as if inadvertently she mixes tones and qualities of feeling, or as if she does not make certain kinds of distinctions.

Mercedes de Acosta says that Mary Desti "worshipped Isadora to such an extent that in a curious way she had taken on some essence of Isadora, although there was certainly no physical resemblance between these two women and they were totally different in character." Yet Mary Desti, in her book, does convey a strong sense of that difference. The very naïveté, the undisguised and human self-praise in her telling makes it possible to see her clearly, and through that opening it is possible to see Isadora in another light.

She begins her story of the birth of Isadora's third child in August 1914 with the statement that she and Isadora had been living at Bellevue, awaiting the birth, but they decided to move to the Hôtel Crillon because all the servants left at the first rumor of war. The pupils of the school were also away at the time: they had been invited to Singer's estate in Devon for a summer vacation.

At the Crillon Isadora was attended by a Dr. Bosson. But suddenly he was notified that he had to report for military service, so he departed, leaving behind a basket of instruments and "the most unsympathetic nurse, who seemed terrified at the idea of his having left her alone."

Fearful that Isadora was about to give birth without adequate help, Mary Desti begged her to leave the hotel and go to a nursing home or hospital at once, but Isadora said she was too tired and would look for one the next day. However, the next morning at four o'clock, Isadora came into Mary's room and told her that they must find a nursing home at once. At this point Mary begged Isadora to stay at the Hôtel Crillon but Isadora insisted on leaving. (This backing-and-forthing between them seems to have been typical, with Isadora usually the one who won, as now.)

Carrying a list of nursing homes recommended by the hotel, they set out in the huge touring car that Singer had given to Isadora. "Often when we would arrive at a certain address, we would have to wait in the car until Isadora had got over a spasm of pain. Then, after they had taken us up in the elevator into one of their rooms, Isadora would utter a shriek, 'Take me out, take me out of this place.' Down the elevator again, into the car, and off to another place.

"Finally in desperation, at nine o'clock, we tried to pass one of the gates out of Paris to go to Bellevue but the guards refused to let us out . . .

"Realizing that there was very little time, I decided to storm the gates and told the chauffeur that no matter who said to stop, at the next gate, he was to rush through. The gate happened to be open when we got there, and as I jumped out, I told the chauffeur to go on and he shot through as the guards yelled at him to stop. I explained that this was Isadora Duncan and her baby was being born and she had to get to Bellevue. They put me through a third degree of questions but I finally convinced them and they allowed me to return to Paris for a doctor."

Mary Desti brought the specialist to Bellevue, where Augustin Duncan was waiting with Isadora (Singer seems not to have been present, though he was in Paris at the time), and an hour later the baby was born. ". . . We understood very quickly that this exquisite little child that looked like a Donatello statue hadn't a chance of living. His lungs refused to expand despite everything science should do."

At Mary's suggestion, the baby was brought in for Isadora to hold. "It seemed to me so horrible that she should never see him, this little being that she counted on for her salvation. So, very pale and with trembling hands, I carried him in and placed him in her arms.

"It seemed as if the gates of heaven had opened for Isadora. We left him alone with her for just a few moments and being too overcome myself, I sent the nurse in to bring him away. Isadora had already noticed something was wrong . . ."

At this moment Singer telephoned and, when told of the baby's condition, arranged to have oxygen sent. The attending physician attempted to revive the baby but his efforts proved useless.

"Then Augustin and I went in and sat one on each side of Isadora. She said, 'Tell me the truth, Augustin.' He said, 'Isadora, poor Isadora, your baby is dead.'

"There are no words to describe the mute sorrow that passed over Isadora. She simply closed her eyes, while Augustin went out and I sat quietly beside her.

"After a little time the doctor had gone and taken Augustin with him to prepare for the interment of the little baby. When Isadora opened her eyes, she begged me to get her a cup of tea. Upon going into the other room, I found the nurse had gone. It was dusk and in this tremendous palace of two hundred odd rooms and about eighty bathrooms, and the great winding, sinister stairs, and the little dead baby lying there alone, my knees shook together as I went down the two flights to the kitchen . . .

"I finally prepared some tea and how I ever got up those stairs again, seeing ghosts and shadows in every corner and groping my way along the now dark hall to Isadora's room, without dropping dead from fright, will always be a mystery to me."

There is something in Mary's telling that opens the event up to view. Is it that her intentions are so obvious and human, as are her responses? Is it that her voice, wavering between naïve self-pride and sudden, almost involuntary revelation, seems innocent of its effect? Is it that it does not have the power of history or legend (as in Isadora's case) impeding our access to her? Is it her artlessness itself that renders her performance transparent so we can see beyond what she says? For sometimes—it is very odd—through seemingly inaccurate words, even through flighty words, one can be led to imagination—to identification: one doesn't argue how.

To imagine what it is to be a witness to this event, to see a child born and then, gasping for life, die, and to be in this almost empty château, dark with death, trying to get a cup of tea . . .

After the birth, alone with the baby, Isadora tells us she whispered, "Who are you, Deirdre or Patrick? You have returned to me."

To go through that pain in childbirth, that hope, that conviction, and to find at the end nothingness—the symbol of nothingness—the actuality of nothingness. How put it into words in its full rawness? To try to find a way of speaking in which words are the equivalent of gestures? But words are not gestures, they are indeed impeded gestures.

There is a pastel by Mary Cassatt, done in 1880 or 1881, called *Baby in a Striped Armchair*. It is a paradoxical work, unlike any other that Mary did, this formal individual portrait of a young baby. It has been identified as a portrait of Lucie Bernard, the youngest child of friends of Cassatt's. In its format, says art historian Suzanne Lindsay, it comes closest to the tradition of "the mortuary portrait, in which a dead child appears most typically alone, laid out in state in its burial attire."

The baby sits in a chair, which is colored an intense blue with darker blue stripes, against a mottled red-orange background. The child's face is intensely alive with startlingly blue eyes, eyes that seem meditative, thoughtful, older. The body of the child is encased in a constricting white dress, blue in the shadows. The body seems wrapped, bundled, inert. In its still-ness and total constriction it suggests nothing so much as mummification.

21

In the second week of August 1914, after arranging for Bellevue to be taken over as an army hospital by the Catholic order of Les Dames de France, Isadora and Mary Desti drove south through the war zone to Deauville. Isadora took a suite of rooms at the Hôtel Normandie, while Mary Desti went to work as a nurse at a new military hospital, housed in the former casino.

Weeks passed, says Isadora, but she did not recover. She remained "so weak that I could hardly walk out on the beach to breathe the fresh breeze of the ocean." However, there were many distractions since the hotel had become a "refuge for many distinguished Parisians," including the Count Robert de Montesquiou (whom we have met briefly through his private diary). In the evenings Isadora listened with great admiration as he recited his poems "proclaiming with ecstasy the power of Beauty."

Soon, however, Isadora felt the need to travel again; but too ill to do so, she moved to a villa nearby. It is this villa, furnished in black and white, that becomes the setting for another incident, framed as she has framed others before, with elements of predestination, of unheeded warning, and of inescapable Fate, an incident of "death-like love."

Sick and desolate she goes to the casino hospital to consult the doctor in charge. Was it her imagination, she wonders, or "did he turn as if to fly when he saw me?" She confronts him and he stammers an excuse, yet continues to stare at her with a "haunted look." When he comes to see her the next day at her "Black and White" villa, she tells him of her sorrow, of "the baby that would not live." He stares at her in the "same hallucinated manner" and suddenly "clutched me in his arms and covered me with caresses.

" 'You are not ill,' he exclaimed, 'only your soul is ill—ill for love. The only thing that can cure you is Love, Love, and more Love.' "

Grateful for "this passionate and spontaneous burst of affection," Isadora accepts his suggestion for a cure. It is, it seems, a double healing, for he—the doctor—André—must also recover, each day, from "the sufferings of the wounded, the often hopeless operations—all the horrors of the horrible War.

"After these hard days and pitiful nights this strange man had need of love and passion, at the same time pathetic and ferocious, and from these fiery embraces and hours of maddening pleasure my body emerged healed and well . . ."

But though her body is recovering, she finds herself oppressed by the atmosphere of death—the death in the war, which is itself a continuing reminder of the death of her children. At the same time, she begins to notice that André's passion is becoming "more sombre in its fantastic intensity." She feels there is some mystery connected with his initial evasion of her and with his "haunted" look. She presses him to explain and André answers, " 'When you know all, it will mean our separation. You must not ask me.' "

One night she wakes to find him bending over her, watching her in her sleep, and she begs him to reveal the "sinister mystery." He moves away from her, he stands with bent head, he asks her, " 'Don't you know me?' . . .

"I looked. The mist cleared away. I gave a cry. I remembered. That terrible day." She recognizes André as the doctor who had come to her Neuilly villa, the day of the children's drowning, promising to save them. He had spent hours with

Deirdre, giving her mouth-to-mouth resuscitation. And now, he confesses, when he looks at Isadora sleeping, he thinks of Deirdre, as she lay dead.

From that night on she realizes that "I loved this man with a passion I had myself ignored, but as our love and desire for one another increased, so also increased his hallucination . . ."

Walking along the ocean, she feels "a great desire to . . . walk straight into the sea, to end forever the intolerable grief from which I could find no relief either in Art, in the rebirth of a child, or in love." However, she does not walk into the sea but starts back to the villa. Halfway there she meets André, who upon seeing her, cries "like a child." Now they both realize that separation is essential, "for our love, with its terrible obsession, could only lead to death or a madhouse."

She adds one further fateful twist to end this story of a "death-like love." Opening a trunk that she sent for from Bellevue, she finds that it contains not her clothes but those of Deirdre and Patrick. She utters a long wailing "death-cry" and faints. "André found me there, unconscious, when he returned—lying over the open trunk with all the little garments clutched in my arms."

It would be easy to fall into an operatic comparison—to use a word like *Wagnerian* or even *mock-Wagnerian* in describing this incident and its telling, but that would be, I think, a kind of intellectual self-congratulation, a stopping point. One has to resist being seduced by Isadora's forms into too easy acquiescence or equally easy pigeonholing and dismissal.

Is it now more possible (after Mary Desti's words) to follow the movement of Isadora's feeling and action here? Or is she once again behind a barrier, hidden by this framed yet unknowing telling? Reading, one gets a sense of her having been encompassed, a sense of her feeling herself forced into stillness and into darkness, into total constraint. Pushed so far, she pushes farther. Pressing for relief from the darkness and death that the gods, once so benign, have accorded her, she turns and embraces sex. (It is a solution familiar to her, one that has served her well in other crises.) In her action there is no indication of deliberation. (In Isadora's actions there is almost never deliberation.)

This time she finds that sex is joined to darkness, joined to death, but she presses on. In this telling, in this incident, there is a kind of passive falling, a falling in which she accords herself power, into which she throws her power, her body leading her through desire, to disregard risk, ordinary event, and ordinary feeling—an assigning of responsibility to the gods, even as she becomes more godlike in her assumptions, throwing herself into this affair, seeking to erase all barriers between sex and death, between life and death, between birth and death. (One cannot go timorously in pursuit of Isadora's feelings and actions in motion. One has to follow her leaps.)

It is not surprising that André finds it is all too much for him, this "death-like love." He breaks down, he cries, he fears insanity. For the force of Isadora's "mirroring" continues, her power to evoke the inner images of others in her motions, and to magnify those inner images through her capacity for reflecting them. He pulls back from his "terrible obsession." And she pulls back. The affair ends. (Later she will say that it was never she that ended an affair, always the man.)

22

There exists a published novel with the following scene: It is Paris in the 1870s. Two artists sit in a café, speaking of their work. He is famous, middle aged; she is his young colleague and disciple.

Together they stroll to his studio. As they stand side by side, examining a print, she turns and looks at him and sees desire in his eyes. Inadvertently she touches him on the arm. He at once assures her that he has reverence for her womanly integrity. He will not try to turn their friendship into more than it is. (Some days earlier, however, he has in a burst of passion, for which he apologized, kissed her.)

Now she declares her own passion to him:

"Edgar, I want you to touch me. I want what you want."

. . . In a moment they were together, arms entwined.

"Edgar, we tried, but we cannot deny this."

". . . Will you come upstairs to my rooms?"

. . . He took her hand and led her up the dingy stairs to his living quarters . . . "Are you worried?" he asked with a hint of a nervous smile on his lips. She looked into his eyes and nodded ever so slightly before their lips met. With the kiss her desire overcame her fears. His body pressed her close and she wanted nothing but his closeness.

. . . So many clothes. Yet to take them off and stand naked before him . . . was painful to contemplate. Nakedness was nothing to them, they had painted dozens of nudes. But this was different . . .

Her gaze met his sensual eyes, and passion flowed. She removed her petticoat, tossing it on a chair, and went to his arms . . . Oh God, how she loved him, wanted him. She found herself caressing his body without shame, her dear perfect god, her genius, for whom she craved hopelessly. This was what life was made of, she thought.

Later, when their passion was spent, Edgar propped himself up on his elbows . . . "Mary, I wish you would let me paint you like this."

"Would you let *me* paint *you* like this?"

Edgar (Yes, Edgar Degas) and Mary (Yes, Mary Cassatt), as imagined characters in a romance of art and life, a work which the author, Joan King, describes as "a story of fantasy as well as fact, born of a need to know her [Mary] better."

In fact, there are no facts about Mary Cassatt's sexual life. There is no record in her history of any sexuality. There is not even a mention of the thought of marriage or an engagement, except once:

In October 1868, when Mary and Eliza Haldeman, a former fellow student at the Pennsylvania Academy of Fine Arts, were studying painting in France, Eliza's brother, Carsten, came to visit. To her mother Eliza wrote, "Carsten was out to see me on Sunday and took breakfast with Mary & I at her Studio. He was impolite enough to say that he did not like the cheese nor the wine, nor the eggs—all the while eating very hardily. He says Mary & he are engaged, I believe it happened this way. We saw one day at [a shop] a wedding veil which was too lovely to describe and cost $1000 dollars, Mary said she would marry Carsten if he gave her the veil for a present which he said he would do, so the thing was arranged. I need not say the veil is *not yet* bought. I suppose they will wait till the day is fixed for the marriage.

"Carsten started for Italy this week . . ."

But beyond this incident (A game? A joke? It is hardly passion, though maybe passion itself is the joke), in Mary Cassatt's life there is not even the slightest suggestion of a sexual involvement, no hint of passion for a man—or a woman.

Once, late in life, according to Nancy Hale, Mary was asked if she had ever had an affair with Degas and she answered, "What! That common little man? What a repulsive idea."

And as for Degas, once, late in his life, suddenly speaking of Mary to the art editor Forbes Watson, he said, "I would have married her, but I could never have made love to her."

Degas, according to his biographer Roy McMullen, "lived, as far as even his close acquaintances could tell, utterly without sexual gratification. He was concubineless as well as wifeless . . . There can be little doubt that . . . [the reason for his celibacy] was impotence—" McMullen quotes references to Degas's impotence in a letter written by Manet and in the journals of Edmond de Goncourt. He also cites a letter from van Gogh to Emile Bernard, which reads in part, "Why do you say that Degas has trouble having an erection? Degas lives like a little notary and does not love women because he knows that if he loved them and spent a lot of time kissing them he would become mentally ill and inept in his art. Degas's painting is vigorously masculine and impersonal precisely because he has accepted the idea of being personally nothing but a little notary with a horror of sexual sprees."

Yet—no matter the evidence—the hint, the rumor, the conviction of, the desire for an affair or at least a "romance" between Mary and Degas has penetrated the work of serious scholars:

"Except for his affair with Mary Cassatt of which we know very little, there were no women in Degas' life . . . The similarity of their taste, *identical intellectual dispositions and identi-*

cal predilection for drawing, were to transform their friendly relations into a love affair, the duration and intensity of which we know nothing."

"So the state of their friendship [between Degas and Mary] was like a changing magnetic field in which objects are given motion by attraction and repulsion. There were no tragedies or scandals. Their love simply grew into a part of the artistic life of Paris."

"As for her true feelings for the irascible Degas, she apparently took care that their correspondence be destroyed before their deaths, protecting their privacy and preventing us from drawing any definitive conclusions. It might be inferred, however, that their relationship was quite warm, even in many ways romantic . . . but not romantic enough to tempt either of them to consummate it."

"She and Degas were the best of friends, and if Degas was in love with her, and he well may have been, she could not reconcile herself to such a relationship, as his bohemian way of living was offensive to her strictly conventional manner of life."

But it is not only in the work of these scholarly writers that this "affair" or "romantic attachment" has its being. It is in the air, it is one of the few things that even well-informed people think they have heard about the intensely private Mary Cassatt. Yes, Mary Cassatt, they will say, she had an affair with some artist, didn't she? Who was it? Degas? Yes, Degas.

It is as if up against—next to—the power of what has been, there always lies another power, the power of what did not happen.

23

Writing to Louisine Havemeyer on January 30, 1913, from the Villa Angeletto in Grasse, Mary Cassatt darts from one idea to another, from one judgment to another, then moves rapidly on again. It is not so much restlessness as a skimming on the surface that creates its own continuity. She refers to the behavior of a woman who is a mutual acquaintance: "she is selfishness incarnate, and has never done anything but flirt since she has been in long skirts . . ."

Next she jumps to James Stillman and doctors, destiny, and H. G. Wells: "Mr. Stillman has no belief in French doctors, and no belief in any but the well known ones, I don't quite agree with him, there is much luck, or destiny rather in our lives . . .

"Have you read Wells's 'Marriage' I found it very interesting his criticism of our modern life. The restlessness and want of purpose . . ."

The weather is "atrocious . . . cold, fog, and drizzling . . ."

But then, as if with a glancing blow or in an aside, the

mention of Egypt: "We had just such days as yesterday here on the Nile only more so."

"If only I felt strong enough to work, then life would be filled with something," she writes on March 12. "I don't feel anything like so much interest in Art. I only want to get to work and think of all I want to do and never will."

"How lonely one can be in this world . . . ," she laments later that month. But immediately after this cry of loneliness comes a lashing out in anger, this time at Matisse and all that he represents. "As to what you write about pictures, I think you flatter Matisse . . . Matisse is a 'facteur' [literally, "postman"; slang for "bad news"]. If you could see his early work! Such a commonplace vision such weak execution, he was intelligent enough to see he could never achieve fame, so shut himself up for years and evolved this and has achieved notoriety. My dear Louie it is not alone in politics that anarchy reigns, it saddens me, of course, it is in a certain measure our set [the Impressionists] which has made this possible. People have been persuaded that composition, pictures, were not necessary that sketches hints were enough. Certain things should not have left the artist's studio nor his portfolios. Then the public accepted everything . . ."

But the anger is not appeased through one letter. There is so much anger, it must be said again, this time in a letter to Mary's niece Ellen Mary Cassatt. There is the same railing against Matisse in almost identical words (as if the rage itself is solidifying in its expression). But rage brings further rage: "As to this Gertrude Stein, she is one of a family of California Jews who came to Paris poor and unknown; but they are not Jews for nothing. They—two of the brothers—started a studio, bought Matisse's pictures cheap and began to pose as amateurs of the only real art. Little by little people who want to be amused went to these receptions where Stein received in sandals and his wife in one garment fastened by a broach, which if it gave way might disclose the costume of Eve. Of course the curiosity was aroused and the anxiety as to whether it *would* give way; and the pose was, if you don't admire these daubs I am sorry for you; you are not one of the chosen few. Lots of people went . . . but I never would, being too old a bird to be caught by chaff . . ."

(Yet Mary had in fact once gone to an "evening" at the home of Gertrude and Leo Stein. According to Nancy Hale, she was taken there in 1908 by a Mrs. Montgomery Sears, to whom Gertrude Stein had expressed an interest in meeting Mary, as they had both been born in Allegheny City, Pennsylvania. "However," Hale reports, "after Mary met a number of Miss Stein's and Leo's friends and looked at their array of early Picassos and Matisses, she went back to Mrs. Sears . . . and said, " 'I have never in my life seen so many dreadful paintings in one place. I have never seen so many dreadful people gathered together, and I want to be taken home.' ")

Anger is an old story for Mary—the containment, the building up, the sudden release of pressure in an outburst. As a young woman, in anger she broke with a fellow student and close friend. In anger she cut one artist "dead" (Cecilia Beaux), and refused to see another (John Singer Sargent) when he came to call. In anger she has expressed her political opinions, her hatred of Theodore Roosevelt, her defense of Dreyfus. In and through anger she has even propelled herself forward in her art. (Once, outraged by a remark of Degas's, she went home and did a painting to prove that he was in the wrong, and, in fact, forced him to admit his error.) Anger has been her intimate, her familiar in action and in talk. She has relied on it as proof of her own strength and power—or perhaps, in its headlong rush in her body, she has called it will.

But now as she approaches seventy, her body having grown increasingly frail and vulnerable, anger becomes an aspect of maintenance. Now anger is in the service of the defense of what has been, of what she has done, against change, which, coming faster and faster in the outer world, seems onslaught as well as degradation—and particularly change in that art in which she was once herself a force for change. The fierceness of her response is like the stiffening of will in the body.

Why now did she single out Matisse to rage against so fiercely? Was it only her correspondent's chance remark that precipitated this outburst? Or was it that she saw something in Matisse's work that she could not turn away from, but had to turn away from?

Yes, Matisse had shut himself away for years. He had

evolved a style that was the very antithesis of containment. He had departed from form to return to another kind of form. If there was distortion in his drawing, there was also the most precise fidelity to movement and to feeling and to the movement of feeling. He allowed himself to move into abstraction while still maintaining the intensity of his expressive force. There was no refusal here (no being refused), no shutting out (no being shut out). All that he allowed himself that she could not allow herself—all that she had not been allowed . . .

Apollinaire, one of those "dreadful people" who had frequented the Steins', had championed Matisse early, as "one of the rare artists who have completely freed themselves from impressionism." At the end of December 1907 he had written a "timid" essay on Matisse, defending him against the accusation of "sketchiness," asserting that Matisse "constructs his paintings by means of colors and lines until he succeeds in giving life to his combinations, until they become logical and form a closed composition from which one could remove neither a single color nor a single line without reducing the whole to a mere chance encounter of lines and colors."

Addressing Matisse directly, he wrote of "your perilous voyage in search of a personality. The voyage begins in knowledge and ends in awareness, that is in total forgetfulness of everything that was not already in yourself . . ."

He quotes Matisse as saying, " 'I created my self by scrutinizing first of all my earliest works . . . I found in them a recurring element, which I first took to be a repetition that made my paintings monotonous. In fact, it was the manifestation of my personality, remaining the same regardless of the varied states of mind that I had experienced.'

"You had rediscovered your instinct. At last, you subordinated your human consciousness to nature's consciousness . . .

"What an image for an artist: the gods, omniscient and omnipotent, but subordinated to Fate!"

Finally, on April 10, 1913, anger having brought its own release, Mary could write to Louisine Havemeyer, "I have begun to work," but she added, "I give out in less than an hour."

(On April 13, Isadora's children died.)

By May 21, 1913, Mary could say: "Perhaps, who knows? I may still have something to do in this world. I never thought I would have. I felt as if I were halfway over the border. I am so much better I think I may still be stronger, strong enough to paint once more."

Now she can go on, no longer isolated by illness with its disabling sense of time, its disorienting sense of place. She has accomplished her flight into safety, into the visible and the real.

Recovering, she begins to regain the weight she has lost. She dropped down to eighty-six pounds the year before, but is now over a hundred pounds. "It is not much but it is a good deal for me who was never fat." She still has occasional small set-backs, as she writes on July 16: "I am nervous about myself, but a hot water bag and dieting made me able to work this morning . . ." Her sleeplessness is a thing of the past. Only, "now that is over my eyes which have always been my strong point, are troubling me. If only I was sure of a good oculist . . ." A fear not dwelled on, skimmed by—

By August 21 she is stronger, "and then my work is exciting, it is so good to be able to work again . . ."

On October 19, again energized by anger, she writes Louisine of a scandal involving the rector of Jennie Cassatt's church. "That horrible immorality went on under their noses for 26 years, and notwithstanding his appearance nobody suspected and even refused to believe when told . . . His latest victim was the sister of one of the curates, and they talk of his marrying her, how will that make matters straight? Really this unsavory story makes one sick, and the blindness of the church authorities. The Christian religion is so simple and clear, why wrap it up in doctrine."

On November 4, from Paris she writes that she has consulted an oculist, who first reassured her about her eyes, saying that she only has conjunctivitis: "He said it was nothing, that I had very good sight, one eye very good, the other not so good but not very bad." However, he wanted to treat her further, to do experiments on her poorer eye. Once more she expressed disgust with doctors: "they . . . see a chance of making money and [do] not hesitate to make you blind! My theory is that they get so hardened with vivisection that human suffering is nothing to them."

She refuses, she does not let him "experiment" on her.

By December 4, sounding as if she is fully back in daily life, once again in a position to give advice, she writes Louisine detailed instructions for the use of copalchi, a medicinal herb used to reduce fever. These directions are to be passed on to the nurse of "Mrs. Havemeyer" (Louisine's mother-in-law?). Mary has sent the instructions in an earlier letter, but the nurse had found them confusing. "They are as simple as 'kiss my hand' . . . a child could understand. I rather wonder at the nurse . . . the powder is steeped in the water eight hours, then the water drunk, the powder left in the bottom of the glass the glass again refilled and left eight hours, the water drunk and the glass once more filled. So that the same powder is used for three glasses in the twenty four hours, the water to stand between each dose eight hours. Could anything be more simple? I have no doubt the remedy is ages old, perhaps may have been used by the inhabitants of the lost continent of Atlantis, as they probably had our ills. We poor humans don't change much . . ."

(Pride and satisfaction in a process that can be controlled; pleasure in the safety of the specific, the simple, the clear, the logical—and the natural; persistence in the reassurance, in the belief that we, "poor humans," don't change much . . .)

She is feeling so much better she hopes that when Louisine comes she will be able to travel with her. However, she wants Mathilde, her housekeeper, to accompany them. "I cannot use my brain all day looking at pictures and pack my trunk and start the next day . . . I suppose you will be as strenuous as ever and leave your maid behind you. Then I must be careful of my diet and also have a hot bath when I can get it . . . I have overlooked my bodily welfare, but I have worked so hard besides, and nothing takes it out of one like painting. I have only to look around me to see that, to see Degas a mere wreck, and Renoir and Monet too . . ."

But she herself is back to work. She writes to Louisine with pride of seven pastels she has just completed: "They were in many respects the best I have done, more freely handled and more brilliant in color."

It has been said of these pastels and of the oil that she completed soon afterward: "blurry, fumbling pastels"; "clumsy handling . . . garish color"; "loss of technique . . . In the pastel the strokes have a random quality and in the oil there is a lack of precision"; "While her palette remained limited, the colors are even brighter, at times even harsh and strident . . . all details have been eliminated . . . The pastel has been applied in quick, slashing strokes crushed into the paper."

These last works are almost all of mothers and children— old feelings, old forms. ("Fancy going back to babies and women, to paint") But there is a restlessness here. The application of chalk seems nervous, hurried, and uncontrolled. It is as if the pastel is being asked to do more than it is capable of doing, as if it is being led to a breaking out but at the same time is being held back, as if there is another intention here, unacknowledged, other than the repetition of the forms that have become second nature to her, as if something else is locked in here, something else not quite seen, an energy unused, somehow forced into a form unsuitable to itself.

So in *The Crochet Lesson,* the woman's right hand guides the girl's right hand, but the girl's hand seems uncontrolled, resistant, clawlike, even as the faces seem so modestly controlled in their domestic task. And in *Mother, Young Daughter, and Son* the arms and legs, head and torso of the child, the enclosing arms of the mother, the mother's profile partially obscuring the face of the daughter, create a unified—even abstract—form out of the three, but the harshness of the color, the elongated shape of the girl's left hand appearing behind the mother, and the too strident white, ostensibly hiding the lolling boy's genitals (but instead calling attention to them), seem to tear the form apart. Yet to Mary it feels accomplished, it feels done; she feels it to be her best.

Did she not see it "right"? It is true that her eyesight was beginning to be affected, but apparently the serious difficulty with her sight had not yet manifested itself. There is another kind of not-seeing that is at work here.

Did daily domestic life, as she had known it, operate to prevent her from going further, from breaking the forms, particularly when her subject matter was that daily domestic life itself? Mary's work from the midnineties on had stiffened into a mold. (It was also highly successful, highly praised—and

therefore even more liable to stiffening.) Her models seem to
hold her in a vise, in their literality, mother, daughter, and boy
child, with his genitals covered.

The painting that Mary did at this time is called *Young
Woman in Green, Outdoors in the Sun.* It is a portrait of a
young woman wearing a hat against the sun, the green of her
hat and dress almost melding into the background of the garden behind her. The brushstroke is loose, opened up. There are
strange disproportions in the image, particularly in the face.
There are things that don't make sense in this painting, an
oddness not realized.

Yet there is a remarkable echo in this painting of one she
did almost forty years before—in 1876, when she was a young
student in France. In this early painting, *Head of a Young Girl,*
the colors are very different, primarily raw umber and burnt
umber, raw sienna and burnt sienna. But there is some basic
similarity in the two faces, in their stillness, in their still gaze.
And there is a strange similarity in the quickness and looseness
of the brushstroke. It is as if, in these two paintings, one so
early and one so late, she was trying to evoke motion without
gesture.

24.

In November 1914 Isadora returned to the United States. For the next four years she would move continuously, from New York to Boston to Naples to Zurich to Montreux to Rome to Naples to Athens to Paris to Geneva to Paris to New York to Buenos Aires to Montevideo to Rio de Janeiro to São Paulo to New York, to Havana, to Palm Beach, to New York, to San Francisco, to New York, to London, to Paris, to Cap Ferrat on the French Riviera—all while the war was still in progress. She kept moving, as if she were powerless to stop her flight, as if motion itself had gained hold of her.

As she moved so rapidly in the world, in her dances she began to move toward stillness, toward the evocation of motion rather than motion itself, toward an intensely dramatic theatricality, achieved through her presence and her posture, particularly through the posture of her face and head and neck. She seemed to be going toward the autobiographical, but it is autobiography as sacred text.

On her programs in early 1915 in New York she danced the *Ave Maria*, a work, writes her biographer Fredrika Blair, "in

which her pupils took the part of adoring angels . . . The Virgin
Mary shrinks back, as if from the Angel of Annunciation, then
makes imploring gestures with her hands and arms. Then,
though her head is bending low over the Child, her arms, wrist,
and hands move backwards in a gesture of surprise. The angels' arm movements in the dance encompass the earth, reach
to the sky, and come from the heart in yearning, as the dancers
offer themselves to the Virgin and the Child."

In the United States, as always, critics were sharply divided in response to Isadora's work. In 1908, on her first tour
of the United States after her European triumphs, a critic had
written:

"Now comes along Miss Duncan with an immense success
in Europe as a recommendation and offers Broadway an entertainment of lofty pretensions to art . . . Miss Duncan is a person
of generous proportions, but handles herself with a smooth,
gliding grace in her slower movements, and with a surprising
lightness in the quicker tempos . . . Her movements, particularly in the manipulation of her hands and arms, are exquisitely
graceful—one might describe it as the sublimation of Delsarte.
In this phase the performance is delightfully perfect, but allowing that, is not it a rather flimsy foundation for an hour and a
half of theatre captivity?"

But to the American artist Robert Henri, "Isadora Duncan,
who is perhaps one of the greatest masters of gesture the world
has ever seen, carries us through a universe in a single movement of her body. Her hand alone held aloft becomes a shape
of infinite significance . . ." "[She] dances and fills the universe.
She exceeds all ordinary measure . . . When we realize her, we
are great as well as she."

In response to these first concerts of 1915, which also included dances to the *Unfinished* Symphony and the "Marche
Funèbre" and readings from the Psalms and the Beatitudes by
Augustin Duncan, one critic wrote, "Her performances are
sicklied over now with the pale cast of some very immature and
hasty thought . . . a most disheartening and amateurish mixture
of music and recited literature . . ."

Increasingly, Isadora responded to such criticisms by
haranguing the audience from the stage, attacking all those in
authority who did not support her in her efforts to create the
actuality of her vision of the new dance. A Boston critic wrote

an article called "The Sorry End of Mistaken Ventures," in which he described these concerts as well-intentioned but unsuccessful exercises recalling "the 'lyceum entertainments' of a vanished New England . . . Isadora sits in humiliation that she relieves by resentful discourse to deaf ears."

Now her work began to incorporate aspects of direct address to the audience as audience. In 1916 in Paris she created and performed *The Marseillaise,* a dance in which she took on the symbolic image of the defender of France. It is a work of direct political meaning, and a work of propaganda, that at the same time aspires to the mythological.

Of her performance in the United States, critic Carl Van Vechten wrote:

"Isadora's pantomimic interpretation of the *Marseillaise,* given in New York before the United States had entered the World War, aroused as vehement and excited an expression of enthusiasm as it would be possible for an artist to awaken in our theater today. The audience stood up and scarcely restrained their impatience to cheer. At the previous performances in Paris, I am told, the effect approached the incredible . . . In a robe the color of blood she stands enfolded; she sees the enemy advance; she feels the enemy as it grasps her by the throat; she kisses her flag; she tastes blood; she is all but crushed under the weight of the attack; and then she rises, triumphant, with the terrible cry, *Aux armes, citoyens!* Part of her effect is gained by gesture, part by the massing of her body, but the greater part by facial expression. In the anguished appeal she does not make a sound, beyond that made by the orchestra, but the hideous din of a hundred raucous voices seems to ring in our ears . . . At times, legs, arms, a leg or an arm, the throat, or the exposed breast assume an importance above that of the rest of the mass, suggesting the unfinished sculpture of Michelangelo . . ."

Simultaneously, in Isadora's private life a different kind of monumentality was taking over, a monumentality of impulse. On impulse she moved from place to place. On impulse she moved from man to man. On impulse she took one drink after another. On impulse, when a potential donor appeared to back her school or her theater, she insulted him or her.

Impulse, as Webster's defines it, is the "act of impelling, or driving onward with sudden force; especially force so communicated as to produce motion suddenly . . ." It was as if, in life, Isadora could not resist any force toward motion, as if she is unable not to move. As a young dancer, Isadora tells us, "in the midst of . . . poverty and deprivation, I can remember standing for hours, alone in our cold, bleak studio, waiting for the moment of inspiration to come to me . . ." But now waiting was not possible for her. As the photographer Arnold Genthe wrote of her, "She was the complete and willing tool of her impulses."

Yet for all her movement, for all her impulses, there was one thing, she says, that did not change for her. Her grief for her children was not alleviated. "The most terrible part of a great sorrow is not the beginning . . . but afterwards, long afterwards, when people say, 'Oh she has gotten over it'—or 'She is all right now, she outlived it'; when one is, perhaps, at what might be considered a merry dinner-party to feel Grief with one icy hand oppressing the heart, or clutching at one's throat with the other burning claw. Ice and Fire, Hell and Despair, overcoming all, and, lifting the glass of champagne, one endeavours to stifle this misery in whatever forgetfulness—possible or impossible . . .

"The sight of any little child who entered the room suddenly, calling 'Mother' stabbed my heart, twisted my whole being with such anguish that the brain could only cry out for Lethe, for Oblivion, in one form or another . . ."

It was as if she lived in two worlds simultaneously, the external world, in which she moved faster and faster, and another world, unchanging, a kind of mental necropolis. Out of these two worlds, these two cities, dwelling in them, she makes her own kind of daily life in a body, itself growing more monumental as she eats and drinks on impulse, amassing herself in motion, even as time alters the contours of her body, makes changes in skin and eyes and muscle.

She is in history, she is out of history. She is in time, she is out of time.

In June 1916 the pianist Maurice Dumesnil went to South America with Isadora to act as her accompanist on a concert tour. He had known her for only a few months in Paris, where he was on leave from the army for a year because of illness. Isadora had engaged him first as an accompanist and then as her conductor for two concerts for war relief in Paris, as well as for two subsequent concerts in Geneva.

In his memoir, *An Amazing Journey*, Dumesnil speaks of the great triumphs of her performances in Paris. Onstage he saw her as a "marvel of personal magnetism and prestige." Of her rendition of *The Marseillaise* he writes ecstatically:

"When I say 'danced,' I am using an improper word. It couldn't be termed a dance. In fact, her impersonation was more on the sculptural order. Her arm extended, her finger stretched toward the invader, her face shining wildly with revenge, sacrifice, craving for heroic deeds, she marched on, while the audience, sprung to its feet, seemed to follow her and sang along with the orchestra. At one moment, one of her gestures broke some seams in her tunic, and the upper part became loosened, uncovering her as far as the lower part of her chest. This incident, which otherwise might have been ridiculous, helped make her figure more realistic, more accurate, more popular. She was the true daughter of the revolution, the inspiration which could lead the masses to run for arms, and start the tremendous feats which freed France from autocracy and, after her, many other nations of the world."

In person he found her to be of "unending generosity, anxious to help the poor." He does note a few irregularities in her behavior, including one incident in which Isadora became drunk and he and several friends had to take her back to her apartment. But that, he suggests, was the exception, not the rule.

In New York, where they stopped on their way to Argentina, he expected to work with her on the dances for the tour, but to his surprise she was so tired from being out at night that she almost immediately gave up rehearsing with him. "She said that it didn't matter as all she needed was to keep fit by going through a few minutes of gymnastics and exercises." As Isadora was being pursued by creditors for bills from her previous trip to the United States in 1914 and 1915, they left New York sooner than they had planned.

But from the moment that they set sail, says Dumesnil, a different Isadora emerged. On the boat, drinking champagne continually, she was occupied with affairs, first with a painter, then with a group of boxers, one by one, then with a gigolo. As Dumesnil puts it, she retired with each of them, in turn, for a "siesta." While he was busy doing his finger exercises, he notes, she was doing a different kind of exercise—and not practicing.

One hot night Dumesnil went up on the deck to sleep, and returning to his cabin at four in the morning, he passed Isadora's cabin and "detected a shadow, someone sneaking from her room." In the darkness he saw "a man . . . gliding along with long steps. I could scarcely believe my eyes, and for a second thought I must be dreaming. What I saw was one of the stokers . . . half-dressed . . . His face and hands were still black from the coal. He looked scared and haggard . . ."

When in the morning, he asked Isadora how she had slept, she said that she had had a "perfectly glorious" night.

" 'You don't mean to say, Isadora, that the object of your delight was the man I saw, sneaking along your corridor . . . Why . . . he was only a stoker!' "

Isadora answered that the men in the engine room had such a hard life, they deserved a little happiness. "And you know," she added, "he had the legs of an Apollo!"

Shortly afterward, observing Isadora on deck, Dumesnil noted "her graceful reclining figure, and the look of reverence, the almost angelic expression of her eyes as she gazed at the sky and the sea. What a curious combination she was! How could she be at times, so supremely intellectual, and at other times so basely material?"

As soon as they got off the boat, there was also the question of Isadora's extravagance with money that puzzled and offended Dumesnil, particularly since, while she was spending so much, neither he nor Isadora's maid were receiving their salaries. Isadora had brought her brother Augustin along as a business manager, but in fact there was not much money to manage. Isadora's way of handling a deficit was to spend ever more grandly. In Buenos Aires, where her first concerts were scheduled, she hired a Daimler with a chauffeur to take her about the city. She spent money lavishly on parties and liquor and dinners and entertainment. The hotel bill mounted. Soon Augustin left, discreetly.

It was all a kind of squandering of herself, and yet there was the sense that she was limitless.

But it was something more than extravagant impulse that disturbed Dumesnil. What he could not understand at all was her deliberate provocation of those who were necessary to make her concerts a success. The night before her first concert she went to the best-known nightclub in the city, drank champagne liberally, insisted on dancing with one of the men who was a "professional" dancer, and then decided to perform a solo dance, her "interpretation" of the Argentinian national anthem. While some of the people present received her dance enthusiastically, others were "shocked beyond words," and the next day, after much unfavorable newspaper publicity, the impresario threatened to cancel her concerts completely. However, he was finally persuaded to let them go ahead as planned.

At the first two performances, the Buenos Aires audience did not react with enthusiasm to Isadora. In response to their indifference she became even more provocative. She decided to schedule an all-Wagner concert for the third performance. (Argentina, though not involved in the war, had a very large pro-Allies faction.) In the middle of this concert, which Dumesnil, as a patriotic Frenchman, declined to conduct, she stopped the orchestra, having heard a noise in one of the boxes.

Isadora stepped forward to the footlights and addressed the audience. "I had been told, before coming here, that I would find the Argentinians very primitive, and uneducated. I had been warned that they would never be able to understand my art. . . . Look at those people [and she pointed to the box], they probably belong to what is called society. Still, they come into their box while I am dancing, making a fearful noise by talking loudly . . . If they do not respect me, they should at least respect the music to which I am dancing. They should respect Wagner!"

And then, she shouted: "The people who warned me were right. You are nothing but a bunch of niggers!"

I have to admit, it is necessary to admit, that I am shocked by this racial slur of Isadora's. Yet why, when Mary Cassatt makes remarks in her letters to Louisine about Jews, am I not shocked (though I am a Jew)? It is not that I condone what Mary said, but then condoning, in and of itself, is not what is at issue here. Whether I like it or not, condone it or not, hate the expression of it or not—to show what this life was or may have been is my primary obligation. In Mary I can understand, or I think I can, that the prejudice against Jews was part of the judgment of that social class she submitted herself to. Or at least so I say to myself. For Mary it was part of outburst, part of seeking an exterior symbol allowed to her for her anger. It is, if not decent, somehow comprehensible.

But with Isadora, who professed such a deep attachment to humanity and to humanitarian values and to the spirit and to the ideal in life, that word does come as a shock. Yes, the words were spoken in rage. Yes, she was using the image of others whom she did not even know. In her childhood in California, then later living in Europe, she had had no contacts with blacks.

In *My Life*, writing of her return to the United States in 1914, Isadora condemned the popular music and dance she saw and heard on her arrival. "At that moment all New York had the 'jazz' dance craze. Women and men of the best society, old and young, spent their time in the huge salons of such hotels as the Biltmore, dancing the fox trot to the barbarous yaps and cries of the Negro orchestra . . ."

"It seems to me monstrous that any one should believe that the Jazz rhythm expresses America. Jazz rhythm," she concludes, "expresses the primitive savage."

Even as she lives a life in which she thinks of herself more and more symbolically, others become symbols to her as well. "Jazz" becomes "the Negro" becomes "the primitive savage" becomes the opposition to her "Ideal," to dance as "spirituality," to the sense of herself as prophetess.

In her "dance of the future," she says, there will be "no rhythm from the waist down [as if only that part of the body above the waist were spiritual and the part below "barbaric"], but from the Solar Plexus, the temporal home of the soul." In that future "long-legged, shining boys and girls will dance . . . not the tottering, ape-like convulsions of the Charleston, but a striking, tremendous upward movement, mounting high above the Pyramids of Egypt, beyond the Parthenon of Greece."

25

Dumesnil published *An Amazing Journey* in 1932, five years after Isadora's death. It is a work that struggles with judgment, frequently giving in to judgment, then finally—as he tells of her death—canceling judgment. He himself is clearly a man who is very susceptible to being evaluated by others.

He presents himself as a man of high moral standards, a serious pianist, devoted to music and to his work, and a serious patriot, devoted to France. He is, as well, a man with a strong sense of privacy, with a sharp sense of the division between the public and the private. Concerned as he is about public opinion, he emphasizes that he and Isadora did not have a "personal" relationship.

His attitude toward Isadora is often one of total puzzlement, even as he seems to take a kind of pleasure in telling of her extravagance. He is the passive observer, watching and listening and noting her affairs, and also judging them. At one point, when Isadora is entranced with a "gigolo," he says, "I

. . . consider the profession as one of the lowest to which a man can descend . . . a degradation, unworthy of a real man."

At times he seems to take pleasure in her being brought down to human scale; at other times he speaks of the divinity in her. He feels that what happened to her in South America was a turning point for her, "after which the road, for her, began to go down . . ." He feels that as the witness to this turning point in her life, it is necessary for him to tell his story.

It is, above all, her excessiveness—in sexuality, in money matters, in general behavior—that intrigues him. He reflects, he resists, he somehow partakes of that excessiveness. And she, seeing him watching, seeing him judging, seeing him struggle between reverence for her godliness and judgment of her "materialism," goads him on.

He reports an occasion in Rio de Janeiro when Isadora suddenly decides to give a large dinner, and insists that he attend. Since he has a previous engagement to be taken by some friends to a high-class French brothel—where, he makes it clear, he will only be an observer—he agrees reluctantly to go to the dinner party, and at the earliest possible moment tries to sneak away. Isadora, seeing him about to go, shouts, "Stop! You can't get away with it, and I'm going to tell everybody!

"Now, listen here, gentlemen . . . what do you think of this? Here's my musical director. We travel together, you know; we work together, we give concerts together. We cooperate and join forces in an effort to express a great ideal. Well, perhaps you'd imagine that with all this, he might pay a little attention to me personally. But not at all! Look at him now. This afternoon . . . was like a holy communion in the genius of Chopin. And you think that anything remains of it? Nothing at all. Now, he's going to his room, and he'll put on his business suit, and he'll go down to some pensions, and to night clubs, and God knows where, to see French girls and flirt around with them, to say the least. Don't you think I have the right to feel that I am badly neglected? Really, gentlemen, my musical director has no taste. He doesn't realize that he's traveling with a Greek goddess!"

Although Dumesnil was embarrassed by what she said, he

was also relieved that no one gossiped about him and Isadora after this.

Once again it becomes clear that telling of another's life, "seeing" another, is a joint act of the viewer and the viewed—a collaboration. Obviously the one being seen acts upon the one seeing, but the reverse is also true. Seeing is never a passive act. It too causes its own reverberations. It is as if the uncertainty principle of physics has its correlate in vision—that the very act of seeing changes the object seen.

Halfway through their South American tour, Dumesnil reports, Isadora regained her godliness. In Montevideo and especially in Rio de Janeiro she was treated with reverence and she responded to this with graciousness and benignity, not with provocation.

In Rio de Janeiro, after the first program, which consisted primarily of Chopin works, followed by *The Marseillaise* the whole audience stood up, shrieking and singing. The next day, the chief morning daily, *O Paiz*, devoted its first three columns on the front page to "Isadora, the divine."

The second concert, also primarily Chopin works, was interrupted after the Chopin Sonata in B-flat Minor by a young man in the top gallery who called for silence and began to speak of his gratitude, "in the name of all other students, for the great lesson, and the message of beauty she had brought to them ... The audience, rather skeptical at first, came under the spell of his remarkable oratory. As everyone began to cheer, he concluded in a lyrical outburst, 'Isadora, you have come to us like a messenger from the gods. You are divine, and we worship you ... you will never realize, Isadora, what this art has meant. It has been the great revelation of truth, the guiding star which will enlighten our lives ...'"

A reviewer in another Rio paper wrote of her performance of Gluck's *Iphigénie en Aulide:* "One knew not if it was she who interpreted the music or if, on the contrary, it was the music which attempted to translate her attitudes, now sorrowful, now joyful, now sad, now nostalgic.

"For when Isadora is possessed by Dionysus she is no longer a human being. She is a cosmic expression. She is a

universal fluid. She is, above all, an unknown force. She is
original, unexpected, more sensed than understood. She is a
vertigo which bears our higher psychism towards intangible
spheres . . . She is emotion itself personified and moving . . ."

Trying to explain the difference in her behavior in Buenos
Aires and in Rio de Janeiro, Dumesnil describes the intense
effects her audience had upon her: "Her nature, artistically,
was of the receptive kind. That is to say, she received the fluid
from that audience, and reacted accordingly . . . Should the fluid
be negative, her spontaneity would shrink, and turn into an
antagonistic disposition. But if it happened to be as decidedly
positive as it was in Rio, she would open up in blooms, like a
flower, and behave like an adorable creature, whose charm
made everybody kneel at her shrine."

Almost as an aside, Dumesnil makes two interesting observations about Isadora's method of working. He notes that in
many intermissions she would go to her dressing room so exhausted that "the maid had to take care of her and undress her
as she would a helpless baby. Her body was in a continual state
of perspiration while she danced, so the maid always had a
number of sponge towels handy. After she was fully dried out
and had put on her fresh garments, she drank a couple of
glasses of champagne, and was immediately revived."

Insisting that Isadora almost never practiced regularly,
Dumesnil describes an instance of her "rehearsing" in São
Paulo. She had decided to dance that night to Beethoven's *Pathétique* Sonata, a work she said she had never done before.
She arrived at the rehearsal session in her street clothes, and
asked him to play the sonata for her. "I started, while she sat
in an armchair near the piano, listening carefully, her head
leaning on her hand. After I finished, she asked that I repeat
it all again. She observed, through this repetition, the same
attitude of thoughtful concentration, and at the end, seemed
satisfied. However, she said:

" 'If it isn't asking too much, would you mind playing it
once more?' and of course, I did so most willingly.

" 'Thank you,' she said after I struck the last chord, 'this
time I have it.' "

If Dumesnil is accurate in his recall and if one credits
Isadora's statement that she had never done the dance before,
this incident suggests how music acted as a spur to the formal

structure of her dances. The incident—if true—suggests that she had, as many great dancers do, the remarkable kinesthetic ability to see herself move in her mind as in actual space. No, more than seeing herself, it involved being in the movement in her mind, feeling it as if she were actually moving, and later being able to transfer that movement intact from mind to realization. Memory and more than memory—the reenactment of thought in and through the body. When she performed the work that evening, she performed it as a finished, an accomplished, work.

(Yet curiously, when asked to teach her dances to her pupils, Isadora could only perform them and ask the pupils to follow. She could not analyze them. She seemed not to have a conscious sense of their structure or form.)

After all his talk of divinity, Dumesnil's final episode about his South American trip with Isadora concerns money. As she had made no attempt to pay his salary, and as he was by now essentially destitute, while she continued to spend lavishly, he approached the impresario and arranged to be paid directly out of the final receipts. When the impresario and Dumesnil went to Isadora and asked her to sign the agreement, "she burst into a terrible fury . . . and exploded . . ." She called them "crooks," "flies," and "deadbeats," and refused to sign. Though Dumesnil was eventually given the money by the impresario, he felt upset and disgraced and wanted to justify himself to Isadora but feared risking her anger anew.

He ends his book with an account of Isadora's funeral, some eleven years later, and his response to her, in memory, after her death: "It dawned upon me clearly that whatever she may have done and however sharply she may have been criticized by puritanical minds, her actions must always have been prompted by spontaneity, generosity, striving toward something beautiful. Her physical impulses were as candidly genuine as those of her heart. She entirely disregarded criticism, and despised hypocrisy and pretense. She could take a prince as her lover, or a stoker, if he only possessed beauty of some kind, either a highly cultured mind, or a simple, naive soul. She gave away everything she had to those who were in need."

Once again he has evaluated her, granting her total adherence to the beautiful and to the good. Reading this ending, one

feels dissatisfaction, uneasiness, even irritation. It is a sentimental reconciliation, one that levels everything, reduces what
is at stake to doing things for "beauty." It is an unearned
reconciliation, dismissing too much that needs to be considered,
all in the name of moral judgment, for all its disavowing judgment. Good, not evil; light, not dark. As if life is something that
has stark edges and contours, when we know . . . we have come
to know . . . that it is not like that at all . . .

But then I should remember too, in Dumesnil's defense,
that it is not only Dumesnil and Isadora who were entwined in
this "seeing." There were all the other eyes in the world, all
those invoked when one speaks of a "media figure" like
Isadora. Eyes that demand, need, devour, eyes that insist on
creating—out of multiplicity—one.

26

In late September 1916 Isadora
returned to New York with almost no money and with many
debts. On arriving at the dock she called one of her good
friends, Arnold Genthe. Singer, who was in New York and had
just come to visit Genthe, answered the phone. "When he heard
that I was alone at the docks without funds, and without
friends, he at once said he would come to my aid . . .

"I felt my return to New York was of happy augury. L.
was in one of his kindest and most generous moods."

According to Allan Ross Macdougall, who was Singer's
private secretary, though the friendship between Isadora and
Singer was "renewed," it was not "as passionate as it once had
been." However, there was once again "a generous stream of
dollars." Singer at once forwarded the money to pay the bill at
the Swiss boarding school where Isadora's pupils had been
living. By this time the younger pupils had returned to their
homes but the six older girls had stayed on and Augustin was
sent to bring them back to the United States.

"L. continued to be in the best and most generous moods,

and there was nothing too good for the children or for me,"
writes Isadora. "In fact, for the time being life became wonderful through the magic power of money." At last the situation
seemed propitious for the founding of Isadora's theater and
school in the United States. But once again there was provocation of Singer by Isadora.

First there was a "small" provocation. At a party given by
Singer for Isadora at Sherry's on Fifth Avenue, Isadora danced
a tango with a handsome young man, whom Macdougall identifies as "Maurice, the well-known ballroom dancer of the period." The onlookers were "shocked," by the directly sexual
expression of the dance, and in particular by "a few earthy
touches of her own." In the middle of the dance, Singer, who
hated exhibitionism of any kind, threw "Maurice" out of the
room.

Arnold Genthe, who was present, says that Isadora
"turned pale and with the air of a prima donna, she called out,
'if you treat my friends like that, I won't wear your jewelry.'
She tore the necklace from her throat and the diamonds scattered on the floor. As she swept from the room, I was standing
in the doorway. Without looking at me she whispered, 'Pick
them up.' "

But that rift being patched over, Singer rented the Metropolitan Opera House for a free concert by Isadora on the night
of November 21, to which he had invited many of the leaders
of the social and artistic worlds. Her program began with her
dance to César Franck's *Rédemption,* a dance of which Macdougall writes, "She merely rose from a crouching position to
stand with arms outstretched heavenwards, reminding the
critic Carl Van Vechten of a phrase of Barbey d'Aurevilly's:
'She seemed to rise towards God, her hands filled with goodness
and charity.' " She ended the program with *The Marseillaise,*
which drove the audience into "enflamed cheering."

Soon Isadora grew restless again and had to be on the
move. She sailed off to Havana accompanied by Macdougall. As
he was an avowed homosexual, his presence with Isadora could
not be considered provocative by Singer.

In her book Isadora tells three curious incidents that took
place during her stay, all characterized by strange disparities

or disjunctions. The first, which Isadora calls a tragic-comic incident, concerns a leper house just outside Havana, with walls "not high enough to prevent us from seeing at times a mask of horror looking over it." The authorities, feeling that foreign visitors might be repelled by this sight, decided to move the leper house. But, says Isadora, "the lepers refused to go. They clung to the doors, to the walls, some got on to the roofs and clung there, and it was even rumoured that some of them had escaped into Havana . . ."

In the second she recounts meeting a beautiful, wealthy woman who had a passion for monkeys and gorillas that she kept as pets in cages. Most of them were tame but others looked frightening, and Isadora asked if they were not dangerous. The woman, in what must have been jest—but Isadora does not take it this way—said that "apart from getting out of their cages and killing a gardener now and then, they were quite safe." What Isadora could not understand was how this beautiful, well-read, and intelligent woman could have this "fantastic affection for apes and gorillas."

The third incident describes Isadora's own actions. One morning, around three o'clock, she found herself in a "typical Havana café . . . [with] the usual assortment of morphimaniacs, cocainists, opium smokers, alcoholists, and other derelicts of life." Suddenly her attention was drawn to "a whitefaced, hallucinated-looking man, with cadaverous cheeks and ferocious eyes. With his long thin fingers he touched the keys of a piano and to my astonishment there came forth Chopin's Preludes, played with marvellous insight and genius." She approached this pianist, who was almost mute in a morphia trance, and suddenly she was overtaken by a "fantastic desire" to dance for this audience of derelicts. She wrapped her cape around her and danced to the preludes; the drinkers stopped drinking, the talkers stopped talking, and many of them wept. The pianist came out of his morphia trance and played as if "inspired."

"I continued to dance until the morning and when I left, they all embraced me, and I felt prouder than in any theatre, for this I knew to be the real proof of my talent . . ."

(Not so, says Macdougall, who was present at the time and recounts a totally different story. Isadora, he says, did dance in the bar of a hotel, but her relationship to that audience was very antagonistic. She likened them to Gadarene swine, whom she would lead into the sea. Further, to the pianist, who was a young woman who had eagerly volunteered to play for her, she was cruelly satiric, about her talent and her appearance.)

But it is not accuracy of fact that I am getting at here. It is rather the quality of disjunction in these three incidents. The repulsiveness of the "mask of horror" of the lepers in the leper house so close to a pleasure resort. The strangeness of a beautiful, intelligent woman who has a "fantastic affection" for apes and gorillas. And in the third story, she, Isadora, placed in an environment of derelicts, of the lost of the earth, redeems them, saves them—even if temporarily—by the beauty and spirituality of her dance. She erases the disjunctions that repeat themselves so often in life—the ugly beside the beautiful, the sick beside the healthy, the repellent beside the sublime—by conquering the ugliness, the sickness, the darkness, by overcoming them through her Ideal Art.

In her mind, in her memory, she was creating Art, but in life there was yet more provocation. From Havana, Isadora went to Palm Beach, where she had an affair with a onetime boxing champion, Kid McCoy. The public flaunting of this affair—if not the affair itself—was, she must have known, something that would enrage Singer. But she went on, as Macdougall says, "playing her portable gramophone in her room with the attentive ministrations of . . . Kid McCoy . . ."

In *My Life* Isadora does not mention McCoy, and only says that she sent a telegram to Singer, who shortly joined her in Palm Beach, bringing with him the American poet Percy Mac-Kaye. "Sitting all together on the verandah one day, L. sketched out a plan for a future School according to my ideas, and informed me that he had bought the Madison Square Garden as a fitting ground-plan for the School.

"Although enthusiastic about the plan as a whole, I was not in favour of starting so vast a project in the middle of the war, and it was this that finally irritated L. to such an extent that, with the same impulsiveness with which he had bought the Garden, he cancelled the sale upon our return to New York."

Arnold Genthe, who was present at the moment of Singer's

"final irritation," tells a very different story. He refers to Isadora's version as incomplete:

> It was my embarrassment to be present when the final break came between Isadora and Paris Singer . . . For some time Paris Singer had had a big plan in his mind. He wanted to do something for Isadora that would carry on her memory and her work for all time. George Gray Barnard, the sculptor, had suggested the endowment of an American Art Center where sculptors, painters and dancers could develop their talents in an atmosphere conducive to work and without financial worry. It was to be a testimonial to Isadora and she was to direct the School of the Dance. Singer took to the idea at once. As he wanted it to be a surprise, he said nothing about it to Isadora. He was going to Florida to visit the home for convalescent soldiers which he was supporting, and before leaving he had taken an option for a large sum of money on the old Madison Square Garden. On his return he gave a dinner at the Plaza for the purpose of telling Isadora about his plan. Among those there were Augustin and Margherita Duncan [Augustin's wife], Isadora's sister Elizabeth, Mary Desti [who omits the incident from her book], George Gray Barnard and myself.
>
> Unfortunately, Singer started to talk of what he was doing for the wounded soldiers.
>
> "Is that what you brought me here for?" said Isadora. "I'm sick and tired of hearing about the war and the sick soldiers. Can't you think of anything else?"
>
> We all began to talk, in the hope of clearing the air, and after a few minutes everything was peaceful again. Then he told her about Madison Square Garden . . .
>
> "Do you mean to tell me," asked Isadora, "that you expect me to direct a school in Madison Square Garden? I suppose you want me to advertise prize-fights with my dancing."
>
> Singer turned absolutely livid. His lips were quiv-

ering and his hands were shaking. He got up from the
table without saying a word and left the room.

"Do you realize what you have done?" we asked
in a chorus of dismay. "You could have had the school
that was your life's dream, and now you have ruined
everything."

"He'll come back," she said serenely. "He always
does."

"He never did," writes Genthe.

Many "explanations" have been suggested for this action
of Isadora's: Macdougall says that the break took place in
Miami, and arose out of a "perverse idea" on Isadora's part that
Singer was going to force her to participate in staging Mac-
Kaye's masques. Alva Johnson, in an article in *The New
Yorker,* wrote that Isadora's anger came out of Singer's objection to her association with Kid McCoy. Fredrika Blair suggests
that Isadora resented Singer's self-confidence, based upon his
wealth, and needed to show her independence, and that perhaps
Isadora "unconsciously identified Singer with her banker father, who by his bank's failure and his desertion of his family,
had left the Duncans to fend for themselves . . ." But then Blair,
growing cautious about "psychoanalysis at long distance," attributes Isadora's actions to a basic difference between
Isadora's approach to life and Singer's. Isadora's life, says
Blair, "had a purpose. She was a 'doer.' Singer, though a man
of taste, intelligence, and ambition, was energetic only by fits
and starts, a beginner and dropper of projects. Being rich, he
lacked the usual incentives for work . . . Only intermittently did
he exhibit his dominating and violent father's compulsion to
make money."

In the first chapter of *My Life* Isadora talks about the
nature of behavior in human beings, as she sees it. (It is like so
many of her other comments, thrown out as if at random, taking little heed of logic or of sequence, often said in contradiction
of what has just been told. These comments are like a sudden
outpouring, a gesture of outpouring, as if words and telling are
insufficient.) "No one is either good or bad. We may not all

break the Ten Commandments, but we are certainly all capable of it. Within us lurks the breaker of all laws, ready to spring out at the first real opportunity . . .

"I once saw a wonderful film called 'The Rail.' The theme was that the lives of human beings are all as the engine running on a set track. And if the engine jumps the track or finds an insurmountable object in its way, there comes disaster. Happy those drivers who, seeing a steep descent before them, are not inspired with a diabolical impulse to take off all brakes and dash to destruction."

Singer sold the option on Madison Square Garden at a loss of one hundred thousand dollars. On March 6, 1917, the day after the incident Genthe describes, Isadora again gave the program she had given at the Metropolitan Opera House in November, and repeated it several times over the next weeks, to great acclaim. The United States entered the war on April 6, 1917.

In 1913, the year before the out-
break of World War I, Mary wrote to Louisine that she was
reading the work of the famous French entomologist Jean-
Henri Fabre. Fabre had worked in isolation for many years in
a small village remote from Paris, in poverty and with only
the most rudimentary instruments. In his studies of insect life
he went directly to Nature for his observations. "I observe,
I experiment and I let the facts speak for themselves," he
wrote.

Several of his most important essays derive from close
observation of the scarab, a family of beetles, of which the most
famous is the Sacred Beetle, the Scarab of the Nile. "We were
going to see whether the Sacred Beetle had yet made his appearance on the sandy plateau of Les Angles," he writes in one
essay on his method of research, "whether he was rolling that
pellet of dung in which ancient Egypt beheld an image of the
world . . ." After watching the scarab intently over a period of
time, he compares his own observations with the writings of
Horapollo, the ancient Egyptian scribe who wrote of the

glorification of the Scarab of the Nile, and concludes that much of what Horapollo said was correct.

A great believer in the immutability and importance of instinct, he writes of the maternal instinct in the Sacred Beetle: "Placed in charge of the duration of the species, which is of more serious interest than the preservation of individuals, maternity awakens a marvellous foresight in the drowsiest intelligence; it is the thrice sacred hearth wherein smoulder and then suddenly burst forth those incomprehensible psychic gleams which give us the impression of an infallible reasoning power."

He describes the pear-shaped pill, where the Sacred Beetle houses its egg, as the work of an artist. "The Scarab does exactly what the laws of aesthetics dictate to ourselves. Can she, too, have a sense of beauty? Is she able to appreciate the elegance of her pear? Certainly, she does not see it: she manipulates it in profound darkness. But she touches it. A poor touch hers, rudely clad in horn, yet not insensible, after all, to nicely-drawn outlines!"

Mary, working, continues to read Fabre, his essays and the biography of him written by C. V. Legros. In the introduction to Legros's biography, Fabre is quoted as saying, "It seems to me that in the depths of my being I can still feel rising in me all the fever of my early years, all the enthusiasm of long ago, and that I should still be no less ardent a worker were not the weakness of my eyes and the failure of my strength today an insurmountable obstacle."

Mary, sending Louisine the biography, adds, "He is now 90 . . . the life most interesting. How little the world knows of its greatest men . . . His theory is that we are here to work. 'Let us work while it is day.' . . . I would rather stay here and read Fabre, and learn something of this great inhuman world beside us than hop about the globe . . ."

28

If the story of Isadora's life is a story of many events, with many different tellings, the telling of Mary's life is a single story: the story of a daily life. It is a story with its own kind of multiplicity. But it is a story that relies ultimately on order, certainty, and predictability.

In August 1914, with the outbreak of the war in France, the certainty of that daily life eroded. Ordinary domestic existence became peripheral, while everything that was large, harsh, and powerful—and at a distance—became the center of life.

When Louisine suggested that Mary return to the United States, she refused, saying she did not want to risk ocean travel. For the last forty years she had made her life in France and her obligations were to that existence. She read in the newspapers of the atrocities committed by the Germans, and felt sickened by these acts. To her the war was a terrible and final assault on civilization. All that she had done in her life was in danger of being obliterated. There had always been in this intensely private woman a sharp demarcation between her private life and the outside public world. But now that demarcation began to blur.

August 18, 1914 (from Beaufresne): "Here the days pass with leaden feet . . . The great drama going on so near us does not interest these young Americans [visiting relatives]. You may imagine how differently I feel . . . The battle in Belgium will be fought out long before you get this. May it be a crushing defeat for Germany. That I think the whole world will pray for . . . My nerves are decidedly on edge, but think how others are suffering—one dare not think of it . . ."

November 8, 1914 (from the Villa Angeletto): "This is the saddest place, war and all its horrors the only subject.

"I have a book from Mr. S. [Stillman] but hear no more of him . . . I begin to wish I were in America, but then I would have got there half dead, so Switzerland or Italy must do for me. After the war no German will be allowed in France. What about me then [without Mathilde, a German citizen, who was at the moment interned in Rennes, waiting for the train to take her to Italy]? I will have to settle in Italy if I am to settle at all . . .

"Half of Brussels Museum has been sent to Germany they have stolen everything at Lille, at Arras, and they fear at St Quentin! A German Art Critic! has advised their stealing all works of Art. The Rubens' at Maline are burnt! It is too sickening Oh! to see that wretched William [the Kaiser] made away with all his brood."

December 3, 1914: "Sat [Mary's nephew Gardner Cassatt] sent me word . . . that I could have all the money I wanted only not to send for it unless I needed it. Now I want my income paid, if there is any & surely there must be some or else the bottom has fallen out of everything at home. You see I don't want to touch on my reserve for who knows what might happen. This is between you and me, and you see I am a prudent person. Perhaps as you say I do know how to manage, for I did have the instinct of what was best to do for Mathilde & her sister."

January 20, 1915: "Now that the Russians have doubled up the Turks, & that Italy & Roumania are to move, & Austria exhausted, things may move quicker & peace be nearer. You have no idea of our state we are weighed down and oppressed. I went over on Saturday to see Tildie. I was so shocked, poor

dear, she has lost 30 lbs pining over our separation . . . [Ma-
thilde] asked me in such a timid way if I thought she could ever
come back. I nearly cried. What this war is, what race hatreds
[?]. No diplomacy can do anything, the stamping out of the
Hohenzollerns is the only thing . . ."

February 1, 1915: "Of course everything here is the same.
We look with apprehension toward Spring and the spread of
disease. Now we have convalescent typhoid patients, & it is cold
& bright, but when the heat comes? . . . War is an infamy
. . . Then the poor soldiers who have recovered from their
wounds & have to go back . . . Mathilde saw Mr. Stillman pass
in an auto at San Remo. I have heard nothing from him . . ."

Yes, she is a "prudent person," as she has always been.
Yes, she is a good manager, as she has always been. Yes, she
is irascible, sharp, irritable, judging as ever.

It is easy to be misled by this "prudent" woman. She offers
none of the ardent expressions of feeling that Isadora glories
in. She offers rather an image of practicality, of rational judgment dealing with the world, distracting us as she darts from
one "practicality," one "judgment," to another. So one has to
refuse and refuse again the ostensible pathways of her
thoughts, or rather one has to follow her thoughts but try not
to be bound by the connections with which *she* binds them. For
words function for her less as an expression of feeling than as
a way of sealing off, of deflecting, of creating a surface.

She writes of women—of the death of men and of the new
power of women to come.

August 18, 1914: "Oh Louie dear women must be up and
doing let them league themselves to put down war."

November 11, 1914: "Do lean Louie on the fact that German 'Kultur' was purely masculine, and for that reason must
disappear. That the victory of the Allies means liberty for Germans, a liberty which they had not temperament to acquire for
themselves. Above all things there was no place for the intellectual qualities of women in their system. I was told the other day
. . . that this war has made men accept the fact of women voting
with more tolerance, the women's movement has progressed."

February 28, 1915, in a letter to a Colonel Paine: "I come

to appeal to you as a patriotic American to lend your Degas to the exhibition Mrs Havemeyer is arranging. [On Louisine's initiative the Suffrage Loan Exhibition of Old Masters and Works by Edgar Degas and Mary Cassatt was to be held in New York in April 1915.] The sight of that picture may be a turning point in the life of some young American painter. The first sight of Degas pictures was the turning point in my artistic life.

"Never mind the object of the exhibition. Think only of the young painters. As to the suffrage for women it must come as a result of this awful war. With the slaughter of *millions* of men women will be forced, are now being forced to do their work, & we have only begun. Far worse is yet to come these next months. Brain and heart are so tortured we cannot settle to anything . . ."

As a young girl Mary had reveled in riding, in scrapping with her brothers. Later, as a young woman and a painter, she often identified with men and preferred their company to that of women. At first she had scorned the movement for women's suffrage but in her later years, and in large part in response to Louisine's urging, she became a supporter. Now she speaks of women and the women's movement as if they—and it—are the last hope for the world's survival. Yet in her speaking of individual women there is no such idealism: she is as critical, as judging as ever.

On March 12, 1915, Mary writes to Louisine: "The rich parvenu manufacturers here are too mean for words. Fancy a woman letting her gardener be at the front since August & not giving the wife or child one sou nor sending a sou to the gardener! Her family are safely 'embarqué.' I tell you dear I am becoming absolutely socialist in my thinking."

On June 8, 1915, in a letter to her friend Theodate Pope: "Mathilde is in Switzerland with her sister she has gone to pieces since the war. I got her safely to Italy she did not have to go to camp. Yet she lost thirty lbs & pined, & drove me nearly crazy—She showed no courage at all—"

At home, the days passing "with leaden feet," she is burdened by her duties, no matter what is happening in the world. She must care for her house, for the servants. She must maintain and maintain ever more fiercely. Yet at the same time she is pulled down by all the deaths in the war, making old deaths new again, reminding her how life can be broken, how hard it is to begin again—and she is seventy and an outsider and alone, having to suffer the seeing, to wait, passively, and to see.

To Theodate Pope, Mary writes, "I am so anxious to see you . . . Since I saw you last I have been so ill, no one thought I would recover—but I did, then I overworked & when the war cloud burst, I broke down under my responsibilities & it has taken me all winter to get well again,—and my sight is enfeebled . . ."

(To Louisine on March 12 she had already written—it was the very last line of her letter, as if an afterthought—"I am not working.")

On June 15 she writes to Louisine: "As to my eyes, Dr. B. [Borsch] says the cells are very young yet . . . therefore I must have patience and above all try and keep well."

(There is some argument as to whether the cataracts she is referring to manifested themselves earlier; but it is clear that by now they are definitely established and her eyesight has begun to deteriorate rapidly.)

To Louisine on July 5, 1915: "Do you think if I have to stop work on account of my eyes I could use my last years as a propagandist [for suffrage]? It won't be necessary if the war goes on, as it must. Women are now doing most of the work. I never felt so isolated in my life as I do now. Your letters are the only things that made me feel not altogether abandoned."

July 13, 1915: "My sight is so enfeebled I cannot read even large print with the aid of a reader."

August 21, 1915, in a cable to Louisine from Paris: "Am here care of oculist must not read or write."

She underwent surgery on October 15.

December 28, 1915 to her niece Minnie: "I have had a great deal of trouble with my eyes . . . Dr. B. [Borsch] promises much but I remember my age and don't look forward but live from day to day.

"In this sea of misery in which we live, an individual case seems of little account. There are ten thousand blind in France.—If only we could see the end of this war!"

June 1916 to Louisine: "I miss the quiet of Grasse, but Dr.

Borsch is treating my eyes, which keeps up hope, he still maintains tho that I shall see to work, but I do not believe it."

Even in this darkness of not seeing, even in this darkness of the world around her, she goes on, she holds on, holding to daily life and its necessities. It is her duty to protect, it is her duty to save, it is her duty to maintain, just as earlier it was her duty to her sister in her illness, her duty to her mother in her illness that was primary, even when it meant putting aside her own work.

To the American collector Harris Whittemore, Jr., in response to his request to purchase a picture from her, after quoting him a price of five thousand dollars, Mary writes, "I don't want the money now, later when the period of destruction is over & reconstruction begins it may be useful." And then she responds to his invitation to visit by saying that she would love to accept but "I feel chained here—& have duties I must fulfill."

July 7, 1916, to Louisine: "My nerves are giving way, & I doubt if I shall ever see again. It would be so good to be over it all, why do we mourn those who go? One tries to do one's duty & the result isn't always best."

To Theodate Pope, who was on the *Lusitania* when it was torpedoed by a German submarine and who survived: "If you were saved it is because you still have something to do in this World—As long as we live, we do not know to what usages we are to be put."

There is one letter to Louisine in which words about duty, about women and the absence of men, and about blindness all come together: "I am still without my papers, & do not know if I can go to Beaufresne with an auto. To be there without any means of communication will be hard, and without a man to attend to anything, but I must go if only for a short time to see about things. It is in such times as this that one realizes one is old and feeble—Add to that dimmed sight and one is helpless." Nevertheless, feeling helpless and with dimmed sight, she "climbed Duret's [Théodore Duret, journalist and collector] stairs to see the Courbet," a painting that she was urging Louisine to buy for her collection (advising her as she had advised her on art matters for so many years).

Once again she speaks of women and what they will have to do:

"After the War is over, Heaven knows when that will be, there will be a great revival; and surely a new view of things. It is then that the women ought to be prepared for their new duties, taking part in governing the world."

PART
THREE

At last she appeared, with the
familiar background of plain black curtains . . . She danced
to some great classical rhapsody, tragic, passionate, world-
destroying, world-creating; and the harmonies of the dead
musician lived a life greater, more formidable, more liberat-
ing, than humanity could have dared to dream they con-
tained. Her arms, her limbs were bare; her nobly modelled
breasts, under some light fabric, outlined themselves as the
breasts of some Phidian divinity.

"Once more . . . she lifted . . . the veil of Isis . . ."

This is fiction, the thoughts of the poet Richard Strong, the
hero of John Cowper Powys's novel *After My Fashion,* as he
watches the performance of the dancer Elise Angel. The novel
was written in 1918 and 1919, after Powys had met Isadora in
New York.

Powys, a novelist, poet, critic, and philosopher, was also a
charismatic lecturer, able to hold his audience spellbound for
hours. In a letter to one of his sisters in 1915 or 1916, he wrote
that he had met Isadora and that she had danced *The Marseil-*

laise for him, as well as sent him "hundreds and hundreds of red roses."

Beyond that, we know nothing of his relationship with Isadora, except for a letter from Powys to her in the Irma Duncan Collection:

> I cannot tell you how poor and sterile New York seems to me now I have lost the knowledge that you are here. It is a wretched irony to me that now I am better able to move about without so much nervousness and discomfort, I have no way of seeing you.
>
> I am still seized at moments with that sort of "whoreson lethargy" and weariness which they say (in their cheerful way) is "the shock of the operation—" but it seems to me much more like a weakness and cowardice of my inmost soul than anything merely "nervous." It seems like an insane terror of having to undertake the struggle of life again. In the effort not to yield to this weakness I keep making use of your friendship; I keep an almost fierce hold upon your hand. I seem to see you always with a secret of courage and of some wonderful, terrible kind of ecstasy that is able to defy everything and springs from the depths. This is your genius and there is none like you in this.
>
> With many it is only art; but with you, as with all the great ones that I love, it is something more, and art breaks down—It is strange . . .

But in Powys's fictional world, when the barrier between art and life "breaks down" in Richard Strong's affair with Elise Angel, the dancer of "divine genius" becomes a destructive image. Strong is thrown "back upon a sort of delicious helplessness and weakness out of which he clung to her blindly, while her love lifted him up, like something strong and immortal into a paradise of peace . . ."

At home with his pregnant wife, he realizes that "the deeper portion of what he felt [for Elise] was a thrilled and grateful response to her genius as an artist . . . On the one hand she appealed so overwhelmingly . . . to his sophisticated senses. On the other hand she inspired in him a pure flame of hero worship . . ." Yet he knows too that the sensual appeal is not "love. It was the old immemorial heathen craving for the beauty that troubled the blood, that aroused insatiable desire. And though he craved for her in that way, he knew very well that he hated her also in that way."

He tries to resist his desire for Elise but he cannot relinquish the "dangerous lure of that perfect skin, 'like cruel white satin . . .' " At one point he attempts to assert his power over Elise physically; he even thinks of striking her, though he does not. To him she becomes a "fatal image 'like a Bacchanal on a Grecian urn,' " a fatal image with a smile of "frank infantile delight," one that speaks with a "caressing infantile naïveté."

At the close of 1917 Isadora arrived in San Francisco, the birthplace she had left twenty-two years before. She had left as a young girl of eighteen, brought up in poverty, convinced that she would make her way in the world by going east. Now she had made her way west again, an internationally famous figure, having won and lost several fortunes.

In San Francisco Isadora seems to have given some thought to those early years, which she had escaped with such vigorous hope. In a hired car she revisited the many places she had lived as a child. (Then too she had moved and moved—with her family—out of economic necessity.) For the first time since 1907, when her mother, Dora Gray Duncan, had abruptly left Europe for the United States, Isadora met with her. She was startled to find that her mother looked "very old and careworn." In *My Life* Isadora relates that she went to lunch with Dora at the Cliff House and there in a mirror she saw the reflection of two figures, her mother with her haggard looks

and she herself with a "sad face." She could not help contrasting that image in the mirror with "the two adventurous spirits
who had set out nearly twenty-two years ago with such high
hopes to seek fame and fortune. Both had been found," she
adds, "—why was the result so tragic?"

It is a mirroring different from all her other mirrorings,
before and after. It is as if in her confrontation with her own
figure in the glass beside her mother, she sees in herself not a
moving image to be reflected back again, confident in its poten-
tialities, but two beings stopped, who have both lost out, who
are losing out, sitting silent and still, subject to time, being
overcome by time.

The language that Isadora uses in describing this incident
is unique for her in its plainness—the stripped-down quality of
the word "haggard," the simplicity of "sad face." Language, as
she generally uses it in her autobiography, is extravagant,
flamboyant, and decorative. It is as if she looks upon language
as a space to be formed; she enlarges upon it, she extends it,
she forces it into everextending meaning.

(And now, I have to ask myself if I have not listened to her
carefully enough. Perhaps it has been my own resistance to the
kind of language she uses that has not allowed me to hear her
properly. Perhaps what she says is not simply for effect—
though it is that too—but is as well an accurate reflection of her
feelings about herself in relation to the world.)

The quality of her language suggests that she lives with
a sense of herself as existing in some continual present. So, in
her autobiography, one thing comes, then another, one thought,
then another, they are put in time, but the time does not feel
like any sequence that we know. With total assurance she can
write of her trip to Egypt, "As the dahabeah voyages slowly up
the Nile the soul travels back a thousand—two thousand—five
thousand years; back, through the mists of the Past to the
Gates of Eternity." But that is not so different from the feeling
one gets of her passage through life day to day.

But, of course, she is living in time, no matter how she
would believe otherwise.

Immediately after telling of seeing herself and her mother
in the mirror, Isadora reflects on the nature of life on earth,

with its "conditions . . . hostile to man," and declares that she
has never met anyone who was "a happy being . . . Perhaps in
this world so-called happiness does not exist. There are only
moments."

At once she slips into her usual extravagant language as
she describes one of her "moments," an affair she had in San
Francisco with the pianist Harold Bauer, whom she calls her
"musical twin-soul":

"When two lovers of the same high ideal of Art meet,
a certain drunkenness possesses them. For days we lived in
a high degree of intoxication without wine, through every
nerve a trembling, surging hope, and when our eyes met in
the realisation of this hope we experienced such vehement
delight as would cause us to cry out as if in pain: 'Have you
felt this phrase of Chopin so?' 'Yes, like that, with something
more. I will create for you the movement of it.' 'Ah, what
realisation! Now I will play it for you.' 'Ah, what delight—
what highest joy!'

"Such were our conversations, continually mounting to a
profounder knowledge of that music we both adored." Isadora
hoped that their collaboration might go on to "an entire new
domain of musical expression together. But, alas, I had not
reckoned on circumstance. Our collaboration ended with a
forced and dramatic separation."

(That puzzling last sentence is elaborated on by Victor
Seroff in *The Real Isadora* with the comment that the cause
of their "separation" was Bauer's wife, who threatened a
scandal.)

Either before or after or during her affair with Bauer,
Isadora also seems to have had an affair with the San Francisco
music critic Redfern Mason. Two letters from Isadora to Mason
still survive. They are undated, their sequence unclear:

> Dear Friend I have had such a beautiful peaceful
> feeling all day—thoughts—& dreams & Hopes—Per-
> haps it was the letter or the prayer—Can you under-
> stand to suffer so that one rushes to the Delirium of
> perhaps a false joy?
> Friday I dance Ave Maria. That will be *all for you*.
>   Isadora

Can you know what it is to have had 3 Babies—&
now have simply—arms? If you can understand you
will forgive.

The second, more enigmatic, reads:

Helas! You have sent me the one message that has
always *terrified* me. (Remember my grandfather's
uncle known as St. Thomas in Cork also walked on his
bare knees on broken glass 3 miles a day for his dinner
of dry crumbs. Do you want me to be walking on my
bare knees on broken glass?) . . . Aren't you glad I can
still dance a Bacchanal & that sometimes in a quiet
landscape I wish for a Faun to part the bushes and
leap forth and seize a not unwilling nymph. I have
shrieked aloud with agony & I have screamed with joy
but I won't no I will never admit—I will tell you the
rest when I see you—soon—n'est-ce pas?

Most lovingly
Isadora

31

There was a witness to Isadora's visit to San Francisco who had known her and danced with her as a young girl. Florence Treadwell Boynton, like Isadora, had been influenced by many of the late-nineteenth-century movements in California that urged a freer, more natural style in dress, in the arts, and in women's lives. She venerated Isadora and eventually created in Berkeley a "Temple of the Wings," a residence for herself and her husband and their five children, built upon the principles of the Greek Ideal, or at least the California version of the Greek Ideal. The temple also served as a school of dance for children, emphasizing the natural quality of movement.

A highly energetic woman, tenacious in the pursuit of her ideals, Florence campaigned to have children wear simple, unconstricting clothing. Spartan in her habits, and urging the same regimen upon her family, she fed them on a strict diet, primarily fruits, nuts, and vegetables. The floor of the temple, which was largely open to the (sometimes very cool) Berkeley air, was heated with hollow tiles embedded in the foundation.

As a dancer and teacher she was, according to Duncan scholar Margaretta Mitchell, the first and most important American disciple of Isadora's, a true disciple, as opposed to many false imitators. She was all in all one of those interesting and original Californians of the time, reconciling an adherence to a Greek ideal with a belief in transcendentalism and a remarkable practicality in her approach to life. The school she established, directed after her death by her daughter Sulgwynn Boynton Quitzow and other family members, survived for almost seventy years.

In her sometimes spiritual, sometimes romantic, sometimes very practical and lively prose, she wrote, first in the thirties and then adding comments toward the end of her life, an account of Isadora's life. In that recounting she struggles with the image of Isadora, identifies with her, is awed by her, and tries to allay whatever contradicts her own ideal of Isadora. Struggling to hold to the Ideal—in herself? in Isadora?—she gives us an image of Isadora that is also dense with mirroring, but, rooted in a real shared past, it has a unique clarity.

Of Isadora's visit in 1917 Florence writes:

> Year after year, Californians had expected Isadora's return. Three times she had been billed to appear in her native State. On each occasion, when she made her plans to come West, some terrible catastrophe had befallen her. Finally the long anticipated visit, incorporating the wonderful possibility of establishing a school, was at hand, but those who years before had rallied to the cause were now scattered or mobilized in War work which absorbed all their time. It had been my intention to meet Isadora's train down the Coast and ride in with her but she arrived unannounced. At her hotel, I received instructions to come right up to her apartment. I shall never forget the arms of love when Isadora opened her door and took me in. It was as if those arms of love could enfold all humanity in compassionate pity. Isadora with the lovely face, the deep thoughtful eyes—a great soul washed of much of the human element through sorrow and tribulations and afflictions! . . . I had taken with me a young musician and my youngest child, three years of age. But

Isadora could not endure the presence of a little child, so the musician and the baby waited in the reception room . . . I said to Isadora, "I did not know you would feel this way or I would not have brought the child." She then apologized as for a weakness, but later referring to the incident said, "Of course no one could understand," in a way entirely foreign to Isadora, as if grief had an aristocracy of its own that only the initiated could understand. I could then see that although her grief, like all grief, was mesmeric (from which all have to be awakened as it belongs to none of us) yet her grief so prolonged was a mesmerism more horribly dense. She was still laboring under the world's multiplied sense of her grief which was like a pall of thousands of minds weighing her down, which she had no power to lift nor knowledge from whence it came. One is not responsible in the face of one grief, but here were millions. Had humanity known better, it would have released her . . .

Abruptly she said, "Look at me, I am a wreck." All one was conscious of was her beautiful face as she was heavily draped like the prophets of the Sargent frieze in the Boston Library. One realized her strength and power and majesty; there was no wreck apparent, but her body was obese, unshapely. Yet the following week at the theatre there stepped forth from that ungainly mass of flesh the maiden of her prime, lithe, agile, with all her purity and loveliness in the bloom of youth, dancing to an exquisite waltz by Brahms . . . During the first visit, which was brief, Isadora seemed to cling to me and want me not to go; she insisted that I return the following evening and told me that I might bring my two little daughters.

The following evening, my husband, the two little daughters, the young musician and I called at the appointed time. The Berkeley poet was there and also a musical critic [Redfern Mason] from one of the local newspapers . . . There ensued a very interesting discussion on Art between Isadora and the critic. For Isadora much was at issue. The success of her tournée depended largely upon impressions made that night on

the critic. Isadora was very beautiful. She was gowned
in black lace. She was brilliant, exquisite in thought
and facial expression. The finest explanation that I
have ever heard of the motive of her school she gave
that night. She described it as the response to a need
in the crisis of the great Greek Tragedies where the
chorus leads the entire audience in thought, lifting
them from the depths, when suffering reaches the
unendurable, to the transcendental, the forever.
Isadora was despondent and talked of death and of her
desire to die, and a tragic sadness tinged all she said.
In Isadora's attitude toward the critic I was impressed
by her complete overcoming of distant formality with
one so formal, beginning the interview as if they had
always known each other and had been the best of
friends. When he departed, early in the evening,
Isadora jokingly and in play asked him when she
should go to the priest to be "shrived and wived" and
he replied in the same playful mood. She also said she
never slept at night and to phone her after midnight.
On our way home, one of our little daughters said,
"She is just like a vampire." Her father, who had been
shocked by the whole interview, was still more so at
this matter-of-fact little miss who always had an apt
way of saying the exact fact in a most unconcerned
manner. "What does this child know of vampires?" her
father asked, and continued, "But it is true."

Isadora in her art remains, as always, awesome to Florence. She describes her reaction to her dance to the Chopin
"Funeral March":

"A figure heavily robed in purple . . . in somber proces-
sional traversed the scene. She was bowed and griefstricken,
dragging each step as if it were the last, until reaching the final
destination, she lies down. To this robed form, now lying still
and deserted in the center of space, comes a tremor of life, and
her arms gently raise. From them drops back the heavy robe,
disclosing a fairer being, enwreathed with beautiful flowers,
slowly rising to the strains of the inspired second movement of
the music. In transcendent joy she is drawn upward and onward
and away in the light of eternal day."

The second dance Florence describes is one of the *Dances of the Furies:* "In the scene of the entrance of Orpheus into Hades, the furies had a deep metaphysical handling. Those qualities described as the haunting fiend spirits of Hades were not depicted as diabolic animal qualities, repulsive or loathsome, but as the more subtle adroitness and divinations of the mental assassin who, like the snake, charms its prey; alert, fascinating, those qualities of the human mind that copy so closely the divine that the elect are deceived . . . The furies surround Orpheus as he descends with his lyre playing the heavenly strains. As his sweet music reverberates through the hollow caves . . . the furies are overcome with remorse and weep, and the gentler emotions awaken in them."

Florence does admit, however, to being very disturbed by one quality in Isadora's dance that she had not seen before:

"All the dramatic power and beauty, tender consideration and compassion as of the saints, all the sweet freshness of youth were portrayed in her Art. Yet now and again was a strain of sadness, almost despair, that had not been there when I had last seen her [in 1910]. This pitiful feature was a repeated effort to bring thoughts of her two little lost children into her dance. She portrayed the parting and lifted them upward, releasing them to the heavenly sphere. This was repeated so incessantly that it was almost insanity. It made me want to scream and rush from the theatre. It was unendurably pathetic."

Yet, Florence reassures herself, a "heavenly state of consciousness" was revealed, "that is home to us all . . ." She is pained by those in the audience who are unreceptive: "The worldly-wise saw nothing. At the first concert an artist and a dramatic reader (both spiritually-minded women) saw and embraced the vision and, rejoicing, went away in tears and in silence. These two women met on the way home and were afraid to speak, each cherishing the vision of beauty, for on leaving the theatre one of them had heard a voice in the audience say of Isadora, 'She is a lobster.' There were those who could only see a repulsive fat woman. But these two finally talked to each other, and exchanged their mutual ideas in appreciation of and joy in her great Art."

Florence struggles to believe that the same Ideal that leads Isadora in her art also governs her in her life. So when she speaks of a visit she made to Isadora at her hotel, she sees in Isadora only the highest of motives.

"Shortly after my arrival Mrs. Duncan came in. In all my life I have never seen a more impressive greeting than Isadora's affectionate expression of filial devotion to her dear mother. It was a poem in motion . . . It was the most exquisite sentiment and tender solicitude toward one who had sacrificed all for her. Isadora was going out to dinner with the critic, and as we bade goodbye, she said to me, 'Florence, go home to your children,' almost like a warning, as if she realized she was taking me from them; and also as if in all the world it was that which she most desired to do, to go home to her own."

But Florence's practicality requires her to acknowledge that this struggle to see only the Ideal in Isadora is not without its cost. There is, for one thing, the problem of Isadora and money:

> Isadora was in trouble; her manager had left the state with all the box office receipts. Of this experience she spoke in the most matter-of-fact way, saying, "Everything I get is taken away from me. I have always gotten everything I have set my heart upon, but I have no sooner acquired my wish than it has been snatched away." This was said in a perfectly complacent manner as if it were the most plausible thing possible; no emotion, no feeling, no bitterness nor resentment, just acquiescent resignation as a matter of course. She explained that the manager was a hard drinker . . . We learned later that the money stolen by the drunken manager was but a mere fraction, that the bulk of the concert proceeds had been squandered by Isadora's dissolute visitors who came later, after tea guests were gone, to eat heartily and drink sumptuously . . .
>
> I never let Isadora know that I knew anything else than her real self. In Truth there is no other. I continually made demands on the ideal Isadora to speak and do and be. She responded heroically and always in my presence every word and deed were blameless. To maintain this attitude was on her part proof of great love and compassion. She suffered in the

thought of my being disillusioned by seeing and hearing aught that would pain me. How like the true Isadora, and what a proof that the actions of the people we know are influenced by our thinking. Other friends had unhappy experiences of seeing her under the influence of liquor through which she sought escape from grief and her pitiful plight.

What Florence and others in San Francisco had hoped for, most of all, was that Isadora's school could be established in their community. In fact, a large tract of land had been given for the school and plans were being made to raise the necessary money. But, says Florence, three obstacles intervened. First, the funds from Isadora's engagement were squandered, so that her own pupils could not be sent for. Second, Isadora pulled out of a scheduled concert for wealthy patrons because she was irritated at the manager. And third, the plan for Isadora to give a great popular concert at the Greek Theater at the University of California for the benefit of her school was deadlocked. Isadora's brother Raymond had previously given a performance of a Greek play there, but had so antagonized the manager that he wouldn't let Isadora perform in the theater.

"Abruptly," writes Florence, "Isadora decided to go East. When I pleaded with her to remain until we could straighten out some of the tangles, and talked to her about the land that had been donated for her school, Isadora was overcome by the old enemy of impatience just on the eve of accomplishment. She replied, 'Land only is not a school.' The land was valuable, and the first building could have been financed. The school, once established, with Isadora at the helm and Elizabeth with the pupils installed, would have soon been paid for . . . Her departure was a great disappointment to the general public and especially to those who had waited years for her coming, to establish her school; but we all believed she would some day in the near future return in full glory to triumphantly fulfill all her hopes and ours."

32

Before I was born my mother was in great agony of spirit and in a tragic situation. She could take no food except iced oysters and iced champagne. If people ask me when I began to dance I reply, 'In my mother's womb, probably as a result of the oysters and champagne—the food of Aphrodite.'"

With these words Isadora begins the account of her life, describing herself as a dancer and as a "revolutionist" from her earliest years. She speaks of the family's poverty and of her mother's divorce from her father. Seeing how divorce had caused her mother to live in disgrace, she decided as a child that she would live "to fight against marriage and for the emancipation of women and for the right for every woman to have a child or children as it pleased her, and to uphold her right and her virtue."

She presents herself as in continual revolt against the narrowness of the society that surrounded her. While her mother worked, giving music lessons to support the family, she and her two brothers—Raymond, who was three years older than she, and Augustin, who was four years older—followed their "vaga-bond impulses." (Elizabeth, the oldest—six years older than Isadora—had been sent to live with their grandmother soon after their father left.) She considered school a prison and was grateful to escape from it and "wander alone by the sea and follow my own fantasies." She expresses scorn for the children of the wealthy and pities them because they are "constantly attended by nurses and governesses."

Convinced that school could teach her nothing, she quit at the age of ten. Thereafter her education came from the reading she did at the public library, assisted by the librarian-poet Ina Coolbrith, who, Isadora says, she later discovered was the "great passion" of her father's life.

Isadora creates a sense of the family alone against the world, making their own enclave of poetry and music and dance, while outside are the philistines. Within that isolated family, Isadora presents herself as heroine. "Of all the family," she writes, "I was the most courageous." She tells how she persuaded the butcher to give them meat on credit, how she peddled some knitted things her mother had made and could not sell. When her father suddenly reappeared after a long ab-sence, the others cowered and hid in fear, but Isadora received him, delighted with this "perfectly charming man."

Some years later the "perfectly charming man," remarried and having made another fortune, returned and presented his former family with a grand house in San Francisco at Sutter and Van Ness. In a few years, however, Joseph Duncan lost that fortune as well, and the house was forfeited with it.

Once again Isadora took command. With Elizabeth, now returned to the family, she began to give dance classes to the children of the wealthy. Her dance teachings, according to Isadora, were totally unsystematic. "I followed my fantasy and improvised, teaching any pretty thing that came into my head." Once she had gone to a famous ballet teacher in San Francisco but had left after the third lesson because she felt his teaching was against nature and ugly. It was to the "wild untrammelled life" she led, to not being supervised by anyone with "don'ts," that she owed the true "inspiration" of her dance.

It is an account laced with errors and contradictions, made murky by all that is hidden and unacknowledged. She never discloses the "tragic experience" her mother was undergoing—

the failure of Joseph Duncan's bank through his own financial manipulations, the loss of money of the shareholders, including Dora Duncan's father, and the imprisonment of Joseph Duncan and the subsequent trial. She forgets, when she insists upon her pity for those children brought up by governesses and nurses, that this was precisely how her own children were brought up. She makes an error in the first paragraph, saying that her mother was suffering from her tragic situation before Isadora was born, while, in fact, Isadora was born May 27, 1877, and the bank failure did not occur until the following fall.

And yet, for all these errors and contradictions, there emerges some coherent whole, a picture of a self convincing in its perfect candor. For the errors are not really errors in Isadora's terms. To see her birth and even her conception as simultaneous with the profound alteration in her mother's life is in keeping with Isadora's remarkable capacity to create a mythical being out of and in herself. When Isadora speaks of her past, there is a way in which that past is not fixed but fluid, a way that allows her to abstract from individual event, to shape individual event, so that the event itself becomes that mythical action which shapes her own destiny.

There is, in this process, a willed certainty in Isadora of her place in eternity that negates ordinary space and time. Yet she tells her story in space and in time. So the reader is alternately pushed and pulled, led and overwhelmed, repelled and seduced by the doubleness of our own human desire for the creating of myth and the destroying of it.

Improvising with thought and with word, she speaks with, seemingly, an almost total lack of self-consciousness. Yet Isadora is never without the consciousness of audience. So, reading, we are not readers—each one responding singly, in silence—but we are made into an audience—one of many, watching at a distance.

From very early on theater, above all, was important to her as well as to the other Duncan children. As teenagers they created their own little theater for the neighborhood. "I danced, Augustin recited poems, and afterwards we acted a comedy in which Elizabeth and Raymond also took part," Isadora writes. At once the little theater became "celebrated." They made a tour down the coast and were very "successful."

Even when she was at school, that place whose teachers

and teaching showed "a brutal incomprehension of children,"
one day at a school pageant she "electrified" her audience by
reciting a poem taught to her by her mother, William Lytle's
"Antony to Cleopatra," a poem from which Isadora quotes the
first lines:

> *I am dying, Egypt, dying!*
> *Ebbs the crimson life-tide fast.*

She omits, or has forgotten, the final lines:

> *Ah, no more amid the battle*
> *Shall my heart exulting swell;*
> *Isis and Osiris guard thee,—*
> *Cleopatra, Rome, farewell!*

33

To think of having known someone early in life who goes away, and the years go by, and then you see her again—how does the image that you have carried with you color and form the image of the one you see now? And how does the present image, entwined, reach back to the image that has been?

Florence remembers first meeting Isadora in Oakland, which was then a place of orchards and large meadows with magnificent oak trees. The Duncans—the mother and four children—lived on Poplar Street in a cottage with a half acre of land and a barn. (The Oakland City Directory of 1888 shows the Duncans living there at the time.) Florence had the impression that the house was bought through some kind of inheritance.

Florence mentions a few facts about her own family: that her father was a lawyer, that the family were Theosophists from England who joined the Universal Church. From what she says, they were a well-knit family, with close ties to the community.

Isadora, when Florence met her, was a girl of eleven with dark brown hair and alert gray eyes. "She had a sweet smile." They used to walk to school together. Florence recalls the schooling as "nationalistic, patriotic." She remembers being taught a poem by James Russell Lowell:

Be noble and the nobility in other men,
Sleeping but never dead,
Will rise in majesty to meet thine own.

She remembers one beautiful young teacher, with whom the lessons were joyous. But for the rest, the pupils had to submit to "harsh and cruel treatment." She remembers that Isadora never completed grammar school, that she persuaded her mother to let her leave.

"The family was improvident. They had either abundance or nothing. There was no frugality, no thrift . . . Often friends and neighbors came to the rescue. There was much needless suffering because of lack of management but also a deal of childish adventure . . . They were governed by impulse . . . On getting a little money, they would go to the city and have a big French dinner with wine. On one meal would be spent money that could, if spent judiciously, have fed them the following week . . . Once they employed a Chinese cook but there was no food for him to cook."

The family would go for picnics in the Berkeley hills in the surrey they maintained for a short time. One Duncan led the horse while several of the others walked, reciting poetry. The horse was finally taken by the hay man to pay for the food bill. The house was also lost, but then the long-absent father appeared, Florence remembers. He presented them with some money and the mother and the four children went to San Francisco.

Florence remembers other fragments: the Duncan theater and their Shakespeare evenings, their recitations and their playing music; Isadora and Elizabeth taking lessons in music and then immediately teaching to others what they had been taught, thus being able to pay for further lessons; the reproduction of Botticelli's *Primavera*, which hung over the bookcase in the Duncan house and which Isadora often gazed at.

She remembers Mrs. Duncan playing Mendelssohn's

"Spring Song" and the family reading the "Rubaiyat." She remembers that Elizabeth, who had been in an accident and had hurt her leg so she could not dance as brilliantly as she once had, was called "May."

She remembers a neighbor, a "Grandmother" Young, a Marie Louise Young, who had come from Germany, who had woodcuts in her house of famous dancers, including one of the ballerina Fannie Elssler. Grandma Young encouraged Isadora and urged her to go to Europe, prophesying success for her there. She helped find a teacher of ballet for her, but Isadora took only a few lessons and refused to continue. Once, says Florence, Grandma Young asked Isadora to dance for her and Isadora refused. Grandma Young was "troubled" that Isadora was ruled more by impulse than by obligation. Still, if rumor was correct, it was Grandma Young who supplied the money for Isadora's first trip east (in June 1895) and also responded to the telegram Isadora sent from Chicago asking for money to go on to New York.

Florence suggests that the Duncans were not entirely the carefree bohemians Isadora suggests. Of Augustin, to whom Florence was once engaged, she says that as "a young man just starting out in life, it was his secret ambition to clear his father's name." Florence, who never met Joseph Duncan, adds, "The family . . . never seemed to realize that their father had been absolved from the taint of criminal interest. They were apparently haunted by a fear of knowing the worst, but there was no worst to be known."

Florence remembers another incident, a sequence, which suggests that fancy and improvisation were not the source of Isadora's dance. As a girl, Florence recalls, Isadora was once very ill, so ill she hovered between life and death. "She emerged emaciated, shorn of her hair . . .

"While still in bed and very weak Isadora used to dance her fingers on the counterpane. In the months following she worked out whole dances while at concerts by dancing them out diagrammatically with two fingers of one hand.

"When Isadora began to put into practice her theories of grace, and apply them to her every motion throughout the entire day, she was painful to behold. Everything that she did was studied (whether she sat down, rose, walked). It appeared to be stilted, overdone, affected, and looked cruder than a slow motion movie. She was never off guard in a single gesture or motion."

Florence remembers Augustin saying, "Isadora knows exactly how she is going to look when she takes a pose. We think we know, but Isadora never makes a mistake."

Florence also recalls that while Elizabeth joined a class in the Delsarte system of movement then "sweeping over" California, Isadora ridiculed these exercises.

Though Isadora may have ridiculed the Delsarte technique to Florence, in 1894, when she was teaching dance in San Francisco, her classes were billed as "Instruction in the Dance and Delsarte." (An entry in the San Francisco City Directory of that year shows Delsarte instruction being given at their Sutter–Van Ness address.)

As a child, Flora Jacobi Arnstein, now 104, took dance classes with Isadora. She recalls going to a large house in an area that had once been wealthy, but was already showing signs of decay. The class began with a series of Delsarte movements, done to the accompaniment of music. She remembers being told to raise her arms slowly and, as she did so, to let her hands trail, with the fingers "dripping." When lowering her arms, she was told to let her hands "float upward." Following these exercises, the children—mostly girls, but also some boys—were given gestural exercises that they performed to Isadora's recitation.

According to Flora Arnstein, the children in the class were never allowed to improvise. The gestures were absolutely dictated by "Miss Duncan, who was attired in a flowing white robe, tied by a gold cord under her bosom. Her dark hair was parted chastely and drawn back over her ears." The recitations included "I shot an arrow into the air" and also "Where are you going my pretty maids?"—this last being particularly impressive to a child because the girls were required to wear organdy aprons and flat lace caps while performing it.

Although Flora Arnstein loved the class, she didn't feel it was a "real" dancing school, and left after some months. She thought of Isadora as a "spirit from another world." Her mother had a different impression of Raymond. "In fact, my mother had left a purse in the dressing room and it disappeared and my mother was always sure that Raymond had stolen it."

34.

The Delsarte system was both a philosophical approach and a practical method to enable the expression of inner emotion to achieve outward form through gesture, through attitude, through timing, through movement in space. It was developed by the Frenchman François Delsarte (1811–1871) after his voice was ruined by disastrous training at the Paris Conservatory in music and acting. He spent the rest of his life evolving a system that he called "Applied Esthetics," the laws of expression in art. In the pursuit of these laws Delsarte spent years minutely observing the responses of people in varied situations in life, at various ages, and under various conditions. At one point he went to the location of a mine disaster to study, as a dispassionate scientist, the attitudes, gestures, tone of voice, and manner of speech of those who waited at the surface to hear what had happened to the victims. He also went through a complete course of medical study, including the dissection of cadavers, to understand the anatomy of the body.

Between 1839 and 1859 his public lectures in France

brought him great acclaim. He illustrated his lectures with gestures, singing, and speaking, and according to observers his performances "had almost magic power to move his audience to laughter or to tears." Around 1860, ill and semiretired, he seems to have fallen into obscurity. Nothing of his work was known in the United States until the American Steele Mackaye, later a famous actor and director, studied with Delsarte for about a year in 1870. It was through Mackaye's work and the subsequent work of Genevieve Stebbins that Delsarte, Americanized, became a great rage in the United States during the last two decades of the nineteenth century and the beginning of the twentieth. Stebbins's book *The Delsarte System of Expression*, first published in 1885, went into a large number of editions that sold nationally. Taken up by innumerable imitators as a fad, Delsarte's work eventually became a butt for popular satire, as in this ditty from about 1910:

> *Her right hand goes this way, her left hand goes that*
> *She flings them both high in the air.*
> *To show her improvement, she makes the wave*
> *   movement,*
> *Impersonates hope and despair.*
>
> *She throws back her head as if she were dead,*
> *Although she's quite hale and hearty.*
> *Oh there's lots of sleepwalking and lots of dumb*
> *   talking*
> *Since Birdie has studied Delsarte.*

Delsarte's system and his principles were crucial to the development of Isadora's work, but only once did she acknowledge this influence. In March 1898, in a dance magazine called *The Director*, there is an article entitled "Emotional Expression," about a Miss Dora (sic) Duncan, "who has been taken up by the millionaire hostesses of Newport." The interviewer quotes her as saying: "Delsarte, the master of all principles of flexibility, and lightness of body, should receive universal thanks for the bonds he has removed from our constrained members. His teachings, faithfully given, combined with the usual instruction necessary to learning to dance, will give a result exceptionally graceful and charming." (Gordon Craig

also reports, according to Francis Steegmuller, that once, looking in Isadora's room for some books he had lent her, he came
upon a copy of a book on Delsarte.)

Even Delsarte's wording about the nature of art was to
become part of Isadora's language about dance. He spoke of art
as "divine in its principles, divine in its essence, divine in its
action, divine in its end." He considered gesture to be the "direct agent of the soul." Speaking of how he obtained his most
important results, he described how he surrendered his will to
become a "passive subject" that "obeyed an inner inspiration
coming from whence I know not, and urging me on to results
I had not aimed at." Of his power to concentrate, he said during
a lecture, "I simply withdraw my vital force into the reservoir
at the base of the brain." There is a clear echo of these statements in Isadora's standing still for hours, achieving her concentration by holding her hands folded between her breasts,
covering the solar plexus.

As part of his analysis Delsarte developed categories of
motion in space and time, which he correlated with correspond-
ing mental, spiritual, and emotional effects. He laid out charts
in which he broke down attitudes of the head and stances of the
feet and legs into at least nine divisions. He worked out a Law
of Correspondences: "To each spiritual function responds a
function of the body; to each grand function of the body corre-
sponds a spiritual act." He believed that the finest gesture was
that which used the greatest number of articulations, and he
insisted, "There is nothing more horrible, or deplorable, than a
gesture without meaning or purpose," a statement that came
to be the very centerpiece of Isadora's philosophy.

In his system Delsarte divided the body into three zones,
the head, the torso, and the limbs, and correlated the emotional
meaning of movement with these zones. So, for example, any
motion above the top of the head served as material for the
expression of ecstasy or aspiration or prayer, a principle that
Isadora clearly made use of in *The Marseillaise* and *Redemption* as well as many other dances.

He divided movement into three types, oppositions, paral-
lelisms, and successions. His theory of successions, movements
passing through any part of the body in a fluid, wavelike pattern, became crucial to Isadora's work. (According to one of the
great early American Modern dancers, Ted Shawn, who wrote

a book on Delsarte, his theory of successions had a profound influence on all later work in American and German Modern Dance.)

Delsarte also presented a Law of Altitudes: "Positive assertion rises, negative assertion falls; in general, the constructive, positive, good, true, beautiful moves upward, forward and outward—the destructive, negative, ugly, false moves downward, inward and backward." He spoke of the Law of Form: "Circular form is, generally speaking, more pleasing . . . angular forms are unpleasant." He noted the Law of Extension: "Movement is extended outwards into space by the 'surrender of the will' and by held breath and sustained posture at the end of the gesture or dance movement." Each of these "laws" was among the many of Delsarte's ideas that were central to Isadora's technique.

Of course it is true that Delsarte was not speaking of dance—he was speaking of movement in its most basic form. Stebbins, as Delsarte's disciple, carried his work into performance through "artistic statue-posing," an expressive imitation of classical Greek statues. What Isadora seems to have done is to have taken over Delsarte's ideas and applied them directly to her vision of dance.

Her own movement vocabulary was limited to basic natural movements: hop, skip, run, walk, leap, bend, fall, et cetera. But even here she seems to have adapted much from Delsarte. In Stebbins's work *The Delsarte System of Expression*, there is, for example, a chapter on "the walk." "The great work of the movement falls to the lot of the thigh, the vital division of the leg," Stebbins writes. She talks about bare feet and about "mother earth" and about the impediment of shoes. She indicates that the torso and head must sway in "harmonic sympathy with every motion of the legs," and she emphasizes the "harmonic poise" in this movement, and talks of how to achieve a majestic stride. In her discussion of the run, Stebbins speaks of the importance of continuous succession, of keeping "the forward leg strong, knee bent, torso thrown forward." Again, all of these points were crucial to Isadora's work.

Moreover, Stebbins, who was apparently greatly influenced by Madame Blavatsky's major work, *Isis Unveiled*, incorporated into her own publications and lectures frequent

references to Isis. According to the dance scholar Margaret
Drewal, in 1892 Stebbins performed *The Myth of Isis* as the
closing pantomime of her recital program and in a work published that year wrote: "The mystic veil of the ancient Isis who
has so proudly boasted, 'I, Isis, am all that has been born, that
is, or shall be, no mortal man hath ever me unveiled,' is at last
being drawn aside by the restless scientific investigations
. . . and ere long our struggling, long-suffering humanity will
stand face to face with divine truth. The pure form of nature
as symbolized in the nude goddess . . . will no longer be able
to conceal her wondrous charms amid her drapery of illusive
matter . . ."

Yet though Isadora may have taken so much from Stebbins
and, through her, from Delsarte, it was in the actuality of
performance that her genius came to bear. And here all sorts
of indefinables enter. Moving, she made herself into the myth
of the veiled goddess revealing herself. In the presence of
an audience she converted all that had been cause for shame before others in her early life—poverty, the divorce of
her parents, the imprisonment of her father—into cause for
reverence.

Critics and other artists have tried to speak of the ultimate
effect. Arnold Genthe spoke of her "divine fluency." Frederick
Ashton wrote, "She had . . . the most extraordinary quality of
repose, she would stand for what seemed quite a long time
doing nothing, and then make a very small gesture that seemed
full of meaning. She also covered the stage in a most remarkable way, she had a wonderful way of running, in which she,
what I call, left herself behind . . ."

The great dance critic Edwin Denby, reconsidering some of
Isadora's technical procedures as he watched one of her students perform, spoke of some indefinable "support" in her
work. He wrote of "the large plain phrases in which a single
gesture is carried about the stage; the large clear contrast
between up and down, forward and back; and the way the body
seems to yield to the music and still is not passively 'carried' by
it, but carries itself even when it yields. It seems to me the
effect of these dances, technically speaking, comes from the
kind of support the gesture has, rather than from the interest
of each new gesture. The gesture in itself, in the softness with

which it begins, in the shape it takes and its accentual rhythm, is monotonous enough; but the support it has is a kind of invention. The support seems continuously improvised and always active, always a little stronger than the gesture in energy and just ahead of it in time . . . It struck me that in the Duncan method the dynamics of movement (the flow and current of the impulse) becomes intentionally the most carefully controlled and the most expressive aspect of dancing."

Differing as they do, these comments converge in an agreement about Isadora's powers. They suggest a simultaneous surrendering and asserting of her will in performance, the ability to convey to the audience the image of her body as if it were their own, and the ability to see herself in their eyes and to have them see her as she feels herself seen.

There is one unusual—and remarkable—description of a dancer by Gertrude Stein in a portrait called "Orta or One Dancing." By all external and internal evidence, the dancer is Isadora. According to Professor Richard Bridgman, one of the alternate titles of this portrait was "Isadora Dora Do." The exact date of the portrait isn't known, but it was written sometime between 1908 and 1912, after Gertrude Stein had become acquainted with both Isadora and her brother Raymond in Paris.

Stein begins the nineteen-page portrait with these words: "Even if one was one she might be like some other one. She was like one and then was like another one and then was like another one and then was like another one and then was one who was one having been one and being one who was one then, one being like some . . ."

(Stein's linguistic circularity, as it moves forward, achieves its own accumulative effect, a kind of narration. In quoting only a few phrases, I do a disservice to the method of the portrait and its effect. Nevertheless, even so truncated, the passages give a sense of the "one" she is portraying.)

> She was one being one. She was one always being
> that one. She was one always having being that one.
> She was one always going on being that one . . .
> She was one believing that thing, believing being
> the one she was being . . . She has been believing this

thing. She always has been, she always is believing being the one she is being . . .

Meaning that thing, meaning being the one doing that thing is something the one doing that thing is doing. Meaning doing dancing is the thing this one is doing . . .

This one has a way of feeling, this one has a way of believing and that is a way of feeling, and that is a way of believing that some have who sometimes look very much like this one looks some of the time. This one is one being one . . .

She was dancing, she was answering, she was carelessly domineering, she was domineering, she was dancing, she was answering . . .

Being that one dancing was then being that one. She was that one, she was completely being that one being the one dancing . . .

She was always being one who was one who was dancing . . .

She always would be one remembering everything about dancing . . .

Being one dancing and being one remembering everything of that thing is something. Being one dancing and being one going on being one dancing is something. Being one dancing and being one believing in feeling in thinking in meaning being existing is something . . .

Stein ends the portrait: "She was dancing. She had been dancing. She would be dancing."

35

On September 27, 1917, Degas
died—Degas, the master draftsman, obsessed by motion, who
created with such a slanted and truncating precision images of
dancers, of horses, of jockeys, of women in their baths, of
women in brothels, of women at work as laundresses or milli-
ners. He observed and drew and analyzed and drew again in his
pursuit of what he called the "essential gesture."

"It is the movement of people and things that distracts and
even consoles if there is still consolation to be had for one so
unhappy . . . ," he wrote in his notebooks.

His earliest work, both paintings and pastels, of ballet
dancers shows an audience, predominantly male, in the dark,
watching a brightly lit stage on which the women perform.
Later he explored images of the backstage life, of the rehears-
als of the young ballet girls called "rats," as they rehearsed and
waited and rehearsed for their performances. In these paintings the observing eye was still an outsider, a man from the
audience, permitted to be part of this backstage life. A detached
observer, looking, looking, with that incisiveness that allowed

him to create new and unexpected designs—slanting, cut off—examining the preparations for illusion, the readying for performance as illusion, stripping it bare, yet creating out of it all new illusion.

In his middle years Degas's vision began to fail. Yet it is the work of his last years that is now acknowledged by many critics to be his greatest, particularly the extraordinary last pastels. They are, almost entirely, images of women—in their baths, drying themselves, bending over as they go in and out of the bath, dancing. In these works the observing eye seems to have vanished, become totally absorbed in the motion, the color itself moving, the forms moving—an arm of a dancer, a shoulder, the head, entwining in essential gesture. It is as if Degas in these last works goes toward an abstraction of motion, or rather that he breaks down the barrier between levels of abstraction, between the abstract and the specific. One looks at these astonishing works of color, one sees motion, particles, waves, one can't tell, life in motion, in color, in form, dissolving, then regrouping to further motion.

The critic-biographer Julius Meier-Graefe, in his book on Degas, speaks of seeing, in the nineties, a large picture of dancers in Degas's studio. "The group teems with heads and arms, placed one above another, a wealth of painted limbs and jagged profiles . . . It is like a mason's work, and it is wonderful how the rhythm of the composition dominates these pointed arches and jagged edges, how the bold curves of the bodies stand out in this blur of motion, how one body seems to grow out of the entanglement of many, how the whole thing has become a mysterious, trembling, swaying mass . . ."

In his later years, as his eyesight dimmed, Degas turned increasingly to sculpture, to what was more immediately malleable through touch. Among these solid figures, here too are dancers, women drying themselves, horses— (Degas studied the Muybridge photographs to determine the exact sequence of a horse's gallop) — old images repeated in new forms. But of all his sculptures the most astonishing, the most enigmatic, and the most radical is *The Little Dancer*. It is of a young girl, fourteen yet still childlike, standing with her feet in an exaggerated fourth position, her legs turned out at the hips, her lower torso thrust forward, her arms straight and pulled back, hands clasped behind her, her head thrust up and back. Exe-

cuted in sculptor's modeling wax over an armature, the figure
stands about thirty-nine inches high and is dressed in clothing
made of real material. The bodice of her costume is of silk faille,
with small buttons, also covered in silk, down the front. Her
skirt is several layers of tulle and gauze. She wears a wig,
probably of horsehair. The dancer's hair and bodice and slippers
are covered with a layer of wax, but the skirt is left untouched.

First shown at the sixth Impressionist exhibition in 1881,
it was received with astonishment and even embarrassment by
many of the viewing public. Many critics were dismayed by its
"ugliness," even as they were awed by it. Joris-Karl Huysmans
spoke of its "terrible realism."

Louisine Havemeyer, with whom Mary had so faithfully
corresponded, wrote of it, "To some it was a revelation, to
others an enigma. The graceful figure was as classical as an
Egyptian statue and as modern as Degas . . . All Paris said, 'Has
the soul of some Egyptian come to our modern world? Who has
achieved this wonderful creation? Whoever he is, he is modern
to his fingertips and as ancient as the pyramids.' "

But Mary herself, commenting on *The Little Dancer* after
Degas's death, made no such distinction between the classical
and the modern. She only said of it, "It is more like Egyptian
sculpture."

Five days after Degas's death, on October 2, Mary writes to Louisine: "Of course you have seen that Degas is no more. We buried him on Saturday a beautiful sunshine, a little crowd of friends and admirers, all very quiet and peaceful in the midst of this dreadful upheaval of which he was barely conscious. You can well understand what a satisfaction it was to me to know that he had been well cared for and even tenderly nursed by his niece in his last days. When five years ago I went to see them in the South, and told them what the situation was, his unmarried niece hesitated about going to see him, afraid he might not like her to come, but I told her she would not be there a week before he would not be willing to part with her, of course she found this true, and now for two and a half years she has never left him . . . I put her in the hands of . . . one of the well known Paris notaries and thanks to his advice everything is as it should be, for Degas's brother had meant to have everything and rob his sister's children of their share. One sometimes can help a little in this World, not often."

It is easy to be misled once again, waylaid by Mary in her evident satisfaction in the fulfillment of her duty, as if that covered over everything. Yet once again—still—words are creating surface—"all very quiet and peaceful." When last she had mentioned Degas to Louisine, it had been in a letter of early 1914, saying "Degas is still wandering." As he did every day the last years of his life, he had wandered through the streets of Paris, unkempt and almost totally blind, frequently following funeral corteges, his hair and beard, grown white, once so impeccably trimmed, now allowed to grow unconstrained.

In his earlier years, according to poet Paul Valéry, Degas had been "elegant . . . his manners, when he had wished, had had the most natural sort of distinction . . . he had been the most sensitive of observers of the human form." But in his late years he was "a nervous old man, nearly always gloomy, sometimes inattentive in a sinister, perfidious fashion, given to sudden spells of anger or wit, to childish impatience and impulsiveness, to caprice."

Degas's biographer Roy McMullen is more graphic:

"Obliged to urinate more and more frequently because of his bladder trouble, he often forgot to close the fly of his trousers. He wore down-at-heel shoes and shiny, greasy clothes around the studio; and if he had to change to go out, he was likely to strip naked in front of a visitor without the slightest sign of embarrassment . . .

"The fatty tissue behind his eyeballs atrophied to such a degree that finally he seemed to be staring out of two dark holes in a tangle of white hair and white whiskers. His admirers compared him to Homer and to King Lear, and [Thadée] Natanson saw him as 'an unemployable Montmartre model for God the Father.'"

What must it have been for Mary, to whom sight was the essential gesture, to have seen this "wreck," as she had put it, of Degas, that one man who had been so crucial to her seeing? There are so many feelings that can surface in a circumstance like this—sorrow, pity, fear—for oneself, for what might happen to oneself in the future. There can be revulsion and then revulsion at one's revulsion. There can be rage at an image betrayed. There can be fear that one may someday, to others, become an image of which one is barely conscious. There may be the resolution to protect oneself. And there may be relief, when death finally comes, in the one seeing, who no longer has to see and feel this alteration of image. So many different feelings, so many different sequences.

Mary, writing to Louisine, follows her own kind of sequence. After the talk of peacefulness she slips at once into "Art Matters," the acquiring of art objects. With Degas's death the contents of his studio will now be available for purchase; there will be opportunities for Louisine to add to her collection. "There [will] of course be a sale. The statue of the 'danseuse' if in a good state you ought to have. Renoir spoke of it enthusiastically to me . . ."

Next come a few sentences about a Veronese and a Courbet a dealer has for sale, and then Mary takes one of her leaps, again without transition. "The sanitary situation is *very* bad, in the country my Doctor told me he had whole families, *all the children* infected by syphilis by the Father when he returns on permission [leave]. An Army doctor told Sat [her nephew Gardner] that such a state of affairs had never been heard of. And I was told yesterday that it leads to leprosy. The Indian and African troops have spread the disease. This when men feel that they are going to be killed they are reckless. Oh my dear Louie humanity is always the same . . ."

From the image of peacefulness to "Art Matters"—and money—and then at once to decay, to disease, to recklessness in the face of death, to immorality. A male image, male images, abstracted, judged—revulsion at a distance.

Even before Mary met Degas, she told Ségard, there had already been a congruency of vision between them. For Mary, "the first sight of Degas's pictures was the turning point in [my] artistic life." As for Degas, at the Salon of 1874 her friend the artist Joseph Tourny had led him to a painting that Mary had done in Rome. When he looked at the painting, Mary told Ségard, Degas said, "It is true. There is someone who feels as I do." Someone who felt as she did, someone who saw as she saw . . .

According to her own statement, Degas had even worked on a painting of hers. In a letter of 1903 to the art dealer Ambroise Vollard, she had written about the painting *Little Girl in a Blue Armchair:* "It was the portrait of a child of friends of M. Degas— I had done the child in the armchair, and he found that to be good and advised me on the background, *he even worked on the background . . ."*

In the painting, in the right foreground, a little girl of about seven leans back in a large armchair. She is dressed in a white dress with lace edging, and around her waist is a large dark-green tartan sash, matched by the tartan socks she is wearing. In another armchair, in the left foreground, a little dog, one of Mary's Belgian griffons, lies almost asleep, its head on its paws, its ears up. In the background are two other armchairs, covered with the same vividly colored pattern, an intense blue, decorated with small, swift, random-seeming strokes of red, dark green, white—colors that pick up the colors in the tartan plaid. The chairs themselves seem randomly placed on an earth-colored gray-green floor. Behind the girl and behind one of the chairs at the upper edge of the painting, light filters in, dimmer than the girl's dress, through several windows.

According to art historian E. J. Bullard, "The portion on which Degas probably worked was the oddly shaped area of flat, gray floor . . . The effect of light penetrating the cool room through curtained windows is also attributable to his brush. The entire picture shows Degas' influence, particularly in the asymmetrical composition, the extensive use of pattern, and the cropping of the painting on all four sides."

There is something both seductive and denying of seduction in this painting. The lushness and intensity of the color of the girl's skin, of her clothing, of the patterned chairs, is offset by the coolness of the color of the negative space of the floor, of the light from the windows. The provocative posture of the child, the left hand behind her head, her legs spread, is countered by the plain figure of the little dog. There is something too in the painting that suggests the child as an object of vision that is different from Mary's other images of children. It is as if, in this painting, a shared vision has been acceded to. There is something in the posture and attitude of the child that suggests she knows she is being seen through male eyes.

There is another painting of Mary's, *Girl Arranging Her Hair*, from 1886, to which Degas has a very different connection. Ségard reports that "one day, in front of Degas, Miss Cassatt, judging a well-known painter, one of their friends, dared to say, 'He has no style.' And Degas began to laugh, shrugging his shoulders in a way that meant: Look at those meddling women who set themselves up as judges. What do they know about style?

"This made Miss Cassatt angry. She went out and chose as a model a woman who was very ugly, a servant of the most vulgar type. She had her pose in a robe next to her dressing table, with the movement of a woman getting ready to go to bed, her left hand holding her meager tresses at the nape of the neck, while combing them with her right. The young woman is seen almost entirely in profile. Her mouth hangs open. Her expression is stupid and weary.

"When Degas saw the painting, he wrote to Miss Cassatt: What drawing! What style!"

To go out and find the "ugliest" model she could find, and out of that to make beauty. Beauty in the curve of one arm, carrying through the curve of the braid of the hair to the curve of the other arm, beauty in the skin tones so skillfully rendered, beauty in the reflection of light off the white cotton shift, beauty in the abstraction of design.

It is a work in which ugliness is used deliberately, as part of a provocation in a fight against male eyes and male judgment. And yet male eyes are still acceded to in this judging of the "ugliness" of the girl, her mouth inert in its slackness, her face expressionless, without consciousness of others.

Of this painting, found in Degas's studio after his death, Mary writes to Louisine that Degas had asked her for it and given her a nude in exchange. "I am glad that in the collection of other painters he owned I will figure honorably, in fact they thought the two, [this] painting, and a pastel were his at first."

Yes, she had been influenced by Degas, had admired him, and after his death called him the "last great artist of the 19th Century." She had wanted to be identified with him, even as she did not consider herself on a par with him as an artist. But she had also feared and fought against fearing his judgment. To Louisine she once said about Degas's critical faculty, " 'Oh, my dear, he is dreadful. He dissolves your will power . . .'

" 'How could you get on with him?'

" 'Oh,' she answered, 'I am independent! I can live alone and I love to work. Sometimes it made him furious that he could not find a chink in my armor, and there would be months when we just could not see each other, and then something I painted would bring us together again . . .' "

A whole history lay between them, of images layering, of eyes fighting eyes. Here was someone who felt as she felt, who saw as she saw. Only there was this crucial difference between them in their work. To him motion was essential; to her, stillness.

And what of the images of Mary as she was seen by Degas?

There is, of course, the painting Degas did of her (which she found to be so repugnant that she got rid of it). But there is also an entire series of works—prints, pastels, a painting— that he did on the subject "Mary Cassatt at the Louvre"—Mary looking, his looking at her looking.

In *Mary Cassatt at the Louvre: The Etruscan Gallery* (1879–1880) two women look at an Etruscan sarcophagus in one of the Louvre's galleries of antiquities. It is a print executed in softground etching, drypoint, aquatint, and etching. The standing figure in the foreground is Mary, leaning upon the umbrella that she holds in her left hand. Her back is to the viewer, to the printmaker. She is wearing a fashionable dark suit with light cuffs above her gloves and an elegant hat. She stands between the sarcophagus and the viewer.

To her left is another woman, seated on a bench, in her hand a guidebook, her face in profile, the features only suggested under the hat, her body three-quarters turned to the front. This second woman is probably Mary's sister, Lydia.

According to the Degas scholars Sue Reed and Barbara Shapiro, in the first state of the print the two women were set against a blank background. But from the third state on, Degas placed the Etruscan sarcophagus in the background. (There are nine known states of the print, evidence of Degas's scrupulous reworking of his images.) The sarcophagus is in a glass case, showing two life-sized stone figures, a man and a woman, husband and wife, reclining upon a couch. Light reflects off the glass in a complex way, showing the reflection of the windows behind the viewer-printmaker.

There is, in this print, something curious about Mary's posture. The diagonal of the left arm, carried through to the umbrella, is separated from the torso by a large negative space.

Mary Cassatt, drawing by Baumgartener, Heidelberg, 1854. ARCHIVES OF AMERICAN ART, SMITHSONIAN INSTITUTION.

Modeling class at the Pennsylvania Academy of the Fine Arts, 1862. From left to right: Inez Lewis, Miss Welch, Dr. Edmund Smith, Eliza Haldeman, and Mary Cassatt. THE PENNSYLVANIA ACADEMY OF THE FINE ARTS, PHILADELPHIA. GIHON & RIXON, PHOTOGRAPHERS.

Mary Cassatt, visiting card. Albumen print, Parma, Italy, ca. 1872. THE PENNSYLVANIA ACADEMY OF THE FINE ARTS, PHILADELPHIA. BARONI AND GARDELLI, PHOTOGRAPHERS.

Mary Cassatt at the Louvre: The Etruscan Gallery, *by Edgar Degas, 1879–1880; etching, drypoint, aquatint.*
MUSEUM OF FINE ARTS, BOSTON; KATHERINE E. BULLARD FUND, IN MEMORY OF FRANCIS BULLARD.

Photograph of Degas ca. 1885 by Barnes. BIBLIOTHÈQUE NATIONALE.

ABOVE: *Louisine Havemeyer, undated.* METROPOLITAN
MUSEUM OF ART. AD BRAUN OF PARIS, PHOTOGRAPHERS.
OPPOSITE: *Mary Cassatt at Saint Trophimes, Arles, 1912.*
FORMERLY, ART INSTITUTE OF CHICAGO.

Mary Cassatt at Beaufresne, 1925. ARCHIVES OF AMERICAN
ART, SMITHSONIAN INSTITUTION.

The right arm hangs by her right side, a minimum of space between the arm and the body. The right shoulder is considerably lower than the left shoulder, yet the right hip is higher than the left hip.

If you try to reproduce this in your own body, you will see that such a posture—leaning to the left, with the right shoulder dropped and the left hip raised—can only be achieved at great effort, by distortion or a severe twist, with parts of the body working under severe tension against each other.

The viewer sees (feels) this tension in Mary, who is ostensibly engrossed in looking, her attention only on looking. But there is something else to be noted in this odd twist within her body. That body, as any body of a self-respecting Victorian lady must be, is surely encased in a corset. Does that encasing contribute to the oddness of this posture? For there is a strange intermingling here: of letting go, in the leaning, and containment—containment through the body's twist, and in the corset. The figure of Lydia, in contrast, slouches as she looks at the sarcophagus and, perhaps, speaks the words aloud that she has just read in the guidebook about these two reclining in their stony embrace. A man and a woman lying together, at ease with their physicality even in death. (It was D. H. Lawrence who was later to say of the Etruscans that they seemed to go on in death as in life, with a kind of joy.)

Degas said about this work that it was intended to show "that bored and respectfully crushed and impressed absence of all sensation that women experience in front of paintings." These are the words of Degas as misogynist, given to cutting and destructive remarks. Yet he too was given to sudden shifts, as when he referred to Mary in a letter as "a good painter" and "this distinguished person by whose friendship I am honored."

Whatever he thought or did not think, whatever he intended or did not intend, it was above all the visual that seized him in this as in his other works, the contrasts in light and dark—the light off the glass case, the light off the dark suit of Mary—and the congruences, the diagonal of Mary's arm and umbrella, the diagonal of the glass case, the curve of the stone couch, the curve of the bottom of Lydia's skirt, the absence of expression on Lydia's face, the absence of expression on Mary's face, as she is turned away, the uncompleted faces of the man and the woman of the sarcophagus.

There is something strangely still in this print by Degas, who was so obsessed by motion, a stillness made up of different qualities of stillness. There is the taut stillness in Mary's figure as she looks, there is the slouched heavy stillness of Lydia, there is the relaxed stillness of the stony embrace of the couple, all in a scene before him, Degas, as he looks at their looking. It is the stillness of vectors straining against each other, of forces in equilibrium, a stillness that implies motion impeded.

37

Once, at work on a biography and in pursuit of my subject, I went to a distant town to interview a woman. (Strange word, *interview*, with its connotation of mutual sight; yet we use it now for seeing only one way—the interviewer seeing the interviewed.) The woman's father had been a lover of my subject many years before. When he died, she became the heiress to his estate, which included, I suspected, some records that might be of value to me.

On my arrival at the bus station in her town, I called her. She insisted that we meet away from her home, in a café for coffee first, and, after, that we walk about the town. We met, we had coffee, we walked. She talked of herself: No, of course she had never met my subject, the affair had taken place long before she was born. When we reached the outskirts of town, we parted. She said she had many things to do that day and could not spare any more time. The next day we met again, away from her house. Again she spoke, not of her father, but of herself. I knew she was trying to judge how I would listen to her life. I listened intently, yet all the time, I was trying to make connections, trying to assess how this might lead me further in the pursuit of my subject.

At our third meeting she invited me to her house. As I walked up the front path behind her, I saw that the front door was nailed shut with a series of overlapping wooden planks. She led me around to the side, saying that there had been a burglary when she was away and the thieves had broken the lock on the front door. She had not had time to have it fixed. (She implied that this had just happened. The nails, however, looked rusty to me.) We entered the house through French doors that opened to a room piled high with boxes. She led me, through a hallway crammed with suitcases, to the living room. She had not yet had time to unpack, she said. (She did not say how long she had lived there.)

In the living room a gray cat was curled upon a white overstuffed chair. Though it was midday, the room was quite dark. A red fabric of some kind was tacked over the large window that faced the front. The woman picked up the cat and motioned to me to sit where he had been. Even in that dim light I could see how the white pillow, covered with a matting of gray hair, still held the outline of his body.

She—my source—quick and birdlike in her movements, sat in a straight chair opposite me, holding the cat on her lap. Now, I thought, she will talk about her father. That is why she brought me here. She sat, for a moment, in silence. From my chair I could see the suitcases piled up in the hallway. "You said—" I began.

"I forgot." She jumped up and the cat, who must have been expecting her move, jumped off her lap at the same moment. "I prepared lunch for us." She darted over to a card table in the corner, upon which was an electric cooker, plates, napkins, and silverware. While she was spooning out the food—it was some kind of stew—the cat circled in a figure eight around her feet. She put a plate of stew on the floor for the cat, then gave me a plate and took one herself. While we ate, we spoke of the house, the garden, the cat, the recipe for the stew.

When we had finished, she touched the edges of her mouth with her napkin. "I have a surprise for you, a tape my father made before his death, about his—meeting with her."

Against the wall behind her was a surprisingly complex stereo system. She got up and turned it on, took a cassette from a small box, slipped it into the slot, and pressed the play button. The voice began, an old man's voice but strong and clear. "I first met..." Suddenly the words ran into each other, dissolving into meaninglessness. "What is that?" I asked in a panic. "I don't understand," she said. "I'm sure it was fine when I played it before. Let me see how the next part is. Maybe it's just a bad piece." She advanced the tape. There was her father's voice, strong and clear, again. "Some sixty years ago, when I first saw ..." Once again, gobbledygook. "Do you have another tape?" I asked, desperately. She shook her head. The voice was going on, sounding as though it had been recorded backward. She shook her head. "I don't know how that could have happened."

In *Mary Cassatt, A Catalogue Raisonné of the Oils, Water-Colors, and Drawings* by the late Adelyn Breeskin, the preeminent Cassatt scholar, there is reproduced a portrait sketch, undated, of Mary Cassatt by Renoir. It is the rendering of a face caught in a moment of stillness. It is not a face that would commonly be called beautiful. It is the face of one who does not resist observation. The facial musculature is not tensed (to willfulness or stubbornness). As much as you can tell in a reproduction, the eyes of this woman are not focused to willful seeing. They have become that through which she is seen. There is a vulnerability here, a softness linked to sight.

There is a dispute among contemporary scholars about this portrait, now lost. One Cassatt scholar doubts that the drawing is of Mary Cassatt. The Renoir expert François Daulte doubts that it is by Renoir. Neither in style nor in technique, he insists, does it have anything in common with Renoir's other works.

But Adelyn Breeskin, who for over fifty years before her death in 1987 had studied Cassatt, never doubted that it was a portrait of Mary Cassatt by Renoir.

38

At the end of 1877, a few months after Mary met Degas and he invited her to exhibit with the Impressionists, Mary's father and mother and sister came to live in Paris. Once again, Mary entered into the household of her childhood. Her domestic daily life became the life of and in that family.

Transplanted though it was to Paris, it remained an island in itself, adhering to old proprieties, to old established behavior. In their intense sense of separateness, the Cassatts did not mix with other American expatriates in Paris. Robert Cassatt wrote to Aleck, "We do not . . . in any way court the [American] colony, and from what we hear . . . we thus escape a deal of very petty scandal."

On occasion they were visited by relatives or members of their Pennsylvania "set." The Cassatts, though not wealthy, lived on a relatively luxurious level in France—certainly luxurious in comparison to the other Impressionists. Robert's income was supplemented by a trust fund established by Aleck, who by this time had become immensely wealthy as vice-president of the Pennsylvania Railroad. In Paris the Cassatts had a large apartment and they also rented a country house for six or seven months of the year. Katharine ran the two households, with the help of four servants. As before, Mary was supported by her family, though Robert did tell her that he expected her studio to pay for itself.

From the letters that Katharine and Robert wrote to their sons, it is clear that they felt pride in Mary's work, or, more precisely, pride in the increasing recognition of her work. But it was always an indulgent kind of pride, modified by the conviction that real work—real accomplishment—and real power lay in the hands of men like Aleck.

Yes, art had a place, but in the world of the elder Cassatts, that place was measured, as were many other things, in monetary terms. Their own understanding of art, in any form, was highly limited. Nancy Hale notes that the Cassatts' "idea of an interesting picture was one with horses in it, with the conformation accurate."

When Mary, somewhat hestitantly, began to buy some early Impressionist pictures for Aleck, Robert attempted to reassure him about the value of a Monet that Mary had bought for him for eight hundred francs: "You will see the day when you will have an offer of 8000 for it."

Mary, sounding uncharacteristically timid, wrote to Aleck about a Degas she was trying to get for him. "I feel it almost too much of a responsibility, am afraid you won't like my selection; & Mother does not give me much encouragement as 'au fond' I think she believes picture buying to be great extravagance."

When the Degas was finally purchased and sent off to Aleck, some misunderstanding arose concerning the exact amount of duty that he would have to pay on the painting. Katharine, as ever, protective of him, wrote that Mary "was very wrong . . . to consent to the arrangement which gives you so much trouble & I hope it will be a lesson to her. I couldn't sleep the night we got your letter and even now I am mortified at the trouble we gave you—"

Within the family structure, it was the men who were paid homage to, whose feelings were the significant feelings to be consulted, to be considered, to be weighed. However, by this time a shift had taken place in the relative power between the men. Aleck, now so successful and so wealthy, so powerful in the external world, had clearly assumed the position of head of the family, while Robert, remaining the titular head, was increasingly seen as ineffectual. Katharine, writing to Aleck, spoke of her husband in words that indicate how much of a change had taken place: "We have been trying to persuade your father to go to Italy, but he is afraid to leave home when there is anything the matter with him . . . he *talks* of going but will take it out in talk I think . . ."

Nevertheless, the shift of the father's power to the son is never directly acknowledged by the women in the household. He is indulged in his sense of his own importance; he is allowed his own small tyrannies. To Aleck he inveighs at Mary for giving in to despair in her worry about Lydia's illness and her mother: "For several days I have been going about with a load on my breast Mame [Mary] being the worst kind of an alarmist does not help me when things look gloomy with her Mother & Sister . . ."

He rails about the "ingratitude" of their servants, who "after the most indulgent treatment and highest wages exhibit base ingratitude lack of feeling and lack of principle. They know that out here [in the country] and in a family circle like this one cannot replace them & they have presumed upon it."

He is allowed to manifest his own self-importance, as when he writes to Aleck that although he is getting older (he is in his midseventies), he is still strong, stronger than Mary: "Yesterday Mame & I returning from St. Germain came by Bas Prunay, one of the longest & steepest hills in this neighbourhood & walked it under a burning sun— I did it with more ease to myself than Mame did to herself— Fact is I was astonished at my own strength & Mame was too—"

It is true that it was not an anomaly for well-to-do unmarried American women of that era to make their home permanently with their parents. But the apparent ease with which Mary fell back into the family is surprising, particularly given her strong sense of independence. She had already left the family once but that leaving was, now, in a sense, undone.

Now she would have two lives—the life she lived in her parents' home in all its Victorian rigor—and intimacy—and the life she lived as an artist. The two seem for her to have been seamlessly interwoven and without contradiction. As an artist, as Nancy Hale points out, "she never mingled socially with the Impressionists." (In contrast, Berthe Morisot, the other important woman painter of the group, was deeply involved with many of the members of the group, but then she was a Frenchwoman married to Manet's brother.) As a proper Victorian woman, Mary would have never even thought of going to the Café Nouvelle Athènes, where the Impressionists gathered and argued.

The family life served as a support for her in many ways, physically, emotionally, and financially. But, in addition, her sister and her mother served as models for her. Lydia, in particular, though a semi-invalid because of Bright's disease, was a model for many of Mary's most important paintings of the domestic life of women of her class.

Yes, limitations were set upon Mary by this reintegration into her first family. Yet she may have welcomed these limitations, maybe even needed these limitations. Was this move by her family—reenclosing her within itself—good or bad for her? Was it good for her work? bad for her work? Who is to say what is "good" or "bad" for lives?

In 1880, the second time Mary exhibited with the Impressionists, the year of her closest association with Degas, she showed a remarkable pastel, usually called *Lydia Leaning on Her Arms, Seated in a Loge.* (Nancy Mowll Mathews believes that the model was not Lydia, but an unidentified young Swedish woman, one of the regular professional models Cassatt was using at the time.) The pastel is so intensely lit, so permeated with light, that it seems to vibrate on the paper. A young woman with red-blond hair, wearing a low-cut yellow evening gown, leans forward, watching a performance. Her back is reflected in a mirror on the loge wall. In the upper left corner of the pastel appears a reflection of the theater chandelier, a stark white, a static image in a field of moving light. The color is applied in layers with great abandon and there is a highly sensual quality to the model's skin, to the line of her shoulders and to her breasts swelling above the edge of the gown. The flesh is both luminous and transparent. It is a work about a woman being looked at, looking. Though there is stillness, there is much energy in the motion of the brushstroke. There is movement in the eye, enflaming what it sees, as if the eye itself is the source of light, or as if light bouncing off a surface is itself a known and felt motion.

Whoever the model was—the Swedish woman or Lydia— the sense that is conveyed by the woman in this pastel (and in *Woman with a Pearl Necklace in a Loge*, also painted in 1879) is of a combination of exuberance and innocence. The pastel and the model alike seem somehow American, she in her posture, in her openness, which is at the same time an openness of the artist, an exuberance in her skill. There is the directness of passion here.

Why not suppose that what passion was to Mary was irrevocably tied to sight, to giving form in line, in color, on a two-dimensional surface, to what she had seen? Why not suppose that what passion was to her was tied to the interweaving of what she had seen and what she made of it and saw once again, changing, and changed on that two-dimensional surface by her making and new seeing?

She herself used the word *passion* about her work in a letter written when she was almost fifty. In a characteristically formal and dispassionate tone she said, "If painting is no longer needed, it seems a pity that some of us are born into the world with such a passion for line and color."

As a young art student, forced to return from Europe by the Franco-Prussian War, she wrote to her friend and fellow art student Emily Sartain about her longing to go to Spain to study, "I have been abandoning myself to despair & homesickness, for I really feel as if it was intended I should be a Spaniard & quite a mistake that I was born in America . . ."

The next month, in another letter to Emily she wrote, "I long to see you & have a talk about art. I cannot tell you what I suffer for the want of seeing a good picture, no amount of bodily suffering occasioned by the want of comforts would seem to be too great a price for the pleasure of living in a country where one could have some art advantages."

In yet another letter to Emily, that October, she wrote, "Oh how wild I am to get to work my fingers fairly itch & my eyes water to see a fine picture again."

A year later, on October 5, 1872, having finally made her way to Europe again, she wrote to Emily Sartain from Madrid. "I got here this morning at 10 o'clock at 12 I had had a bath was dressed and on my way to the Academie Museo or whatever they call it. Velázquez oh! my but you knew how to paint! . . . Oh dear to think that there is no one I can shriek to, beautiful! lovely, oh! painting what aren't you."

Why not call that shrieking "passion"? Who is to define the proper uses and objects of "passion," its range, its intensity, the shape that it takes? For what if her efforts to become what she had to become, in opposition to what was expected of a woman of her class and world, consumed what passion she had, focused it and narrowed it, into this single channel of her work? And what if the very making of her choice of profession left her in her life without room or opportunity or chance or even desire for other passions? For payment has to be made in one way or another for hard choice.

In 1881, Mary painted *Woman and Child Driving.* It is a work ostensibly about motion. The painting shows Lydia in profile, holding the reins of a pony cart, driving in the Bois de Boulogne. Next to her on the seat is a young child, perhaps five or so, Odile Fèvre, a niece of Degas's. Behind Lydia, with his back to her, sits a young groom, his face barely detailed in profile. The left half of the painting shows the rump of the pony, the harness, and the forward panel of the pony cart, to which is attached a lamp. The cropping of the painting, with the front part of the horse absent, has suggested Degas's influence to many critics. But as Suzanne Lindsay points out, Degas's carriage scenes are imbued with motion, and this painting is a study in immobility.

The figure of Lydia, though driving, is without force. The child beside her sits, inactive, her face slack, on an edge of boredom. The groom, a stylized figure, stares into the space from which they have come, but the stare has no sense of intensity in it. The landscape in the background is of an over-hanging darkness, only here and there the suggestion of light. It is not a background that beckons the viewer into the painting. It is abstract, flattened, promising no way out of the bound inertia of the three figures, driving but unempowered. Even the potential power in the scene that might derive from the horse is absent. Its haunches seem static. It is a painting about driving, but there is no going. It is a painting of power not taken.

Lydia (who was to die the following year), driving, is still.

They are all still, all being moved, yet without the sense of motion. They are separate from each other, enclosed within themselves, enveloped by a vision that holds them apart, untouching and untouched. The line from the harness, through the reins, to Lydia's hand, down to the carriage wheel, back again to the harness, suggests an eye moving but constrained. It is motion become turgid, a going toward, a going away, a pulling and a pushing, a stasis of motion. It is passion turned into indirection.

39

After the death of Lydia in 1882, the burden of the day-to-day care of Mary's aging parents fell increasingly upon her. A change in authority began to take place within the family of three. Mary, aided by her mother, began to assert herself against her father's domination, which brought forth an immediate and irate response. To Aleck, Robert complains: "Mame is lamentably deficient in good sense about some things unfortunately the more deficient she is the more her Mother backs her up—It's the nature of Woman to make common cause against the males and to be especially stubborn in maintaining their opinion about matters of which they are ignorant. They try my patience to the last point of endurance sometimes . . ."

After a trip to England, he complains again: "Mame was very sick in crossing—had to be carried off the boat, & never was such madness as for her to undertake a journey of pleasure in which crossing sea water was included—She is dreadfully headstrong in some things and experience is lost upon her."

He wants to see only pleasantness and agreement about

him, but Mary, who has grieved for many months after Lydia's death, though she finally goes back to work in her studio, "is not," he writes Aleck, "in good spirits at all— One of her gloomy spells—all artists I believe are subject to them—"

Now he often sounds in his letters to his older son like a latter-day Polonius, giving counsel about money, emphasizing the need for discipline in training his grandchildren: "Do not forget that a governess to be successful must be supported by the parents & therefore lend her any necessary aid. I do hope that Katharine [Aleck's daughter] will not only like her but respect her as well, else she will not likely prove a very tractable pupil—which would be a great pity . . ."

In July 1883, he writes to Aleck about his son Eddie, who has been spending some time with the Cassatt family in Paris: "As the time approaches for his departure he is growing anxious to be off already anticipating the freedom he will enjoy when he gets home—The discipline he has been subjected to here has undoubtedly been serviceable to him and it will be a shame if you allow it to be relaxed at home. He needs to be aided in obtaining self-control and it is your duty to aid him."

His words to his son are consistently words of the need for self-control and for self-discipline, with a hint of self-pride, suggesting that these principles have ruled his own life. If Mary and her mother do on occasion protest at his statements and join forces against him, the general tenor of their treatment of him is still to indulge his sense of self-pride, his image of himself as the ruler of the household. But as he grows more demanding and more obstinate, it becomes harder and harder for Mary to maintain this image and do what is best for her mother, who is ill with a heart condition.

In January 1884, when she has taken her mother to southern Spain for her health, Mary appeals to Aleck for help: "I feel very badly about leaving Father in Paris, more especially as he evidently considered the whole [trip] perfect nonsense, he really cannot be made to understand Mother is a sick woman and that if we want to keep her with us, she *must* be taken care of . . . The fact is, that apartment is too much for her, those five flights of stairs; Father does not feel them, and thinks nobody else ought to. When you write to him, you might say you are glad to hear he intends to move, that you are sure it is too much for Mother, and that you hope he is going into a house with a lift. Now *please* don't forget this . . . I dare not open my mouth, he won't listen to a word I say. He thinks I want to move for my own pleasure . . ."

In her next letter to Aleck she thanks him for his intervention: "I am glad you wrote to Father about the apartment. He . . . is now willing to change; before that he kept saying he would, but whenever it came to the point he backed down . . ." She assures Aleck that they can afford the new flat. "Our apartment we could have rented easily, and no doubt will find a tenant again; but Father, the moment we left for Spain, told the concierge not to allow it to be visited by any one . . . he is all wrong about money matters."

By April 17, having shuttled back and forth between Biarritz, where her mother was now staying, and Paris, she has moved the household to a new apartment, as she reports to Aleck: "The apartment in Paris is very nice and even Father seems satisfied . . . Father went on like a crazy man the first three weeks and nearly killed me, but latterly he seems reconciled and . . . no doubt will much prefer this apartment to the other. He was so unreasonable about allowing me to rent the other, that we lost about 100 francs by his obstinacy. He begins to realize, I think, that he is no longer able to manage matters for himself."

Perhaps he realized it, perhaps he did not realize it. Few, aging, can accept the waning of everyday powers with all its implied surrenders and needs. Mary, bit by bit, taking over the power in the household, is still cautious about protecting his image of himself for him—and for herself.

In 1885 Mary did a large pastel of Robert on horseback, horse and man turned three-quarters away from the viewer. The background of tree and leaf is an intense blue-green, with here and there contrasting yellows to indicate filtered sunlight. Robert, in a blue coat and top hat, his face barely visible in profile, sits straightbacked yet inert. He seems stiff, as if propped up. Any power in the portrait resides in the horse. In fact, the horse, Isabella, belonged to Mary.

In 1888, while out riding with her father, Mary had a bad fall. It was the first of a series of accidents that she would have involving horses and carriages, but as a result of this first accident she would never be able to ride again. Of this accident Degas wrote to his friend Henri Rouart that Mary "had had a fall from her horse, broke the tibia of her right leg and dislocated her left shoulder . . . She is going on well, and here she is for a long time to come, first of all immobilized for many long summer weeks and then deprived of her active life and perhaps also of her horsewoman's passion.

"The horse must have put its foot in a hole made by the rain on soft earth. HE [Mary's father] hides his daughter's *amour-propre* and above all his own."

(*Amour-propre* can be translated as "self-pride," "self-respect," or "even self-love.")

In the last years of Robert's life his letters to Aleck begin to sound softer, as if feelings not previously acknowledged insist on being heard. Still Polonius-like, though a softer Polonius, he writes to Aleck on hearing that his younger son, Gardner, is depressed: "This is not a natural or safe state of mind for one of his age and unless there is a cause for it is dangerous and ought not to be indulged in lest it become chronic. Now not a word about what I am going to say beyond our two selves. May there not be some domestic chagrin to account for it? You know he is a domestic fellow and if he has any trouble of the kind I hint at, he has not a soul to whom he can open himself to on such a subject except you and his pride will keep him from seeking your confidence. Therefore my dear son do have your powers of observation on the alert and try to find out where the trouble is—*for trouble there is I am sure*—Court his confidences or do what your own good sense shall dictate to be of use to him in his trouble. His present state of mind has been going on too long . . ."

By July 1891, Robert is suffering from great weakness—his legs are swollen and he is very short of breath. Katharine writes to Aleck: "I didn't tell you that he sleeps a great deal in his chair & sometimes in the carriage—indeed he has failed greatly since you saw him last summer."

In one of his last letters Robert tells Aleck about Mary's continuing successes as a painter and printmaker, then goes on to talk about the house they are renting for the summer and discusses the cost of renting. He ends, "That is as much as you will care to hear about it—and will I know have some trouble to decipher it all. Since I wrote you your mother & Mame have been pretty well—not so with me— I have been *very* unwell I may say ever since we came out— I need not particularize—Old age—general breaking up . . . Why I keep on telling you all this I don't know so I stop with a God bless & keep you all . . ."

He died on December 9, 1891.

To Aleck, a week later, Mary wrote: "Neither Mother nor I have felt able to write to you since Father's death. It was very sudden at the last . . . he was taken with paralysis of the brain on Sunday & never recovered consciousness . . .

"It was the cold he caught on coming back to town that made him so ill, he got up one morning at four o'clock & opened all the windows to give air & that after sitting over the heater.

"I think if we could have gone South in the winter it would have prolonged his life, but he would not listen to that. I don't think he had enjoyed living since his health began to fail four years ago . . .

"All our friends have been very kind. We are going South for a little. I think it will do Mother good, & I am very much depressed in every way and long for a change."

In the following year, 1892, she painted the most mysterious, most disturbing work of her entire career, *The Woman with the Red Zinnia.* It is a painting that belies the sense that many have of Mary Cassatt as uniquely a painter of mothers and babies, a sense that she herself in later years both acquiesced in and encouraged. Certainly it is true that from 1880, when she began focusing on the mother-child theme, as suggested by Degas, until the death of her father, this was the main emphasis in her work. But *The Woman with the Red Zinnia* is a sudden and radical shift, a break with what has gone before.

"There are two ways for a painter," Mary once said, "the broad and easy one or the narrow and hard one." But *The Woman with the Red Zinnia* takes neither the broad and easy way nor the narrow and hard one. It is a study in contradiction; in change erupting; incorporated, yet thrust out; welcomed, yet refused.

A figure of a woman sits almost squarely before us. A woman, one of Mary's models, from the surrounding countryside. A country woman. Yet she wears an elegant dress, sewn— and painted—with the greatest complexity. The tucks and braids, the shadows and the highlights are wonderfully and

delicately rendered, creating a costume for a figure to which it
does not seem to belong. Her left elbow leans upon the back of
the bench on which she sits. The left side of her face leans
against the knuckles of her left hand. There is leaning, but
there is no sense of weight placed, given over into the lean.

In her right hand she holds a red zinnia, a startling intense
red upon its stiff green stalk. It is held and looked at not as an
object for meditation, but as something at a distance, barely
recognized. It is held as if it was placed there to be held and she
looks at it not comprehending the holding any more than the
flower.

The face of the woman is at odds with the gesture of the
hands. The face reveals neither emotion nor interest. The eyebrows are washed out, the nose large, the mouth set. The skin
of the face is mottled with red. The auburn hair is pulled tightly
back from the wide brow. The ears are large, the neck is massive, the width and breadth of a man's neck. As one continues
to look at the painting, the contradictions in the figure begin to
create further contradictions. What is flatness here, what is
distance? What is the relationship of foreground to background? The strong dark diagonal of the back of the bench, a
dark green with black in it, seems about to tilt the entire painting in a clockwise arc.

The head of the seated woman above the thick columnar
neck, with the top of the hair so close to the top of the painting,
suggests a geometric shape. The realistic elements of the painting begin to verge on abstraction, but abstraction is refused.
The delicacy of the dress—white with blue-violet trimming—
the deftly brushed-in meadow-garden (a sketch of trees in a
space too formal to be a meadow, too irregular to be a garden),
pull it back across the line to realism.

Something is seamed together here that wants to split. The
woman looks at the red zinnia and we look at her looking.

We know that the woman who was the model for this
painting was used by Mary in other paintings, but the quality
evoked here is different from the way she is portrayed in any
other work. There is a vibration between masculine and feminine here, as if the two are in tension in the same body. It is like
a reflection, a derivation, a repetition of that early painting-
sketch of the servant Mrs. Currey and Mary's father done on
the same canvas but here it is not error, not a chance happen-

ing, but something deliberate, meant, arranged, painted.

Or is it deliberate?

Years later, when questioned about her use of "ugly" models in such elegant clothes, Mary answered, "So you think my models unworthy of their clothes? You find their types coarse. I know that is an American newspaper criticism, everyone has their criterion of beauty. I confess I love health & strength. What would you say to the Botticelli Madonna in the Louvre. The peasant girl & her child clothed in beautiful shifts & wrapped in soft veils. Yet as Degas pointed out to me Botticelli stretched his love of truth to the point of painting her hands with the fingernails worn down with field work!"

Yet, despite what Mary wrote, we must still be wary. Words are—were—still her way of creating surface impenetrability. It is her eye, her hand, her brush that we must listen to, look at. And they are saying something else—about stillness enforced, about stillness placed, about refusal, about feeling retracted, contradicted, and atomized, and about women—and men and women. The eyes that have made this painting are eyes in which a woman's eyes struggle with a man's—man's eyes through which a woman has seen.

From the fall of 1892 through the early spring of 1893 Mary worked on a commission for the Woman's Building at the World's Columbian Exposition (the Chicago World's Fair) of 1893. She was painting a mural for the south tympanum (a semicircular space within an arch) of the Woman's Building.

When first approached to do the work, she was "horrified," as she wrote to Louisine Havemeyer, "but gradually I began to think it would be great fun to do something I had never done before. The bare idea of such a thing put Degas in a rage, and he did not spare any criticism he could think of. Now, one has only to mention Chicago to set him off."

Degas's objection, according to Pissarro, was the use of painting as "decoration." Pissarro wrote to his son, "I am wholly of his opinion: for him [a mural] is an ornament that should be made with a view to its place in the ensemble, it requires the collaboration of architect and painter. The decorative painter is an absurdity . . ."

Despite—or perhaps because of—Degas's objection, Mary accepted the project and set to work on her preparations, which

included the construction of a glass-enclosed studio at her summer home and the digging of a trench so she would not have
to stand on a ladder to work on the mural.

Mary described her intention for the work in a letter to
Bertha Palmer, the chairman of the board of Lady Managers
of the Fair.

> I have tried to express the modern woman in the fash-
> ions of our day and have tried to represent these fash-
> ions as accurately and as much in detail as possible. I
> took for the subject of the central and largest composi-
> tion Young women plucking the fruits of Knowledge
> and [or] Science. That enabled me to place my figures
> out of doors and allowed of brilliancy of color. I have
> tried to make the general effect as bright, as gay, as
> amusing as possible. The occasion is one of rejoicing,
> a great national fete. I reserved all the seriousness for
> the execution, for the drawing and painting. My ideal
> would have been one of those admirable old tapestries
> brilliant yet soft. My figures are rather under life size
> although they seem as large as life. I could not imag-
> ine women in modern dress eight or nine feet high. An
> American friend asked me in rather a huffy tone the
> other day, 'Then this is woman apart from her rela-
> tions to man?' I told him it was. Men I have no doubt,
> are painted in all their vigour on the walls of other
> buildings; to us the sweetness of childhood, the charm
> of womanhood, if I have not conveyed some sense of
> that charm, in one word if I have not been absolutely
> feminine, then I have failed. My central canvas I hope
> to finish in a few days . . . I will still have place on the
> side panels for two compositions, one which I shall
> begin immediately, is Young Girls Pursuing Fame.
> This seems to me very modern and besides will give me
> an opportunity for some figures in clinging draperies.
> The other panel will represent the Arts, Music . . .
> Dancing and all treated in the most modern way. The
> whole is surrounded by a border, wide below, narrow
> above, bands of color, the lower cut with circles con-
> taining naked babies tossing fruit, etc. I think my dear

Mrs. Palmer that if you were here and I could take you
out to my studio and show you what I have done that
you would be pleased indeed without too much vanity
I may say I am almost sure you would.

The mural has not survived, but some photographs of it
still in existence reveal it to have been a very odd work of
"decoration." The women in the central panel pick fruit in a
manicured arbor. Wearing elegant clothes, they give no sense
of effort or toil. Neither suffering nor work enters here, and
most certainly no sense of death or loss. It was a work of
"woman apart from her relations to man," or so she said.

The left panel shows three young barefoot women and four
ducks running after a small enigmatic flying figure (a round
face with a tail? a kite?) representing Fame. The right panel
shows a group of three women in a meadow. They too wear
elegant dresses. One is seated playing a mandolin, the second
is seated listening. The third holds up her skirt in preparation
for a "skirt dance," a rather formal and well-defined ladylike
kind of folk dance. Around the border, here and there, a fat
baby holds fruit in each hand, ready to toss them (at the ladies?
into the meadows? at Fame?).

It is a work of contrivance and externality, even as it attempts to be about "Modern Woman." It is, in some way, the
denial of both men's eyes and women's eyes, a vaporous Ideal
that is at the same time bizarre and incongruous. The women run but they are not free. The woman dances, but she is
fettered.

About sequence in painting: How sometimes it happens in
painting, as in any art, that one can follow a sequence, say this
painting derives technically from that painting or the theme of
this painting derives from that work. At other times, as in any
art, something will appear, as if out of nowhere, sometimes
seemingly without preparation, sometimes out of desperation
or even out of casual disregard. But then it can also happen that
suddenly a theme or a technical capability that has erupted
suddenly disappears, becomes lost, is hidden, perhaps to surface again, perhaps not.

And sometimes it seems that what is being sought by the

artist is—and always was—a single image, and that this act of seeking is repeated over and over again, only from different starting points.

In 1893 and 1894 Mary painted *The Boating Party*. A man, a woman, and a child in a boat. (Before this Mary had almost exclusively painted women alone, women with other women, children alone, women and children. On rare occasions she has painted a man. Once she painted her brother Aleck with his son. She has never painted a man and a woman together. She has never painted a man and a woman and a child together before this.)

In the background, the horizon almost at the top of the canvas, the sea and the line of the shore. In the foreground, a man rowing, his back to us. His figure is a dark blue with black in it, his left arm visible, his hand on the oar, an even darker cap on his head, his head turned so that his profile is barely visible. In front of him and to his left, at the back of the boat, is the woman, seated facing him, holding a child. On the woman's face, not a looking, but an inner look, or a look of being looked at. The child, on her lap, seems to be looking at the man. The oar and the interior of the boat are an intense yellow.

A vibration is set up between the blue-black of the man and that intense yellow of the boat. Sunlight shines on the hat and costume of the woman and on half of the face of the child, but even in sunlight the man is dark. He seems to be looking at the woman, but it is not clear whether or not she is looking at him. On her face there is an unclear expression—is she lost in memory?

The entire painting is tightly tied together, by angles and through curves, by arms leading to the child, by parallel forms. Everything is foreshortened, tipped up, the influence, surely, of the Japanese prints Mary had been studying. (It is also a work that seems to have been influenced by Manet's *Boating Party*, painted twenty years before, a work that Mary had persuaded her friend Louisine to purchase, but it is a work of a very different emotional power.)

The lightness of the woman and the child seems to lift the painting. The darkness of the man weights it down. Yet it is he who rows, he who is responsible for motion. The mother and child sit, waiting, still, being rowed. There is no joy in this painting, this is no fête. There is something else here.

The three of them are caught by the lines of force, in the enclosed space of the boat, in the enclosed space of the painting. Unmoving, they move. They are tied together. They are isolated. They are upon that sea that she fears so, the horizon lifted so high, the shore unattainable. Yet there is no narrative in this painting; it negates narration.

The man looms, threatening in some way, a darker aspect of the sea. He is between the viewer and the woman and the child. It is a painting that is called *The Boating Party.* But Mary, herself, some years later, referred to it in a letter as *"The Man in the Boat."*

4.0

"All my childhood seemed to be under the black shadow of this mysterious father of whom no one would speak," writes Isadora in *My Life*. Once, she says, when she asked one of her aunts whether she had ever had a father, the aunt replied, " 'Your father was a demon who ruined your mother's life.' After that I always imagined him as a demon in a picture book, with horns and a tail, and when other children at school spoke of their fathers, I kept silent."

Her father is mentioned in that early chapter three times, first on the occasion of his visit to the family when she was seven; she alone received him, surprised that he was a handsome gentleman without the horns and tail she had pictured. He is mentioned a second time when, having made his "fourth fortune," he reappears to give the family the house in San Francisco. His name surfaces again when the fourth fortune and the house are lost: "Before the collapse I saw my father from time to time, and learned to know that he was a poet, and to appreciate him. Among other poems of his was one which was in a way a prophecy of my entire career." Beyond that, he is never mentioned again by Isadora. He simply vanishes.

In 1899 Isadora arrived in London with her mother, Raymond, and Elizabeth on a cattle boat, determined to make her way in the Old World, to be received and recognized as America had not received her. As Isadora tells it, despite their poverty they were all in a "state of perfect ecstasy" over being in London, over having all the cultural resources of the great city before them. She speaks of being forced out of a hotel, of having to wander the streets and sleep on a park bench, but nevertheless they spent their days in absolute delight in the British Museum.

(Macdougall notes that the Duncans' situation was not exactly as Isadora describes it. Isadora had already performed in London with the Augustin Daly company in 1897—a visit she does not mention—and had in fact taken classes there with the ballerina Ketti Lenner. Further, a number of influential acquaintances of Isadora's, as well as several of her New York society patrons, were then living in London. They would undoubtedly have been available, says Macdougall, to open doors for Isadora in society and to other art patrons.)

After a miraculous invitation for her to dance in a wealthy lady's drawing room, Isadora continues, she received many invitations to dance in many "celebrated" houses, even performing once before royalty. But when autumn came and the fog set in, the family was still penniless. "Even the British Museum had lost its charm," writes Isadora (a line later immortalized in Ira Gershwin's lyrics for "A Foggy Day"). But then came another magical meeting, this time with Mrs. Patrick Campbell, who—just by chance—saw Isadora and Raymond dance in the gardens of Kensington Square. As a result of that meeting Isadora was introduced to the painter Charles Halle, and he, in turn, arranged for her to give a series of evenings at the New Gallery, of which he was a director.

From the programs of those evenings it is clear that Isadora, by the spring of 1899, had made many important contacts with men in the artistic community of London. The committee sponsoring her New Gallery evenings was made up of sixteen prominent artists, including Halle; Andrew Lang, the translator of Homer; Lawrence Alma-Tadema, a painter of ancient Greek scenes; and J. Fuller-Maitland, a musicologist and critic. It also included Henry James, that observer of the innocent young American woman abroad, of whom he once wrote:

"The most general appearance of the American (of those days) in Europe [was] that of being almost incredibly unaware of life—as the European order expressed life . . . Conscious of so few things in the world, these unprecedented creatures [American women] were least of all conscious of deficiencies and dangers; so that, the grace of youth and innocence and freshness aiding, their negatives were converted and became in certain relations lively positives and values."

Certainly Isadora had rapidly converted any negatives in her situation to positives. As she herself writes, "I . . . awakened a frenzy of enthusiasm and admiration in such men as Andrew Lang, [George Frederick] Watts, Sir Edwin Arnold, Austin Dobson, Charles Halle—in all the painters and poets whom I had met in London . . ." But conscious of her own deficiencies—in music, in art, in history—she did more than bask in their admiration.

She listened to Alma-Tadema as he guided her in the museums and pushed her toward the studies of the ancient Greek vases that allowed her "to reconstruct the movements of the antique dance." She asked Fuller-Maitland to recommend music that she could "illustrate" in her art. He suggested to her the use of Chopin in her work and particularly emphasized how important it would be to "have the *rubato* of Chopin carried out in her dance." From all of them, pan-Hellenists as they were, she drew upon their experience and incorporated into her work an emphasis upon the early Greek Ideal.

She had arrived in England a talented and beguiling beginner, relying on sentimental music, using neoromantic verse as background for her performances. By the time she left London the following year her direction was clear to her. It was a transformation that was intuitive, not intellectual—or, at least, not what we commonly think of as intellectual, with its melding of eroticism and thought, its conversion of admiration to influence. Seen by these men as fascinating and innocent, she opened herself to their ideas and opinions as if she were opening herself to a sexual act. (It is an interchange reminiscent of Yeats's "Leda and the Swan," in which Yeats speaks of Leda,

after her encounter with the Zeus figure, as putting on "his
knowledge with his power.")

The poet Douglas Ainslie was one of those artists who,
according to Isadora's statement in *My Life*, fell in love with
her in England. A number of letters from Isadora to Ainslie,
dating from 1899 and 1900, reveal a tone of childlike sweetness
in her approach to men, a charming self-deprecation even as she
is clearly aware of how much she is admired.

> Dear Mr. Ainslie—
> Thank you for your note. I will look forward to
> seeing you tomorrow. Was this not a bright beautiful
> day—If tomorrow is as fine you might come at twelve
> and take me for a walk and stay to lunch if it would
> not bore you—but if you do not like that idea then I
> will expect you at three. This is written between
> dances—Am I not a hard working small person but is
> this "Task that I love a painless toil"
>
> > Until tomorrow
> > Terpsichore

With an innocent gracefulness she asks him for help, sure
that her request will be granted:

> Dear Mr. Ainslie—
> It is so kind of you to ask me for Sunday evening
> and I should like to go—but that is my eve at home and
> So I can not come—
> I want to ask your help in putting together Some
> Choruses for my recital if you can spare Some after-
> noon or evening . . .
> Do you know I feel quite grateful to you for hav-
> ing introduced Mr. Clayton he is one of the most de-
> lightful of men— . . .

In a later letter, however, Isadora's tone shifts. She grows
bolder, even as she terms herself "meek":

> Dear Friend—
> I but wish you Good Morning in Paris. Then not
> for a long week will you think of me but will See many

wonderful Things and people and think beautiful Thoughts—I remaining here will lose you Seven days and Nights . . . only being happy in remembering the precious minutes you cared to Spend with me—and wishing also that—what am I wishing?—

On your return if you have any need of me—here am I filled with all the love and longing you have caused in me.

Good Night and a happy stay in Paris

In all meekness
Terpsichore

I lost my little pocket book on the way home and I must guess the address—am I not a small lunatic?

She encloses a sonnet that she has written to him:

When first you kissed my finger tips.
Although my heart was glad.
No answering smiles came to my lips.
Which drooped wan [?] and sad.
My mind would then the question ask
Why should this strange thing be?
Found the puzzling quite a task
But this it seemed to me
The kiss you gave my finger tips
Was envied by my amorous lips.

Dec. 13—1899 Terpsichore

Two fragments of letters suggest, however, that Isadora miscalculated Ainslie's intentions, or that Ainslie may have been put off by Isadora's increasing boldness.

Ideas are eternally satisfactory, always there to welcome one, if one comes in the right Spirit. People on the Contrary are most unsatisfactory and cause pain—Therefore I have come back meekly repentant in sack cloth and ashes to my particular Good Angels and I do not want to feel any more as I did. Do you mind my being So honest?—

. . . I have been thinking a great deal about you—from quite an intelligent standpoint and from that standpoint I shall look forward to seeing you *Friday at 2:30*—. . . Good Night-most dear to Me—and forgive the ravings of   Terpsichore

Dear Mr. Ainslie—
　　All today I have had a pleasant remembrance—of yesterday's rain and wind—I was rather glad you did not come today—for today I liked best to remember you—and I have regained the perfect balance-. I think your note helped me to that—I was holding the Thyrsus wand in the right hand and needed a little extra weight for the left side. Anyway I regained the poise with new Harmony and feeling once more Secure— look back with Terror to those chords I will not say discords, but certainly they do not belong to me, which you caused—And now I am once more happy and in my own element. I have been dancing Greek friezes—all afternoon Impersonal little friezes—of figures that have kept the same attitude for years and years— intent on their own inclining [the letter breaks off].

　　The following year, in Paris, Isadora again attempted to shift the terms of her relationship with a reverent admirer. Soon after her arrival in the city she met the writer André Beaunier, whom she describes as pale, round-faced, fat, and with small eyes, but, she adds, "what a mind!" She was convinced that his name "will go down the centuries as one of the most exquisite writers of his time."
　　He came to see her every day and read to her from the works of Molière, Flaubert, Maeterlinck, introducing her to "the finest" French literature. "I was always a *'cérébrale,' "* Isadora comments, "and although people will not believe it, my love affairs of the head, of which I had many, were as interesting to me as those of the heart."
　　Cérébrale or not *cérébrale,* after a year of this "quaint and passionate friendship," Isadora felt she would like a change. As she puts it, "In the innocence of my heart I had dreamt to give it another expression." Arranging for her mother and Raymond to be out of the way, she bought a bottle of champagne and set the stage for a seduction scene. (Earlier Beaumier apparently had tried to indirectly convey that he was

a homosexual, by telling of his terrible suffering over the fate of Oscar Wilde, but Isadora, bent upon her own intentions, had chosen to ignore this or did not understand it.) When Beaumier arrived, he was "terribly embarrassed" by Isadora's behavior. When she began to dance for him, he suddenly got up and left, saying he had a lot of work to do.

Despairing at the failure of her effort to turn this "love affair of the head" to one of the body, she initiated a "violent flirtation" with another admirer. This time she got the young man to go to a hotel room with her, and arrived at the moment when she found herself "submerged in a storm of caresses . . . every nerve bathed in pleasure . . ." But this young man suddenly took fright and refused to go on, insisting that she "remain pure."

Isadora's own interpretation of the failure of her plan is that this entrance into "the strange land of Love . . . was denied to me . . . by this too religious and awe-inspiring effect which I produced upon my lovers . . ."

In the spring of 1902, in Budapest, Isadora had her first great popular triumph. By this time she saw and presented herself and her work as closely allied to the ancient Greeks. To a newspaper reporter she used the word *sacred* in speaking of her dance and told of her greatest dream, "to erect a temple in Athens where she would educate young girls to become priestesses . . . of the dance." Here, for the first time, she was treated as a "visiting goddess from another world."

Following her performance at the Urania Theater, one critic raved: "This is, in fact, the magnificently free dance of nymphs of a Greek chalice where the feet carry the slender body with breathtaking ease." Another said, "The audience gazed at her as if they would like to absorb through their eyes the sunshine and springlike flavor of her sweet soul."

Isadora in turn gazed with absorbing eyes at the Hungarian actor Oscar Beregi, who participated in her first programs, reciting the classical odes that accompanied some of her dances. She describes Beregi, whom she refers to as "Romeo," as someone with "two large black eyes that burned and glowed into mine with . . . ardent adoration . . . He was tall, of magnificent proportions, a head covered with luxuriant curls, black, with purple lights in them. Indeed he might have posed for the David of Michael Angelo himself . . . From our first look every power of attraction we possessed rushed from us in mad embrace."

Enthralled by his performance onstage as Romeo, she invited him to her apartment at night, when her mother was asleep. It was there that Beregi finally accomplished the seduction she had so desired.

Writing her autobiography more than twenty years later, Isadora spoke of that first passion—and later passions—as a conflict between intellect and the senses. In sex, she says, her intellect is at first detached, and even acts as "critic of the senses." But soon the brain capitulates and "cries, 'Yes. I admit all else in life, including your Art, is as vapour and nonsense to the glory of this moment, and, for this moment, willingly I abdicate to dissolution, destruction, death.'"

41

Isadora's encounter with intel-
lect—with thought—is something that is difficult to even begin
to understand. Ideas do not seem to come to her as idea. They
are bathed in an aura of excitation, of eroticism. Certain words
and expressions seem to become talismanic to her, work on her
so as to create a readiness within her for her own expressivity,
her own creativity through movement, for the creation of her
own personal myth.

In *My Life* she speaks of herself in Germany in 1903 returning from a performance "where the audience had been
delirious with joy," and sitting reading "far into the night in my
white tunic, with a glass of white milk beside me, poring over
the pages of Kant's 'Critique of Pure Reason,' from which,
Heaven only knows how, I believed I was finding inspiration for
those movements of pure beauty which I sought."

She speaks of her initiation into the mysteries of Nietzsche's work, at that same time, in terms of seduction. The
writer Karl Federn came to see her every afternoon and read
Thus Spake Zarathustra in German, "explaining to me all the

words and phrases that I could not understand. The seduction
of Nietzsche's philosophy ravished my being . . ." She identified
with Nietzsche's principles—or more precisely with what she
took to be his principles—and subsequently became the "Diony-
sian" she thought him to be.

Through contact with maleness, through men's power—
intellectual and artistic—she increasingly found within herself,
within what she calls the "soul's mirror," the "Spiritual Vision," which she would "express . . . in Dance," in motion and
gesture of continual upwardness.

Yet at the same time through contact with maleness—with
the direct sexual power of men, with and through her body, she
came ultimately to an experience of willing abdication to "dissolution, destruction, death."

It seems that, after all, that black shadow of the male from
her childhood has not dissipated. Rather, on the one hand, she
converts, transforms, and transmutes it, so that men become
the guide for her impulse to motion and form in dance. But on
the other hand, through sex she follows their lead to where that
dark shadow takes over—she surrenders to it—and willingly
goes down into "dissolution."

Returned from a tour of other cities and towns in Hungary,
Isadora, after being greeted continually as a "goddess from
another world," finds a "strange change" in her Romeo. Now
he is playing Mark Antony on the stage. Is this the cause of the
change in him? she wonders. He speaks of marriage, but without enthusiasm. They go to look for an apartment. She feels
despair; she sees that she is no longer his "central interest."

One day when they are in the country, she says, "he finally
asked me if I did not think I should do better to continue my
career and leave him to his. These were not his exact words, but
that was his meaning."

Once more she goes to see him perform—this time as Mark
Antony. The audience goes mad with enthusiasm. She swallows
her tears and feels as if she has "eaten bushels of broken
glass." She says good-bye to Beregi, "who seemed stern and so
preoccupied that the journey from Budapest to Vienna was one
of the bitterest and saddest I ever experienced." In Vienna she
falls ill and is placed in a clinic, where she experiences "utter
prostration and horrible suffering." Beregi comes to visit her in

the clinic. She sees that he is tender and considerate, but she has heard the "knell of Love's funeral."

In an article "Isadora Duncan in Hungary," the Hungarian dance scholar Dr. Gedeon P. Dienes cites an article written in 1982 by another Hungarian critic, T. Ungvari, telling of a recently discovered photograph in which "Beregi and Isadora are tenderly looking at each other, yet even the pleated and ample skirt of the dancer cannot conceal her being pregnant."

4.2

In December 1904 Isadora met Edward Gordon Craig.

He was thirty-two, divorced, with a current mistress, a man of great sexual magnetism who had already had seven children in the course of his many affairs. Poetic and inspired in his talk, extraordinarily handsome, a brilliant actor, a skillful draftsman, he was to become one of the great figures of the twentieth-century theater. A man whose abstract, mysterious inventions for stage design would change the nature of stage performance, he proposed a "kinetic" theater, a synthesis of form, light, sound, scene, figures, and movement. Yet through his arrogance, his need for control, his fear of what others might do to his work, he was only rarely able to bring his brilliant concepts to fruition. As he once wrote, "I am as it were cut off from the theatre I who possibly happen to *be* THE THEATRE."

Absolutely committed to his work and to his talent, he was to live until his nineties, often an isolated figure, but always with someone—a woman—to care for him. He was obsessive in his accumulation of everything that pertained to him, his life, and his work. He kept diaries, copies of letters he sent, scraps and masses of his own writing. He also kept almost all of Isadora's letters to him.

Since her affair with Beregi, Isadora had devoted herself to her work, choreographing and performing with enormous success, particularly in Germany, where her carriage was drawn through the streets by ecstatic young men proclaiming her divinity. With her family she had made a pilgrimage to Greece, an enthusiastically impractical journey to the past, which the modern residents of the country greeted with astonishment. (With some of the proceeds from Isadora's performances, the Duncans bought property on which they planned to erect a temple, which would also serve as a dwelling. Only after a considerable amount of construction was completed did it occur to them that there was no water on the land.)

As for her personal life, since her affair with Beregi, Isadora writes, "I had lived chastely, relapsing, in a curious manner, to the state in which I was as a virgin." In Bayreuth, in the summer of 1903, she had had an intense "affair of the head" with the writer Heinrich Thode. It was an affair that Isadora had not been able to convert to a true physical encounter, much though she suffered from its limitation.

At the time Isadora and Craig met she was performing and living in Berlin and was also in the process of setting up her long-awaited school for children.

In his diary *Book Topsy* (Topsy was his name for Isadora) Craig recorded his meeting with her. He thought her, at first, "a nice Greekish lady by art & a fine American girl by nature . . . She at once suggests the amateur-hypnotic lady & I should distrust her if she were not beautiful & Beauty is the only thing we can entirely trust. This reference to her beauty is rather strange, for in features she was not beautiful, but in *movement* she made up for the lack of . . . Lily Langtry features—"

In a BBC radio talk in 1952 Craig spoke of going to see Isadora dance. She appeared on stage, stood still at first, and only after the music had begun did she begin to move, he said, "just moving . . . speaking her own language . . . telling to the air the very things we longed to hear and until she came we had never dreamed we should hear; and now we heard them, and this sent us all into an unusual state of joy, and I . . . I sat still and speechless."

After the performance, Craig continues in *Book Topsy*, he went to a gathering at her house. There she sat beside him. "The next thing she does is to —no, I will not write it—but I remember it, and how she discovers (bless her) that I am just an ordinary gentleman.—for her anyhow!!!" They talk and, Craig says, "we know that we know each other . . . she can read me with ease . . ." When he leaves, she gives him a picture of herself and writes upon it, "with Love Isadora."

"A regular hussy of a girl," he writes in his diary, "one would say if one thought about it—but that only proves that to think is often a mistake—and leads to error . . ."

The next day she comes to see his exhibition. Observing her, he feels that she is seeing and feeling things the others do not. The following morning he spends with Isadora and her brother Augustin and his lover Sarah and they go to visit Isadora's new school. "I find it all ugly except her," Craig writes, noting that she has told him the "fairy tale of Psyche—" He invites her to his studio to see his drawings and is upset when she does not come at the appointed time. "When next I go to see her dance I am asked round to supper. Then she tells me she had come round to my studio & missed it, looked & looked & had to go away.

"Then I find she is the she I thought she was."

On December 16 Isadora "says she will come & see me the next day 'to tea' at my studio at 4 . . . At 4 she arrives—away we drive for an hour in her carriage. Then tea. Then carriage dismissed—Then supper—then we sleep together on our balcony. 17 December— our marriage night on the floor of the dear studio. I tell her I am going to marry in about 4 months time— she does not believe in marriage."

They attend a reception for her the next day. Isadora's family, says Craig, is chilly to them. Still they spend four days and nights together before she goes to St. Petersburg to dance. "In those nights," writes Craig, "she gives herself to me & reserves nothing."

On the day she leaves, December 23, 1904, she writes to him:

> Thank you Thank you Thank you for making me Happy—whole Complete I love you love you love you & I Hope we'll have a dear sweet lovely Baby—& I'm Happy forever
>
> <u>Your</u>
> Isadora

As soon as she gets to St. Petersburg, she sends him a letter:

> You dear—dearest sweetest & Best. I think the best thing to do with St. Petersburg is to forget it— and pretend I'm not here. I'll not see it—I swear I won't—Darling—Sweetest Love—I shut my eyes and think of it and I heard you Breathing—but when I awoke I was alone—alone alone—

But Craig writes in *Book Topsy*:

> All has been easy & without regrets & silly things. All has been as it should be between a woman and a man who attract each other as we do.
> Do I love her?
> Does she love me?
> I do not know or want to know. We love to be together . . .
> Is that love? I do not know.
> She says she loves me. What does that mean from her? I do not know . . ."

Twenty years later, writing in *My Life,* Isadora gives her version of the first meeting with Craig. In the midst of a performance one night, she says, she became "psychically aware" of the presence of a personality in the front row. After the performance a "beautiful being" came to see her and immediately accused her of having stolen his stage designs. Isadora answered that the blue curtains she used were her own invention. Craig insisted they were his. " 'But you are the being I imagined in them. You are the living realisation of all my dreams.'

" 'But who are you? . . .'

" 'I am the son of Ellen Terry.'

"Ellen Terry," Isadora says to her reader, "my most perfect ideal of woman!"

And immediately afterward, Isadora gives us a description of Craig as she saw him then: "Craig was tall, willowy, with a face recalling that of his wonderful mother, but even more delicate in features. In spite of his height, there was something feminine about him, especially about the mouth, which was sensitive and thin-lipped . . . His eyes, very near-sighted, flashed a steely fire behind his glasses. He gave one the impression of delicacy, a certain almost womanly weakness. Only his hands, with their broad-tipped fingers and simian square thumbs, bespoke strength. He always laughingly referred to them as murderous thumbs—'Good to choke you with, my dear!' "

Isadora then tells of their first night together at Craig's studio: "Here stood before me brilliant youth, beauty, genius; and, all inflamed with sudden love, I flew into his arms with all the magnetic willingness of a temperament which had for two years lain dormant, but waiting to spring forth. Here I found an answering temperament, worthy of my metal. In him I had met the flesh of my flesh, the blood of my blood. Often he cried to me, 'Ah, you are my sister.' And I felt that in our love was some criminal incestuousness."

To her he is like Endymion, he is like Narcissus, he is like Perseus, he is like an angel of Blake. Her eyes are "ravished by his beauty," she is "drawn toward him, entwined, melted." They are "two halves of the same soul."

But this is still the same Isadora we have met before. Soon after they meet she tells him the "fairy tale of Psyche." It is the Greek myth of a young maiden of whose beauty Venus becomes jealous. In her jealousy she orders her son Cupid to cause Psyche to fall in love with a monster. Instead of carrying out his mother's orders, Cupid himself falls in love with Psyche. He marries her, so the myth goes, but refuses to reveal who he is. He will not even let her see him; they are only together in darkness. Warned by her sisters that he must be a monster to behave in this way, Psyche lights a lamp in the darkness to see him and thereby destroys their marriage.

A story about the body and the soul—a story about a woman and a man—a story of a woman who must see the dark figure of the man.

4.3

It seems, at first, an affair that will conform to all expectations of high romance—he and she, two beautiful passionate geniuses. But its shape is not the shape of high romance, a plot of obstacles placed in their way and then obstacles overcome. Here they themselves are the obstacles.

They meet in Berlin, then they must part as she has to leave for Russia; she returns, they have a passionate reconciliation. But what appears to be rebinding is only the prelude to the next separation. She wants him to tour with her, which he agrees to do for a while. But proximity is not the solution she hopes it will be. Uncertainty keeps surfacing in him. He thinks he loves her, he thinks he doesn't love her. He comes to her, he goes away, he comes to her, he goes away. She holds fast to desire and the more he pulls away, the more she holds to it. He blames her, admires her, castigates her, seems unable to tell self-loathing from anger at her, uses anger to propel himself away, for he has to get away. For all his agreeing, on occasion, for all his saying they are one, he is fearful of being one.

And she, expressing desire, need, longing, falls into jealousy. "The mark of the green-eyed monster . . . the stigmata of the slave," she will call it many years later, speaking of what she saw as a child in "the faces of the married women friends of my mother." But she, unmarried, disdaining marriage—or so at least she has said, becomes slave to it herself. She provokes an incident with him. For finally, it seems, she has learned more than she wanted to know of the other woman, of the other children in his life.

According to Francis Steegmuller in *Your Isadora*, a narrative of the affair between Craig and Isadora, based upon her letters and his letters and diaries, in March 1905 Isadora apparently opened a letter from Elena Meo to Craig. Elena Meo's third child by Craig had been born on January 3, 1905, at the very time Isadora and Craig were having a passionate reconciliation after her return from St. Petersburg.

There is no way of knowing what Craig had told Isadora about his other lovers and his children and, if Craig did tell Isadora, whether she believed him. For what she wanted to believe in clearly was the permanence and exclusivity and total absorption of the passion she was feeling and was sure she was seeing in Craig. But now, with the opening of the letter, she could no longer not see what was going on. And evidently she flew into a rage of accusation.

Afterward she wrote to Craig:

> Dear—I feel awfully ashamed—ashamed is not the word.
> I feel dust & ashes—it was an awful kind of rage that took possession of me—
> Let my pain atone for it—I'm afraid you will never be able to think of me in the same way again.
> And I didn't mean to tell you.
> That is the worst of it—
> You are so dear & kind
> but I know what you must *think* of it
> I would give   I can't write about it—I hate myself—I am in despair over it—
> forgive me—
> but you can't make it *undone* can you—

Jealousy has come, dark and ugly—but she fights it off, with the help of his words and his lovemaking, which she so desperately needs and wants. He writes to her, "Be Calm Big Clear & Cool." And she takes his words to heart, telling him she has absolved herself from her sins. "I'll put it down to Primitive Instincts, Inherited Tendencies . . . ," she writes, then adds, "You need not write 'Never not love me'— I love all that is beautiful and I will always adore you because you are beautiful." She says she has been thinking of words of Plato and Marcus Aurelius and Dante about living in terms of the reasoning soul, in Peace and in Harmony. Then she adds: "As Christ said— 'Love one another.' Also he said some things about *little children*—and Isadora considered these things and prayed: 'Save me from the *Green Demon Jealousy!* and the *Red Devil Desire for Complete Possessorship . . .*' "

She tries to make herself a "reasoning soul," capable of accepting everything. By the next year, when she is in Holland, pregnant with Craig's child, and he is away in England, visiting his mother and Elena Meo, she makes this offer to him, "If there is anyone you care for very much who feels unhappy and wants to come with you she [Elena Meo] can have half my little house with *all my heart.* It will give me *joy*—and Love is enough for all—"

But jealousy will recur, no matter how much she tries to transcend it, struggling against the kind of humiliation that her mother had experienced and that she as a girl had vowed never to experience.

It seems to be about high romance, but, in fact, it is a struggle for power. (Is that what all high romance is?)

In a notebook entry—probably from early 1905—Craig wrote about his love for Elena Meo and his paradoxical feelings for Isadora:

> . . . I am in love with one woman only, and though others attract me how could it ever obliterate what exists of her in my heart and soul, or how could it alter my heart and love towards her— But I am keenly attracted to another woman, who may be a witch or a pretty child (and it really doesn't matter which) and I find it hard to be away from her. She not only attracts

me, she revolts me also. One moment I instinctively smile with her and love to be with her, and the next I want to be away from her and I shrink from her. It is not that she is at all ugly or repulsive—but merely that I am delighted with her or bored.

When she talks about herself incessantly for a quarter of an hour—when she drinks more wine than she needs or wants—when she cuddles up to other people, men or women, relations or not relations—it is not that she does so repulsively but I see they are equally attracted as myself—and I object to be equally anything in such matters.

And my confession is that I have a contempt for her and do not like to feel that I have a contempt— because I find her so dear and delightful.

Still I cannot trust her, and even friendship, much more love demands absolute trust.

Not that I love her—it is not possible to "Love" twice.

And that is where perhaps a clever idiot would get mixed, for though I do not love her, I tell myself and her that I do—Still I also tell her that I am unable to tell what love is— So I am—Love is something a bit less restless and wayward than this. Love regards no other thing or person except through the eyes of the loved one . . .

Love which torments is not love . . .

He is back and forth, back and forth—he wants equality, he wants more than equality—she is a witch, she is a pretty child. He feels "contempt" for her, yet he is persuaded she is a genius. To his friend Martin Shaw he writes of her dancing: "If you could see *one* dance you would understand how wonderful it is. Beauty & Poetry is art when it is created, no matter how, by a living being—"

He wants, he says, a love that is without torment, "without fluster or excitement, something at ease and gravely sweet . . ." Yet he prizes the excitement that comes from being with her: "Inspiration is given out by the thousand volt per second from Miss D. And I am alive again (as artist) through her. You know how life-giving or -taking one artist can be to another."

She meanwhile is caught between power and powerlessness, the power of her own desire for him and her powerlessness to refuse it:

From Brussels in March 1905, she writes:

> . . . I'm dying for you . . .
> Come along quick—*quick as you can*
> I'm half dead for you . . .
> I feel I'm like an Amazon
> Amazon persued & brought the stalwart Warriors home—'n Kissed 'em to death. [*Kissing* was their word for scx] . . .
> I think I is an Amazon—
> If you like the persuing idea you'll have to put up with me persuing at the same time & Clash Bang Crash *Collision* in the Middle—

According to Edward A. Craig, Craig's son, who was also his biographer, Craig never made the first overture to a woman until he was well into middle age. So great was his attractiveness as a young man, says Francis Steegmuller, "that he had only to be still; the woman would advance, and eventually a child was born . . ."

Whether or not Isadora made the first move in their affair, it is clear from her letters that throughout their relationship she was the one who pursued, he was the one who was pursued. She was the one so overcome by desire for him that she could not bear to be parted from him. She tells him he is the other half of herself, she says she doesn't even exist without him. She presses and presses him to be with her, to make love to her, and he, clearly, withdraws. When he withdraws, she becomes frightened, she tries to control herself, she pulls back. But then once they are together again, she presses him more. There is, in her, with all the expression of love and desire and the fulfillment that he brings her, the sense of an insatiability—desire possessing her, out of control.

Of their first night together Isadora writes, in *My Life*, that her joy was "so complete" that "one should not survive" it. But, she adds, as Craig had "neither the nerves nor nature of a voluptuary," he "preferred to turn from love-making before satiety set in, and to translate the fiery energy of his youth to the magic of his Art." Clearly, Craig was a man who saw to his own protection. No death, dissolution, destruction for him.

Many years later, writing on what had happened between them, Craig said, "I loved her—I do still—but she, the complex she, might have wrecked me, as she wrecked many—and finally herself. And she did not wreck me? No, she did not. She was a strange, lovely, strong creature, but it seems I was the stronger."

Reading Craig's diary entries and the hundreds of letters between them, one gets a sense not of sequence in a single line but of entanglements that are pulled tighter and tighter. There is, first of all, Isadora's entanglement of the affair with her art. On that trip to Russia, just after she had met Craig, she gave a speech about her intention in dance, which the painter Alexander Benois later reported on:

"In her opinion, the only thing that matters is beauty, the pursuit of beauty in order to make all life beautiful. In the presence of beauty even suffering has no terrors, even death does not frighten . . ." Benois added that when asked by a writer " 'What are we to do about ugliness, since it exists in the world?' Miss Duncan . . . replied without hesitation, 'Il faut la tuer, la laideur! Il faut la tuer!' " (It is necessary to kill ugliness! It is necessary to kill it!)

And just as her dance is the realization for her of all that is beautiful, idealized, and transcendent, so is Craig. Before leaving for St. Petersburg she wrote to him:

> Dearest Sweetest Spirit
> You will never know how beautiful you are. Only I know that. You will never know what an immense Joy *Giver* you are . . . What shall I give you in return— All all that I have in my power to give & that is not enough—but perhaps you will find a cold empty corner for it . . .
> You have the most beautiful eyes in the world— and the dearest hands. You contain the sweetness of all the flowers & soft winds & sun—& I love you—as the essence of all that is good & sweet in creation—& I am above every thing else Grateful—Grateful—

Grateful to you—& will always be grateful to you. We
were born in the same star and we came in its rays to
earth, & for a little I was in your heart & then I wandered far away & now I am back. That is our History.
No one could understand it—but us . . .
        I am your love if you will have me—if not—
        but I am
            Your
            Isadora

He is Beauty to her, he is the opposite of darkness and of
ugliness to her, just as her work is Beauty and the opposite of
darkness.

In 1906, when Craig was working with Duse on a production of Ibsen's play *Rosmersholm*—and as usual having difficulty with his co-worker—Isadora wrote to him:

"Beauty—Inspiration Genius— *You not Ibsen* . . . Of
course Ibsen has a sort of genius but O Damn it all it's just the
reverse of Beautiful and if D. [Duse] goes that way she will
wander in Darkness—No—*not* Ibsen great as he may be—but
You you have the divination of *Beauty* . . . Dam Strindberg
Dam such stuff it is *Poison*—No such mixtures for *you* . . . not
these grubby darknesses . . . Lets go *upwards* & onwards."

It is through Craig, above all, that Isadora seems determined to reconcile her art with her life. It is as though she goes
even further by applying the principles of her art, the method
of her art, to her relationship with him. All that she knows of
art she tries to make real in life with him. He is her work of art,
he and she together are her work of art. The obsession with
Craig, in fact, makes her begin to doubt the importance to her
of her own work. In a way, he begins to replace her own art.

"O you you you—I am slipping away from myself and
becoming nothing but a longing and reflection and I tried to tell
you the other day my *work* was the principal thing. *Work*—I
haven't a thought or feeling left for it—that's the truth—it's
this Infernal feminine Coming out at all places . . ." she writes.
And in another letter: "How do you find *me* as an inspiration?
You give me only one inspiration and that is to run away from
all Publics and the like and rush to you—& then die or what
ever—"

There is an entanglement, as well, in the affair with her

own mythology and mythological urgings. They are twin souls, they were born in the same star, they are brother and sister as well as lovers. When she is near him, she only wants to "fly into" him and "die." From and through him she will be reborn into a new and different kind of woman.

She reads Walt Whitman's poem "Think of the Soul," and copies the line, "Think of womanhood and you to be a woman;" for Craig. She adds, "How can I? With you I had some faint hints of it— what it might be. Darling, you don't know— I think I have died & passed among the shades . . ."

4.4.

It all lies together for her in this entanglement of the affair—art, myth, the meaning of the feminine—she imagining, creating herself and the idea of him. (And he too, imagining, creating himself and his idea of her out of his own myths—but that is not our story here.) They mirror each other but there is much she does not see.

For all she sees that they share—the need, the love for beauty, the need to break old barriers, even a life history that has similarities (he too had a dark shadow of a father, an absent father, who had never married his mother)—she does not acknowledge their sharp and crucial differences.

She does not see that there is a deep rhythmic disparity between them. He functions with breaks sharp and sudden, starting, stopping, starting, stopping. She wants continuity, going on and on in a wave form with no breaks, no sharp edges.

She does not see that something in him requires that he live in essential isolation. Unable to work with others, unable to see with others' eyes, he must live as if he himself is his only audience. He is a man of the theater for whom there will never be the right kind of theater on earth.

In a letter he drafted but did not send to Isadora, in September 1907, just before his final break with her, he writes:

"Only true loneliness which is not seen, not felt by others but is an *internal, eternal joy* can submit to play the game for its own sake—the sake of the *game* not the sake of the *goal*. The game is to encircle the earth, to press one's lips upon the face of the world—that is called 'thinking one's maker,' or 'filial love.' Only that is LOVE. All else is death . . ."

But she wants and needs the admiration of others, lives through their eyes, performs in some kind of melding with her audience. She cannot bear to be alone, ever. In 1907 she writes to Craig from Nice, where she has been recuperating from an illness: "The feminine spirit has a *special* aversion to entering in that land of abstract idea where work is—Indeed only a few in History have succeeded in doing it alone—& then only through suffering, & I object to suffer."

She wants to hold off darkness with beauty, she wants to hold off what she calls "brutal reality," she wants to live through the imagination, but also through the body. It's as if she is going to conquer life itself with her capacity for idealization, by uniting it with art, making her body the luminous manifestation of the spirit, while still holding to the physical delights of sexuality. No, she does not care about contradiction. But mediated as it all is through her body, she finds herself at the mercy of her body.

In 1906 Isadora became pregnant. When she could no longer perform, she went to Noordwijk, a seaside town in Holland, where she rented a villa and awaited the birth of the child. Craig came to visit her on a few occasions, but essentially he was absent. In her letters to him she continued to present herself as tranquil, even happy, in her waiting state, only occasionally revealing her anguish in not hearing from him. But the sculptress Kathleen Bruce, who stayed with Isadora before the birth, says that although Isadora was sometimes peaceful and radiant, she also had "terrible days and nights when a fierce cloud of doubt, fear and loneliness would descend upon her."

As a child Isadora had walked beside an ocean, dancing, she says, freely, learning movement and the joy of movement from the waves. Now, with Craig absent, bearing his child, she attempted suicide by walking into the sea. To Kathleen Bruce, who found her in the water, she said, "with a faint childlike smile . . . 'The tide was so low, I couldn't do it, and I'm so cold.' "

Her daughter Deirdre was born on September 24, 1906, after an extremely difficult labor. Craig was present but left shortly afterward. In November Isadora and Craig, with the baby and the nurse, went to Florence to arrange with Duse for Craig's production of *Rosmersholm.* By mid-December Isadora was performing again, this time touring in Poland for almost a month. Returning to Berlin, where she met Craig briefly, she left almost at once for a tour of Holland. (The baby had been sent with the nurse to San Remo on the Italian Riviera when Isadora left for Poland.)

In Amsterdam Isadora was overcome by "a strange illness" and after the performance "fell prone upon the stage and had to be carried back to the hotel. There for days and weeks I lay in a darkened room packed in ice bags," she writes. "They called it neuritis, a disease for which no doctor has been able to find a cure. For weeks I could eat nothing and was fed on a little milk with opium, and went from one delirium into another, and finally into unconscious sleep.

"Craig came flying up from Florence and was devotion itself. He stayed with me for three or four weeks and helped to nurse me . . ."

(Francis Steegmuller notes that Isadora's recollections are "inaccurate." Craig came to see her in Amsterdam, briefly, and then left to continue his work with Duse, in Nice.)

Writing to him, Isadora kept apologizing for her illness: "Silly me, to get so ill—Can't understand it—forgive these stupid lines . . ." "Dr. says *perhaps* I may travel Saturday but I'm afraid not till Tuesday—but then I will be *quite* well & *never* be ill again . . ."

She traveled to Nice, thinking Craig was still there, but by the time she arrived, he had already taken off for Florence, after an argument with Duse about the production. From Nice, where the nurse and baby joined her, she wrote to him about her pains, in one sentence mentioning their severity, in the next apologizing for them. "I am getting ashamed to regale you always with my pains . . . This getting well is very difficult. I

still take these powders which make my head continually spin—
A tedious business . . . I look at the Baby & look out over the
sea & think of you— & if my poor body is racked with silly pains
my heart is filled with love & love—& so it's all right . . ." "It
is true I am still somewhat ill & a good deal of pain but your
power of giving me joy is so great that the dear lines you write
me make up for all else . . ."

"Are you my pulses & my blood & do I only exist because
of you—and if you turned from me would I die—. . . & do I exist
when apart from you only by your thoughts of me— . . . does
my spirit beat itself to death out there trying to get to you &
leave me with nothing but a body & a dulled brain . . ."

When a letter comes from Craig, after what has seemed to
her a long silence, she writes, "O I tell you I have no caution
or care, & if I don't see you soon I will pull myself up by the
roots & throw myself into the Sea— . . .

"What are nerves—are they little demons who when they
find the soul forces weak rush in & strike with pitchforks all
over?—& did a thousand little spirits jump from your letter just
now as I opened it & demolish them all? . . ."

After all, she miscalculated. She had thought to impose the
principles and esthetic of her art upon her life. But it had not
worked. There was no continuity, no wavelike motion, only
breaks and more breaks. And she, growing more and more
fearful of losing him, censored what she said, keeping from
herself the realization of her own self-containment. No, in this
affair she was not as she was in her dance, moving freely,
unconstrained, with wildness surfacing now and then, but in
control. (You can see that wildness in the drawings of her by
Abraham Walkowitz and Antoine Bourdelle and others—particularly in the way the thigh lifts as she prepares to run.) Here
wildness is only an outcry not acted on, a threat—a suggestion—that she may throw herself into the sea. And here body
asserts its power through the one way available to it, throwing
her into neuritis, neuralgia, whatever . . .

Meanwhile, Craig, in Florence, kept her at a distance, no
matter whether she wrote of pain or transcendence of pain. He
was ready to break off the affair and the actuality he called upon
to break it was money.

Almost from the beginning of the affair, Isadora had supported Craig so that he would be free to do his great work.

From the money that she made from her performances she also supported her mother, the school in Germany that Elizabeth ran for her, and, on occasion, one of her brothers. Craig and Isadora had formed a financial partnership, at first managed by an unlikely entrepreneur, Maurice Magnus. (Magnus was later to become famous through the introduction written by D. H. Lawrence to his *Memoirs of the Foreign Legion.*) At other times Craig himself had seen to the managing of Isadora's money, a vexing arrangement for the both of them since Isadora was very extravagant, in Craig's terms.

But now, in Florence, after his break with Duse, Craig was working on his new project for his immense marionettes, great "Black Figures" that were the "antithesis of the actor, singer & dancer," and he desperately needed funds to pay his craftsmen and assistants. He kept pressing Isadora for the financial help, which she had promised him. In the spring of 1907, having recovered her health, Isadora returned to performing. She managed to send Craig some money, but by the summer she wrote, "My money is at an end."

In answer Craig begged her to try to borrow the money if necessary, telling her that his work was "going ahead with fearful & divine energy & success," but that he desperately needed money to conclude it. Isadora replied that she could not help him, adding that they were both not "very practical" people. "Dearest Dreamer this is a pretty silly world & I'm afraid you needed someone a bit stronger than your poor Topsy to help you."

She then traveled to Venice for a rest, staying at an expensive hotel, as she always did, and begged Craig to come to see her there. He did not come, so she went to Florence to see him. It was there that Craig made it clear to her that the affair was over.

Writing many years later about the termination of the affair, Craig quoted Isadora as having promised that she would keep him "sufficiently supplied in funds to pay your 2 workmen & to get wood & canvas & do the rest."

"This was not an immense undertaking," Craig insisted, "her receipts might be anything between 3000 & 8000 marks per performance & she would send 1000 marks per show to let the work go on.

"I went off to Florence— waited, not a word— not a mark arrived . . . I waited & began work— I got 2 men to commence— one a young artist from Bordighera gave up his house there on the strength of my assurance & damme if Madame Duncan didn't let me down & him down & what's worse sent no word of excuse.

"From that day I have never forgiven this: I don't mind what anyone does or says to me— but if they in any way show disrespect for my work once I am at work (when warm at it) then click goes the apparatus & it's all over between me & whoever has played me the trick."

Yet Craig finally came to see—or at least to say—that money was only the immediate cause of the break. In 1943, reflecting on the end of the affair, he wrote about their last meeting in Florence. "I think that I deliberately made her think ill of me. I think I did this that she & I (she whom I loved and I who I knew she loved) might get out of our muddle— *we were getting in each other's way.* Strange but true— for we were made for each other. She couldn't fit in to me—I couldn't dream of her doing that—her genius could fit into nothing—& although *like a woman* she wouldn't have minded at all if I could have fitted into her place of things, I was not able to do that."

In *My Life* Isadora gives her own version of the immediate cause for the break. "I adored Craig—I loved him with all the ardour of my artist soul, but I realised that our separation was inevitable. Yet I had arrived at that frenzied state when I could no longer live with him or without him. To live with him was to renounce my art, my personality, nay, perhaps, my life, my reason itself. To live without him was to be in a continual state of depression, and tortured by jealousy, for which, alas! it now seemed that I had good cause." (In fact, according to Francis Steegmuller, she did not have any particular "good cause" at this moment. But as Victor Seroff, so much later her lover, writes, "Jealousy was, astonishingly, one of the most pronounced traits of Isadora's character. She could be jealous of everything and everybody, and that trait sometimes led her to the most exaggerated behavior.")

She was assailed by visions of Craig in another woman's arms "in all his beauty . . . looking at them with that winning smile of his—the smile of Ellen Terry . . ." She says that she desperately wished for a remedy, and the remedy came in the person of a young man called Pim, who suddenly appeared and whom she took to Russia with her on tour. "The presence of Pim gave me new life, new vitality," she writes. "I . . . lived in the moment and was careless and happy. As a consequence my performances bubbled over with renewed vitality and joy."

(According to Victor Seroff, "Pim" was "pretty, blond, blue-eyed, homosexual, the possessor of eighteen trunks containing suits, shoes, neckties, linen, and extra fur-trimmed waistcoats, all of which he took with him . . . to Russia. Once in that country, Pim disappeared and left no trace in her life.")

In the course of writing about her affair with Craig, Isadora gave a further explanation—if *explanation* is the right word—about its difficulties. Although, she says, she never spent a dull moment with him, "he was always either in the throes of highest delight, or the other extreme, in those moods which suddenly followed after, when the whole sky seemed to turn black, and a sudden apprehension filled all the air. One's breath was slowly pumped from the body, and nothing was left anywhere but the blackness of anguish."

45

There is one association with Craig that recurs in Isadora's story. "An ordinary walk through the streets with him was like a promenade in Thebes of Ancient Egypt with a superior High Priest," she writes. "Whether due to his extraordinary near-sightedness or not, he would suddenly stop, take out his pencil and paper-block and, looking at a fearful specimen of modern German architecture, a *neuer kunst praktisch* apartment house, explain how beautiful it was. He would then commence a feverish sketch of it which, when completed, resembled the Temple of Denderah of Egypt."

The association occurs again when she describes Craig's design for the set of *Rosmersholm* as "a great Egyptian Temple with enormously high ceiling, extending upward to the skies, with walls receding into the distance. Only, unlike an Egyptian Temple, at the far end there was a great, square window."

But it was not only later, writing in the midtwenties, that she made and felt this connection. In July 1906, when she was in Noordwijk, awaiting the birth of her child, Craig was in Berlin, "reading daily about Egypt." He apparently sent or recommended several books on Egypt to Isadora, including *L'histoire de l'art dans l'antiquité* by Charles Chipiez and G. Perrot. In a letter to him from Noordwijk, she says, "I study each day from the Chipiez books & am becoming awfully learned." In a later letter she writes, "I am becoming so learned about ancient Egyptians that *you'll* be *awe*struck."

After the birth of Deirdre and after Craig had left Noordwijk, she writes to him that she is reading "the new Egyp. book today—Prayers to Ra—very Beautiful . . ." And on October 11 she again mentions studying about Egypt: "Two nice Egyptian books by Budge made today pass quickly—"

There is an ancient Egyptian legend in which Isis longs to possess the power of Ra over gods and men. Knowing that the only way to obtain that power is through the knowledge of his secret name, Isis took some earth and mixed it with Ra's saliva and formed it into the shape of the great hooded snake, the emblem of all goddesses. She hid the serpent in Ra's path and when Ra passed, the serpent bit him. Burning and trembling with the poison, Ra called for help. Isis, responding, said she would cure him if he told her his secret name.

"Thy Name, thy true Name, thy secret Name . . . Tell me thy Name that the poison may be driven out, for only he whose name I know can be healed by the might of my magic."

Then the Majesty of Ra cried out and said, "Let Isis come with me, and let my Name pass from my breast to her breast."

And he hid himself from the gods that followed in his train. Empty was the Boat of the Sun, empty was the great throne of the God, for Ra had hidden himself from his Followers and from the creation of his hands.

When the Name came forth from the heart of Ra to pass to the heart of Isis, the goddess spoke to Ra and said, "Bind thyself with an oath, O Ra, that thou wilt give thy two eyes unto Horus [her son] . . ."

Thus was the Name of Ra taken from him and given to Isis, and she, the great Enchantress, cried

aloud the Word of Power, and the poison obeyed, and
Ra was healed by the might of his Name.

And Isis, the great one, Mistress of the Gods,
Mistress of magic, she is the skillful Healer, in her
mouth is the Breath of Life, by her words she destroys
pain, and by her power she awakes the dead.

In January or February of 1908, after their affair had been
ended for some months, Isadora sent Craig an invitation from
St. Petersburg: "I have a wild not yet defined plan to go to
Egypt! . . . Would you join me for a look at the Pyramids?"
Craig made his own note upon this letter: "I.D. is expecting me
to drop my work & follow her to Egypt!!!!great Gods what is her
head made of?"

(Craig himself never did get to Egypt.)

In October 1909, in his publication *The Mask*, Craig (under
the pseudonym Adolf Furst) wrote "A Note on Marionettes"—
on those "Black Figures" he was creating:

"Very far back across the centuries may we trace the procession of this silent race to their remote origin in the figure of
the gods in Egypt . . .

"Two of the most salient characteristics which chiefly im-
press us in them are their simplicity and their calm . . . Each
little figure, strangely human in its repose, hangs upon its nail
in the dim light, gazing before it with eyes as inscrutable as
those which yet meet ours from under the quiet brows of the
gods of Egypt and Etruria. It is their silence, their passionless
gaze, their profound indifference which give so supreme a dignity to the frail little bodies tricked out in gauze and tinsel. As
in the fallen descendant of a great family some one trait may
yet remain to recall a noble origin, so does that impassive gaze,
that air of seeing *beyond* all the transitory and the accidental,
still proclaim for the marionette his kinship with the grave
stone images of the ancient eastern world."

PART
FOUR

46

On May 9, 1918, in a shaky hand-
writing that is like a staggering and then an onrush, a staggering and then another onrush, Mary Cassatt writes to Louisine
Havemeyer from the Villa Angeletto in Grasse: "Oh the world
Louie! . . . Is it possible that France can recover the losses?
. . . it is the end of a civilization."

June 25, 1918: "Americans have the defense of Paris in our
hands, the French say we are as good soldiers as they are,
better than their nearest allies. I wonder if there could be any
doubt about that . . . Heaven help those who are prisoners.
What a breakdown of civilization, when women's votes begin to
tell will it be better?"

July 19, 1918: "Everything is difficult now . . . If this goes
on who will be left to enjoy the millennium: Are we never to get
to the end . . ."

August 16, 1918: "I have given up the idea of going to
Beaufresne, Gothas are flying over the country there and also
over Paris where is it to end. The 'Times' says 3 more years!
. . . our soldiers say that they are here to kill the Germans, but

oh! what a change from our ideals! The world will never be the same again . . ."

August 24, 1918: "My sight is getting dimmer every day . . . I look forward with horror to utter darkness and then an operation which may end in as great a failure as the last one. Renoir says the finest death is a soldier's, why don't they send all of us who are old and useless to the front Death is a release, you would miss me [but?] you have so many . . ."

September 22, 1918: "Everything will be changed after this war, no place for my generation."

47

From the Savoy Hotel in London in early 1918 Isadora wrote to Mary Desti:

Had bad luck to fall down dark stairway on ship [from America] first night out & sprained hip. Was laid up for trip & am still. Mr. S. [Gordon Selfridge, the owner of Selfridge's department store in London] was charming en route but have not seen him since!!! I'm afraid it needed you—& London needs you I find it a bit dark & triste—I have only seen Comm. [Commandant?] B. He is delightful but seems very vague about any possible performance! I have not been able to find Angelo [?] . . . I wish you were returning I feel rather lost—I have taken some rooms 8 Duke Street Piccadilly as here is trop cher—Cable me if you are returning. I am afraid there is no hope of further news from S. [Selfridge] I will stay here a week & if nothing comes more hopeful I will return to Paris.

Please see [Singer] & tell him to cable me some

thing—Keep me posted as I'm afraid Augustin won't write. Will you tell him it is *very* necessary to find my curtains carpets—left in charge of Oppenheimer in S.F. and music. If I suddenly made an engagement to dance I could do nothing without them—& will you try . . . to save my collection of Spanish shawls which he is holding for money [owed] . . . Please let me know what is going on what has been decided about the girls [the six Duncan Dancers] . . . Give my dearest love to all . . . I am still dizzy from Boat & cannot move from fall—I will write clearer later.

 With all my dearest Love to you . . .

Shortly afterward, from the Duke Street address, Isadora wrote to Mary again:

 How can I ever be grateful enough to you— New York seems like some awful nightmare. *Do return soon.* It is lonely here. Commandant [?] B. is charming he takes me each day to lunch or dinner—Angelo is also very kind. I have been laid up with a sprained hip—from fall on boat—

 My dancing here depends on my being able to get my costumes carpet music programmes & press books . . . I have cabled Augustin to send them—I also cabled *you* to Biltmore. If you can Persuade Paris to cable 1000 it would be salvation—as A. [Angelo] & B. are delightful but *poor* . . . The best news I could hear is that you are returning—Mr. S. has disappeared I think rather frightened—The more I know him the more I realized that what you did was a *Miracle!* [Mary had persuaded Selfridge to pay for Isadora's passage to London] . . .

On April 16, from the Hôtel Palais d'Orsay in Paris, Isadora wrote another entreating letter to Mary:

 Have sent you 6 letters & 4 cables—Have you rec[eived] anything I have no reply from you or Augustin. Ruth Mitchell [a young American who was always ready to help Isadora] cabled. Mr. Mason is sailing Apr 30 with my theatre materials music etc—I could do *nothing* without them—With them I can accept an engagement for Spain—

Will you also send gramophone plaques—and the remaining trunks with shawls—summer dresses—*Photos* papers—etc. S.A. [South American] *press* book etc— Will you be so sweet as to get my belt made to order by Riker 1263 Bdway and send it—I can get nothing like it here—

S. proved to be an illusion! Angelo— Boris [Commandant B.?] & others quite helpless—I could do nothing in London—Perhaps you might have—

On April 26, again from the Palais d'Orsay, she wrote:

Still not a word from any one—only a letter from Jim [?]— I cabled you about 8 times—fr[om] London & here! I am waiting anxiously for my curtains & carpet—Can do *nothing* without them—

Please write me news—I have heard nothing— What is Augustin doing—& the girls—?—

Are you returning?

I am living here on Hope—if you can persuade Paris to send me something do so . . .

Love to Preston & to all—for Heavens sake Write.

A change has taken place in Isadora's letters. From now on, with a few exceptions, they are begging letters. They speak of her money troubles, of her despair, of her sense of isolation, of her sense that no one is helping her, of her feeling that she has been bypassed, abandoned. She who was courted and revered by others, her very presence a benediction, now finds herself seeking rescue from others. She asks and asks again by letter, by cable, to Mary Desti, Singer, Ruth Mitchell, Jim—the list goes on; the more there is no answer, the more tenaciously she asks. All asking seems the same asking, a torrent of asking, innocent and childlike in its assumptions. There is no sense of shame or humility in the asking, no sense either that these requests are a burden to the other. She is, as she says, living on Hope, on the hope that all will be granted, that she will once again be what she has been.

But her sense of herself, of her place in the world, has diminished. It is as if that power which was once resident in her is leaking out—has leaked out—when she wasn't looking. Yet she refuses to give up hope, grasping at others for help. As always, she cannot bear being alone.

"I spent some terrible and gloomy weeks in that melancholy lodging [on Duke Street], completely stranded," she writes in *My Life*. "Alone and ill, without a cent, my School destroyed and the war appearing to go on interminably, I used to sit at the dark window at night and watch the air raids, and wish that a bomb might fall on me to end my troubles . . . In despair I cabled to L. but got no reply . . ."

From her letters and from the evidence of others she was not alone, but in her memory, in her sense of how things were, she was alone. But then "by chance," she continues, she meets "a charming member of the French Embassy, who came to my rescue and took me to Paris. There I engaged a room in the Palais D'Orsay, and resorted to money-lenders for the necessary funds."

Yes, she can still find a man who will help her, someone who sees with the eyes of the past, who sees what she was, who beholds her, as it were, in her past glory. One can hear her with this "charming" man, charming him in her melodious, soft voice, speaking of her temporary reverses, asking for help.

48

In 1919, operated on once again for cataracts, Mary struggles against too much hope, as if it were deception. "The operation was a very daring one as the cataract was not ripe . . . He [the doctor] hopes and promises great things more than I believe possible . . . I must be grateful if I can see to recognize people and read some . . ."

But by New Year's Day 1920 she cannot find gratefulness for her state—or the world's. "Those who have gone have escaped much and who knows what is reserved to us in this fall of civilization. No slow decline and fall, all goes quickly in this period [?] of invention and Science . . . the cinema preferred to the theaters photography to Art."

On March 31, 1920: "Oh Louie dear my eye has another cataract growing after all his assurance. Oh dear *do* wish for my end. I am so tired . . ."

On April 13, 1920: "If only I could get back Mathilde [who was still interned], and at least partial sight in the eye on which such promises were given."

On April 30, 1920: "I am so tired and so hopeless . . ."

The theme of death and hopelessness is like a recurrent dark melody. But in and out of it entwine other themes, juxtaposed, creating a surface dense and contradictory, in which feeling is never articulated without an adjacent contradiction. (It is all of a piece with Mary—the way she writes, the way she thinks, the way, finally, that she paints. There is the interweaving, the going from depth to surface without transition, the not resting, not staying in the depth, the refusal of depth, the evasion of depth, finding in surface that resolution which is not ultimately resolution, but only a stopping place.)

There is rancor, there is outrage, and there is sudden tenderness, barely articulated before it is retracted into self-pity:

"It is too nice what you say about me dearest Louie, how I wish I could say to you all I feel about you, you are the only one who cares."

But self-pity for Mary is not a state into which she falls and stays. If anything, it is often a prelude to new outrage.

There is outrage at ingratitude: she who has created, has cultivated, has held to an image of herself as a grande dame helping others, dispensing aid, in the village of Beaufresne and elsewhere, to others less fortunate, asking no exchange but gratitude, now finds that "even the nurse who has been able to open a bank account since I took her affairs in hand she said, 'Oh you like to do that sort of thing it amuses you.' Yes, I like to help people but they might acknowledge it." Yet, in sudden softening, she adds, "You, you dearest Louie, write too much of what I have been able to do for you."

There is outrage at her own sense of helplessness. Of a Swiss maid she writes to Louisine, "She reads me my letters in English without understanding a word now I must appeal to English nursery maids, oh what it is to be helpless if only one could leave the world when one's work is over . . ."

Forced to be so dependent, to ask others for help, she rages at the thought that others might think she has been dependent before. People think it was her brother Aleck who supported her, but they never acknowledge, she tells Louisine, that it was she who got him to buy great Impressionist pictures when they cost next to nothing. "People think I lived on his money, but with these pictures his heirs will make as much as all my capital. He left 12 or 14 Manets . . . early manner, and certainly his best."

"Do you wonder that I feel a certain bitterness," she repeats a few days later, "people think I was a pensioner on my brothers bounty but for the Degas and the three Monets he paid 8125 francs! and I dont think he paid on an average 1000 francs a piece for the 12 or 14 Manets he owned."

Outrage at helplessness, outrage at having to ask others for help, when she has done what she has done—what no other American—man or woman—of her time has done—and done it by herself . . . Even her family—what is left of it—her brothers' children—even they don't acknowledge her—or at least so she feels, writing to Louisine about an upcoming visit by some young relatives. "My dear Louie no one who is coming here wishes me to be known they secretly resent my reputation for which I care so little—Enough of me . . ." But then a few lines later, "Pity me dear and dont worry about me I shall pull through no doubt and if I collapse after they go why I shall at least be alone . . ."

At least she will be alone . . . It is a state she knows well, one that chance and fierce pride and independence have brought her to, one that has come to her, without her asking.

She has been bypassed in life, but even more in art, by that movement in whose early stages she was an eager participant. She worked in opposition to the accepted, but now her work has become the accepted that the young oppose. What has all her work meant then, in the face of this devaluation? Sometimes she knows, then she is not sure. She keeps looking to external judgments as proof of what that work was and is, who she was and is.

She writes to Louisine of praise and acceptance:

"I wanted to tell you of the Petit Palais they have made another room with all the pictures of our set [the Impressionists]. One of my pictures is in that room, probably also my sisters portrait . . ."

She writes of opposition: "When I think of my life and how I was sneered at and my friends too, opposition is the only thing."

She writes of the monetary value of her work, of paintings and prints sold and resold. It is something she is familiar with, the buying and selling of paintings. For so many years she has advised Louisine, and her judgment with respect to others' work has usually been unerring, but that judgment applied to her own work is another matter:

> I sold to the DR's [Durand-Ruels] all I had left of my own dry points and a lot of pastel drawings, and amongst them one unique etching of Degas . . . in all there were 95 or 100 things. I asked them 10,000 francs for the lot . . . They refused in the most decided manner alleging that there was no sale for my dry points and etchings at any good price, the most they could get was $4 or $5 . . . as I wanted a reserve with them I let them have the lot for 5000 fcs. Just after that was concluded I had a letter from a Club asking if for $100 I would let them have something "a pencil sketch." Then came the picture of the man in the boat [*The Boating Party*] which I offered to give to Brown [Ellen Mary Cassatt], she forgot to even thank me, seeing she did not care I sold it for the *very* moderate price of 10,000 fcs. Now the DR's will find a purchaser. I disposed of my sketches because I knew at least they would be preserved. Now I have another picture in their hands, probably you know it the woman in shadow holding a child in her arms, if I sell it to them I want dollars, do you know at what price my pictures will sell. It seems to me I ought to have $3000. They never got over my selling that round picture to Harris Whittemore for [?] $5000, and oh! how they behaved about the pastel you bought . . .

But after all the talk of money, of external valuation, something else slips in, another more interior judgment. She ends the letter with the statement "I have not done what I wanted to but I tried to make a good fight of it."

One day in November 1920 Mary discovered among her possessions a portrait of her brother Aleck that she had painted many years before. Immediately she wrote to Louisine that it was "by far the best that has been done of him, the coat a little cracked which makes it necessary to reline it . . . If only I could show it to you and have your opinion. I have been very foolish in despising my work too much, but all artists are like that. It has seemed like old times to be busy over pictures . . ."

The next week she wrote to Louisine again: "What an irony life is . . . my eyes in no better state. I am taking piqures given by the doctor to reduce the arterial pressure which is not high only too high for my sight. We die by inches." And then without transition, without break, "Yes my dear I know that I have nothing to complain of do you remember Mrs. Browning's poem, The Lost Bower? . . .

I have lost oh! many a pleasure
Many a hope and many a power
Studious health and merry leisure
But the first of all my losses
Was the losing of the Bower.

I have lost the dream of doing
And the other dream of done—

In Egypt in 1911, she had written, "I did not feel I was equal to a man's portrait but now I must, to work off if possible this overpowering impression . . ." Yet it seems it had already been done. As she wrote to Louisine, "Well my dear the dream of done came back again when I rediscovered my brother Aleck's portrait."

"The Lost Bower," one of Elizabeth Barrett Browning's *Poems of 1844* (coincidentally the year of Mary's birth), is a poem of loss and redemption. In seventy-four stanzas, the woman narrator recalls an experience from childhood, of climbing to the top of a hill and looking behind her to where

> *shining hills on hills arise,*
> *Close as brother leans to brother*
> *When they press beneath the eyes*
> *Of some father praying blessings from the*
>   *gifts of paradise.*

Ahead of her, on the ridge, she sees a wood that looks impenetrable. Tearing apart the brambles, the child is astonished to find, hidden in the midst of the wildness, a bower of such perfection that it seems "Finely fixed and fitted" with "seeming" art, a marvel that cannot be the work of Nature alone. Seated in the bower, she hears a sound, "a sense of music which was rather felt than heard."

> *In the song, I think, and by it,*
> *Mystic Presences of power,*
> *Had upsnatched me to the Timeless, then*
>   *returned me to the Hour.*

The next day the child tries to go back to the bower, but she cannot find it and, in fact, she is never able to find it again. Years have passed, says the narrator, and she still laments its loss. Then, in the poem, come the two stanzas that Mary copied for Louisine: "I have lost—oh many a pleasure . . ." And immediately afterward, the long-lost image of the bower appears to the narrator, lying upon her couch, and it is just as if she were within the bower once again.

> *Is the bower lost, then? who sayeth*
> *That the bower indeed is lost?*
> *Hark! my spirit in it prayeth*
> *Through the sunshine and the frost,—*
> *And the prayer preserves it greenly, to the*
>   *last and uttermost.*

> *Till another open for me,*
> *In God's Eden-land unknown,*
> *With an angel at the doorway,*
> *White with gazing at his Throne;*
> *And a saint's voice in the palm-trees, singing—*
>   *"All is lost . . . and won!"*

But Mary, telling Louisine of the poem, does not cite these last stanzas. It is not through spirituality or the vision of some "Ideal" that Mary seeks resolution, but in the "real" world.

In 1913, writing to Louisine of a woman she had met "who only cared for spiritual things, the spiritual side," Mary said, "I cannot follow her nor can I follow Florence Nightingale altogether, I am now reading F. N.'s life & she certainly had the 'saintly' side . . . I wish I could feel as they do people like F. N., towards God, but I cannot understand a *personal* God, Master of the Universe, I think we are surrounded by spiritual forces but I agree with Fabre in thinking the human brain unfit to grasp the universe."

So now, immediately following her words to Louisine about the "dream of doing" and the "dream of done," Mary turns to the real world. She speaks of what will happen to the portrait of her brother Aleck. "It goes to New York in a few days. I do hope you will see it and let me know if I am mistaken in thinking it one of my best things."

50

"Please don't let anyone per-
suade you to try to dance to Debussy. It is only the music of
the *Senses* and has no message to the Spirit," Isadora wrote to
her six "girls," her older pupils, who had remained in the United
States. "And then the gesture of Debussy is all *inward* and has
no outward or upward. I want you to dance only that music
which goes from the soul in mounting circles."

Telling them to work on the Beethoven Seventh and the
Schubert Seventh as well as seven minuets of Beethoven and
the Mozart Symphony in G which she had choreographed for
them, Isadora continued,

> Plunge your soul in divine unconscious *Giving* deep
> within it, until it gives to your soul its *Secret.* That is
> how I have always tried to express music. My soul
> should become one with it, and the dance born from
> that embrace. Music has been in all my life the great
> Inspiration and will be perhaps someday the Consola-
> tion, for I have gone through such terrible years. No

one has understood since I lost Deirdre and Patrick
how pain has caused me at times to live in almost a
delirium . . . Sometimes quite recently I feel as if I
were awakening from a long fever. When you think of
these years, think of the Funeral March of Schubert,
the *Ave Maria,* the *Redemption,* and forget the times
when my poor distracted soul trying to escape from
suffering may well have given you all the appearance
of madness.

I have reached such high peaks flooded with light,
but my soul has no strength to live there—and no one
has realized the horrible torture from which I have
tried to escape. Some day if you understand sorrow
you will understand too all I have lived through, and
then you will only think of the light towards which I
have pointed and you will know the *real* Isadora is
there. In the meantime work and create Beauty and
Harmony. The poor world has need of it, and with your
six spirits going with one will, you can create Beauty
and Inspiration for a new Life . . .

She continues to hold up for them a vision of herself and
her work that they, as her "daughters," will carry on for her.
(The six young women—Anna, Margot, Irma, Maria-Theresa,
Erika, and Lisel—had changed their last names to Duncan in a
New York court in 1917, although they were not officially
adopted by Isadora.) But the intensity of Isadora's feelings, her
call for pity, her hatred of anything that is not of the Spirit, her
presentation of herself as the "Mother," belie what she herself
must have come to see by now: that she was no longer sought
after by impresarios; she was no longer in demand as a performer. She too had been bypassed, was being bypassed in the
onrush of the modern.

"Much as we loved Isadora and venerated her as an artist
and teacher . . . we nevertheless ardently wished to be independent," writes Irma Duncan of herself and the five other Duncan
pupils. "Not merely financially but also artistically independent
. . . This overwhelming motivating force in our new relationship
with Isadora, unfortunately, placed us in opposition to our mentor. It unavoidably became a constant cause of friction and

contention between us which, with the passing of time, threatened to come inevitably to a head-on collision of wills. For she continued to treat us like children, subject to her every whim."

Isadora insisted that the girls perform only with her, when and as she arranged it. In 1917, when she was in California, she had angrily canceled a contract for the girls to perform. After she returned to Europe in early 1918, Augustin, recognizing that they had no money at all to live on, had arranged a series of performances for them at various military camps throughout the United States. Subsequently, they had gone on to make a successful national tour, still without Isadora's permission.

They were, of course, dancing pieces that Isadora had choreographed. For Isadora had never allowed her pupils any measure of independence in terms of their own movement. Just as she had insisted on absolute compliance when she had instructed Flora Arnstein so many years before, she still only allowed the students to perform what she told them to dance, her dances. In her words she named it freedom of the dance, but in fact it was a paradoxical freedom she gave them.

She was and saw herself as the Mother who gives, the Mother who has suffered, the Mother who grants love, and the Mother who is the source of all creativity. But at the same time she was another, more personal mother, a mother rooted in the experience of giving and withholding, of winning and losing in ordinary life, a mother jealous and possessive.

In 1895, the year after Mary completed *The Boating Party,* her mother died. No longer the child in the family (even though she had long been the care-taker), she was now, in her own right, sole mistress of the château. From her mother she had learned to manage the household well, to deal scrupulously with the servants, and to demand obedience in return. Living on money she had inherited from her father plus money sent to her by Aleck plus money she earned from her own work, she was, if not immensely wealthy, now able to do exactly what she wanted, without the continual pressure of family obligation.

At Beaufresne her role in relationship to the people of the nearby village of Mesnil became that of a stern benefactress. She paid the salary of the teacher at the village school and also paid for the furniture at the school. In addition she helped a number of young women who worked at the local button fac-tory, where the pay was low and the working conditions poor. Some of them she hired to work for her at her château. Others she sent to Paris to work at the homes of friends. Among the country people who lived nearby she became known as "l'Impératrice" (the Empress).

As a " 'grande dame' of the art world" she was as disciplined as ever, continuing to work almost daily. But in work as in life something had altered. The willingness to risk, the ambiguity of *The Woman with the Red Zinnia* and *The Boating Party*, had given way to repetition, to an immersion in the safety of well-known forms and themes. She was to create a series of paintings and pastels, almost exclusively of mothers and children, often in brilliant colors, in well-designed forms, but severely limited in emotional range. Excellent though they were in execution, in their effect they moved toward decoration. They began to slip toward sentimentality.

In the winter of 1898–99 Mary crossed the Atlantic to the United States for the first time in over twenty-five years. Her brother Aleck had just come out of retirement to take on the position of president of the Pennsylvania Railroad. Upon her arrival in Philadelphia, the *Ledger* carried a social item: "Mary Cassatt, sister of Mr. Cassatt, President of the Philadelphia Railroad, returned from Europe yesterday. She has been studying painting in France and owns the smallest Pekingese dog in the world [actually it was a Belgian griffon]."

But, as Suzanne Lindsay points out, Mary was not without recognition in terms of her own accomplishments in her native city. Another newspaper wrote of her as "an artist of the first rank, and while we of Philadelphia may take just pride in claiming her as a member of our community, she is one of the brilliant galaxy of cosmopolitan painters whose fame is world wide and who are citizens of the world of art."

Returning to France in the spring of 1899 (a month or two before Isadora's voyage to England on the cattle boat), she embarked on another activity in the outer world, one that combined finance with art. With customary vigor she began to advise Louisine and her husband Henry Havemeyer ("The Sugar King of the U.S.") on purchases for their art collection. She traveled with the Havemeyers in Italy and Spain, working relentlessly at tracking down major works of art that she thought would be suitable for their collection.

Through her efforts the Havemeyers obtained a remarkable number of great masterpieces, including works of Goya and El Greco, as well as the works of Courbet and the Impressionists. To this activity Mary brought two remarkable talents: an almost unerring eye in evaluating works of art (unerring with the exception of anything that postdated the Impressionists) and a shrewdness in financial matters.

This new work became remarkably exhilarating to her. In a letter to Henry Havemeyer in 1901, she wrote, "I am glad the Veronese is to hang in *your* gallery it is on the ocean now, perhaps Louie & I will get you the Prado if you only give us time, & even if I have to take more journeys with disappointments at the end. I really enjoyed the journey & felt so proud of myself for being able to do it. I owe it all to Louie, apart from the pleasure of my journey last winter, the benefit I derived from it I can never be sufficiently grateful for; I am ready to be off again if any other prize is in view . . ."

In a letter to Louisine in 1903 she wrote, "Here is a letter from poor 'Pepita' which I think will interest you. If only we can circumvent Casa Valencia you may yet possess the [painting of the] Cardinal at a reasonable price. I answered her letter at once strongly impressing her with the necessity of secrecy as regarded the name of the would be buyer, for if the Condé suspected Mr. Havemeyer of wishing to buy the picture he would create all the difficulties possible. It would be rather a triumph to possess a really fine Greco, for with all their crowing none of them, not Manzi more than the others has a really good specimen of that artist. I imagine this is the finest thing outside the Public Galleries in Spain . . . my head is set on your having that picture . . ."

In gaining the "prize" for the Havemeyers, she was winning out over all the other American collectors like Harriman, Morgan, and Carnegie, who were then actively seeking to purchase art works in Europe through their agents. As representative of the interests of the Havemeyers, always intent on getting them a good price, she also triumphed over the owners of the pictures, as well as over any artists whose work she acquired. Even in the case of her "set," the Impressionists, she was on the side of the buyers and not on the side of the artists.

From another viewpoint, of course, there was a rational justification for this toughness in the pursuit of these great works. According to Adelyn Breeskin, Mary sensed "the great need for great art works to strengthen our [American] civilization . . . to persuade . . . wealthy friends to buy art works which would in the long run benefit the entire American public. This, then, became her great ambition. It diverted her from her own art, but how can we judge if the sacrifice was not worth the great end in view? She thus became a worker in a cause . . ." (In fact, she was the one who was primarily responsible for the great Havemeyer collection that now hangs in the Metropolitan.)

But rational justification or not, in terms of Mary's own life, this activity represents a very curious turning. For Mary to put so much of her energies into acquisition suggests that a strange split had taken place in her—as if, in putting herself on the side of the Havemeyers as purchaser, not on the side of the artist (which she now consistently did, even with Degas), she was allowing the practical, outward-seeking part of her personality to conquer the artist in herself.

With the death of her mother, Mary began to demonstrate forcefully the very quality that Katharine Cassatt so admired in her sons, particularly in Aleck—the capacity to make his way to the top in the business world, to win out over his rivals. For through this activity she was winning (as a surrogate) in the outer world in a way that one does not win as an artist. (Or at least as one did not win then—though now, of course, with the new relationship between art and money, all of that has changed.) In a sense she had become the son who was preferred by her mother; she had turned away from those very symbols that had held mysterious power for her.

In December 1904 Mary refused a prize of five hundred dollars from the Art Institute of Chicago for her painting *Caress*, a study of a mother and two children that had been loaned for exhibition. In a letter to the director of the institute she wrote, "The pictures belong to Messrs. Durand-Ruel, and were loaned by them under the proviso that they were not to be in competition for any awards. I was one of the original 'Independents' who founded a society where there was to be no jury, no medals, no awards. This was in protest against the government salon, and amongst the artists were Monet, Degas, Pissarro, Mme. Morisot, Sisley, and I. This was in 1879, and since then we none of us have sent to any official exhibition and have stuck to the original tenets . . ." Mary suggested that the money be awarded to a young student.

The new recipient, a young American artist, Alan Philbrick, came to see Mary in Paris and later said of that visit, "I was scared to death of her . . . A fiery and peppery lady, a very vivid, determined personality, positive in her opinions."

At the end of 1904 Mary was made a Chevalier of the Legion of Honor, an award that she did accept. As was the custom among the recipients, she wore for a year the red ribbon conferred upon her.

Reporting an interview with Jean de Sailly, whose parents had known Mary well at Beaufresne during the years after her mother died, Nancy Hale quotes de Sailly as saying that Mary did a good deal of calling about the countryside

> "dressed elegantly, from Redfern. She did not come in. People came out to her car. Her French? It was—queer but okay. Her intelligence?" The elderly gentleman placed the tips of his fingers together. "It was irrational. Emotional. I should say that Miss Cassatt's political judgments were always emotional. Yes. She bobbed about in her judgments, politically. Emotionally she was what we French call da-da—bobbing about. Her food was, however, very good . . .
> "Her teas were excellent . . . it was for tea that I was generally invited— being, you understand, a child at the time . . .
> "My sister and I used to pose for her, and we definitely considered the experience agreeable, since we were well supplied with books and toys. We were, however, driven to distraction by those little . . . griffons, nipping at our heels . . . Miss Cassatt . . . took excellent *care* of children. For example, her models among the village children had to be disinfected—their hair deloused—before she would permit them to have tea with her nieces or ourselves."

From Mary to Louisine, March 10, 1908 (in reference to a woman of whose morals Mary disapproves): "You and I, you see, are as you said once, old-fashioned . . . By the way do propose a limited vote for women in America, only native born white women one native born parent, I assure you the men I have spoken to about this are rather struck, the only objection they find, is that it will never pass."

From Mary to Emily Phillips Cassatt, who is separated from her husband, Eddie, Mary's nephew—August 25, 1902: "You may not have complained. I am afraid there has been the mistake, you ought to have complained and loudly— Come over & see me & then I can say more than I can write; I cannot see this affair as final— After all you are not divorced, Ed is weak as most men . . ."

According to the art dealer René Gimpel, at Pissarro's funeral in 1903, Mary said to Degas, "You're nasty to your brother, you're beastly to your sister; you're bad, you're bad." In response, says Gimpel, Degas "uttered a raucous snarl."

In 1897 or 1898 Mary did a color print with drypoint and aquatint, *By the Pond.* It shows a mother holding a child in a landscape of pond, trees, and meadow. The mother, her face in profile, gazes adoringly at the boy, who is blond-haired with ringlets. There is a curious quality in the rendering of the child's face and intense yellow hair. It is a face that is reminiscent of a cartoon, with eyes drawn like curls around a dark center. The quality of the face, gazed at so worshipfully by the mother, is unsettling against the lush and abstract background in deep greens and blues. Threat has been simultaneously waylaid and deflected in this image of a little boy, whose curls are like round unseeing eyes.

52

In April 1920 Isadora sent a cable to her "daughters," the "Isadorables," as they had come to be called, inviting them to work with her in Europe from June to October. Irma, who was afraid that Isadora would not let them return for their winter tour of the United States, insisted on a written contract, which Isadora signed but which, says Irma, "I instantly realized . . . was just a piece of paper."

The girls joined Isadora in Paris, where she was now living on the rue de la Pompe with a new lover, the pianist Walter Rummel. After Isadora sold Bellevue to the French government, she and Rummel and the six pupils set out for Greece, where she had been invited by the Greek official Eleuthérios Venizélos. They stopped off first in Venice. There, Irma noted in her diary, Isadora "appeared to be in a state of shock. Very taciturn and morose. It seems she and the Archangel [Rummel] had a serious quarrel."

Irma's diary entry a few days later adds: "Anna [one of the

Isadorables] and the Archangel have fallen in love. Isadora is awfully jealous."

In *My Life* Isadora says that when Rummel appeared, it was like the realization of a song of Wagner's, "The Angel," which "tells of a spirit sitting in utter sadness and desolation, to whom comes an Angel of Light . . .

"When he entered I thought he was the picture of the youthful Liszt . . . so tall, slight, with a burnished lock over the high forehead, and eyes like clear wells of shining light. He played for me. I called him my Archangel."

She began to work with Rummel and composed new dances "to the inspiration of his playing, dances all comprised of prayer and sweetness and light, and once more my spirit came to life . . . This was the beginning of the most hallowed and ethereal love of my life." In his performances he was "all gentleness and sweetness, and yet passion burned him. He performed with unconsenting frenzy. His nerves consumed him, his soul rebelled. He did not give way to passion . . . but, on the contrary, his loathing was as evident as the irresistible feeling which possessed him." But then Isadora, in her telling, adds this strange sentence: "Loathing of love can easily turn to hatred of the aggressor."

Seroff, attempting to explain the words "loathing of love," reports that Isadora told him that Rummel " 'preferred to make love to himself behind the closed doors of his room,' rather than to her, lying frustrated in her bedroom . . ." Seroff adds that since Isadora was "desolate, penniless, almost abandoned by her friends" at the time, "in her worn-out state and with her shattered nervous system she . . . adjusted herself to a relationship that was incomprehensible to her, and offensive as a woman."

Whatever Rummel did or did not do behind his bedroom door, he apparently withheld himself from her physically, while she settled for an Ideal Love, for what she describes as "holy hours, our united souls borne up by the mysterious force which possessed us. Often as I danced and he played, as I lifted my arms and my soul went up from my body in the long flight of the silver strains of the Grail, it seemed as if we had created a spiritual entity quite apart from ourselves, and, as sound and gesture flowed up to the Infinite, another answer echoed from above . . .

"If my Archangel and I had pursued these studies further, I have no doubt that we might have arrived at the spontaneous creation of movements of such spiritual force as to bring a new revelation to mankind."

But the studies were not pursued further. The young women arrived in Paris and it soon became clear, even to Isadora's eyes, that this was not an "Ideal Love" between the thirty-two-year-old Rummel and Anna. Now the "mother" in Isadora became even more estranged from the Ideal "Mother." Jealousy erupted in her, the mother recalling all the "Mother" had given to the daughter, by her own teachings having helped to "create" the loveliness of the daughter, who was now "winning out" over her.

Isadora writes that "a spasm of rage seized me with such violence that it frightened me . . . I loved, and, at the same time, hated them both . . ." By the time they arrived in Greece, where Isadora hoped to reestablish her school, the romance between Anna and the Archangel had become ever more obvious. And to make it even worse from Isadora's viewpoint, there were all the memories associated with this country to which she had come as a triumphant beautiful young dancer in 1904.

Whether she was with them or away from them, the image of Rummel and Anna together took possession of her, "gnawing at my vitals and eating like acid into my brain." Though she kept trying to teach her pupils "Beauty, Calm, Philosophy and Harmony," she was "inwardly writhing in the clutch of the most deadly torment." Her solution, she says, was to assume an air of exaggerated gaiety and to drown her sufferings in wine. "There might certainly have been a nobler way, but I was not then capable of finding it."

According to Irma, Isadora did finally manage to begin working with her pupils by the end of September, teaching them dances to music by Beethoven and Tchaikovsky. But by now it was almost time for the young women to return to the United States to fulfill their contract for their winter tour. At this point Isadora refused to allow them to return to New York. Irma had a fierce argument with Isadora, and Isadora ordered her to go back to America alone.

In great distress at this argument with her "mother" and

"mentor," Irma wrote a letter to Isadora in which she tried to make clear her allegiance to Isadora's ideals and yet defend the necessity for doing her own work. "Your art . . . is the highest expression of all that is pure and divine in man." But then, she added, it did not seem right for Isadora to insist on total sacrifice from them "for the school," when she, Isadora, for all her words about the Ideal, had never sacrificed herself for the school. (Irma did not mention directly—although it obviously rankled in her—that Isadora had in fact, on and off, for many years, been irresponsible about the school and the girls, not only financially, but even in terms of attention to how they were taught. Almost all of the teaching responsibility had devolved upon Elizabeth—and oddly, or perhaps not so oddly, it was Elizabeth that Irma hated, not Isadora.)

In answer to Irma's letter Isadora sent her a conciliatory note with a picture of "the Greek goddess Demeter, Mother Earth, handing on a torch to her young daughter Persephone, the new life, bringing light to the world."

The trip to Greece and the hope of founding a school there were terminated suddenly by the death of the young Greek king as a result of a monkey bite and the subsequent fall of Isadora's sponsor Venizélos. She and her young dancers were forced to return to Paris. Isadora writes, "What a strange, torturous memory is this last visit to Athens in 1920, and the return to Paris and the renewed agony and final separation and the departure of my Archangel, and my pupil, who was also leaving me for ever. Although I felt I had been the martyr of these happenings, she seemed to think just the opposite, and blamed me very bitterly for my feelings and lack of resignation about it all.

"When at length I found myself alone in that house in the Rue de la Pompe, with its Beethoven Salle all prepared for the music of my Archangel, then my despair had no words . . . I believed that the world and love were dead for me. How many times in one's life one comes to that conclusion!"

And now comes one of Isadora's leaps. "Especially do I resent the conclusion formed by so many women that, after the age of forty, a dignified life should exclude all love-making . . .

"How I pity those poor women whose pallid, narrow creed precludes them from the magnificent and generous gift of the

Autumn of Love. Such was my poor Mother, and to this absurd prejudice she owed the aging and illness of her body at the epoch when it should have been most splendid, and the partial collapse of a brain which had been magnificent . . ."

53

Dora Gray Duncan, Isadora's
mother, is a curiously vague figure in the "real" world. In part
this stems from the lack of accurate information about her
earlier years. The records of her birth, marriage, divorce, et
cetera were destroyed in the San Francisco earthquake. But
even in unofficial records, there is little evidence of Dora Duncan's existence.

If she wrote letters or if letters were written to her, they
were never kept. A few photographs of her remain, but even in
them she is obscure. In one, as a young woman, she poses
formally, her shoulders rounded, her face blank, somehow re-
sisting expression. In a photo of 1903 she stands with Isadora
in front of the sculptor Walter Schott. She is heavyset, in
shadow. No expression can be detected on her face. She looks
at Isadora, who serenely faces the camera. (In a newspaper
article of 1898 she had been described as "a large mama in a
blue gown that was monstrous and unnatural.")

The facts of Dora's life seem to be—roughly—as follows:
She was born in 1849 in San Francisco into a devout Irish

Catholic family. (Her father's sister was a mother superior in a convent in St. Louis.) Her father and mother had come to California in a covered wagon. At age twenty she married the divorced fifty-year-old Joseph Duncan and in 1878, after having borne him four children, she divorced him. In 1895 she went east with Isadora, first to Chicago, then to New York, then to London and the Continent. She returned to the United States in 1907 and lived quietly in the San Francisco Bay area. In 1922 she returned to Paris to be with her son Raymond and her daughter Elizabeth and died there. She is buried in a niche in a wall in the Paris cemetery Père la Chaise, near Isadora and Isadora's two children.

In *My Life* Isadora never mentions her mother's name. She begins her account with a blurring of the experience and identity of herself and her mother. Describing her mother's suffering, her "agony of spirit" in her "tragic situation," coincident with her own birth, Isadora says that her mother, divorced and with four young children, the lone breadwinner in the family, was away from home "all day and for many hours in the evening," giving music lessons at the houses of pupils. In the evening she "played . . . Beethoven, Schumann, Schubert, Mozart, Chopin or read aloud . . . from Shakespeare, Shelley, Keats or Burns," and taught them poetry by heart. Having given up Catholicism after her divorce, she became an atheist and frequently read the works of Bob Ingersoll to her children.

Isadora speaks of her as a "beautiful and restless spirit," who was "too busy to think of any dangers which might befall her children . . ." Isadora calls this lack of supervision (when she was three? at five?) a great gift of freedom. Isadora also says that, while playing the piano or reciting poetry, her mother "quite forgot about us . . . oblivious of all around her." Isadora takes this oblivion to be further proof of her mother's poetic spirit. But one can also see in this oblivion the indication of Dora Duncan's desperate need to escape from the overwhelming burden of real life into an "ideal" world.

Even as Isadora speaks of her own courage as a child, it becomes clear that the actions of this "beautiful spirit" were often ineffectual. When the long-absent father comes to call, Dora Duncan cannot face him and goes into the next room, locking the door behind her. When she cannot sell some caps that she has knitted for a shop, she sits and weeps. When she is refused credit by the butcher or baker, she sends Isadora, still a child, to wheedle further credit.

In Isadora's account, from an early age she becomes the one who leads, her mother follows. Whatever she suggests, her mother agrees to. She wants to quit school, her mother says yes. She insists on leaving San Francisco, saying: "We *must* leave this place, we shall never be able to accomplish anything here." Her mother agrees to go with her, "somewhat dazed, but ready to follow me anywhere." The picture that Isadora presents is of a totally acquiescent mother, childlike in her following of the child-mother.

In 1899, when Isadora left for England on the cattle boat, her mother was once again the follower. In England and later on the Continent, Dora played for Isadora in the studio, she traveled with her, she did whatever she could to further her daughter's career. There was never any indication of resentment, only willingness to go along, to follow, to do whatever was necessary to help Isadora achieve what she must achieve—fame and fortune.

It was with the appearance of Gordon Craig, at the end of 1904, that a drastic change took place in the relationship between mother and daughter; the mother, for the first time, seems to have tried to assert her authority. (There had been some small difficulty earlier over an Ivan Miroski, a poor forty-five-year-old poet Isadora had fallen in love with in Chicago, but that had been hastily settled when Isadora's brother had found out that Miroski was already married.)

Now, in the midst of Isadora's enormous success in Berlin—that dream they had both struggled for—Isadora went to Craig's studio and did not return for the night—or for several nights and her mother "went around to all the police stations, and all the Embassies, saying that some vile seducer had run off with her daughter . . ." When Isadora finally did return to her family, she says, her mother on seeing Gordon Craig, "cried, 'Vile seducer, leave the house!' "

And then Isadora adds: "She was furiously jealous of him."

Isadora concludes her account of this episode by saying that her mother left Europe for the United States "shortly afterwards."

In fact, however, Dora Duncan did not leave Europe "shortly afterwards." She remained in Europe for two more years, until the end of 1907. She was not with Isadora at the time of Deirdre's birth in September 1906. (Of her absence Isadora says, "Why wasn't my dear mother with me? It was because she had some absurd prejudice that I should be married.") But her mother was with her and the baby in March 1907 in Nice, when Isadora was ill, after Craig escaped to Florence.

It was in October 1907, shortly after Craig terminated the affair, that the true break took place between Isadora and her mother. To Craig, Isadora wrote, "I have been having awful time with Mother— Wild horses would not hold her & she has now left for London. I spent a small fortune in Drs. & nurses trying to hold her to no avail—"

In a subsequent letter to Craig she added, "Mama insisted on taking the steamer to America & she is now on her way there. She has cost me a small fortune & now I think dear Brother Gus may take care of her for a time."

Indeed Isadora was not to "take care" of her mother again. She would, in fact, see her only once again, on that "sad" occasion, in San Francisco in 1917, when looking into the mirror she saw her face and her mother's face together in grief.

She was not present at her mother's death.

For all of her remarkable capability as a performer to open herself to others in her audience, in the situation with her mother (and in fact in most situations in her life) Isadora could not put herself outside herself imaginatively into the place of the other.

Apparently feeling called on to "explain" to her readers her mother's departure so soon after her affair began with Craig, Isadora suggests boredom combined with the pressures of sexual frustration plus the realization of having "wasted" her life on her children. Isadora writes, "My mother, who had, during all the times of privation and disaster, borne her troubles with such extraordinary courage, began to find life very dull. Perhaps this was on account of her Irish character, which could not stand prosperity as well as adversity. Her temper became most uneven. Indeed, she was often in such moods that nothing pleased her. For the first time since our voyage abroad, she began to express a longing for America . . .

"I think that this turning of her character was probably

due to the habitual state of virtue in which my mother had lived, for so many years devoting herself only to her children. Now that we found interests so absorbing that they continually took us away from her, she realised that she had actually wasted the best years of her life on us, leaving nothing for herself . . . These uncertain humours on her part increased more and more and she continually expressed the desire to return to her native town, until at last she did so, shortly afterwards."

Isadora does not acknowledge, though she herself has given us the grounds for such acknowledgment, the crisis that Craig's entrance into their life introduced for Dora in terms of her own past history. A devout Catholic, she had married a divorced man, choosing the idealization of love over religion, and had then been betrayed by him and exposed to shame before others. He had betrayed her with other women and he had also betrayed her financially, having involved her own highly respected father in his fraudulent banking scheme. Left alone with her four children, she had turned her back on love as well as Catholicism. But then she had found a new belief, a new ideal, in atheism as advocated by Bob Ingersoll, the popular American lecturer and writer.

"Art in its highest forms increases passion, gives tone and color and zest to life," Ingersoll wrote in one of his most famous essays.

> [Art] is the highest manifestation of thought . . . It is the highest form of expression, of history and prophecy . . . [Art] deals with the beautiful, the passionate, with the ideal . . .
>
> The great lady, in velvet and jewels, makes but a poor picture. There is not freedom enough in her life. She is constrained . . . In all art you will find a touch of chaos, of liberty; and there is in all artists a little of the vagabond—that is to say, genius . . .
>
> The nude in art has rendered holy the beauty of woman . . . The Venus de Milo . . . is a miracle of majesty and beauty, the supreme idea of the supreme woman . . .
>
> Genius is the spirit of abandon; it is joyous, irresponsible. It moves in the swell and curve of billows;

it is careless of conduct and consequence. For a moment, the chain of cause and effect seems broken; the soul is free . . . Limitations are forgotten; nature seems obedient to the will; the ideal alone exists . . .

Dora had conveyed his words and ideals to her daughter, her child-mother, reading to her from Ingersoll night after night. The daughter in return had become the one to act upon the words, making the "ideal" real in performance. (One can hear the cadences and even the words of Ingersoll in Isadora's writings about the dance.)

But the appearance of Craig was to bring the ultimate betrayal to Dora. By choosing passion in the world over the passion for art, Isadora broke the almost symbiotic link between her and her mother. This was no simple revolt of daughter against mother—if there can ever be a "simple" revolt between the two. From a very early time, there had been a blending of mother and daughter at the edges of their lives. Daughter slipped in and out of mother; mother slipped in and out of daughter. Out of this meshing and through the means of Isadora's great talent, a third being had been created, a mother-daughter, a virgin goddess, the daughter of Isis, the "Ideal" of a woman, a "superior being," a holy goddess in the world.

But now, by choosing Craig as her lover—a Craig who in so many ways was so like Joseph Duncan—by submitting herself to him—as Dora had once submitted herself to Joseph—by valuing that passion for him above all else in life, even dance, Isadora had forsaken that meshing with her upon which Dora had built her life. And once that had happened, though she might come back to help Isadora abandoned by Craig, the mutuality of selves could not be reestablished. And so she left.

There is a short entry about Dora Duncan in her last years in the United States in an oral history at the Bancroft Library, an interview with the descendants of Florence Boynton. One of the Boynton children remembered that "Isadora's mother used to stay with us. We children just loved her because she would stay in the nursery, she wasn't interested in the grown-ups at all.

"She would tell us stories about Isadora as a little girl, sneaking down in her nightie and dancing while Mrs. Duncan played—And she would make believe that she didn't see her because she was disobeying orders . . ."

Preferring to stay with the children, uninterested in the adults, Dora spoke of her child as a child to children.

54.

Mary's mother, Katharine Kelso Johnston Cassatt, was born October 8, 1816, into a Protestant family of Irish extraction that traced its history back to the Revolutionary War. As a child, Katharine received a "proper" French education, having been taught by a woman who had "attended Madame Campan's select establishment in Paris." At Madame Campan's, Katharine later proudly told her children, "girls of the Imperial aristocracy" were enrolled, as if this linked her in turn with that aristocracy.

At the age of eighteen, on March 22, 1835, she married Robert Simpson Cassatt, ten years older than she. It was a marriage to which both partners brought a sense of "position" in the social world. She bore seven children, five of whom survived infancy. She was by all accounts an admirable mother and housekeeper, who held firmly to the traditional standards she had been brought up to revere. As a wife, she recognized her duty to defer to her husband's needs. If he wanted to move once, twice, ten times, though she might not want to move, she moved. She considered obligation to husband and children as superseding her own needs. She never doubted—or never seems to have doubted—for herself, as for other women, that true fulfillment came from devotion to home and family.

Her relationship to Mary's work is puzzling and contradictory. She seems early to have been pleased that Mary did well and might even sell a picture or two. She arranged for her to obtain a commission from a bishop to copy a picture in Italy, to help defray her expenses in Europe. Yet she also seems to have considered Mary's passion for painting as something of an indulgence. In the summer of 1873, when she visited Mary in Europe, Mary asked for some money to pay for models, but Katharine "absolutely refused . . . considering them an unnecessary expense."

At sixty-one, when she and Robert and Lydia came to France to live with Mary, she brought with her an unchanged and unchanging vision of a domestic world, ready to be transferred from Pennsylvania to Paris. The family's "position," even—especially—in this strange land, remained important to her. As she wrote to Aleck, "We . . . make no acquaintances among the Americans who form the colony, for as a rule they are people one wouldn't want to know at home, and yet they are received as specimens of the best society in America . . . They say [the Mackays, an American family] are as low and common as it is possible to be."

She carried on a frequent correspondence with her sons and her grandchildren, whom she had undoubtedly left reluctantly. The letters show her devotion to them, her interest in the children's education, her interest in almost anything her son Aleck is involved with, including his racehorses.

Her relationship to her husband remained one of deferring to his needs, though now and then a hint of irritation shows through. "This morning I had a letter from your Father which has upset all our plans—," she writes to Aleck. "Mary and I had decided to start for Divonne on Sunday evening, but he writes that the novelty of the thing having worn off he is tired of it and wants to come home—& is even in such a hurry that he says we had better telegraph as otherwise he will be here before we look for him. Now with his ideas of housekeeping I can't leave him with our cook alone—I must stay and superintend—and then another trouble is that he can't bear not to see everything finished about the house . . . so we were glad to get him away until things were all in order. Now he comes back just as we are in the midst of work . . ."

But though she may allow herself a small complaint to Aleck, she still fulfills her obligations, she is a "realist," she does what she must do as wife and mother in the world of the family. As to the world of art, it is neither comprehensible to her nor totally to her liking, an attitude that aligns her closely with Aleck. In a letter to him in 1880, she writes about Mary trying to find the "right" Degas for him. "I didn't encourage her much as to buying the large one being afraid that it would be too big for anything but a gallery or a room with a great many pictures in it—but as it is unfinished or rather a part of it has been washed out & Degas imagines he cannot retouch it without painting the whole over again & he can't make up his mind to do that I doubt if he ever sells it . . ."

After this irritation with Degas's impracticality, and a paragraph about children and the question of buying or renting a summer home, she goes on to say, "I see you are going to have the famous 'Sarah' [Bernhardt] . . . I never saw her but once & didn't like her at all; but then it was one of Octave Feuillet's worst pieces 'the Spring' & they said she didn't care how she played it as Croizette had the best role— I like to be amused & consequently don't like french tragedy so I never was tempted to go to see Sarah a second time . . ."

There is difficulty enough in life—so much worry about health, with Lydia so ill from Bright's disease, Robert not as strong as he used to be, and Mary and she only "tolerably" well. "We are not a robust family," she tells Aleck. No wonder, from her viewpoint, she doesn't need or like tragedy, French or otherwise.

After Lydia's final illness and death Katharine developed a severe heart condition. Increasingly Mary was the one who took care of her and Robert. In 1886 Katharine wrote to Aleck, "I don't know what we would do without Mary to look for us—she has a knack of finding out what is to rent & don't mind scaling the stairs when the lift is not yet in working order."

Yet her view of Mary's work did not alter. Though by the early nineties Mary had become a well-known painter, accepted and praised by her fellow artists, when Katharine wrote to Aleck about Mary's work, it was still in external terms—her fame somehow a matter of "luck": "Mary is at work again, intent on fame & money she says, & counts on her fellow country men now that she has made a reputation here— I hope she will be more lucky than she is in horseflesh— her new horse has been down—this time while driving him . . . Mary firmly believes she has bad luck & it looks like it—happily for her she is immensely interested in her painting . . . After all a woman who is not married is lucky if she has a decided love for work of any kind & the more absorbing it is the better . . ."

Shortly before Katharine died, Louisine Havemeyer visited Mary and later wrote: "Anyone who had the privilege of knowing Mary Cassatt's mother would know at once that it was from her and from her alone that [Mary] inherited her ability. In my day she was no longer young, [but] she was still powerfully intelligent, executive, and masterful, and yet with that sense of duty and tender sympathy she had transmitted to her daughter."

Certainly for Mary her mother was and remained an "executive, and masterful" presence. For all Mary's independence, her rebelliousness, she was obedient to her mother in her mother's lifetime, and even in her death. As late as 1920, twenty-five years after her mother died, Mary would write to Louisine: "Nothing that my mother ever told [Mathilde] has been forgotten, and the order and method of her housekeeping, all her recipes [?] she has kept . . ."

Even later, in the spring of 1924, when the young Philadelphia painter Adolphe Borie came to visit her, Mary said to him, "My mistake was in devoting myself to art, instead of having children." It is a clear reflection of her mother's words and presence, still held to, never surrendered, mirrored, repeated.

In 1873, when Katharine was visiting Mary, first in Paris and then in Holland, Mary painted her portrait. It shows a woman of middle age with an overlarge head and a slight body, with sharply sloping shoulders. She is dressed as for a social call, wearing a hat and a jacket. Placed against a dark background, she looks out of place, unsettled yet severe, determined, a visitor in a foreign land.

In 1878, shortly after Katharine arrived in Paris, Mary painted another portrait of her mother. It is considered by many critics to be the best portrait Mary ever did, reflecting the new

energy and confidence that came to her with her acceptance by
the Impressionists.

Called *Reading Le Figaro,* it portrays Katharine sitting in
a chintz-covered chair, intently reading the newspaper. In the
left background of the picture a mirror reflects the back of her
hand and the newspaper. She is wearing a white dress, in which
even the shadows are warm-toned, a warm gray and violet in
the white. Her dark hair is silhouetted against a wall several
tones darker than the gray in the shadows of the dress. In the
mirror is a reflection of a background of a still darker gray. The
chintz pattern of the chair picks up the darker gray of the
mirror and entwines it with an even darker gray and red.

It is a portrait of a woman at home, in place, intent, vigorous, any sternness in her appearance offset, modified by the
light that floods the canvas.

Mary did a third portrait of her mother in 1889: now Katharine is nearly seventy-three. She is shown sitting on a straight
chair, wearing a black dress, over her shoulders a shawl. She
is not occupied; she simply sits, neither seeing nor not seeing,
weighted as if she had been set in stone. Her left arm is propped
on the left arm of the chair; her left hand is placed against the
left side of her face. Her right hand holds a starkly white
handkerchief. This hand is excessively large, like the hand of
a hardworking peasant woman, the skin tone overlaid with dark
gray. The face worn, though not wrinkled, shows neither vigor
nor determination nor severity, but endurance. Her hair, still
dark but overlaid with a film of gray, is silhouetted against a
background of a painting on a wall, drawn in rapid and broad
brushstrokes. There is no clear demarcation between the head
of the sitter and the painting behind her. In contrast with the
starkly and precisely drawn face and hands and the dense im-
pacted black body, an imprecise image erupts in the upper
right-hand corner of the painting—it seems to be a vase with
flowers. But this breaking loose is partial, limited, held down by
the weight of the image in the black dress, by the face with its
resignation, by the peasantlike hand. In the lower left of the
painting, the chair is left unfinished, the shawl is left unfinished, edging off to a corner that is light gray, a negative space,
unfilled. The viewer's eye leaps from this gray area along the
diagonal to the opposite corner, upper right, also gray, also

unfilled. Or rather the eye would leap, but the darkly solid figure, whose body is hidden under the darkness of the dress, is like a barrier between. It is not a light-filled painting. It is a painting in which there is stillness but no rest. There is the suggestion of a presence forcibly held in place.

A portrait—three portraits—works of an artist preoccupied with color and with form, with surfaces and reflections. A daughter looking at a mother and a mother sitting, knowing she is being looked at by a daughter. A mother who sees in paintings pretty colors and takes the point of a painting to be the making of a "likeness." A mother who sits for her painting, believing, knowing that being a mother is more central to existence than the painting of existence, no matter how accurate.

The painting of 1873—the eyes of a daughter of twenty-nine looking, not knowing, trying to separate out, to see the mother, a traveler, seeing the set, determined face, the refusal of the face against the invasion of her own eyes—trying to see, to penetrate, but not too far, for is that not betrayal? The mother allowed her containment, granted her containment, in her shoulders, in the look on her face—and the daughter looking, seeing that look, does she wonder will it someday be hers? Is it hers now? A painting of attempted separation, and of attempting to know what is here of love, of not being loved, of sons preferred to daughters . . . A painting of entanglements unacknowledged.

The portrait of 1878. A portrait of a woman sure of her world, the world of daily life. Light has entered the painting. Reflection has entered the painting—though in the mirror, in the painting, the one who is painting is not seen. There is incorporation here, the body of the sitter has been taken in. There is softening here. The light that illuminates the mother has been granted to the mother, is a gift given by the daughter. There is a surrounding of the figure, an enveloping of it with light, the light itself, in and of itself, a penetration, a flowing through the form, a kind of love given and received.

The portrait of 1889. In it there is the knowledge of death coming soon to the one who is seen. In it there is the struggle between mother and daughter giving way in the face of death. There is sharpness of contrast and fusion here. The black of the sleeve is set against the lightness of the shawl, the white of the handkerchief is set against the black of the dress. The deep violet of the painting in the background fuses with the top of the mother's head. There is form sharply articulated and there is form only hinted at. There is the pull to abstraction, there is the pull to actuality. There is an expressiveness in this work that resists its own expression.

55

In the summer of 1920 Forbes
Watson, editor of the American journal *Art News,* visited Mary
Cassatt in her apartment in Paris on the rue de Marignan. He
found her "an embittered old woman, blind and lonely, unreasonable and vituperative . . . [yet] still a burning force and a
dominating personality, capable of a violent burst of profanity
in one breath and, with the next, of launching into a plea to save
the coming generation of American art students from turning
into café loafers in Paris and from all the other forms of the
uprooted ex-patriatism that had 'destroyed so many of them.' "

"Officially the war was over when I made my last visit to
her . . . Indeed it had been over for more than a year and a half,
but she was still violent, not, strange to say, about Germany
but about Wilson, Clemenceau, about everyone except the So-
cialists . . ." (According to Nancy Hale, "Watson told a friend
that Mary called Wilson 'a syphilitic son-of-a-bitch,' and then
put her hand to her mouth and said, 'I suppose if I were a lady
I wouldn't have said that.' ")

"She launched instantly into a semi-violent series of questions about artists or rather about the condition of art in America. But the subject of politics constantly intervened. At one point she exclaimed, tapping her cane on the floor: 'If I weren't a weak old woman I would throw away my limousine, give up this apartment and live without luxury.' "

56

In July 1921 Isadora Duncan
went to Russia.

At the end of *My Life* Isadora tells the beginning of her
journey: "I had the detached feeling of a soul after death making its way to another sphere . . . With all the energy of my
being, disappointed in the attempts to realise any of my art
visions in Europe, I was ready to enter the ideal domain of
Communism . . .

"As the boat proceeded northwards, I looked back with
contempt and pity at all the old institutions and habits of bourgeois Europe that I was leaving . . .

"Now for the beautiful New World that had been created!
. . . The dream that had been conceived in the head of Buddha;
the dream that had resounded through the words of Christ; the
dream that has been the ultimate hope of all great artists; the
dream that Lenin had by a great magic turned to reality. I was
entering now into this dream that my work and life might
become a part of its glorious promise . . ."

In going to Russia she will finally be given the money for

the school she has said she so desires. She will have a thousand pupils whom she will teach, all of whom will be supported by the state. Under her guidance as teacher, as prophetess, these children will become "free" spirits in "free" bodies. Their example will serve to inspire all of the Russians in their search for a higher form of humanity. So Isadora believes, or wills herself to believe.

It was a departure for Isadora, but in another sense it was not at all a departure. She had long sympathized with the poor against the rich, with the downtrodden against the persecutors, in some vaguely formulated way. In this she was still following the teachings her mother had read to her of Bob Ingersoll, who as early as the 1870s was writing, "I believe there is to be a revolution in the relations between labor and capital . . . I would like to see all working people unite for the purposes of demanding justice . . . All my sympathies are on the side of those who toil . . . of those who carry the burden of mankind . . ."

Only now, for Isadora, the new Ideal world will be one that will incorporate an actual revolution, one in which life, art, politics—everything—will be merged in a new vision of daily life. In this life she will pursue a "priestly" art totally divorced from commerce: "I am sick of the modern theatre, which resembles a house of prostitution more than a temple of art, where artists who should occupy the place of high-priests are reduced to the manoeuvres of shopkeepers selling their tears and their very souls for so much a night. I want to dance for the masses, for the working people . . . for nothing . . ."

But, of course, this was no ideal dream she was entering, as she found when she arrived in the Soviet Union. It was a society in the grip of poverty and disorder. All the ordinary amenities of Western civilization were absent. The machinery of daily life was in disarray. In many areas there was actual starvation.

Isadora saw, but yet she did not see. She persisted in her belief that she would help bring about the ultimate reconciliation between the Ideal and the real, between Art and life. (There is something about Isadora's refusal of the real in Russia that is like her refusal of the death of her two children, like her belief that through the birth of a third child she could bring them back to existence.)

What is astonishing is that, given the conditions in the Soviet Union at the time, she managed to make any headway at all, let alone exist. Of course, the Soviet government saw some advantage in being able to announce that the famous dancer had defected to Russia. But beyond that, there seems to have been something in Isadora that managed to touch and even move certain officials in the government—perhaps it was the force of her reputation or the tenacity of her expectations or her belief in their intentions, which she now identified so closely with her own.

Anatole Lunacharsky, the commissar of education, had been responsible for sending a telegram to Isadora, inviting her to come to the Soviet Union. An intellectual, a man of wide education in all of the arts, he had seen Isadora dance in Paris in 1913 and had admired her performance greatly. He had invited her to Russia, in the spring of 1921, after hearing that she was interested in coming, but he apparently hadn't really expected her to follow through. Startled by her actual appearance on the scene, he attempted to see to it that she was given a chance to start her school, though of course the economic situation was so grave that funding for a school of dance was hardly of first priority when compared with the need to provide for food.

Meanwhile, however, Isadora, having fallen into the dream of the Ideal, was exploring the new world in which she would be one of the "comrades." Dressed in one of the Paris creations she had brought with her, she went into the hotel dining room, where a dozen or so men, lucky enough to be able to pay for a meal, were seated at a long table, wearing their hats and coats—for of course there was no heat—while they ate "a dark greasy looking soup" and black bread. Isadora "greeted them cheerfully, 'How do you do, *Tovarishti,*' giving them her most sweet and ingenuous smile. But the *tovarishti* went on eating, after having glanced up sidewise for a moment—the time to take in this 'comrade' in a 'Callot Soeurs' creation . . ."

Next Isadora found herself invited to an official reception. She prepared herself for this event by dressing in a red tunic and the scarlet cashmere shawl she wore when she danced *The Marseillaise,* and by winding around her head a red tulle scarf as a turban. But when she arrived at the reception (held in a former mansion), instead of finding comrades in boots and peasant dress as she had anticipated, she discovered that the officials were wearing evening clothes, eating well-prepared food, and listening to French court music. At once, the heroine of her own dream, she launched into a diatribe—not in Russian, since she knew no Russian—attacking those present for betraying the Ideals of the Revolution. Then she stalked out, much to the bemusement of those left behind.

Isadora, never one for consistency, seems to have forgotten, or perhaps simply ignored, her own departures from "Ideal" behavior. She had come to Russia, accompanied by her maid, as always, and had brought with her a "six-foot high pile of trunks, hampers, hatboxes, and suitcases," including a special "Bolshevik" creation made for her by Paul Poiret, a black satin jacket and a white satin waistcoat with a red border.

By the middle of August there was still no help forthcoming from the Soviet government for her school. Perhaps to appease Isadora, Lunacharsky sent his private secretary with a Comrade Krasnostchokoff, the president of the Far Eastern Republic, to take Isadora to visit a children's colony at Malakofka. According to Irma, who had come to Russia with Isadora to be her assistant teacher, at the colony "Isadora gathered the children about her on the front lawn and gave them a lesson. They, not to be outdone in rhythmic courtesy, danced some of their peasant dances for her. Through an interpreter she spoke to them saying: 'These are the dances of slaves you have danced. All the movements go down to the earth. You must learn to dance the dance of free people. You must hold your heads high and throw out wide your arms as though you would embrace the whole universe in a large fraternal gesture!' "

Soon afterward, by chance, Isadora met her "Ideal" commissar. He was Nikolay Podvoysky, a close friend of Lenin's, who during the October Revolution had been in charge of the Military Revolutionary Committee in Petrograd. Isadora was "strangely impressed" by him, according to Irma, so impressed that soon after the meeting Isadora wrote a "portrait" of him, which she immediately sent off to an English newspaper. She describes him standing on the high balcony of a ruined palace, "the red flag waving in the free heaven above his head, looking down on his troops with an infinite love and clairvoyance in his eyes, such as one does not meet in the eyes of a human being, but only dreams of in the eyes of a God . . ."

After meeting Podvoysky again, she wrote yet another eulogy of him, saying that he "might if he wanted, live in luxury in a palace with a Rolls-Royce. All these things are at his disposal, but he prefers to live in two bare rooms, and he eats every day exactly the same rations that every soldier eats. He said to me:

" 'That is why my soldiers follow me and listen to me, because they know that, war or peace, I share the same hardships and eat the same food as they do. And that is why, when the White Army was near, and we were a mere handful of half-starved soldiers, we could force them back. It was because my soldiers knew that, for the Ideal, I had lived and suffered and starved just as they. And so they were ready to follow me to death, or anywhere!'

"And as Podvoysky spoke to me, I felt just as one of his soldiers; that I could follow him to death, or anywhere . . ."

According to Ilya Ilyich Schneider, Isadora's private secretary and translator while she was in Russia (and also the author of *Isadora Duncan: The Russian Years*), Isadora herself did as much talking as listening in her meetings with Podvoysky. He reconstructs her conversation, in part as, "The last few years all my thoughts have been of Russia and my soul has been here. Now that I have got here, I feel that I am following the paths which lead to the kingdom of universal love, harmony, comradeship, brotherhood . . . I despise riches, hypocrisy, and those stupid rules and conventions I had to live with. I want to teach your children and create beautiful bodies with harmoniously developed souls, who, when they grow up, may show their worth in everything they do . . . A free spirit can exist only in a free body, and I want to set free these children's bodies. My pupils will teach other pupils, who, in their turn, will teach new ones, until the children of the whole world will become a joyous, beautiful, and harmonious dancing mass . . ."

Apparently Podvoysky was "strangely impressed" with Isadora as well. Once again she was exerting her "magical" power, and under the most unlikely circumstances. That power is certainly not in the words Schneider reports to us. But then it is clear that Isadora's power had little to do with words. What was conveyed by her always had more to do with her presence, her daring as a performer, her years of knowing how she af-

fected others, how she looked, her years of perfecting gestures—whether in the turn of the head or a lift of the shoulder,
whatever—so that their ultimate effect was mythic, secret, un-
predictable, not susceptible to analysis, at a distance from ordinary life, filled with meaning beyond the apparent meaning.
She was never not performing, she was never not believing. As
Gertrude Stein wrote in "Orta, Or One Dancing," "She was one
believing that thing, believing being the one she was being
. . ." And Podvoysky, commissar or no commissar, must have
felt that same mirroring that so many others had felt, that
brought with it that sense of overcoming, crossing over a
boundary, finding the true vision of one's self in another—the
mutuality of believing and being.

According to Irma Duncan, Isadora was so impressed
with Podvoysky that she decided to follow his example by
going to live in a two-room log cabin, with her maid and Irma.
Irma, in collaboration with Macdougall, writing in *Isadora
Duncan's Russian Days,* says about this stay: "If Freedom
means living in an *isba*—three people in two rooms—sleeping
on the floor, enduring the most primitive hygienic arrange-
ments, eating rough food and drinking goat's milk, then
Isadora suffered Freedom for about a week in the woods of
Sparrow Hills."

After meeting Isadora, Podvoysky had begun to pressure
Soviet officials to assist her with the setting up of her school.
Returning to Moscow, Isadora was given a mansion, formerly
the residence of a ballerina and her millionaire husband. She
was also provided with a large staff including porters, maids,
and a chef, to assist with the running of the school. True she
did not get the thousand children she wanted. But she did get
fifty, and the school finally opened its doors by the middle of
October.

At Lunacharsky's request, she agreed to give a public performance during the celebration of the fourth anniver-
sary of the Russian Revolution, on November seventh. The
press, announcing the performance, told of the "world-famous
artist who had courageously left a crumbling capitalistic
Western Europe" to come to Russia to work with the Soviet
children.

To a packed house—no charge was made for the seats—at

the Bolshoi Theater, Isadora presented a program of Tchaikovsky's *Pathétique,* followed by the "Marche Slav." According to Seroff,

> Isadora's interpretation of the latter, which she had
> introduced in public performances in London and
> Paris, was even more poignantly felt by the Russian
> audience as it watched a chained slave, symbolically
> representing the Russian people, who, after valiant
> struggles, broke his chains and overcame his oppres-
> sor. "It was not dancing in the ordinary technical
> sense," *Izvestiya* reported in its front-page article on
> the following day: "It was the most beautiful interpre-
> tation in movement and miming of a musical *chef
> d'oeuvre;* and also an interpretation of the Revo-
> lution—the music of a hymn to a monarchy, paradoxi-
> cally enough, sounding revolutionary.
> "The thrill of the evening came at the closing
> number of the program, when, after her solo perfor-
> mance to the first stanza of the *Internationale,* the
> audience saw Irma Duncan come from a corner of the
> bare stage, leading a little child by the hand, who was
> followed in turn by another and another—a mass of
> children in red tunics moving against the blue cur-
> tains, then circling the vast stage, and finally sur-
> rounding with their youthful outstretched arms the
> noble, undaunted and radiant figure of their teacher.
> "The audience sprang to its feet, and with one
> mighty voice sang fervently the words of their hymn;
> they seemed like a great antique chorus celebrating
> the heroic gestures of the central figure on the stage.
> And no one failed to see that Lenin, keeping his eyes
> on the stage, stood in his loge and sang the *Interna-
> tionale* with the rest of the audience."

Unfortunately for Isadora, this dream of the "Ideal" was
soon shattered. Lunacharsky came to call upon Isadora a few
days later and announced that under the New Economic Policy,
all funds promised by the government were withdrawn. From
now on she would be allowed to charge for tickets and out of

that income she was expected to support the school. The government would, however, continue to provide her with the mansion.

So now at the end of six months in Russia, she was back where she had been in Paris. She must support the school herself. She must charge money for her performances. The Ideal state had rejected her vision, after all. But still something in Isadora would not accept that refusal. She kept asking and asking, not only for money for the school but also for several new projects, including the financing of free performances on Monday nights at the Bolshoi Theater.

In an article for *Isvestiya* she spoke of the necessity of expressing "Heroism, Strength and Light." Again she castigated the government for its capitulation to bourgeois ideas, in particular for its support of the ballet, which she had always considered a decadent art form. She spoke of seeing the ballet *Raymonda* and called it "a glorification of the Czar. The subject of the ballet had nothing to do with the rhythm and mood of our present life. It was EROTIC without Heroism. It is sufficient to watch the part the man is taking in our contemporary ballets. He is not natural but effeminate . . . Whereas man should first of all express courage in his dancing . . ." (Isadora herself had never worked with male dancers.)

Nevertheless, despite her outrage, Isadora decided to stay in Russia, even if it meant having to earn money for the school by touring. Besides, staying in Russia now offered her a new opening into the Ideal, a new possibility for the reconciliation of Art and Life, a chance for the "EROTIC with Heroism," through the person of the twenty-six-year-old Sergei Esenin.

Esenin, one of the great lyric poets of twentieth-century Russia, was the son of a peasant, born in a peasant village of an illiterate mother. As a young man he had come to Moscow and St. Petersburg and, when he was twenty-one, published his first book of poems. Inducted into the army, he deserted, was caught, and was forced to serve again. After the revolution in 1917, he deserted once more, this time briefly joining the revolutionary forces. In 1919 he and the writer Anatoly Mariengoff and several other poets published the Imaginist Declaration, an affirmation of the theory that image is the essence of poetry.

As a poet, Esenin always remained an independent and idiosyncratic voice. He considered himself the "last village poet." His great lyrical gift was capable of sudden shifts into a gross, violent mode. He was called "a poet of death and a poet of eternal youth."

By the time Isadora met him in 1921 he had been married twice and had had three children. He was also apparently deeply attracted to men and had had, according to some sources, a number of homosexual affairs.

Ambitious for fame, he was described by a fellow poet when he first came to St. Petersburg as appearing to be modest, but "his modesty was a fine cover under which beat a greedy, unsatiated striving to conquer everyone with his poems, to subjugate, to trample." He was capable of playing many parts, from the innocent young poet to the dandy to the hooligan. He exhibited sharp mood swings and also drank excessively. He was extremely handsome, with blond hair and blue eyes.

Though Isadora and Esenin became lovers soon after they met, they shared no common language; Esenin spoke only Russian. They shared no "interests." He knew nothing of music and the dance; she understood nothing of his poetry, though she still claimed to know he was a genius. Esenin's friends and Isadora's friends equally condemned the relationship, finding it a gross mismatch.

Mariengoff tells of being brought to visit Isadora at her studio by Esenin. Isadora, at Esenin's suggestion, proceeded to dance an "apache" dance to an Argentine tango, with herself as the apache and a pink scarf as the woman. Later Mariengoff wrote "Esenin became her master. Like a dog she kissed the hand that he raised to strike her . . . [in his eyes] burned more often hate than love. And yet he was only the partner. Like the bit of pink stuff, a partner tragic and without a will. She danced . . . It was she who led the dance."

It was a very daring dance that Isadora was leading. She told Mary Desti and others—and in fact Esenin himself came to know it—that when she looked at Esenin, she saw her blond-haired son Patrick. Isadora knew nothing about Esenin and his life when she met him, nor did she ever learn anything about his history, for she was living out another story, a myth, un-related to the Esenin who existed.

In the Egyptian myth, Isis and Osiris, the first-born chil-dren of the god of the earth and the goddess of the sky, fell in love and mated within their mother's womb. Once out in the world they pursued their mission to train mankind to revere the gods. But Seth, Osiris's brother, grew jealous of him, killed him, and threw his body into the Nile. His corpse floated out into the Mediterranean but was eventually found by Isis, who brought it back to Egypt. There she resurrected her husband-brother, giving him eternal life, and simultaneously she bore his child Horus, who upon his death became Osiris. In the leg-end of Isis in any of its manifold forms—Plutarch's is only one of the retellings—husband is brother is son; birth becomes death becomes life.

Isadora, pursuing Esenin, pursued her own variation of the myth, blocking out all that she did not want to see, holding tenaciously to him despite his drinking, despite his rages, de-spite his beating her, despite his leaving her. Each time he left, she begged him to come back and he came back. (What myth of his own was he pursuing?)

Mariengoff describes an incident in which Esenin appeared at Mariengoff's residence, carrying a packet of two shirts, a pair of drawers, a pair of socks—

He said: "This time it's definite. I said to her: 'Isadora, Good-bye.' "

Two hours later the porter from Pretchistenka [Isadora's residence] came with a letter. Esenin wrote a reply, laconic and definite. An hour after came Mr. Schneider, Isadora's secretary.

At last in the evening, she herself appeared. Her lips were pursed, and her blue eyes still shone with tears. She sat down beside his seat and put her arms about his legs, her hair falling about his knees.

"Angel!"

Esenin pushed her away brutally with his foot.

"Go to Hell," he said, using a foul word.

Then Isadora, smiling still more tenderly, said

very softly: "Sergei Alexandrovitch, lublu tebia." [I love you.]

And always this ended in the same fashion: Esenin took up his little bundle and went away.

He was a wayward, wilful little child, and she was a mother passionately enough in love with him to over-look and forgive all the vulgar curses and the peasant blows . . .

Believing that Esenin's friends were intriguing to get him away from her and telling her friends that she wanted to find a cure for his drinking, Isadora decided to take him abroad. To provide the school with funds in her absence, she conceived of a "brilliant festival," a program of dancing by her and the children, to be followed by a large party with Russian food and drink, accompanied by gypsy singing and dancing. Isadora planned to invite members of the American Relief Organization; she expected that they would contribute substantial sums to the school.

Lunacharsky, hearing about Isadora's plan, telephoned Schneider and told him that Isadora's announcement of the festival had met "with an unfavorable reception by our Party leaders. I must warn you that everything you do should be kept within the limits of strictest decorum . . ."

In reply, Isadora wrote Lunacharsky: "Dear Comrade, The words 'within the limits of strictest decorum' do not exist in my vocabulary . . ."

57

On October 1, 1922, Isadora and Esenin arrived in New York from Europe. In May, just before leaving Russia, they had been married. To her friends she had justified this surprising step by saying that it was a matter of prevention. Otherwise, she said, they would be harassed by the authorities in the United States while staying in a hotel as an unmarried couple.

But on their arrival, they met with another kind of harassment. They were detained on the dock by the immigration authorities. According to Sol Hurok, her manager, when he came to meet her at the boat, he was told by an immigration inspector that "they were very sorry. The law by which an American woman who married an alien automatically forfeited her citizenship had gone into effect two months before. With a Russian passport and a Bolshevik husband—the whole proposition was too hot for them to handle on the spot." The two would have to undergo questioning on Ellis Island.

After reporters interviewed Isadora and Esenin, New York papers headlined Isadora's detention. The next morning she

and Esenin were taken to Ellis Island for questioning and then
released. (A statement was issued later "that she had been held
by the Department of Justice because of her long residence in
Moscow, and because there was some suspicion that she and
her husband might be acting as 'friendly couriers' for the Soviet government . . .")

Still followed by reporters, Isadora and Esenin took the
ferry to Manhattan. Landing at the foot of Manhattan,
"grandly gesturing the taxicabs aside . . . [she] set forth on foot
to the Waldorf-Astoria. In her red-leather Russian boots and
Russian caracul hat, with her startling hennaed hair and her
long cape flying, she marched from the Battery up Broadway,
up Fifth Avenue, a triumphal parade of one," followed by Esenin and Hurok, who adds, "Thanks to the United States Government and the New York newspapers, three performances [at
Carnegie Hall] were sold out within the next twenty-four
hours."

That triumphal parade was, however, the prelude to disaster. Esenin, in the five months that he and Isadora had been in
Western Europe, had exhibited further signs of violent behavior while drinking, alternating with sudden moments of homesickness and then rage. But in the United States, Isadora's
native land, his moods swung wider and wider, his drinking
became more desperate. At least in Europe there had been
many who recognized his genius as a poet. Now he was almost
totally in Isadora's shadow.

As for Isadora, here she was, coming out of that dream
(Ideal) state that had turned out not to be a dream, returning
with her husband, who was part of another dream, to that
native country with which she had long had a love-hate relationship—that country that had never accepted her as she wanted
to be accepted, which she had felt forced to leave so many years
before in order to be recognized.

Here in America, she grew ever more expansive, wanting
to conquer absolutely as the heroine of her own drama; he,
attached to her, beside her, unable to speak the language, cut
off from his own language, spoke of his hatred for this bourgeois world (but went out and bought everything he could lay
his hands on), and drank and drank more (she too was drinking), growing more and more disruptive, as if he—this child-

husband-brother—were performing on this stage of the New
World (though her old world) his own drama of destruction,
darkness, downgoing.

He was living a public life with her, their activities continually chronicled in the press: the gossip of drinking and brutality,
of the destruction of hotel rooms, supplemented by Isadora's
statements defending Esenin as a genius. As the tour went on
her pronouncements became increasingly rancorous, many
delivered from the stage during her performances.

A travesty of a private intimate life, caught in a web of
mythical intricacy, was now converted to public view. At the
same time they were caught in another public image, the identification by many Americans of anything—anyone—Russian as
demonic and as morally and sexually depraved. Who is to say
how Isadora and Esenin, themselves so intent on their own
image making, were reflecting and being ruled by that image
among all the others?

In 1921, in New York, Edwin Denby, still a very young
man, saw Isadora dance for the first and only time. Many years
later he wrote: "I watched a program from up in the Carnegie
Hall gallery, from where she looked, all alone on the stage and
facing the full blare of a Wagnerian orchestra, very small indeed. But the slow parts of her Venusberg dance and her Siegfried Funeral March remain in memory two of the very greatest
effects I have seen; I can still feel their grandeur and their
force."

H. T. Parker, the dance critic of the *Boston Evening Transcript,* had been a great partisan of Isadora's dance from 1908,
the first time she returned to the United States from Europe.
In Isadora's dance Parker had seen "exquisite innocence," "exquisite lightness," "exquisite plasticity."

He had caught echoes in her work of the dancing figures
of the Greeks and Romans, and of the pictures of Botticelli.
"Quite as sedulously, seemingly she has observed the rhythmic
movements of natural objects, like the leaves of the forest or
growing grain swept by the wind, and of children and other
spontaneous natural folk. Out of all these strands she has
woven the form, the manner, and the artistry of her dancing

. . . Most of all she has woven it out of her own imagination, skill, and ambition of intuitions, experiment, and trials . . .

He spoke of her dance seeming "to spring spontaneously into being, to be the instinctive translation of the rhythm and the mood of the music, or of some vaguely indicated episode, in wholly natural and seemingly unfettered movement . . . She moves often in long and lovely sinuous lines across the whole breadth, or down the whole depth of the stage. Or she circles it in curves of no less jointless beauty. As she moves, her body is steadily and delicately undulating. One motion flows or ripples, or sweeps, into another, and the two are edgeless. No deliberate crescendo and climax ordered her movements, rather they come and go in endless flow as if each were creating the next."

No dancer, he believed, could be freer from "the grosser bonds of flesh and muscles and nerves, from all physical and material conditions that would bind her to the earth" than Isadora was. "Her dancing is as intangible, as un-material, as fluid as are sound or light. There is spirit-like quality in it."

Parker had seen her dance again in 1911 and had felt that she had "grown somewhat too stout of leg and body." The audience was much less receptive to her than it had been before and he himself thought she was "reading too much" into the music of Bach and Wagner, "cloth[ing] them in her motions with a plastic imagery of her own, and it was not interesting." Nevertheless, he had found moments of pure sculptural beauty and sensual beauty in her work. And in her dance of the Bacchanale in the Venusburg music of Wagner, he saw once again the idealization he had found in her work earlier. "There is no sense of time, place, audience—only of the dance and the moving body sublimated, idealized, of the spirit and not of the flesh."

But now, in October 1922, at her first concert in Boston he saw not spirit but flesh:

> Miss Duncan, who is frank enough about tell-tale dates, is no longer a young woman, except in the bright-eyed wistfulness, the half-eager and half-waiting smile that, under the lights of the stage, still haunt her face. Miss Duncan, as always, is likewise fertile in theories of the dance—theories, a cynic might say,

that fructify in the practice of her mounting years. In a sense, then, Isadora no longer dances—or dances only after the work of the evening has made her anew free-motioned and supple. So, for easy analogy, a singer, at odds of spirit with relentless time, "limbers up" her voice until at the end of a concert she is again capable of highly ornate and elastic music. Similarly as extra numbers, at the close of the appointed program, Miss Duncan dances—in the full sense of the word—to the light, flowing measures of two waltzes by Brahms—if recollection holds, exercises from the earliest days of her grace, charm and light fancy. She not only renewed these qualities but in plastic, finely modulated motion followed the contours, inflection and rhythm of the music.

When, however, in the preceding piece, the so-called "Bacchanale" from "Tannhäuser," Miss Duncan sought to gain the arrow-like swiftness, the dartings and the flashings, the joyous wildness, the exultant beauty of those earlier years, she was far from corybantic. By thought and effort she would summon anew the lithe lightness of old; but the merciless years have perceptibly stiffened it . . . Even the vivid life of that outflung pose and motion of joy—now part of the working capital of every dancer the world around—no longer vibrates upon eye and ear. Eagerness, though it still burn white in Isadora with thought and will to blow the flame, may no longer enkindle a body, loth to light, swift, instantly supple motion.

So it is that, nowadays, Miss Duncan most engrosses the eye and quickens the imagination when she is semi-static; most achieves beauty when she seeks it, so to say, in sculptured pose and gesture, in surface and plane, rather than in movement . . . Isadora is ceasing, inevitably, to be a dancer in the sense of vivid motion. Instead, she is becoming sculptress, while the medium upon which she works is her own body . . .

In Isadora's dance to the music of *Götterdämmerung*, Parker saw "mourning translated into sculptural beauty, . . .

deep grief transmuted into line, plane and mass . . ." But he could not avert his eyes from something else that he saw in Isadora's soliloquy of Isolde mourning over the dead Tristan: "constricted poses and [a] gorgon-like visage."

Parker returned to Isadora's second concert, the next night, as if he were determined to find the young Isadora in the old, to reconcile the disparate images he had to face. In his review of the second and final performance, labeled "Isadora Incontinent," he tells first of Isadora's speech to the audience, of her railing about her reception in Boston, comparing the United States unfavorably with the Soviet Union. He watched and listened to this "minor excess," as the audience received her remarks with "obvious merriment."

But he saw a far more serious affront, a "grave offending," in Isadora's costume, or rather in her lack of costume during the performance. Dancing to music of Tchaikovsky, she wore only a few very transparent scarves on a stage that was brightly lit. "The outcome, especially when Isadora answered recalls or stretched a congratulatory hand to the conductor, was a degree of bodily revelation unbecoming to a middle-aged woman, too obviously high in flesh. It was the negation of the sculptural beauty that she professes to seek.

"It was also one more evidence of the irritation that tends more and more to curdle the exploits of these, her final years. Miss Duncan will not accept with resignation the coming of middle age and the inevitable end therewith of her dancing. She gropes after a substitute for it; she releases her rebellion in such excesses as those of Saturday; she dispenses sensation for the sensation's sake . . ."

But even more disturbing to Parker was the monotony evoked by her "posturing" to the lengthy *Pathétique* Symphony of Tchaikovsky. "Now, monotony, a lack of variable and viable resource was the shortcoming of Miss Duncan's dancing days. The very technique that she then professed to disdain would have suggested means that she much needed. Still more did monotony beset her present posings upon a music in itself long-drawn. Wearisome and meaningless to watch became her reiterated lifting of crossed arms . . . of certain carriages of the head. Often she maintained a crouching posture as in the first and last movements, until it declined from formal beauty and emotional suggestion into a mere carven immobility . . ."

He admits that he still saw in her work attitudes of "truly sculpturesque beauty; while the transition from one to another was now and then as fluid as rippling water or as darting as quick flame." But in her "Marche Slav," he saw only a "more ordinary and obvious miming. She bowed and crouched and writhed to the sombre measure of the beginning like a moujik-like captive fettered in woe. As the music warmed, quickened, brightened she was as that prisoner struggling into freedom, gaining it, exulting thereby . . . Any accomplished mime would do neither more nor less with so obviously graphic a music. If he were intelligent, he would also remember that few and far between are the dancers who can rise with grace from a crouched or a recumbent position—a tenet of the dance . . . which somehow, in these latter days, Isadora quite forgets."

What are we to make of Parker, who was so distressed at the sight of a middle-aged woman, high in the flesh, no longer able to leap and run and rise as she once had? Was it just that, as the conservative man he was, he saw in the immediacy of the sagging flesh a violation of the distancing necessary to all art? Was this the real "affront" for him?

But what then of Balanchine, who saw Isadora dance in Russia and, many years later, was still incensed by that memory: "I thought she was awful. I don't understand it when people say she was a great dancer. To me it was absolutely unbelievable—a drunken, fat woman who for hours was rolling around like a pig. It was the most awful thing. It is unbelievable how people can be hypnotized so nobody dares to say what he thinks. I don't believe she ever danced well. She was probably a nice juicy girl when she was young . . . There was no reason to be so bad at forty. I can't believe she was excellent when she was thirty. Those ten years couldn't make such a difference."

It is true that for Balanchine slenderness was essential to his idea of beauty. It is true that for Balanchine control and discipline were at the core of expressiveness, that he hated what was lax, self-indulgent, flabby, unrealized. Was that all that was behind his outburst?

Or is it possible that there was something never acknowledged in this interchange of motion and sight, an ugliness that she had once said had to be killed, now leaking out through her face, through her body? A body moving her in its own uncontrolled independence, making use of her expressiveness, taking charge of that expressiveness, no matter how erratically. A darkness seeking expression, all the more terrible for not being acknowledged by the instrument of its expression, who still mouthed words of "beauty" and "soul" and "spirit" and the "Ideal."

Was this what the two men, choreographer and critic, saw in her, the one calling her "pig," the other "gorgon-like?" (And yet, we have all seen performers who have stayed past their prime. We have all felt the regret, the pain at having to look at someone who has lost their power to hold, to entrance. Was it simply that Isadora no longer knew how she was seen?)

There exists a small ancient terra-cotta statue of Isis carrying a mystical ladder in her arms, as she sits naked with outspread legs on a pig. Erich Neumann, in *The Great Mother: An Analysis of the Archetype,* says of this figure that in the ancient world "the pig is a symbol of the Archetypal Feminine and occurs everywhere as the sacrificial beast of the Earth Goddess."

As for the gorgon, she was the terrible face of the Great Mother, the goddess with snaky hair whose gaze turned men to stone.

58

In April 1891, after Pissarro saw a set of ten color prints Mary had just completed, he wrote to his son Lucien: "It is absolutely necessary, while what I saw yesterday at Miss Cassatt's is still fresh in mind, to tell you about the colored engravings she is to show at Durand-Ruel's at the same time as I . . .

"You remember the effects you strove for at Eragny? Well, Miss Cassatt has realized just such effects, and admirably: the tone even, subtle, delicate, without stains on seams, adorable blues, fresh rose, etc. . . . The result is admirable, as beautiful as Japanese work, and it's done with printer's ink . . ."

These color prints—in drypoint, aquatint, and soft-ground—were, in fact, inspired by the 1890 exhibition in Paris of Japanese woodblock prints. To Berthe Morisot, with whom Mary was at the time on cordial—though not intimate—terms, she had written in great excitement, "If you would like, you could come and dine here with us and afterwards we could go to see the Japanese prints at the Beaux-Arts. Seriously, *you must not* miss that. You who want to make color prints you couldn't dream of anything more beautiful. I dream of it and don't think of anything else but color on copper."

The subjects of these ten prints, dreams of "color on copper," are women in daily life. One is of a woman alone bathing, one is of a woman alone dressing her hair. One is of a woman sealing a letter, one is of a woman sitting alone beside a lamp, one is of a woman giving a child a bath, two are of a mother caressing her child, one is of a woman being fitted at a dressmaker's, one is of two women and a child in a tram, and one is of two women at an afternoon tea party. They are all portrayals of women in their private lives. Even the print of the two women and the child in the tram, though ostensibly in a public space, sets them in isolation in an intimate private space. There are no other passengers, there is no bus driver.

In these highly stylized works, taking their cue from the Japanese woodcuts, the forms of the women and of objects are flattened. There is a compression of space, a sense of two-dimensionality. The Japanese works are alluded to further by the use of objects that have Eastern rather than Western shapes, by the setting of the women against backgrounds as if they were before screens. (Mary, at first, even called one of these works *An Imitation of the Japanese.*) The color in these works is of a remarkably contained delicacy, which emphasizes the tone of formality, of ritual, even of ceremony in the daily acts of the women.

The French critic and art historian Claude Roger-Marx, who judged these ten color prints, "together with the sets done by Bonnard, Vuillard, and Toulouse-Lautrec," as "the most successful color engravings we have," saw in Mary's use of drypoint something characteristically appropriate to her work. "The term *drypoint* describes not inaptly the remoteness and dignity always preserved by Cassatt . . ."

The technique of drypoint involves working with a tool—a diamond- or ruby-point pencil—directly on the copper plate. Using this drypoint pencil, the artist, working against the resistance of the metal to the tool, achieves a line—a cut in the plate—at the same time throwing up the excess metal as "burrs" on either side of the channel. It is a difficult technique to control precisely, but Mary, using a minimum of lines in her drawing, achieved a precision, even a mastery, in these prints that she had never been able to find before. Apparently, at

times, she even drew directly on the copper plate with no pre-
liminary drawing on paper. "In dry point," she once said, "you
are down to the bare bones, you can't cheat."

In these prints everything seemed to come together for
Mary, as she worked with precision, in containment. The tendency toward decoration that could have been a danger here is
held precisely within bounds, just as the various colored areas
of the prints are held so precisely in place. Even her tendency
toward distraction is eliminated. One can see this distraction in
the paintings, in, for example, *The Girl Arranging Her Hair*,
where the glass bottle and the washbasin behind the girl dis-
tract the eye and leave in the viewer's eye a sense of confusion,
or, as in the last painting of her mother, where the background
acts as diversion from the main thrust of the painting. In these
paintings and others, it is as if she herself has not chosen
precisely, as if she is painting more than one painting.

But in these ten color prints there is neither distraction nor
digression. Everything has become subsumed into color and
line. Nothing irrelevant bursts out or even threatens to burst
out. The work is the style and the style is the work. There is
none of the discordant tension of *The Woman with the Red
Zinnia.* In that painting the woman's face is at odds with her
clothes, the figure at odds with the background, the red zinnia
threatening, promising a breaking through into another style
that almost occurs but does not occur.

Here in these prints, with colors so complex and fertile,
nothing leaks out, nothing breaks across borders. Everything
is held to the flattened surface, but that surface is complete in
itself, as if it has interchanged meaning with depth. Passion
for line and color has found its own proper, its own necessary, containment . . . through limitation, through distancing,
through turning away from the process and power of direct
gaze. It is as if, in turning away to the strangeness of another
culture, another way of seeing, she allowed herself to become
the willing instrument of her own contained strangeness.

And for the viewer, looking, what and where is feeling
here? It seems that feeling in these prints is not the primary
intention, at least not the direct expression of feeling. A print,
by the very process it goes through in its creation, is absolved
of directness. In a drawing or a painting, we can see at once,

immediately, the work of the hand on paper or on canvas. But in a print, there is a step between. One sees on the paper the mark, the indication once removed, of what the hand did on the plate. One does not see the plate. There is a barrier. There is a transformation.

And yet, paradoxically, through this indirection, taking its clue from indirection, feeling here is given its due. One looks at these prints and one sees appropriateness, one feels pleasure at the achieved beauty of the colors and forms. One is distanced, but held confidently, accurately, unwaveringly, at this distance. It is a triumph of feeling made formal, of feeling itself become formality.

There is a haunting quality in these works, in the stilled gestures that are simultaneously foreign and familiar. Here surface is containment, surface is repose, is its own secret.

59

It is the afternoon of October 31, 1923. Mathilde Vallet, Mary's housekeeper, is cleaning out a closet in the apartment on the rue de Marignan. Suddenly she comes across twenty-five copperplates worked in drypoint. Examining them, she thinks they look as if they've never been printed. Immediately she takes them in to Mary, who is lying down for her afternoon rest.

Mary, of course, cannot see the plates well enough to make her own judgment, nor can she remember, since they were done so many years ago, when or if they have been printed. That evening, when the American artist George Biddle comes to visit, Mary shows him the plates. He, like Mathilde, concludes that they have never been printed. A day or so later Mary shows the plates to Delâtre, a printer, whose father did all of Mary's earlier printing. Delâtre agrees with Biddle. In great excitement Mary asks Delâtre to make six sets of prints from the plates. She then sends two sets to Louisine Havemeyer, and asks her to take them to William Ivins, the curator of prints at

the Metropolitan, to see if he is interested in exhibiting or purchasing them.

Louisine dutifully takes the prints to Ivins, who looks at them and tells her immediately that the proofs have been made from old worn-out plates. In fact, he adds, the Metropolitan already has in its collection earlier and better prints of the same plates. Now Louisine writes to Mary what Ivins has said. She suggests that Mary has been misled by Mathilde or Delâtre or Biddle.

To Joseph Durand-Ruel, Mary writes: "It seems Mr. Ivins has no desire to exhibit my dry points, according to him inferior, the plates worn. Mrs. Havemeyer didn't say a thing. She accepts Mr. Ivins's opinion! I am obliged to believe him . . . Obviously they embarrass Mrs. Havemeyer. Strange way to treat a friend."

To William Ivins she writes, "I must at once correct a wrong impression first as to my sight & then as to my memory. I can perfectly see my etchings & am not likely to forget those I have done, I see them every day when at home they are framed & line the walls— As for poor Mathilde What has she [done] to Mrs. Havemeyer [who] wishes to make her a scape goat for what I have done—it isn't necessary. I take all responsibility for my acts . . ."

To Durand-Ruel she writes again,

I must be boring you with all these stories, but I have another letter from Mrs. Havemeyer, who is completely beneath contempt in this matter . . . The first person to see the drypoints was Mr. George Biddle who is a printmaker. It was one evening and I told him what we had just found and since I don't see work on copper very well, I showed them to him. He immediately saw the work and told me that there was still some black which one applies to help see the line and also the oil on the plate which facilitates the stroke of the needle. Now as you might imagine there was still a burr beside the line. When a plate is to be steel plated it must be brushed to remove all the oil. That also removes the burr. Delâtre told me that me that my plates or rather my proofs show the burr. This is what

proves, it seems to me, that they are not old worn out plates, as that imbecile said . . . Mrs. Havemeyer assures me that what they all want is to protect my reputation! to prove that I am not a fraud! I will never forgive that. I told her that I could take care of my own reputation and that she could take care of hers. Poor woman, there wasn't a word, a gesture, nothing that one might have expected. But since she has become a politician, journalist, orator [for the suffragette movement], she is nothing anymore . . .

Still raging four months later, she writes to Harris Whittemore: "I have no respect for the opinion of Mr. Ivins. I had a note from him a few years ago when he told me that Whistler's etchings looked as if spiders had been running over the plates! A most unbecoming attitude for the Director of Print Department of a great museum to sneer at Whistler indeed. Ivins cannot touch Whistler's fame. Mine is different. He has accused me of fraud and Mrs. Havemeyer has accepted the charge—of course all is over between us . . ."

In the midst of a daily life of barely seeing when seeing was once almost all, in the midst of confinement, of helplessness, these unfinished images have appeared. With no warning they have brought, once more, the possibility of old work made new, the reassertion of lost power—the dream of doing and the dream of not quite done that is yet to be done . . .

One of the prints was of her mother, the others apparently of mothers and children. To Ivins she had written in her own defense, "But I have a joy from which no one can rob me— I have touched with a sense of art some people once more— They did not look at me through a magnifying glass but felt the love & the life. The greatest living optician when he saw the etching of the naked baby burst out oh! the baby is living & told me he had spent two hours the evening before looking at the etchings two hours of delight— Can you offer me anything to compare to that joy as an artist—"

But once again granted that joy, it is as suddenly taken away—and moreover, at the same time, she is accused of fraud.

So joy turns back upon itself and becomes rage, feeding on itself, amassing itself with all the other rages that can be called

on—rage at the body, rage at the hand no longer instrument of the eye, rage at the eye no longer guide to the hand, rage at darkness, at being alone, at being bypassed, having been bypassed by the "modern," at no longer being able to work, at work that might have been . . . rage at Louisine—Louisine, whom she had met more than fifty years before, in 1873, when Louisine, then Louisine Elder, was a schoolgirl in Paris—Louisine, who had idolized her, Louisine whose private collection she had made into one of the world's finest, Louisine whose ideas on the vote for women she had accepted as her own . . .

Mary recants her sympathy with the Women's Movement, she cuts off Louisine completely, Louisine, who had been "the only one who cares."

A. F. Jaccaci, the publisher and writer on collecting, said of her, "She's become a viper."

An old woman, blind and raging. . . . In a man it might be called Lear-like. But in a woman? She is seen as a viper. For what can there be of cosmic rage in an old woman living a daily, domestic life, alone, raging?

60

Yes, I am leaving America. I am shaking the dust of your narrow-minded, hypocritical, loathsome United States from my feet," Isadora wrote in Hearst's *American Weekly* of January 1923.

"America makes me sick—positively nauseates me. This is not a mere figure of speech. America produces in me a definite malady—I know the symptoms; I have felt them here on other visits.

"Stupid, penurious, ignorant America disgusts me and I am going back to Russia, the most enlightened nation of the world today."

At her last performance in Boston she had waved a red scarf and proclaimed herself "red," full of life and vigor, as opposed to Boston and Bostonians, who were "gray," lifeless. After Mayor Curley banned her from any further performances in the interests of preserving "decency," many concerts in other cities were canceled. Further, the departments of Labor, Justice, and State began an investigation of Isadora, based on reports of her nude "immoral" dancing and of her proclamation of herself as "red," a word taken in its political context. Together with Esenin, who was still raging—drinking, fighting, and buying—they continued to be daily "copy." Now, leaving, Isadora wrote her own text of rage:

> You feed your children here canned peas and canned art, and wonder why they are not beautiful. You will not let them grow up in freedom. You persecute your real artists. You put them under the heels of fat policemen, like the ones who sat on the platform of my concert in Indianapolis. You drug your souls with matrimony. You import what art you have, which isn't much. And when anyone tells you the truth, you say, "they are crazy!"
>
> I am absolutely, unutterably and vehemently opposed to all legalized marriage. I think the wedding ceremony is a most pernicious foe to the poor little victims of marriage—the children . . .
>
> What do parents do in their holy wedded life? They browbeat, intellectually and spiritually, every child that is born to them. They commit malpractice upon the souls of each of their offspring . . .
>
> Maybe some people may think I do not practice what I preach, since just a year ago I got married myself. Well, I was forced into matrimony by the silly laws of the lands I had to travel through as an artist. I married my husband to get him past the customs officers. I married my husband because if I were not married to him in our—huh! huh!—"free America," two burly policemen would have the right to raid my hotel and take us into court because we were natural enough, and sane enough, and loving enough to live together without this throttling wedding ceremony . . .
>
> [If children were cared for by the state,] mothers of the world would be free to experiment as to fathers for fit children, as a botanist experiments as to fertilizer for fit seed. What a preposterous thing that a woman should give children to the world by only one father! The Russian Communists have the right idea.
>
> Look at the race of run-down, lily-livered, stoop-

shouldered, dreary-minded American men who yearly
are becoming the fathers of the new generation of
little Americans. Why should a woman who is really a
mother at heart have to bear the children of one of
these sublimated essences of fiddle-dee-dees of fathers
to the sixth or eighth child? . . .

Perhaps, in some cases the father, in his youth,
was fit to be a father. But in his knock-kneed fifties he
is too hardheaded for anything spiritual to spring from
him. Then let his wife rotate the children crop just as
sensible farmers rotate the crop of potatoes. Let her
look about for a young father, fit to be perpetuated in
a child . . .

But it is not alone on the score of the family that
I so object to my native country. I object also because
my country has no imagination. When I tell my friends
that I love my husband because, when I slept, my soul
traveled off into space and joyed in finding his soul
there, they think I am crazy. When I explain that I was
a dancing girl on the Nile ten thousand years ago, and
that my husband was then a soldier, and that we two
were lovers and merely renewing the ancient associa-
tions now again centuries later in the year 1921, they
again think I am crazy. Ah, they understand not true
love which means to them nothing but a stereotyped
wedding ring.

It's the smugness, the sanctimonious righteous-
ness, the "God bless me and my wife, my son John and
his wife, us four and no more, Amen" quality to America which crushes my soul. As for me, I would rather
be free than be out of debt. I would rather see with
clear eyes than be a millionaire. I remember some
years ago a millionaire whom I associated with for
eight years. He wanted to marry me. But I shuddered
at the stall-fed project . . .

And I spurned the millionaire . . . said I, "I could
never be happy with matrimony which always ends it
all. I want revolution which cleanses. I want debts, if
I must have them. I want suffering and hardships and
love that is more cruel than pain. I want life and adven-

ture and the whole world. Who are you, with your millions, to try to capture my soul?" . . .

The curse of the United States is its humdrum old life, same yesterday, today and always. The curse of my country is its slavishness, mental and spiritual. Most of us in the United States are dead—all dead—at the top. Nothing new and progressive, like the Russian Revolution, can come out of America—[not] just yet, at any rate . . .

Bah! I am tired of the American hypocrites who lift their eyebrows at the barefoot dance; at the exposure of our bodies which should be the temple of god in man. Bah! Bah again! I have had about as much of a chance this winter in America as Christ had before Pilate. We both were doomed before we even spoke. When I think of some of the experiences I have lived through on my American tour it makes me want to be a Christian. It makes me feel even that mean . . .

There are, in the world, persons of three colors. There are the whites. Their color typifies a purity which is useless; a starved quality of the body and mind and emotions . . .

The next color is gray. They paint the walls of their Symphony Hall gray in Boston because that is the color of polite funerals and hearses where too much sadness is not desired. Gray is the color of Boston—people who are dead and buried already . . .

The last color of all is red. That's the color of the people who do the real work of the world . . . That's the color of the artists and the creators, the great soldiers and fighters and poets. And that's my color, praise the Lord! For you see, the color of my blood—I am glad, glad to say—is still red even after my American tour.

I have been in sad financial straits in America. That is one grudge I feel toward my country. She lets her artists starve. And my manager had me by the throat . . .

Routine, weary routine, the same old table in the middle of the same old floor, the same old books on the same old table—that's America.

But I will predict. I have seen the Russian revolutionists in Moscow standing in the street, some so poor that their feet are done up in newspapers for lack of shoes. I have seen the freedom in their faces, as they sang the *Internationale*, waving the red flag. I have seen your workers parade, also, down Fifth Avenue. I have watched the poor starved bodies, their weak backs and shrunken limbs. Yet I see, in those downtrodden, exploited ones, the promise of America.

Wake up, in time! Or else those crushed will start thinking . . . And on Fifth avenue, they will start up the *Internationale*, while the red flag is waving all about. After all, since red is the color of youth and promise and vigor and initiative and all virile creation, that may be the only cure possible for these dreary, routinized United States.

Once she had stood in silence with her hands on her solar plexus waiting for her soul to speak through the medium of her body. Now there is no waiting. There is only immediate outcry.

It is an accretion of rage, a confusion of rage, that merges past and present affronts indiscriminately.

It is rage against the Ideal, against all the Ideals that have been shattered—in France, in England, in Russia (yet only here does she feel free to express it).

For all its apparent sense of onslaught, it is rage deflated by a sense of impotence. No longer does she evoke herself as the daughter of Isis; when she speaks of her "Egyptian" connection, it is of having been an Egyptian "dancing girl."

PART
FIVE

61

In early 1923, while living quietly in London with her new husband, Howard Perch, Mary Desti received a wire from Isadora in America: "If you would save my life and reason meet me in Paris . . ."

Scraping together what money she could, Mary hurried to Paris to greet Isadora as she came off the boat train. Shortly afterward four guards descended from the train, "lifting and pulling what seemed like an enormous bundle of elegant furs. They righted the object which took the form of a man, plus an enormously high fur hat, which made him seem very tall and ferocious," writes Mary. It was Esenin, whom she had never met.

At once Isadora, though almost completely out of money, decided to take rooms at the expensive Hôtel Crillon. Her home on the rue de la Pompe was occupied by a tenant who would neither pay nor leave. At a "delicious little dinner Sergei recited some of his poems, and truly looked like a young god from Olympus, Donatello come to life, a dancing faun. He wasn't still a second, bounding here and there in ecstasy, now throwing himself on his knees before Isadora, laying his curly head in her lap like a tired child, while her lovely hands caressed him, and a Madonna-like radiance streamed from her eyes."

As Isadora had refused to order champagne, Esenin began to run out of the room at intervals. "Each time he returned he looked a bit paler," says Mary, "and Isadora more nervous. The last time he didn't come back for quite a while, so Isadora rang for the maid.

"The maid then told us he had come several times to her room and ordered champagne, but now he had gone out." At this point Isadora grew "melancholy" and told Mary that "Sergei is just a wee bit eccentric, and the longer he stays out the more eccentric he becomes. In fact if he does not come very soon, it might be as well for us to move to some other part of the hotel where he can't find us."

Appalled at the thought that he would hurt Isadora, Mary asked her why she put up with it, and Isadora answered, " 'Mary dear, I can't explain it. It would take much too long. And then there's something about it I like, something deep, deep in my life. Have you noticed a resemblance between Sergei and some one you once knew? . . . Can't you see the resemblance? He's the image of little Patrick . . .' "

Mary begged Isadora to leave, but Isadora insisted that she couldn't go until "I hear him coming." Soon they did hear him, storming down the hall, pounding on the door. "I dragged Isadora out and down the hall," writes Mary, "and we flew like fiends down the five flights of stairs," though Isadora insisted on stopping to ask the concierge to go up and look after her husband and to be "very gentle with him," as he was ill and she was going out to find a doctor for him.

From Mary's hotel room, Isadora telephoned the Crillon, only to learn that six policemen had just taken Esenin to the station, but not before he had beaten up a hotel porter, pushed a dressing table and couch through the window "without the precaution of first opening it" and had "broken every bit of furniture in the place." He had also threatened to shoot the police but couldn't find his revolver.

"Isadora almost swooned when she heard this. 'What shall we do, Mary? I haven't a cent. Sergei has the last of the money Lohengrin [Singer] sent us, and that is only a few dollars.' "

At last Mary and Isadora found a doctor and took him to

the police station to examine the raving Esenin. "The doctor now declared he was an epileptic and most dangerous; under no condition, should he be set at liberty. This last blow completely prostrated Isadora."

Returning to the Crillon at four A.M., they were asked to leave but Mary "took the manager aside" and persuaded him to allow them to remain until the morning. In the room, or rather what was left of the room—the beds were broken, the springs on the floor, and the sheets torn in shreds—Isadora calmed herself with a drink of brandy. Then she opened the (still intact) wardrobe and there discovered Esenin's locked attaché case. Reluctantly, at Mary's suggestion, Isadora opened the case with Esenin's keys (given to her by the police) and, to her astonishment, found two thousand dollars, all in small denominations. " 'My God, Mary, can it be possible that I have been harboring a viper in my bosom?' " she said, but immediately relented. " 'No, I can't believe it, poor little Sergei. I'm sure he didn't really know what it was about.' " Isadora decided that Esenin had only taken the money—and her clothes, which she also found in his trunks—for his poverty-stricken relatives and friends in Russia.

The next day the police informed Isadora that either Esenin must go to an institution or leave the country. At once Isadora sent her maid, with two tickets and "the last money that she had in the world," to take Esenin to Berlin. Then Mary and Isadora moved to another hotel, where, confined to bed with a fever, Isadora "could not be left alone for a second, night or day."

According to Mary, Esenin and his friends now "bombarded" Isadora with telegrams asking her to come to Berlin; otherwise he would commit suicide. " 'If you are really my friend,' " Isadora said, lying on her sickbed, " 'take me to Sergei or I will die. I can't live without him. I don't care what he has done. I love him and he loves me.' " Suddenly recovering, she told Mary to find out where they could get a car to take them to Berlin.

"Heavens!" writes Mary. "Here we were without a penny, yet she wanted to go by auto to Berlin. Nothing ever seemed impossible to her. She declared she could not get in a train."

The next day Isadora borrowed money from "an old rogue," giving as security three of Carrière's paintings that she treasured, and, evading the reporters who kept pursuing them, they rented a car and set off for Berlin.

"Now began one of the strangest journeys. Isadora must have thought herself the Flying Dutchman. She acted like a person demented; that nothing could stop. First the wretched car and chauffeur would go no farther than Strasbourg, leaving us completely in the lurch. Nothing daunted, Isadora immediately hired another, which almost at the moment of starting ran into the side of a bridge, breaking down. This forced us to stay the night in Strasbourg."

Refusing to sleep, Isadora insisted on going from restaurant to restaurant, from nightclub to nightclub, "anywhere and everywhere for excitement. And when I remonstrated with her, she replied in the most pathetic way, 'Why does no one ever let me enjoy myself as I like? I am doing no harm; I who pass my life giving happiness to others. Why must I always sit on a pedestal like a Chinese god?' "

When they returned from their night out, Mary fell into bed, but Isadora woke her soon after, telling her that they were on a great adventure and couldn't waste time sleeping. "Heavens! I thought I would go to sleep standing up. So on we went, I grumbling a bit, but Isadora was like the sun; she smiled and you would go to your death foolishly, feeling you were doing some great brave deed. She always made you feel so wonderful, that you were a superior sort of God-sent being . . . And to me she was always as near perfection as any one on earth could ever be."

In the morning, with the car repaired, they traveled on as rapidly as possible. By midnight they found themselves in a small village, "high in the mountains." Now this driver refused to take them any farther. Once again, exhausted, Mary fell into bed, this time in a "dismal" hotel. But within an hour, Isadora, bearing champagne and sandwiches, woke her up and told her she had arranged for yet another car. " 'Up, Mary, up,' she said . . . 'I have a presentiment that Sergei is dying; that he has shot himself.' I was so tired and sleepy that I really didn't mind if he had, but Isadora was beside herself, and I thought if she could endure it, so could I. It was one of the terrible nights of my life."

What are we to make of this word *terrible* in the midst of this tale that reads like farce? Is Mary accurate in her reporting? Or is that not the right question to ask about Mary's writing?

In the rush of events, of telling of one life and then another, do all voices begin to "jam" each other? Where is Isadora's rage that we heard in the letter to Hearst's *American Weekly*? Was it dissipated by its expression, or has it simply been transformed into something else, into motion, into anxiety, into further motion producing more anxiety? Or was it never "simply" rage to begin with?

Seroff, of course, believes almost nothing Mary Desti says. Blaming her for almost everything that happened, he insists that the "very sight of this obese, loud-mouthed, middle-aged woman repelled Esenin." He suggests that "Sergei would have been well advised to supply her [Mary] with a gigolo for her more pressing needs, for her role of policeman only incited him to an almost routine violence"—as if Mary's sexual frustration—which he assumes—were to blame for Esenin's behavior. But what does any of this have to do with "blame," anyway?

What is all this about, if it's not about the terrible seen yet rejected, the image of the terrible converted into and through motion?

"All through Germany we saw nothing but the greatest suffering. Women were climbing on milk wagons begging for just a drop of milk," Mary writes of one stopping place. But they do not stop for suffering. Only momentarily aware of the anger of the villagers watching them, they continue in their headlong rush.

Undeterred by fog or bad roads, or their car being without headlights, Isadora urges the driver on to full speed to get to Berlin. "Isadora was always happy in an automobile going anywhere," Mary tells us. "Swift movement was as necessary to her as breathing. She only lived when going like mad, resting now and then for food and drink, which usually consisted of rare roast beef, salad, and champagne." But Mary cowers in the car; she is "doubly anxious" now.

On impulse, in the midst of this mad dash to Berlin, Isadora ordered the driver to make a detour. "In spite of Isadora's anxiety about Sergei, she couldn't resist passing through Bayreuth, although it took us hours out of our way. No, we must once more embrace Frau Cosima . . ." Isadora had met Cosima

Wagner in the summer of 1904, when she had danced at the Bayreuth Festival and Mary had been with her at the time. Now, almost twenty years later, they appeared unannounced for a reunion with her in Bayreuth at midnight. "As we could not see Frau Cosima, we begged the host of the inn to be kind enough to send her in the morning one hundred of the most beautiful American Beauty roses possible to find with love from both of us."

At dinner at the inn Isadora struck up a conversation with a "very charming" young man, on his way to Leipzig, who also happened to be a racing driver and had his hundred-horsepower car with him. "He offered to take us; so we bade goodbye to the old tin can we had been riding in and started for Leipzig at one A.M." With Isadora in front next to the driver, urging him on to ever greater speed, Mary, alone in the back, "passed a few unhappy hours." Suddenly something white loomed up in front of them, and the car hit a pile of broken stone on the highway. "We hadn't noticed that the road had been barred, but the car righted itself and started on its way as if nothing had happened."

This time even Isadora seemed "shaken," and when Mary threatened to get out and walk if they didn't slow down, Isadora quieted the "racing chauffeur." Leaving the young man in Leipzig (madly in love with Isadora, says Mary), they rented another car and finally arrived in Berlin at ten at night.

"As we drove up in front of the Hotel Adlon . . . a flying leap landed Sergei in our car, he having bounded straight on to the engine, over the chauffeur's head into Isadora's arms . . ."

From this moment on, it is as if Isadora's rage to motion has been transferred to Esenin. She is once again the famous performer, spending grandly, taking over elegant hotel suites, giving lavish parties with expensive food, with vodka—all on credit. And he is gathering momentum for yet more leaps, yet more outbreaks. It is as if the two of them are caught in a dance from which they cannot extricate themselves. He grows violent, she endures the violence, he takes the violence further, she retreats from him, he brings the episode to a crashing, destructive climax. He becomes still—is stilled. She relents, feels love for the "poor wild little boy," this "sweet little impractical child," who knows no better, and returns to him. The dance begins again. The scenes repeat, but they are of increasing intensity, of greater destructiveness. It is finally not possible to tell who is driving whom.

Mary herself begins to wonder: "What had come over the gentle, timid Isadora? Russia had surely changed her, changed her character. I do believe that if he had never attacked her, she would never have resented these spells [of his], as they were so in keeping with the awful inner torment from which she never ceased to suffer. They had the same soothing effect on her as a mad, racing auto or airplane—the utter disregard for everything conventional and for all life that had so brutally destroyed her, seemed to give her some respite from sorrow."

But even Mary finds she is "getting pretty well fed up." Though by now, she says, she is only an "onlooker," Isadora will not let her go; nor indeed is Mary able to let go. Isadora now insists that they must return to Paris, and Mary promises that she will help her get there. Mary takes the train to Paris, manages to raise some money, and wires it to Isadora, who hires yet another car and finally arrives, with Esenin in tow.

At once she takes a suite at one of the best hotels, the Carlton. The management invites her and her party to be their guests at a gala dinner. In the midst of the celebration, Isadora gets up and dances a tango with a professional dancer. Esenin, drinking more and more champagne, rants at her dancing of the tango, and she in turn insults him. Esenin walks out of the hotel, comes back and breaks up the furniture in his own room, and then tries to break into Isadora's room. She calls the management and requests a "strong porter" to restrain him. The hotel replies that they have no such porter, but that they will send for the police. Isadora yells this to Esenin through the door; he gives the door a kick and leaves. She, "wild with excitement and fearing some one would hurt him," blames it all on the hotel.

"I had never seen her in such a mood," writes Mary. "She seemed to be searching utter destruction . . ." Rushing out to find him, Isadora leaves the hotel and goes to a café, where she orders the most expensive Napoleon brandy, which she distributes liberally to the "dancing girls" at the other tables. Meanwhile, Esenin, who has gone to a Russian restaurant and insulted the owners, formerly officers in the czar's army, is beaten up and thrown into the gutter. He is picked up by a taxi and is brought back to the hotel.

"Isadora went to bed more dead than alive, and the next morning the manager was up bright and early, saying we must leave immediately. I told him it was impossible, that Miss Duncan was very ill. He said that didn't matter, they would carry her out the back way where they had a special entrance for sick people and the dead. Isadora was so ill that I was afraid she was dying. She lay with glazed eyes, not seeing or understanding anything.

"Sergei was all tenderness and greatly worried about her, besides being greatly frightened that the police would come and lock him up. As I didn't go mad with all this, I believe I am safe forever. The management finally refused to talk about the thing, simply insisting that we leave.

"I sent for Raymond [Duncan], begging him to come at once with a good doctor, which he did. The doctor gave a certificate stating that it was absolutely dangerous for Miss Duncan to be moved at all, and that she had been poisoned . . . This poisoning rather frightened [the manager] as she had dined in the hotel . . . the night before . . .

"They didn't bother us any more and the next day we all went to the Reservoir Hotel at Versailles. It was a delightful little pavilion . . ."

According to Irma Duncan and Allan Ross Macdougall, soon after the return from Berlin, Isadora and Esenin were able to move into her house on the rue de la Pompe, as the tenant had finally vacated it. Here Esenin's frenzy (and Isadora's) seemed to abate. As they were still penniless, however, Isadora began to sell pieces of furniture to be able to buy food and drink for herself and Esenin and their staff and their continual dinner guests.

Suddenly Isadora decided to give several performances, but she was unable to find an impresario to arrange them. Raymond and her secretary took it upon themselves to manage two performances for her at the Trocadéro, one on May 27 and the other on June 3. After the first performance, by no means a full house, Isadora gave a talk to the audience, insisting she was not a "Bolshevist," and asking for money for her school in Russia. Of the children and her dance she said, "Place your hands as I do on your heart, listen to your soul, and all of you will know how to dance as well as I or my pupils do . . . There is the true revolution. Let the people place their hands in this way on their hearts, and in listening to their souls they will know how to conduct themselves."

Following the performance, Isadora held a reception for friends at her home. Once again Esenin fell into violence, threw a candelabrum at a mirror, and when the servants tried to hold him, kicked and screamed. The police were called and he was taken to a sanitarium. After the second performance, Isadora decided to return to Russia with Esenin.

62

For the fifteen months that Isadora was away in Europe and America, Irma had maintained the Russian school, teaching the children and acting as the director, with the assistance of the secretary, Ilya Schneider. While Isadora was present, Irma had never been allowed to perform in the Soviet Union, except to lead the pupils on stage for the "Internationale" during the finale of Isadora's concerts. But in the spring and early summer of 1923, while Isadora was in Paris, Irma had given a series of successful performances in Moscow on her own.

Now—August 5, 1923—she went with Schneider to the train station to meet Isadora and Esenin. Esenin, according to Irma, was wild with drink and with joy at being back in Moscow, and in his fervor had smashed all the windows of the coach.

In the afternoon Isadora hired a car—"a rare and expensive thing in the Moscow of those days"—for the drive to Litvino, a village fifty miles from Moscow, where the children of the school were spending the summer. But the next day, Esenin insisted on returning to Moscow, and Isadora and Irma accompanied him. The moment Esenin got to the house in Moscow, he left and no word came from him for three days. On the third day Isadora opened one of his trunks—one of those same trunks that Mary had seen in Paris. As Irma tells it, Esenin, returning at that moment, screamed "like one demented, 'My trunks! Who's been meddling with my trunks? Don't you dare touch my trunks. I'll kill the person who touches my trunks . . .' "

A pulling match occurred, with Isadora and Esenin fighting over a dress of Isadora's, one of the innumerable objects he had squirreled away in the trunk. Finally, Isadora told him, as he prepared to leave once again, that if he went away without telling her where he was going, it was the end between them. Further, Isadora added, she was going for a vacation to a health resort in the Caucasus that night. Esenin left but appeared at the train to tell her good-bye. Isadora tried to persuade him to come with her and Irma but he refused.

After a week at the spa, Isadora grew restless and decided to tour the Caucasus with Irma. Despite not having practiced for months, she felt able to—she needed to—perform. She danced at theaters and at workers' clubs; she gave free performances for the children of workers.

One matinee, when Irma was ill and could not dance her part of the program, a group of Isadora's early works, Isadora danced them herself. Irma watched while she danced these "creations of love and adolescent joy, of ecstasy and happy grace . . . that she had not danced for many seasons. To the music of Gluck, Schubert, Brahms, Chopin," Irma writes, "she danced all the girlish ecstasies and raptures with an artless joy and an effortless grace. By the great power of her dominating will and the magic of her genius, she caught the spirit of fleeting youth and held it captive for an afternoon."

Here was Irma, a young woman in her twenties, watching her "mother," now forty-six but looking older than her age, thirty or forty pounds overweight, re-create those pieces that she had created when she was a young girl, going back in time, becoming that young girl. (Perhaps it was always there, waiting to be brought forth in Isadora, this idealized image of that innocent, virginal girl—and the more it was refused in life, the greater became the urgency for it to surface in dance.)

But if Isadora, performing, before the eyes of others, grasped that image, overcame it, even became it in her dance, in that other dance—the one with Esenin—the image she had grasped for—the mother-sister-wife—was slipping away irrevocably.

According to Gordon McVay, Esenin's biographer, all of his friends who met him again after his return from abroad agreed that "he was 'a broken man,' 'a different person,' ill and irritable . . . 'A kind of impenetrable darkness enveloped his sick consciousness.' "

He seemed simultaneously to have become more an actor in appearance and less so in behavior. " 'There was something strange about his face, powdered like an actor's, and his hair, which had been curled at the hairdresser's. And only when I went up to him did a sad feeling of alarm oppress my heart,' " one friend said. Mariengoff noticed that " 'whereas, before his foreign trip, the poet's scandals were calculated and cunning (he hurled unbreakable plates on the floor, and broke windows after first taking the precaution of protecting his fist), now they were uncontrolled and sick.' "

Along with his obsessions about the trunks, which he had moved to Mariengoff's lodgings, Esenin had another obsession—that he had to get away from Isadora. Yet he could not break with her directly; he needed help to be able to do it. From the Caucasus, where she was still performing, Isadora kept bombarding him with telegrams and letters, expressing her undying love for him, saying she was expecting him to come and join her, entreating him, summoning him. By late September, however, Esenin had moved into the flat of Galina Benislavskaya, a young woman who had become his "devoted friend and nurse." He kept asking her to help him to extricate himself from his present state and to break finally with Isadora. He had once felt, he said, a "great passion" for Isadora, but now it was over. " 'When I felt passion, I saw nothing but now . . . my God, how blind I was?! Where were my eyes?' "

In October Esenin sent a telegram to Isadora, saying, "Don't send any more letters telegrams [to] Esenin he is with me and won't join you must count on his not returning to you." And he signed it, "Galina Benislavskaya."

At first frantic over his telegram, then persuaded that

Esenin was being misled by his friends, Isadora returned to Moscow and tried to find him. In fact, he had left the city out of panic over meeting her again. He returned to Moscow shortly afterward, and eventually showed up at Isadora's house, raving and drunk. The first time he came he screamed at Isadora that he loved another woman and that he had made two other women pregnant, and Schneider threw him out of the house. He appeared a second time, one day in November, so drunk he could barely stand, yet insistent on retrieving a wooden bust of himself, carved by an artist friend. It was as if he feared even to leave an image of himself in Isadora's possession.

After this visit, Isadora never saw Esenin again.

Mary Desti has a different story of Isadora's last meeting with Esenin, though she was not in Moscow at the time, so her version, says McVay, "presumably deserves little credence."

"When alone," writes Mary, "Isadora would sit for hours with an immense album of her children's pictures . . . One evening when Sergei came home unexpectedly, he found Isadora seated weeping over this book of her dear lost ones. In a paroxysm of rage he snatched the album from her and before she could stop him, threw it in the roaring fire. Isadora would have torn it from the flames but he held her with his mad, superhuman force, taunting her about her children."

Irma and Macdougall repeat the same episode, though they put it in a different sequence, placing it in Berlin in 1922, and conclude the incident with Esenin crying out in a drunken rage, "You spend too much time thinking of these [deleted expletive] children!"

Seroff also reprints this version of the last meeting between Isadora and Esenin. He presents it only as "a much discussed scene," without attribution, and gives it yet another ending. In his version, when Esenin came upon Isadora crying over the photographs of her children, he shouted at Isadora, "I am your husband—your man . . ."

Seroff, though himself opposed to the idea that Isadora's feelings toward Esenin had any relation to her feelings for her son, does add a remark made by Esenin to Nina Tabidze, the wife of a Georgian poet: "When we first met," Esenin told her,

"Isadora was stunned by my resemblance to her dead boy. This was the main thing that brought us together, but I saw something unnatural in it . . ."

On New Year's Eve, Isadora telephoned Mariengoff's wife and asked her to come to her house to spend the evening. Madame Mariengoff said that at the moment she had guests at her house and asked Isadora to join them. She warned Isadora, however, that among the guests was Augusta Miklashevskaya, a young actress to whom Esenin had recently dedicated a cycle of love poems. "Then I will come right away," Isadora answered.

Miklashevskaya later wrote an account of that meeting with Isadora:

> She astonished me by her unnaturally theatrical appearance. She was wearing a transparent pale-green chiton with gold lace, belted by a golden braid with golden tassels. She had on golden sandals and lace stockings. On her head was a turban, adorned with colorful beads. Over her shoulders she had something that resembled a raincoat, or a cape of dark green velvet texture. This was not a woman, this was some kind of theatrical king.
>
> She looked at me and said: "Esenin is in a hospital, you should take him fruit and flowers." Then suddenly she tore the turban off her head, as if to say, "I have made an impression on Miklashevskaya—now I can throw it away," and she threw the turban into a corner of the room.
>
> Then she became more simple, more animated. One could never be offended by her—she was much too charming. "All of Europe knows [said Isadora in her faulty Russian] that Esenin was my husband and suddenly—he sang about love—to you, not me! There is a bad poem: *You are so simple like all . . .* That is for you . . ."
>
> It was getting late, a long time past the hour to go home, but Duncan did not want to leave. It began to be daylight. We had turned off the electricity. Gray dim light changed everything. Isadora sat bent down,

looking older, crushed. "I do not want to leave. I have no place to go. I have nobody. I am all alone."

Esenin was to die in late December 1925, a suicide by hanging. A month previously he had published "The Black Man," a poem about his double—something Isadora refused to recognize—the dark side of his being.

63

In the early spring of 1924, reports Irma, Isadora toured the Ukraine. In one town after another she had an enormous success, giving eighteen performances in Kiev. She opened her concerts with two funeral marches dedicated to Lenin, who had died in January.

A number of the works Isadora choreographed in the Soviet Union had a direct tie to what was taking place in the society at the time as well as to the existing ideology. Yet to the eyes of today's viewer—I should say, to my eyes—these dances (as reconstituted) to work songs, or popular revolutionary songs, hold two conflicting strains in uneasy juxtaposition. The Duncan technique—upward motion, idealized, arising from the solar plexus, continuous, carried, sustained, flowing—strains against a technique that seems superimposed—of motion downward into the earth, of exaggerated realism, focusing on the limbs or the lower part of the torso.

But it was these very dances that her audiences applauded so ecstatically, as if through these works they were seeing the creation of their own secular mythology.

Offstage, on the streets of the famine-ridden Ukraine, Isadora "was hailed and cheered by the people," write Irma and Macdougall. "The beggars followed her about crying, 'Duncan, Duncan, Beautiful Lady, give us bread!' And Isadora, like a queen, scattered largesse in the form of copper kopecks. She had a theory that one must never knowingly incur a beggar's curse . . . One day as the beggars crowded about the restaurant where she was dining, she ordered the waiter to give all the snivelling, whining army, plates of *borscht*. After that she was never rid of them . . ."

No longer a goddess, dispensing light and joy, she was now, out in the world, a queen with an audience of "beggars" who demanded and demanded—not spiritual but actual—food.

In June she started out on yet another tour of the Ukraine, this time with Irma, fifteen pupils, and a full symphony orchestra. That this was a totally impossible project financially became evident after the first two weeks in Kiev. The orchestra and Irma and the pupils were sent back to Moscow. Only Isadora, her pianist, Mark Metchick, and the manager, Boris Zinoviev, went on.

According to Seroff, "Anyone with even the most elementary knowledge of the geography of that country, and its climatic conditions, would have known better than to suggest a tour through the provinces, scorched by summer heat. But to Isadora a boat trip on the Volga River, and the Oriental splendor of Samarkand and mysterious Tashkent, sounded so romantic that . . . she set off with her two companions . . . on this ill-chosen adventure."

Whatever Isadora was pursuing—romance, as Seroff thinks, or escape into new myth—what she found was, in her words, "catastrophe." Heat, dirt, bedbugs, poverty, absence of transportation, and rejection by the public all came together, as she told Irma in a series of letters that summer:

Samara, June 20, 1924:
Here is more catastrophe. We can't get from one town to another!!! and the curtains have not arrived. I have given three horrible performances before grey scenery and *white* lights. And we have not a kopeck. We leave this Volga, which I prefer to remember from a distance. No public, no comprehension—Nothing.

Boats frightfully crowded with screaming children
and chattering women . . .

This journey is a *Calvaire* . . .

Yours in unholy martyrdom,

Poor Isadora

Hell of a life, anyway.

Samarkand, the end of June:
We go from one catastrophe to another. Arrived in
Tashkent without a kopeck. Found theatre full of
Geltzer [the ballerina, Yekaterina Geltser], whole
town occupied. We had to go to an awful hotel where
they demanded "dingy" [money] in advance and, fail-
ing, would not give us a samovar. We wandered round
the town *without even a cup of tea* all day. In the
evening we went to see Geltzer dance to a packed
house! After a second hungry day Darling [Zinoviev]
pawned his valise with two costumes for just enough
to come here . . . I feel a bit dilapidated . . . The country
here is divine, fruits and trees and all like a garden—
very hot but lovely. But it's a terrible sensation to
walk about without a penny . . . Well, we're hoping for
better luck. So far the tour is a tragedy. Why did we
leave Friday the 13th? . . .

Taskhent, July 10:
This tournée is a continual catastrophe . . . Again no
hotel . . . Spent two days wandering around the streets
very hungry . . . Finally we found rooms in this fearful
hotel over-run with vermin. We are so bitten as to
appear to have some illness . . .

Courage; it's a long way, but light is ahead. My art
was the flower of an epoch, but that epoch is dead and
Europe is the past. These red tuniced kids [of the
school] are the future. So it is fine to work for them.
Plough the ground, sow the seed, and prepare for the
next generation that will express the new world. What
else is there to do? . . .

You are my only disciple and with you I see the
Future . . .

Tashkent, July 19:
In fifty degrees [Centigrade] heat and . . . in a fearful room . . . I think my last hour is come. Metchick was a gay and wild Lothario when you knew him, compared to what he is now . . . Darling [Zinoviev] also receiving a lot of starving telegrams, has settled into a fearful gloom. I spend my nights in feverish bed-bug hunts and listening to the dogs howl. *C'est très amusante.*

Wednesday is the first performance but—no sale.

When you have an inspiration to save us, for heaven's sake act on it for it is the last moment . . .

I keep on making jokes which are not appreciated; but it's my Irish way.

Well, farewell.

This is probably my last gasp.

With all my love to everyone.

Poor Isadora.

Ekaterinaburg, August 4:
You have no idea what a living nightmare is until you see this town . . .

Our two performances were a *four noire* [failure], and, as usual, we are stranded and don't know where to go. There is no restaurant here, only "common eating houses" and no coiffure . . .

Darling rushes from one bureau to another in search of dingy only to learn that *they* don't like me at all, and don't approve of me. In fact this town is as near Hell as anything I have ever met . . .

Vyatka, August 12:
I haven't a bottle of eau de cologne, no soap nor tooth paste since a month. The beds are made of *boards* and populated. The stains and pistol shots in the mirror. *C'est très amusante.* My hair is quite white from lack of henna shampoo and I feel extremely *kaput* . . .

With love to the children and love to you

Sterbende [Dying] Isadora

It is all of a piece, this tale of the catastrophic—the exaggeration, the joking, the mythmaking, the fearful energy that drives her on, from which she draws yet more energy. At the same time, it is prelude to an ending, as shown in several sentences, tossed off as if they were an afterthought of the moment, in a letter from Tashkent: "But this is a primitive, wild place, and anything can happen to one. It's the sort of place to come with Lohengrin and his millions; very like Egypt. The heat is forty degrees [Centigrade], more in the shade and flies, bugs, mosquitoes make life unbearable."

Whatever she was looking for on this "ill-chosen adventure," she has found another Egypt—not the Egypt of mystery, of transcendence, of mystical vibrations, but an Egypt of heat, of flies, of bugs, of mosquitoes, an Egypt become life "unbearable."

64.

Two women traveled up the Nile —one who lived through sight, the other who lived through motion—to see the enormous stone still forms, to see the immense verticals in the "low and level" landscape, to see the tombs with the wall paintings, the world of ancient Egypt.

It was a world that did not think in terms of sequence as we know it, of cause and effect. It was a world in which all phenomena were only momentary flashes of a timeless and boundless universe. It was a world that saw its own existence as a mirror image of the realm of the gods, that saw the particular only as an aspect of the vast and un-differentiated. It was a world that made no sharp distinc-tions between states of being—human and animal, living and dead, human and divine. It was a world that saw all phenomena as essentially of one substance, "blended in-to a great spectrum of overlapping colors without sharp margins."

It was a world in which a single word meant both "celestial glory" and "daily utility."

If to the ancient Egyptians their daily existence was a mirror, revealing the order of the gods, to these two women, who came so many centuries later—at a time in their lives and in their world, when everything was about to change—Egypt was another kind of mirror. (For one whose mirror image had always given her delight—for the other who had looked and had flinched and had looked again, not accepting what was given . . .)

One woman who came to Egypt had embraced the mythic as Ideal and the Ideal as mythic in her own being, in her own body, and if she did not refuse the daily, she thought of it as what had to be transcended. The other woman who came to Egypt had refused the Ideal, refused the mythic, had found her being, her purpose, in that which she saw—in surface, on surface, in the visible object, in the way light reflected from surface, a woman who lived in and through the daily.

Still young, one came believing herself to be the daughter of the goddess, but a daughter who chose only beauty, who refused the ugly, who refused suffering, who was treated as a goddess, daughter of a woman who was mother-child to her, daughter of a dark shadow, still shadowed by the male, bearing a child . . .

The other woman came to Egypt no longer young, never having borne a child, having become the painter of mothers and babies, having fought off death for mother and sister and having lost them, and having lost as well father and brothers, having held off darkness—though once, twice, ten years before, she had almost allowed it—having chosen above all to see the visible, the specific, the daily, having wanted the power of the male, daughter of a mother who had preferred her sons, having seen or chosen to show in the female image what was charming, loving, "the mother," not the "Mother."

To the ancient Egyptians the Great Mother, the Great Goddess, the one who put the king on the throne, the one who was the throne itself, was Isis. She tolerated all, she refused nothing; she was the destroyer as well as the giver of life.

Isadora at age three, 1880. SAN FRANCISCO PERFORMING
ARTS LIBRARY AND MUSEUM. PHOTOGRAPH BY EICHEN-
BERGER, OAKLAND.

ABOVE: *Isadora at twelve; photograph taken in Fresno, California.* SAN FRANCISCO PERFORMING ARTS LIBRARY AND MUSEUM. PHOTOGRAPH BY CREVEL.

OPPOSITE: *Isadora Duncan by Arnold Genthe (ca. 1915– 1917).* MUSEUM OF THE CITY OF NEW YORK.

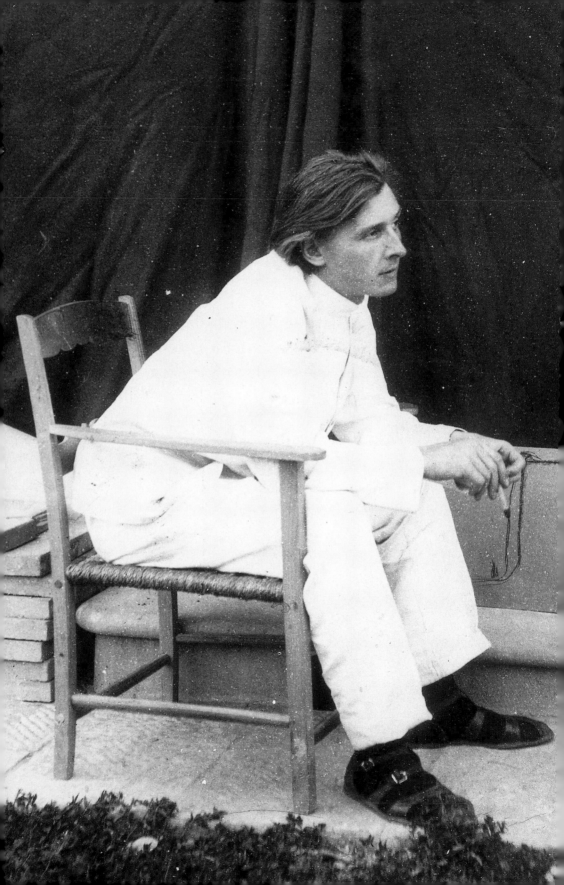

ABOVE: *Isadora Duncan by Arnold Genthe (ca. 1915–1917).*
MUSEUM OF THE CITY OF NEW YORK.

OPPOSITE: *Gordon Craig, 1907.* DEPARTMENT OF SPECIAL
COLLECTIONS, UNIVERSITY LIBRARY, UNIVERSITY OF CALI-
FORNIA AT LOS ANGELES.

ABOVE: Isadora and Esenin in New York, 1922. SAN FRAN-
CISCO PERFORMING ARTS LIBRARY AND MUSEUM.

OPPOSITE: Isadora and Paris Singer. MUSEUM OF THE
CITY OF NEW YORK.

Isadora by Genthe. MUSEUM OF THE CITY OF NEW YORK.

65

It has been fifteen years, give or take a few, since they went to Egypt, fifteen years since what we call the modern—we have no better word—has taken hold.

Fifteen years in which the relation between cause and effect has altered—the relation of the present to the past, the present to the future, the relation between levels of abstraction, between the specific and the general have all altered.

There has been a change in the way people see, there has been a change in the way people move.

Now there is an uncertainty about vision, about the place of the observer relative to the object, about the way seeing itself alters vision, about the way the observer alters the object.

There is an uncertainty about motion, even, especially in one's own body. As early as 1902 Rilke foresaw how these "new gestures" were taking hold:

> The gestures of mankind . . . have become more impatient, more nervous, more abrupt and hasty . . .
> These movements have at the same time also

become more hesitant. No longer do they possess that gymnastic and resolute directness with which earlier men came to grips with everything. They are not like those movements preserved in ancient works of sculpture, gestures for which only the starting point and the end point were important. Numberless transitions have been introduced between these two simple moments, and it is evident that the entire life of contemporary man, all his actions and his inability to act, has taken place within these intervening states. His grasp has changed, his beckoning, his letting-go and holding. In everything he is much more experienced, and yet at the same time unknowing. He exhibits much less spirit and a perpetual concern with opposition, more despair at loss, more deprecation, judgment, deliberation, and less spontaneity.

Predictable patterns—wavelike forms—have given way to quantum forms, to discontinuities. Distinctions have grown blurred between the private and the public, between inner and outer, object and subject, depth and surface. It has become necessary to allow what is not beautiful, not good—to see in the ugly, the repugnant, the terrible, all that has been held so grimly in shadow: awesomeness . . .

Then how could lives, the idea of a life, the story of a life not change?

66

December 7, 1924, from the Central Hotel in Berlin, Isadora to Mary Desti:

"I am here *stranded* in this awful city—since two months & can't move—I think you'll be hearing of my funeral very soon. If this reaches you for Heaven's sake send me a word—I also wrote to Augustin without an answer Beginning to feel haven't a friend in the World . . ."

March 24, 1925, from Nice, Isadora to Mary Desti:

"You never answer my letters . . . I got nervous prostration since Margot's death [Margot was one of the Duncan Dancers]—it opened too many old wounds—I could find no place to live or work in Paris—I have taken a *Studio Theatre* here by the Sea . . . I am stranded as usual and have no money to fix it up—on receiving this if you can telegraph me $200 I could get my carpet from Paris & a Piano—& work again . . . Conditions in Russia make my return there impossible unless the Government does something for the School as the Children are starving & no one will help me . . ."

Late spring of 1925, from Nice, Isadora to Mary Desti:

"I am installed in my studio but that left me with 50 francs—that is $2. I am quite *alone* here. The wound in my arm is healing [apparently an infection from an insect bite] but I still can't use it—

"I asked Augustin & Margherita [Augustin's wife] why they don't come over for the summer—They could play in the Theatre & swim in the Sea—Are you coming over?—What are your plans? I have had two or three strange fainting fits—& think I'm almost ready for the next world—Say nothing to Augustin but still if you all want to see me again you better come rather quickly—

"If you could manage between you to send me $50 a week till the Autumn when I have a *Contract*— I could repay you by November—"

From "Isadora Really," a memoir by the English artist Sir Francis Rose:

> I was a precious, spoilt youth, full of Jean Cocteau's ideas, when Isadora Duncan swept into my life like an exotic wind with all her red veils, lobsters, baskets, and "pigeons" flying. She was a goddess of madness—of mad freedom—and of liberty without a torch . . .
>
> It was in the hot summer months of an empty Riviera in 1925 that I met her. She was drunk on the terrace of the wooden shack of a fisherman's bar in Villefranche . . .
>
> Isadora was half asleep; her Grecian face was resting on her plump folded arms on the dirty table top. A large glass of acid-green "pastis" was next to her. The wind blew her untidy orange hair in all directions. Around her were a mess of magenta and red draperies. Somewhere amongst the folds she had lost a wicker basket, covered with peeling gold paint, filled with a couple of live green-grey *langoustes* and one rosepink cooked one.
>
> Isadora looked at me and said something rude as she groped about in the folds. She had taken me for one of her two "pigeons," a couple of pretty American

homosexuals she had found bathing . . . on the beach
at Nice. "For Christ's sake, stop those lobsters screaming," she mumbled sleepily in a thick American voice.
Then she woke up and she looked at me again, and I
knew that we would immediately become friends.
"Hello," she said, with a marvellous smile and suddenly sobered blue eyes. From that moment her voice
became beautiful to me.

Isadora Duncan had an exceptional voice combined with the eyes of a genius. She was a generous
and a very great artist. Even at that time . . . every
gesture she made was a statement. She was far away
in a shrine of her own to any young man; even in her
drunkenness she was stimulating. Her perpetual faux
pas were amusing, as though she were as simple as a
child . . .

Jean Cocteau and René Crével occasionally visited
her to see if this curiosity of the past was still alive.
She was surrounded by a couple of old cronies, women
who were devoted to her . . . Her friend Mary stood
firmly by her side.

The two young "pigeons" looked after her . . . and
for a long time I visited her daily in a flat on the first
floor of an Art Nouveau building which stood up all
alone like a thin sandwich at the very end of the Promenade des Anglais in Nice, facing the ramshackle fret-
work porches of the Henri Plage . . .

On a dusty vacant lot next door, with a couple of
dying palm trees, stood a kind of large shed or garage,
stuccoed a faded pink salmon; the windows were
boarded up, and on the peeling blue paint on the small
door were a lot of graffiti; in the centre a heart, with
the signature Jean deeply engraved. This was Cocteau's symbol at this time . . . This building looked
abandoned and unoccupied, as a lot of rubbish was
piled around it . . . but it was here that Isadora worked
and danced . . .

Every day Isadora drove down the Promenade des
Anglais, in an open fiacre drawn by a very old horse,
wearing one of her red, orange, or magenta togas,

chosen to clash with the color of her hair. These togas looked as though they were made of sheets dyed in a hurry for a party in an American art school . . .

From *Miss Mary Cassatt: Impressionist from Pennsylvania*, by Frederick A. Sweet, an entry on Mary's last years:
"Mary Cassatt's life went very much by routine, and she would allow for no change in her accustomed mode. Her chauffeur, Armand Delaporte, recalls her motoring habits:
" 'Mademoiselle had only the one automobile from 1906–1926, a 20 horsepower Renault landau, license number of the car registered in Oise 702-1-3. She enjoyed and expected a daily drive, regardless of the weather as she was never cold. She insisted that the car be in a running order and would not allow a breakdown. She would not permit this despite the severe blindness with which she was afflicted. She was keenly aware of the places in which she was, to the point that one day February, 1925, Miss Cassatt severely reproached me for having changed the route which we were accustomed to take to Saint Cloud.' "

From writer Robert McAlmon's section of *Being Geniuses Together*, an incident, undated, probably 1925 or 1926:
"Laurence Vail had an exhibition of paintings in Mina's [Mina Loy's] shop [in Paris], and Isadora Duncan attended it. She drank copiously of the punch that was furnished, and went across the street to drink more at a bistro bar, and returned to talk grandly of what paintings she would purchase. As she was then living more or less on charity, nobody took poor Isadora seriously."

From *Here Lies the Heart*, the autobiography of Mercedes de Acosta:

The night I returned to Paris [in 1926] I ran into a man I knew who said, "I know you are a friend of Isadora Duncan's. I hear she has behaved so badly that everyone has abandoned her. I am told that she is in a hotel on the Left Bank, practically starving." I had not heard any of this and I hoped it was only gossip, but when I went to bed I couldn't sleep. Around two o'clock in the morning I could stand it no longer. I got up and dressed, hailed a taxi, and explained rather hopelessly to the driver that I was looking for someone in a small hotel . . . At three in the morning I gave up and we started back, but driving along the Boulevard Raspail we came to the Lutetia. I had not thought of it before because it was large and expensive. (Little did I know Isadora in those days—nothing was too large or expensive for her at any time.) . . . A porter was washing the sidewalk and as a last effort I stopped the taxi and asked him if by any chance Madame Isadora Duncan might be staying there. To my intense delight he assured me that she was . . .

"Room sixty-seven," the porter said . . . I knocked timidly [on Isadora's door] and hearing *"Entrez!"* I opened the door. Facing me and sitting up in bed was Isadora. A small lamp was lighted on the table beside her, but a scarf (the eternal scarf) was thrown over it, and the room was in semidarkness. "Archangel!" exclaimed Isadora.

(I was dressed in a white cape without a hat and she afterwards told me she had been lying there praying for help at that moment. As I stood in the doorway the light from the ceiling in the hallway fell on my head in rays, and for a moment she really thought I was a celestial being.)

"I thought you were an archangel from another world come to help me in answer to my prayers," she said . . .

I told her what I had heard about her and how I had found her. I discovered that she owed the hotel a large bill and that the management had refused her any further service . . . She did not have a sou and was staying in bed because she had been living on biscuits for nearly a week . . . I asked her why her friends hadn't helped her.

"I have spent their money and not repaid them," she said, in that childlike voice she often assumed.

"Did they ever think you would repay them?" I asked, laughing.

"That's just it. I spent their money which is just what they should have expected me to do. What else is money for but spending?" . . .

"Yes," I said. "I suppose money is to be spent—at least if it's your own money."

"Money is only dirty paper and dirty silver and dirty copper. Everyone knows that money is full of germs. People should be glad to have those horrid germs taken from them," she said.

I was forced to laugh at this. Then she plaintively added, "Please don't scold me. I am hungry."

I called the porter and, tipping him well, told him to go to the nearest café and bring us a roast chicken, bread, butter, and a bottle of wine. "Two bottles!" Isadora called out . . . "And some strawberries . . ."

As a matter of fact, I took Isadora's starving saga with a pinch of salt. I knew only too well how many loyal and true friends she had. None of them would have let her starve. The truth was that Isadora's feelings were very easily hurt. Probably someone spoke severely about her continually asking friends for money and always spending it recklessly, and she had just retired to bed without communicating with any of her real friends. That she owed a large hotel bill . . . was certainly true . . .

All that first day she begged me not to leave her. She came back to my hotel and I talked to her about her life, and said that she absolutely must stop squandering it and pull herself together and dance again.

"I am no longer believed in. No one believes I can still dance. I could be saved if someone would organize a recital for me. I only drink and waste my life to forget my little dead children and that no one will let me dance any more."

An inspiration came to me.

"Isadora, if you will behave and concentrate on writing your life, I promise you on my solemn word of honor that somehow I will arrange a dance recital for you, and I will help you get the book published."

She did not react to this suggestion.

"I am not a writer and I would not have the energy to write, and perhaps now, after so many years, I cannot even dance."

"Nonsense," I said. "You will be helped to do both."

"Who will help me but you, my Archangel?"

"You will be given Divine Energy, if you will only call upon it," I said . . .

A letter from Tommy Smith, editor at Boni and Liveright, to Mercedes de Acosta:

"Isadora Duncan will not mind my saying, I am sure, that her temperamental reputation is rather well known, and it is this which causes us, as it will certainly cause any editor, to be certain of all the manuscript, or a greater part of it, before entering into, or paying any substantial sum of money for its publication . . ."

From *Here Lies the Heart:*

"One of Isadora's most charming traits was her impatience when anyone she loved was coming to see her. If I had promised to come at eight o'clock, the telephone would ring at half past seven, and I would hear her voice asking, 'Are you on your way?'

"When I arrived she would be waiting impatiently at the top of the stairs. She would stretch her arms wide when she saw me. I always think of her like this, with her arms outstretched in the form of a cross. I think of the words she once wrote: Perhaps I am *La Madonne qui monte le Calvaire en dansant.*

"Some women can cry easily. For me it is difficult. There are only a few people before whom I would let myself go. Isadora was one of them. She used to laugh and say that she was the only person before whom I could enjoy a good, comfortable cry."

A letter from Isadora to "Angel" [Mercedes de Acosta] in the de Acosta Archive at the Rosenbach Museum:

"I await your coming as the Soul in Hell the *Last Day* of

Ten Thousand years of tortures—In your absence of five Centuries I have been feeding from the hand of the Super Demon
misnamed Seraphita [?]—a diet of Live Coals & *Vitriol*"

A poem from Isadora Duncan to Mercedes de Acosta in the
de Acosta Archive:

Beneath a forehead
Broad & Bright
Shine Eyes
Clear wells
  of light—
A Slender Body
Soft [above "Soft" is written "Hard"]—White
To be the Source
Of my delight—

Two sprouting breasts
round & Sweet
Invite my hungry
mouth to Eat
from whence two
nipples—firm &
pink persuade my
thirsty soul to drink
& lower still
a Secret place
where I'd fain
hide my burning face

Arch Angel
from Another Sphere
God Sent to
light my pathway
here
I kneel in Adoration
  dear

My kisses like a swarm of Bees
Would find Their way
between thy knees

& suck the honey
of thy lips
Embracing thy
Two slender hips

Isadora
to
Mercedes
1927

Isadora to Mercedes, de Acosta Archive, undated, upper corners of the two pages torn:

Adorée J'ai jouée avec les flammes de Toi et je suis horriblement brulé—J'ai pensée que j'avais connu toutes les Souffrances mortelles mais je Comprends maintenant que la plus Cruelle m'etait reservée—Je souffre *attrocement* mais je l'accepte puisque la Source est si *belle* [illegible] *fuire* vers la Mer—mais Comment vivre avec cet poison dans mes veines que j'ai bu de ta bouche divine—Je te supplie ne te moque pas de moi—j'en mourrai peutetre—j'ai l'horreur de comprendre que je connais l'Amour pour *la premiere fois*—ne ris pas [torn here] . . . un petit mot—Est-ce que il y'a dans ton Coeur un peu de pitié pour moi— Respecte mon Secret Je suis torturé au degrée de Crier Pitié—*

Isadora

There is a photograph of Mary Cassatt taken at Beaufresne in 1925. It shows her seated in a white slipcovered chair. On her fingers are three or four rings (those rings from Egypt?). In her lap, her hands around him, she holds one of her small dogs, a Belgian griffon. She is wearing very thick glasses,

*(Translation:) Adored one I have played with the flames of your being and I am horribly burned. I thought I had known all mortal suffering but I understand now that the greatest cruelty has been reserved for me. I suffer *atrociously* but I accept it since the source is so *beautiful* [Illegible] to *flee* to the sea—but how live with this poison in my veins that I have drunk from your divine mouth—I beg you not to mock me— perhaps I will die of it. I feel horror at recognizing that I know love for *the first time*. Don't laugh [torn here] . . . a little word—Is there in your heart a little pity for me. Respect my secret. I am tortured to the extent that I cry out for pity—

upon which the light glints—from a window behind us, behind
the camera. Through the lenses of the glasses the eyes look
very large. They seem to be looking at the camera.

Wrapped around her head is a white lacelike cloth, tied in
a bow at the crown. A matching cloth is tied about her neck. She
is wearing a loose jacket over her slanting shoulders. She looks
frail, impeccable, stern. (Except for her hands, she looked, said
Forbes Watson, like a "lean, bent, over-worked Puritan
housekeeper gone blind in her old age after incessant domestic
drudgery.")

Behind her, at the left of the photograph, a doorway leads
to another room, with a desk, a chair, a small rug on the floor,
and on the wall a print that seems to be of a woman. Behind her
and above her head, at the right of the photograph, a wall. On
it, a Japanese print. One can barely make out the forms. They
seem to be three women, seated on the floor, at tea.

From *To Whom It May Concern*, a memoir by Victor Seroff, published under the pen name M. R. Werner, in 1931:

> While I was playing the piano [in Paris, at the
> home of a Madame Marvine; the date isn't given, but
> probably 1926], a woman came in, and somebody whis-
> pered, "Isadora Duncan." I went on playing until the
> end of the piece and thought of the first time I had ever
> heard that name . . . when I was a child of nine my
> mother spoke of seeing her dance. She came up to the
> piano after I had finished. She was a woman of medium
> height, who had now grown somewhat stout. One no-
> ticed at once her lovely arms, with their fine, small
> hands, and the line of her neck and shoulders was
> magnificent. Her whole body moved beautifully as she
> walked calmly and gently across the room . . . Her
> voice was low and gentle, and it had a tone which gave
> her whole character a quality of naïveté. Her face was
> tired and looked as if she had rouged it without looking
> in the mirror, and around her eyes, which were green,
> witty and gentle, she had streaks of black and blue
> makeup which did not quite hide the small wrinkles
> under the eyelids . . .
> After I had finished, she thanked me, and her eyes

were filled with tears, as she gave me her hand to kiss. She talked to me in the few words of Russian she knew, and then, looking round the room, and smiling in the most naïve way, she said, "He's a genius. Doesn't anybody know he's a genius? I have a nose for genius." There was an embarrassed silence. She looked at Mrs. Marvine and said "Is he your lover?" Mrs. Marvine hastened nervously to deny the possibility: "Why, no, Miss Duncan . . . He is my guest." Isadora continued to look around the room, smiling: "He must be somebody's lover?" she asked. The guests were shocked and embarrassed . . . Then, turning to me, she said to the assembled company: "Well, he is nobody's lover, then I will take him for myself. I always take genius for myself. Genius needs me."

A statement by Armand Delaporte, Mary's chauffeur, written after Mary's death:
"No one but Mademoiselle Cassatt had a right to cut a rose. She always did this herself, when she wanted to make a gift."

From "Isadora Really," by Sir Francis Rose:
"I remember her last concerts [1926] in the dark and dusty studio. They were generally disastrous. She was either drunk, afraid, or in a bad mood. Her public no longer existed, and she was aware of it. At the end, her greatness was reserved for a few such as myself. She danced alone for a young boy because she knew I would remember and record it in the future. She danced as wonderfully as she had ever done. It was great, great, great!"

From *Paris Was Yesterday*, by Janet Flanner, writing of several recitals given in September 1926 by Isadora in Nice, on a program with Jean Cocteau and Marcel Herrand:
"Her art was seen to have changed. She treaded the boards but little, she stood almost immobile or in slow splendid steps with slow splendid arms moved to music, seeking, hunting, finding. Across her face, tilting this way and that, fled the mortal looks of tragedy, knowledge, love, scorn, pain. Posing through the works of Wagner, through the tales of Dante, through the touching legend of St. Francis feeding crumbs and

wisdom to the birds, Isadora was still great. By an economy
(her first) she had arrived at elimination."

From Kay Boyle's section of *Being Geniuses Together*, an
incident, undated, probably 1925 or 1926:
"Once McAlmon and I had dinner with the [James] Joyces
. . . and the talk that night was almost entirely about Lucia's
[the Joyces' daughter's] eyes . . . and Joyce himself shook his
head and asked if she wasn't continuously too nervous, too shy
. . . McAlmon suggested that perhaps her dancing would be a
better release for her tensions . . . 'Do you think so, McAlmon?'
Joyce asked, seizing eagerly on this . . . Yes, yes, she was born
to dance, he repeated in some relief, and he explained to me that
she was going to Salzburg to study with Elizabeth Duncan, as
the more famous sister, Isadora, was not holding classes now.
'She's not even holding her liquor,' McAlmon said, and, 'Ah, the
poor soul,' said Nora Joyce . . ."

Paris, May 7, 1927, Mary Desti to her son Preston Sturges:
"I went to see Isadora—found her in almost as bad a condition [as B., a suicidal friend] and between the two of them life
is terrible— Isadora insisted I go to live in her hotel—over at
Montparnasse—Someone's prayer saved me from that folly—
and in spite of [B.'s] fearing she would have to commit suicide
(and I wishing she would) and Isadora tearing at me to save her
school, as it was the last moment and I advising her to give all
thought of the bugbear up forever—I say in spite of all this I
managed to slip out & find myself a dear little flat . . ."
Paris, June 3, 1927, Mary Desti to Preston Sturges:
"Isadora is dancing the 28th—she is in very bad circumstances—but—I refuse to be [illegible] with her any longer—
she won't try to economize refuses to eat except at the best
restaurants, and wants to drink the most expensive wines—she
feels the world owes it to her—well I guess it does—but if she
is hungry she can come here any time and share what I have."

From *The Real Isadora*, by Victor Seroff, an account of
Isadora's final concert in Paris, July 8, 1927:
"The amateurish management was far from achieving a
packed house on the day of her performance. But distinguished
members of the artistic world and Isadora's faithful old admir-

ers made an enthusiastic audience nonetheless. Her interpretation of Franck's *Rédemption* was monumental, and her *Ave Maria,* with maternal arms lulling an imaginary babe, was so personal and so heartrending in its simplicity that it provoked unashamed sobs throughout the audience. At the end of the performance she was cheered and called back to the stage again and again."

From *Isadora: A Revolutionary in Art and Love,* by Allan Ross Macdougall, a description of Isadora's last concert in Paris:
"The theatre was packed by a distinguished and enthusiastic audience of the dancer's American and French admirers . . . The matinee opened with the *Allegretto* from César Franck's Symphony and followed with Isadora's rendition of the French master's *Rédemption,* one of the monumental creations of her last years. Then came the Schubert *Ave Maria* danced with such moving beauty that there were those in the audience who unashamedly sobbed aloud. (Will they ever forget the ineffable gesture of the maternal arms cradling nothing? The moving tenderness and simplicity of it?) Then the orchestra alone played the first movement of Schubert's *Unfinished Symphony,* and Isadora danced her conception with a more tragic profundity than ever before.
"After the intermission came the Wagnerian part of the programme. In this she did her well-known 'Bacchanal' from *Tannhäuser* and the 'Love-Death of Isolde.' Between these two grandiose creations the orchestra played the 'Funeral March' from *Siegfried.* "

From Robert McAlmon's section of *Being Geniuses Together:*
"Her last dance program at the Théâtre des Champs-Elysées was not without its depressing moments. Although she must have known that her dancing days were over, she had tried to do one leap, and it was grotesque and sad, and she was aware of it. But long before this I had seen a constantly despairing and rather shameful look in her eyes."

From Sewell Stokes's *Isadora Duncan,* a description of the last room where she lived:

"The room at the Negresco—which was probably not paid for at the time of her death—was like an actress's dressing-room, after she had invested it with her flowing personality. I always had the impression when she left it that she was going to make her appearance on the stage. It had the makeshift qualities of a temporary place, and it was difficult to realise that at the time it was Isadora's only home. The furniture was pale grey and gold, like the bedroom suites in musical comedy. Out of some of the drawers hung tails of colored clothing. A trunk stood half-open on the floor. The bed became a divan during the day, and was invariably littered with newspapers. On a table near the window, were piled up books of press-cuttings which Isadora was looking into to help with her memoirs. On her dressing-table, propped against a bottle of perfume, was a large photograph of Mitri [Seroff] looking happy in a brilliant pull-over; and tucked into the corner of the mirror, in true theatrical style, a snap-shot of Gordon Craig as a young man in a white linen suit. Even during the day the room was lit by artificial light. Isadora had ceased to appreciate the sun."

From George Biddle's *An American Artist's Story*, an account of his last visit to Mary at Beaufresne in 1926:

> She lay, quite blind, on the green bed I knew so well from the painting in the Metropolitan Museum and from other paintings . . . She was terribly ema-ciated. Her thin gray hair straggled from under her lace cap, over the blue veins of her high white fore-head. Her hands, once such big, knuckled, capable art-ist's hands, were shrunken and folded on the quilt. When she began to talk they waved and flickered about her head, and the room became charged with the electric vitality of the old lady.
>
> "Well [she shouted], have you ever seen such weather? My doctor says that in forty years there has never been such a storm."
>
> She was terribly put out that the weather pre-vented her from coming down to lunch [Biddle had dined alone] . . . She would have ordered chicken, but really hadn't expected me at the last moment . . . She hoped the Château Margaux was really good

. . . It was the last bottle in a case . . . presented to her by her brother just before his death some fifteen years back . . .

Miss Cassatt as usual did all the talking. Her mind galloped along, shaking the frail human body lying propped up, thin and impotent. Every few minutes her memory would fail her, and her face became tortured in the effort to recall or concentrate on a word. She writhed about, frantically snapping her fingers. The faithful Mathilde leaned over the bedhead, painfully intent on interpolating the missing links of the conversation. She could almost read her mistress's mind, and would make hurried suggestions to the snapping fingers. Miss Cassatt would pounce upon the right one and gallop along in her talk. Every now and then, for but a moment, she would gently subside . . . There she sat . . . prim, erect, intent, the corners of her eyes slightly raised, looking very straight and hard at one. She wished Mathilde to go and fetch the Egyptian jewelry of lapis lazuli and carnelian. Now there was a terrible snapping of fingers . . . At last the jewelry was brought in and spread upon the bed . . .

The witness was, after all, Mary Desti.

Despite the irritation with Isadora that she had expressed to her son, Preston, Mary was with her again in Nice. She kept trying various schemes to get money for Isadora, at the same time knowing Isadora would immediately spend whatever funds were received.

On the eleventh of September or so in 1927—chronology here is somewhat hazy, as it usually is in Mary's telling—Isadora begged Mary to go to Singer, who was living in a château nearby, to ask for help.

"I hated to do this," writes Mary, "but I just couldn't see Isadora unhappy." Hiring a "passing auto" on credit, Mary drove to Singer's palatial home reluctantly, feeling that he had always been "magnificently generous, and I knew that he was now himself going through a great financial crisis . . ." (Singer had lost most of his money in a real estate venture in Palm Beach.)

Nevertheless, once she got to Singer's home, she did ask him for money for Isadora. Singer refused, saying the money would only be wasted—"he believed nothing would check Isadora's downward rush." On Monday the twelfth, however, he relented and came to see Isadora. Agreeing to cover her living and working expenses until her situation improved, he promised that he would return at four in the afternoon on the fourteenth with a check. Isadora was ecstatic, says Mary, feeling that she was once again "loved."

In the meantime, however, with Seroff away in Paris, trying to raise funds for her, Isadora had developed an "interest" in a handsome young Italian garage proprietor, Bénoit Falchetto. He drove a Bugatti, a two-seated sports car, and was also an agent for the firm. Isadora arranged for him to take her for a drive in his Bugatti, ostensibly to see whether she wanted to buy one.

He arrived on the afternoon of the thirteenth while Isadora was asleep, and Mary sent him away. When Isadora found out what Mary had done, she "sprang from the couch like a tiger," saying Mary should have awakened her, that it was terribly important, that she had to see him.

Why? Mary asked her. " 'What can this chauffeur have to do with you?'

" 'I tell you he's not a chauffeur, but a messenger of the gods. He's divine.' "

Mary's view was less exalted. "I had seen him dressed as a simple young workingman," she comments, "certainly very handsome, but that's all."

Singer did not appear at four P.M. on the fourteenth, but Falchetto, having been contacted again by Isadora, showed up at five-thirty. Shortly afterward Singer arrived. He found Isadora "sitting beside Bugatti [as Mary calls him], telling him about her art, dancing, etc."

To Isadora, Singer said, "I see you haven't changed."

Isadora protested that the young man had actually come to see Mary, as she was thinking of buying a car from him. Singer, aware that Mary's own financial situation was precarious, was clearly not taken in by Isadora's story but he made no issue of it. He only said that he had not had the time to get the check that day but would bring it the following day. After Singer left,

Isadora told "Bugatti" to return at nine in the evening—with his car.

To Mary, Isadora said, "Now we will see what we will see . . . I don't believe he will come or Bugatti, either."

As they were finishing dinner at a nearby restaurant that night, Mary writes, "an immense dark cloud seemed to descend on our table between Isadora and me. I gasped, 'Oh, my God, Isadora, something terrible is happening.'

"Isadora cried, 'Mary, for Heaven's sake, what's the matter? I never saw so tragic a face. What is it? Why are you trembling? Waiter, bring a glass of brandy.' I said I didn't want any brandy and would be all right in a moment. The waiter brought the brandy, and Isadora insisted that I drink it. This was just nine o'clock.

"Isadora said, 'It's just nine o'clock, we must hurry.' She took my arm and said, 'Now, Mary, what is the matter?'

"And I answered, 'Please, Isadora, don't go in that auto. My nerves are terribly unstrung; I'm afraid something might happen to you.'

" 'My dear, I would go for this ride tonight even if I were sure it would be my last. Even then, I would go quicker. But don't worry, Bugatti is not coming.'

"We went into the studio, and she turned on all the lights and the gramophone and began to dance wildly. Suddenly from the window she saw Bugatti drive up with his car. She started for the door. I pleaded, 'Isadora, please put on my black cape, it's quite cold.'

" 'No, no, my dear, nothing but my red-painted shawl.' "

(The shawl was one Mary had had made for Isadora some years before, a huge rectangle of densely woven red silk crepe, six feet by five feet, with a fringe of silk tassels eighteen inches long on each side.)

"I ran out ahead of her and said to Bugatti, 'I don't believe you realize what a great person you are driving tonight. I beg of you to be careful, and if she asks you to go fast, I beg you not to. I'm terribly nervous tonight.'

" 'Madame, you need have no fear,' he replied. 'I've never had an accident in my life.'

"Isadora came out; seeing her red shawl, he offered her his leather coat."

But Isadora insisted on wearing only the red shawl. Throwing it across her shoulders and around her neck with a characteristic gesture, she called out, "Adieu mes amis. Je vais à la gloire."

The car started up. The long fringe of silk tassels, reinforced by intricate tying, spilled over the side of the low-slung car. As the car started forward the tassels caught in the spokes of the wheel, which had no mudguard. The wheels turned, the strands pulled tight. Isadora's head snapped down and to the side, her larynx crushed, her neck broken.

Mary ran for a knife, she tried to cut through the strands. She called for a scissors, for a doctor, for help. A passing car stopped and several onlookers helped lift Isadora's body into it. "I sat beside her in the back seat," Mary writes, "and held her in my arms, while the driver and his wife sat in the front . . . All the time I was trying to get Isadora to breathe . . .

"At last we arrived at the hospital, where they did not want to let us in, believing she was dead, and they are not allowed to take dead people in. But I so insisted . . . we carried her inside."

One of the doctors said to Mary, "Madame, calm yourself. There is nothing to be done. She was killed instantly."

Isadora's body was brought back to her studio, which was then sealed by the police. In the morning, after the coroner had left, Mary "dressed Isadora in her red dress and her dancing veils, and there, in the midst of her great couch, surrounded by myriads of the flowers she loved best, she looked like a little Tanagra figure lying in a garden."

Singer, who stayed with Mary throughout the day, arranged for Isadora's body to be taken to Paris by train. "The train had scarcely started to move," Mary reports, "when the most extraordinary thing happened. It had been pouring rain all day, but the instant that the train started, the sky darkened, and a perfect hurricane almost blew every one out of the station. They say they had never known anything like it before in Nice."

On the morning of September 19, Isadora's body was carried out of her brother Raymond's studio in Auteuil into the waiting hearse. The purple velvet cloak in which she had danced

The Resurrection covered the coffin and at one end Raymond placed an American flag. Mary rearranged a spray of red flowers on the coffin so the accompanying banner, The Heart of Russia Weeps for Isadora, was clearly visible. (It was Mary, not the Russian government, says Seroff, who had ordered and paid for the flowers and the banner.)

The funeral was held at the cemetery of Père Lachaise, where Isadora's two children and her mother had preceded her. Four thousand people greeted the cortege at the cemetery gate. At the service within the chapel Schubert's "Ave Maria" was sung and Bach's "Aria in D Minor" from the D-Minor Suite for Violin was played. The poet Fernand Divoire delivered the eulogy.

Behind a heavy curtain where the cremation was performed, Mary stood with Elizabeth and Raymond as Isadora's ashes were drawn out of the furnace on an asbestos couch. To Mary, watching, the ashes seemed to form an outline like the breath of one of Isadora's dances, "like a white drawing of her."

For Mary Cassatt it was to be a death of slowness, a death that had been awaited a long time, a death in domesticity, a death among known things, a death that had been resisted, a death that had been prepared for, a death like a test of will, an almost imperious death, surrounded by servants, an ebbing in stillness, a letting go . . .

She died at Beaufresne on June 14, 1926, at eight o'clock in the evening on the arm of Armand Delaporte, her chauffeur.

Many years later Delaporte wrote in response to a letter from Sweet:

"For a long time Miss Cassatt had diabetes which imposed on her a most severe regime which she observed rigorously. She had a great desire to get well and to live. Mlle. had given orders in case of her death, to open a vein. This was done by Dr. Gillet of Auneil (Oise). Miss Cassatt was buried at Mésnil-Théribus in the family vault, the care of which I have taken upon myself, out of gratitude, during the time that I continue to live. In this tomb are placed her father, her mother, her brother, her sister . . . Miss Cassatt had a most imposing ceremony (of the Protestant religion) with military honors in view of her Legion of Honor and accompanied by the Mésnil-Théribus band. She had a splendid turnout and quantities of red roses. The day of her burial the weather was sullen gray and raining but during the funeral procession there was a clearing."

68

Two women who went to Egypt.
Two women who never met . . . Two stories—or perhaps all
stories of a life or lives are only one story at the moment when
death becomes—takes over—memory. Perhaps it does not matter how they have been told, backward, forward, in fragments.
There remains something beyond our reach in the telling . . .

As if the residue, the core, the center of the being had not
been listened to enough, had not been told enough . . .
As if every telling of a life were a journey past immense
unknown statues, hidden then revealed then hidden again, by
waters covering and uncovering, and we, drifting down on the
surface of those waters, trying to see, trying to tell, hold to the
belief that there is yet more to be seen, more to be told . . .

NOTES AND SOURCES

In letters by Mary Cassatt and Isadora Duncan quoted in the text, a number of silent corrections have been made of casual errors that impeded the flow of the narrative. Errors were left uncorrected if they made an essential contribution to the tone of a particular excerpt.

The following abbreviations are used:

    MC Mary Cassatt
    ID Isadora Duncan

ARCHIVES

  AAA Archives of American Art, Smithsonian Institution
 APSF San Francisco Performing Arts Library and Museum, Duncan Archive
  BAN Bancroft Library, University of California at Berkeley, J. Redfern Mason Papers

BEIN   Beinecke Rare Book and Manuscript Library, Yale
        University Library, Appa-Craig (Oenslager)
        Collection
HRC   Harry Ransom Humanities Research Center, Uni-
        versity of Texas at Austin
MMA   Metropolitan Museum of Art, Archives: Letters
        from Mary Cassatt to Louisine Havemeyer
PARC-CD Performing Arts Research Center, The New York
        Public Library at Lincoln Center, Craig-Dun-
        can Collection
PARC-ID Performing Arts Research Center, The New York
        Public Library at Lincoln Center, Irma Dun-
        can Collection of Isadora Duncan Materials
PHIL   Philadelphia Museum of Art, Archives of Ameri-
        can Art/Carl Zigrosser Collection
ROSE   Rosenbach Museum and Library, Philadelphia,
        Mercedes de Acosta Archive
UCLA   The University Library, Department of Special
        Collections, University of California at Los
        Angeles, Sturges-Desti Archive

BOOKS ON MARY CASSATT

CAR   Carson, Julia M. H. *Mary Cassatt.* New York:
        David McKay, 1966.
HA   Hale, Nancy. *Mary Cassatt.* New York: Double-
        day, 1975.
LET   Mathews, Nancy Mowll, ed. *Cassatt and Her Cir-
        cle: Selected Letters.* New York: Abbeville,
        1984.
SW   Sweet, Frederick A. *Miss Mary Cassatt: Impres-
        sionist from Pennsylvania.* Norman: Univer-
        sity of Oklahoma Press, 1966.

BOOKS ON ISADORA DUNCAN

ISA   Blair, Fredrika. *Isadora: Portrait of the Artist as
        a Woman.* New York: McGraw-Hill, 1986.
US   Desti, Mary. *The Untold Story: The Life of
        Isadora Duncan 1921–1927.* New York: Hor-
        ace Liveright, 1929.

AJ Dumesnil, Maurice. *An Amazing Journey.* New York: Ives Washburn, 1932.

DD Duncan, Irma. *Duncan Dancer.* Middletown, Conn.: Wesleyan University Press, 1965.

IDRD Duncan, Irma, and Macdougall, Allan Ross. *Isadora Duncan's Russian Days and Her Last Years in France.* New York: Covici-Friede, 1929.

ML Duncan, Isadora. *My Life.* New York: Boni and Liveright, 1927.

RAL Macdougall, Allan Ross. *Isadora: A Revolutionary in Art and Love.* New York: Thomas Nelson, 1960.

RI Seroff, Victor. *The Real Isadora.* New York: The Dial Press, 1971.

YI Steegmuller, Francis, ed. *Your Isadora: The Love Story of Isadora Duncan and Gordon Craig.* New York: Random House and the New York Public Library, 1974.

PART ONE

Page

7 "My impressions here . . .": MMA, January 4, 1911.
8–9 "We are distinctly . . .": ibid., January 17, 1911.
9 "Nonsense," says Mary: *CAR,* p. 145.
10 "It is all so Heavenly . . .": ID to Mary Fanton Roberts, January 25, 1910, *ISA,* pp. 205–206.
11 "As the dahabeah . . .": *ML,* pp. 242–43.
11 "I am called Isadora": ID to Gordon Craig, January 15, 1905, *YI,* p. 56.
11 "It would have been . . .": *ML,* pp. 242–43.
11 "The dahabeah moved . . .": ibid., p. 244.
12 "We are glad . . .": MMA, January 20, 1911.
12–13 "Oh Louie would . . .": ibid., January 28, 1911.
13–14 "Now she is . . .": ibid., February 11, 1911.
14–15 "had the heart": ibid., March 8, 1911.
16 "obsessed . . . everything to life": *ML,* p. 245.
17 "The English people . . .": ibid., pp. 247–48.
17 "what he always considered . . .": ibid., p. 249.

17   "hours every day . . .": ibid., p. 250.

17–18   "To drown my ennui . . .": ibid., pp. 250–51.

18   "tremendous force under constraint": *ISA*, p. 212.

18   "great Amphitheatre . . .": *ML*, p. 253.

19   "in him I had met . . .": ibid., pp. 182–83.

19   ". . . I had discovered that Love . . .": ibid., p. 254.

19–20   "Isadora has not danced . . .": Leo Stein to Gertrude Stein, undated, Edmund Fuller, ed., *Journey into the Self: Being the Letters, Papers, and Journals of Leo Stein* (New York: Crown, 1950), p. 47.

20   "I saw S. who has finished . . .": Leo Stein to Gertrude Stein, August 22, 1911, Fuller, *Journey into the Self*, p. 48.

20–21   "Between Luxor and Aswan . . .": *DD*, p. 119–123.

22–23   "All that Egypt . . .": MMA, March 17, 1911.

23   ". . . the photos of the Saint . . .": ibid., March 24, 1911.

23–24   "I met them at the station . . .": ibid., March 31, 1911.

24   "Doctors order rest . . .": ibid., April 12, 1911.

24   "could never weep again": MC to Theodate Pope [1903], quoted in *HA*, p. 207.

24   "What a book! . . .": MC to Theodate Pope, October 1903, *HA*, p. 210.

24   "The more I read . . .": MC to Theodate Pope, November 1903, ibid., p. 211.

24   "They think the religion . . .": MC to Electra Havemeyer Webb, ibid., pp. 211–12.

26   "I commenced a study . . .": MC to Emily Sartain, June 7, 1871, *LET*, p. 74.

26–27   "The elder Mr. Cassatt . . .": *HA*, p. 48.

27   "Robert Cassatt's constant shifts . . .": *SW*, p. 15.

27   "he was never . . .": ibid.

27   "the only being . . .": *HA*, p. 13.

27–28   "had really no great interest . . .": *SW*, p. 14.

29–30   "Robert Kelso Cassatt . . .": *HA*, p. 20.

30–31   "I did think . . .": Robert S. Cassatt to Alexander Cassatt, August 5, 1883, PHIL.

32   "Ever since her liaison . . .": *DD*, p. 124.

32   "I am working . . .": ID to Paris Singer, undated, BEIN.

33   "meeting place and a haven . . .": *ML*, p. 273.

33   "I will leave . . .": ID to Paris Singer, undated, BEIN.

33 "Dearest I wonder . . .": ID to Paris Singer, undated, ibid.

33 "The misunderstanding on Craig's part . . .": ID to Paris Singer, undated, ibid.

34 "Your idea of the cheaper places . . .": ID to Paris Singer, undated, ibid.

34 "Please, if I really . . .": ID to Paris Singer, undated, BEIN, quoted in *YI*, p. 397.

35–36 "My studio was . . .": *ML*, pp. 261–62.

36–37 "Here I'm living . . .": *ISA*, p. 219.

38–39 "Yes I *am* better . . .": MMA, December 1, 1911.

39 "This is the 8th day . . .": ibid., December 14, 1911.

39–40 "auto cure . . . nine and ten hours": ibid., December 29, 1911.

40 "I was there . . .": ibid., December 1911.

41 "I confess to feeling . . .": ibid., January 9, 1912.

41 "of two women . . .": ibid., January 16, 1912.

41–42 "I have had a relapse . . .": ibid., January 26, 1912.

43 "to end all hopes . . .": *ML*, p. 267.

43–44 " '. . . all the children are dead!'. . .": ibid., pp. 263–64.

44 "Living there at Neuilly . . .": ibid., pp. 265–66.

44 "icy breath . . . strong scent . . .": ibid., pp. 266–67.

45 "approached the foot of the bed . . .": ibid., pp. 267–68.

45 "as never before . . .": ibid., p. 270.

45–46 "And the direct thought . . .": ibid., pp. 271–74.

48–49 "Paris, April 20 . . .": *San Francisco Examiner*, April 21, 1913.

50 "a man of sanguine . . .": *San Francisco Evening Bulletin*, October 8, 1877.

50–52 "the struggle of the people . . .": Joseph C. Duncan, "The Tri-Color (A Tale of the Three Days of July)," in *The Prairie Flower* vol. 1, no. 1 (1841), pp. 8–10, APSF.

52 "Joseph Charles Duncan . . .": *San Francisco Examiner*, November 13, 1898.

53 "the sculptor Antoine Bourdelle . . .": *ISA*, p. 221.

53 "The mourning mother . . .": *RI*, pp. 189–90.

54 "All men are my brothers . . .": *ISA*, p. 224.

54 "Today Europe . . .": "Notes et réflexions inédites de Robert de Montesquiou," Bibliothèque Nationale. Author's translation.

54 "long days and nights . . .": *ML,* p. 75.

54 ". . . was almost unbelievable . . .": ibid., p. 179.

55 ". . . phantom ship upon a phantom ocean": ibid., p. 267.

55 "I had some definite plan . . .": ibid., p. 277.

55 "entered a dreary land . . .": ibid., pp. 278–79.

56 "Do you remember . . .": ID to Gordon Craig, May 31, 1913, *YI,* p. 323.

57 ". . . the most wonderful excursion . . .": MMA, February 18, 1912.

57–58 "I often think . . .": ibid., early March 1912.

58 "That is a sad prospect . . .": ibid., March 12, 1912.

58 "if I am well again . . .": ibid., March 23, 1912.

58 ". . . Yesterday I went to Beaufresne . . .": ibid., March 29, 1912.

58–59 the sinking of the *Titanic*: ibid., April 16, 1912.

59 "All my doctors . . .": ibid., August 1, 1912.

60 "You have been sent . . .": *ML,* p. 287.

60 "following an irresistible impulse": ibid., p. 289.

61 "the sound of the familiar music . . .": ibid., p. 290.

61 "took me in her arms . . .": ibid., p. 292.

61 " 'You have on your brow . . .' ": ibid., p. 294.

61 " 'If you knew how short . . .' ": ibid., p. 295.

61 "my heart was too heavy . . .": ibid., p. 296.

63 "the central spring . . .": ibid., p. 75.

63 "This so called *real* world . . .": ID to Gordon Craig, June 23, 1913, *YI,* p. 326.

64 "I thought I would swim . . .": *ML,* p. 296.

64 "One grey, autumn afternoon . . .": ibid.

65–66 "a pitying hand . . . console me on earth": ibid., pp. 296–97.

66 "I am half mad . . .": ID to Gordon Craig, September 2, 1913, *YI,* p. 328.

66 "I embrace you . . .": *DD,* p. 137.

66 "a sculptor named Romano Romanelli . . .": William Weaver, *Duse* (San Diego: Harcourt Brace Jovanovich, 1984), p. 293.

66 "Nothing of that . . .": *RI,* p. 203.

67 "far from entering into the spirit . . .": Mercedes de Acosta, *Here Lies the Heart* (New York: Reynal, 1960), pp. 51–52.

68 "draw a line . . .": MMA, June 4, 1912.
68 "One would like to leave . . .": ibid., March 10, 1908.
68–74 "A very aristocratic woman . . .": This and all subsequent quotes in this chapter have been taken from Achille Ségard, *Mary Cassatt: Un peintre des enfants et des mères* (Paris: Librairie Paul Ollendorff, 1913). Author's translation.
75 "After he left . . .": MMA, June 7, 1912.
75 "I am no use to anyone . . .": ibid., August 1, 1912.
75 "I am sick of the doctors": ibid., September 6, 1912.
75–76 "I must tell you . . .": ibid., September 26, 1912.
76 "if you can call it dinner . . .": ibid., October 2, 1912.
76 "beautiful child . . . What sunshine . . .": ibid., November 1, 1912.
76 "the Balkan business . . .": ibid., November 8, 1912.
76–77 "The war cloud . . .": ibid., November 15, 1912.
77 "the Crown Prince . . .": ibid., November 30, 1912.
78 "It has qualities of art . . .": quoted in *CAR*, pp. 149–50.
79 "The essential cubism . . .": John A. Wilson, *The Burden of Egypt* (Chicago: University of Chicago Press, 1951), p. 53.

PART TWO

Page

85 "You are the only Mother . . .": MMA, November 29, 1907.
86 "I am passing through Florence . . .": ID to Gordon Craig, [autumn 1913], *YI*, p. 338.
86 a telegram from Singer: *ML*, p. 298.
86–87 "magnificent suite of rooms . . . Dance of the Future": ibid., p. 299.
87 "I bought for . . .": ibid., pp. 300–301.
87 "I spent hours . . .": ibid., pp. 303–304.
88 "Nietzsche says . . .": ibid., pp. 323–24.
89 "How describe Isadora? . . .": *US*, p. 63.
90 "She was about Isadora's age . . .": *RI*, p. 64.
90 "This obese, loud-mouthed . . .": ibid., p. 334.
90 "an illiterate megalomaniac": ibid., p. 395.

90   "worshipped Isadora to . . .": Mercedes de Acosta, *Here Lies the Heart* (New York: Reynal, 1960), p. 80.

91–93   "the most unsympathetic nurse . . .": *US,* pp. 63–65.

93   "Who are you . . .": *ML,* p. 307.

93   "the mortuary portrait . . .": Suzanne G. Lindsay, *Mary Cassatt and Philadelphia,* exhibition catalog, Philadelphia Museum of Art, 1985, p. 53.

95   "so weak that I . . .": *ML,* p. 310.

96   "death-like love": ibid., p. 314.

96   "did he turn . . . healed and well": ibid., pp. 311–12.

96   "more sombre in . . .": ibid., p. 313.

97   "I loved this man . . .": ibid., pp. 313–15.

99–100 "Edgar, I want you . . .": Joan King, *Impressionist: A Novel of Mary Cassatt* (New York: Beaufort, 1983), pp. 189–91.

100   "a story of fantasy . . .": ibid., p. 7.

100–101 "Carsten was out . . .": Eliza Haldeman to Mrs. Samuel Haldeman, October 15, 1868, *LET,* p. 59.

101   "What! That common . . .": *HA,* p. 86.

101   "I would have . . .": ibid., pp. 85–86.

101   "lived, as far . . .": Roy McMullen, *Degas: His Life, Times, and Work* (Boston: Houghton Mifflin, 1984), pp. 264, 268.

101   "Why do you say . . .": ibid., p. 397.

101–102 "Except for his affair . . .": Pierre Cabanne, quoted in *CAR,* p. 34.

102   "So the state . . .": T.B.H., "The Degas-Cassatt Story," *Art News* 46:53 (November 1947), quoted in ibid., p. 35.

102   "As for her true feelings . . .": *LET,* p. 13.

102   "She and Degas . . .": *SW,* p. 182.

103–104 "she is selfishness . . .": MMA, January 30, 1913.

104   "If only I felt . . .": ibid., March 12, 1913.

104   "How lonely one . . .": ibid., [March 1913].

104   "As to this Gertrude Stein . . .": MC to Ellen Mary Cassatt, March 26, 1913, *LET,* p. 310.

105   ". . . a number of Miss Stein's . . .": *HA,* p. 199.

106   "one of the rare artists . . .": Leroy C. Breunig, ed., *Apollinaire on Art: Essays and Reviews 1902–1918* (New York: Da Capo, 1988), p. 66.

106   "constructs his paintings . . .": ibid., p. 38.

106 "your perilous voyage . . .": ibid., p. 37.
106 "I have begun . . .": MMA, April 10, 1913.
107 "Perhaps, who knows? . . .": ibid., May 21, 1913.
107 "It is not much . . .": ibid., April 30, 1913.
107 "I am nervous . . .": ibid., July 16, 1913.
107 "and then my work . . .": ibid., August 21, 1913.
107 "That horrible immorality . . .": ibid., October 19, 1913.
107 "He said it was nothing . . .": ibid., November 4, 1913.
108 "They are as simple . . ." ibid., December 4, 1913.
108 "blurry, fumbling pastels": *HA*, p. 254.
108–109 "clumsy handling . . . garish color": ibid., p. 256.
109 "loss of technique . . .": Nancy Mowll Mathews, *Mary Cassatt* (New York: Harry N. Abrams, 1987), p. 149.
109 "While her palette . . .": E. John Bullard, *Mary Cassatt: Oils and Pastels* (New York: Watson-Guptill, 1976), p. 82.
111–12 "in which her pupils . . .": *ISA*, p. 246.
112 "Now comes along . . .": *RAL*, p. 119.
112 "Isadora Duncan, who . . .": Robert Henri, *The Art Spirit* (New York: Harper and Row, 1984), p. 55.
112 ". . . dances and fills the universe . . .": ibid., pp. 198, 245.
112 "Her performances are . . .": *The Boston Transcript*, February 4, 1915.
113 "the 'lyceum entertainments' . . .": *RAL*, p. 153.
113 "Isadora's pantomimic interpretation . . .": Carl Van Vechten, "The New Isadora," in *Nijinsky, Pavlova, Duncan* (New York: Da Capo, 1979), p. 30.
114 "in the midst . . .": *ML*, p. 84.
114 "She was the complete . . .": Arnold Genthe, *As I Remember* (New York: Reynal and Hitchcock, 1936), p. 179.
114 "The most terrible part . . .": *ML*, pp. 331–32.
115 "marvel of personal magnetism . . .": *AJ*, p. 39.
115 "When I say . . .": ibid., p. 47.
115 "She said that . . .": ibid., p. 64.
116 "detected a shadow . . .": ibid., p. 88.
117 "shocked beyond words": ibid., p. 134.
117 "I had been told . . .": ibid., pp. 152–53.
118 "At that moment . . .": *ML*, pp. 317–18.
118 "It seems to me . . . the primitive savage": ibid., p. 341.

118   "no rhythm from the waist down . . .": ibid.
118   "long-legged, shining boys . . .": ibid., pp. 341–42.
119–20   ". . . unworthy of a real man": *AJ*, p. 95.
120   "after which the road . . .": ibid., p. 178.
120   "Stop! You can't . . .": ibid., p. 272.
121   "Isadora, the divine": *ISA*, p. 266.
121   "in the name of all . . .": ibid., pp. 267–68.
121–22   "One knew not . . .": *RAL*, p. 164.
122   "Her nature, artistically . . .": *AJ*, p. 268.
122   "the maid had to . . .": ibid., p. 196.
122   "I started, while she . . .": ibid., p. 287.
123   "she burst into . . .": ibid., p. 302.
123   "It dawned upon me . . .": ibid., p. 311.
125   "When he heard . . .": *ML*, pp. 327–28.
125   "as passionate as . . .": *RAL*, p. 166.
125–26   "L. continued to be . . .": *ML*, p. 329.
126   "Maurice, the well-known . . .": *RAL*, p. 166.
126   "turned pale and . . .": Genthe, *As I Remember*, pp. 183–84.
126   "She merely rose . . .": *RAL*, p. 167.
127   "not high enough . . .": *ML*, p. 329.
127   "apart from getting . . .": ibid., p. 330.
127   "typical Havana café . . .": ibid., pp. 330–31.
128   "playing her portable gramophone . . .": *RAL*, p. 169.
128   "Sitting all together . . .": *ML*, p. 332.
129–30   "It was my embarrassment . . .": Genthe, *As I Remember*, pp. 184–85.
130   "unconsciously identified Singer . . .": *ISA*, pp. 274–75.
130–31   "No one is either . . .": *ML*, pp. 4–5.
132   "I observe, I experiment . . .": Edwin Way Teale, ed., *The Insect World of J. Henri Fabre* (New York: Dodd, Mead, 1949), p. xiv, Introduction.
132   "We were going to see . . .": ibid., p. 93.
133   "Placed in charge . . .": J. Henri Fabre, *The Life and Love of the Insect* (London: A. and C. Black, 1911), p. 1.
133   "The Scarab does . . .": ibid., p. 31.
133   "It seems to me . . .": quoted in Teale, *Insect World*, pp. xv–xvi, Introduction.
133   "He is now 90 . . .": MMA, May 7, 1913.
135   "Here the days . . .": ibid., August 18, 1914.

135   "This is the saddest place . . .": ibid., November 8, 1914.

135   ". . . I could have all the money . . .": ibid., December 3, 1914.

135–36   "Now that the Russians . . .": ibid., January 20, 1915.

136   "Of course everything here . . .": ibid., February 1, 1915.

136   "Oh Louie dear women . . .": ibid., August 18, 1914.

136   "Do lean Louie . . .": ibid., November 1, 1914.

136–37   "I come to appeal . . .": MC to Colonel Paine, February 28, 1915, ibid.

137   "The rich parvenu manufacturers . . .": MMA, March 12, 1915.

137   "Mathilde is in Switzerland . . .": MC to Theodate Pope, June 8, 1915, *LET*, p. 323.

138   "I am so anxious . . .": ibid.

138   "I am not working": MMA, March 12, 1915.

138   "As to my eyes . . .": ibid., June 15, 1915.

138   "Do you think . . .": ibid., July 5, 1915.

138   "My sight is so . . .": ibid., July 13, 1915.

138   "Am here care of . . .": ibid., August 21, 1915.

138   "I have had . . .": MC to Minnie Cassatt, December 28, 1915, *SW*, p. 192.

138–39   "I miss the quiet . . .": MMA, June (?) 1916.

139   "I don't want the money . . .": MC to Harris Whittemore, Jr., July 8, 1915, AAA, Adelyn Breeskin papers.

139   "My nerves are . . .": MMA, July 7, 1916.

139   "If you were saved . . .": MC to Theodate Pope, June 8, 1915, *LET*, p. 325.

139–40   "I am still . . .": MMA, June 26, 1916.

PART THREE

Page

143   *At last she appeared . . . veil of Isis*: John Cowper Powys, *After My Fashion* (London: Picador, 1980), pp. 179–80.

144   "hundreds and hundreds of red roses": quoted in ibid., p. 5, Foreword.

144   "I cannot tell you . . .": J. C. Powys to ID, undated, Irma Duncan Collection of Isadora Duncan Materials, PARC-ID.

144   "back upon a sort . . .": Powys, *After My Fashion*, p. 183.

144–45   "the deeper portion . . .": ibid., p. 213.

145   "fatal image 'like a Bacchanal . . .' ": ibid., p. 24.

146–48   "very old and careworn . . . only moments": *ML*, p. 337.

148   "When two lovers . . .": ibid., p. 338.

148   That puzzling last sentence: *RI*, p. 242.

148–49   "Dear Friend I . . .": ID to Redfern Mason, undated, BAN.

149   "Helas! You have sent . . .": ID to Redfern Mason, undated, ibid.

150–56   Florence Treadwell Boynton: All information on Florence Boynton and all quotes in this chapter are from an unpublished memoir by Florence Treadwell Boynton, now being edited for publication by Margaretta Mitchell.

151   Duncan scholar Margaretta Mitchell: from *Dance for Life: Isadora Duncan and her California Dance Legacy*, catalog of exhibition and multimedia presentation, The Oakland Museum, 1985; also published as *Dance for Life*, a portfolio of photogravures and text by Mitchell (Berkeley: Elysian Editions, 1985).

157   "Before I was born . . .": *ML*, p. 9.

157   "to fight against marriage . . .": ibid., p. 17.

158   "vagabond impulses": ibid., p. 11.

158   "wander alone by the sea . . .": ibid., pp. 10–11.

158   "great passion": ibid., p. 23.

158   ". . . the most courageous": ibid., p. 20.

158   "perfectly charming man": ibid., p. 16.

158   "I followed my fantasy . . .": ibid., p. 21.

158   "wild untrammelled life": ibid., p. 11.

158   "tragic experience": ibid., p. 9.

159   "I danced, Augustin . . .": ibid., p. 20.

160   "a brutal incomprehension of children": ibid., p. 13.

160   "*I am dying, Egypt* . . .": ibid., p. 20. The complete poem appears in William H. Venable, ed., *The Poems of William Haines Lytle* (Cincinnati: The Robert

Clark Company, 1894), p. 63. (The first line, though unacknowledged, is from Shakespeare's *Antony and Cleopatra.*)

162–64 "She had a sweet smile" . . . "sweeping over": All quotes in this section are from the unpublished Boynton memoir.

164 "Miss Duncan, who . . .": Conversation with poet Flora Jacobi Arnstein, May 1984.

166 "had almost magic power . . ." Ted Shawn, *Every Little Movement: A Book About François Delsarte* (New York: M. Witmark and Sons, 1954), p. 16.

166 *"Her right hand . . .":* I owe this recollection to poet Janet Lewis, 1984.

166 "who has been taken up . . .": Quoted in Shawn, *Every Little Movement,* p. 80.

166–67 Gordon Craig also reports: *YI,* p. 263.

167 "divine in its principles . . .": Quoted in Shawn, *Every Little Movement,* p. 24.

167 "I simply withdraw . . .": ibid., p. 57.

167 "To each spiritual function . . .": ibid., p. 31.

167 "There is nothing . . .": ibid.

168 "Positive assertion rises . . .": ibid., p. 48.

168 "Circular form is . . .": ibid.

168 "Movement is extended . . .": ibid., p. 65.

168 "artistic statue-posing": Genevieve Stebbins, *The Delsarte System of Expression* (New York: Dance Horizons, 1977), p. 444.

168 "The great work . . .": ibid., pp. 156–57.

169 "The mystic veil . . .": Quoted in Margaret Drewal, "Isis and Isadora," *Proceedings of the Society of Dance History Scholars 1987,* p. 190.

169 ". . . extraordinary quality of repose . . .": Quoted in David Vaughan, *Frederick Ashton and His Ballets* (New York: Alfred A. Knopf, 1977), p. 5.

169–70 "the large plain phrases . . .": Edwin Denby, *Dance Writings,* Robert Cornfield and William Mackay, eds. (New York: Alfred A. Knopf, 1986), pp. 87–88.

170 one of the alternate titles: Richard Bridgman, *Gertrude Stein in Pieces* (New York: Oxford University Press, 1970), p. 96 n.

170–71 "Even if one . . .": Gertrude Stein, "Orta or One Dancing," in *TWO: Gertrude Stein and Her Brother and Other Early Portraits 1908–12* (New Haven: Yale University Press, 1951), pp. 283–304.

172 "It is the movement . . .": *Degas in Motion,* Norton Simon Museum, 1982, unpaginated epigraph.

173 "The group teems with heads . . .": Julius Meier-Graefe, *Degas* (London: Ernest Benn, 1923), p. 82.

174 "ugliness" . . . "terrible realism": George T. M. Shackelford, *Degas: The Dancers* (Washington: National Gallery of Art, 1984), p. 66.

174 "To some it was a revelation . . .": Louisine W. Havemeyer, *Sixteen to Sixty* (New York: Metropolitan Museum of Art, 1930), p. 254.

174 "It is more like . . .": MMA, June 26, 1918.

175 "Of course you . . .": ibid., October 2, 1917.

176 "Degas is still wandering": ibid., February 15, 1914.

176 ". . . natural sort of distinction . . .": Quoted in Roy McMullen, *Degas: His Life, Times, and Work* (Boston: Houghton Mifflin, 1984) p. 462.

176 "Obliged to urinate . . .": ibid., pp. 461–62.

176 "The fatty tissue . . .": ibid., p. 464.

177 ". . . The statue of the 'danseuse' . . .": MMA, October 2, 1917.

177 "the first sight . . .": MC to Colonel Paine, February 28, 1915, ibid.

177 "It is true . . .": *SW,* p. 31.

177–78 "It was the portrait . . .": MC to Ambroise Vollard, [1903], *LET,* p. 281.

178 "The portion on which . . .": E. John Bullard, *Mary Cassatt: Oils and Pastels* (New York: Watson-Guptill, 1976), p. 24.

178–79 "one day, in front of Degas . . .": Achille Ségard, *Mary Cassatt: un peintre des enfants et des mères* (Paris: Librairie Paul Ollendorff, 1913), pp. 184–85.

179 "I am glad . . .": MMA, December 12, 1917.

179 "last great artist . . .": MC to George Biddle, September 29, 1917, *LET,* p. 328.

179–80 " 'Oh, my dear . . .' ": Havemeyer, *Sixteen to Sixty,* pp. 243–44.

180 in the first state: Sue Walsh Reed and Barbara Stern

Shapiro, *Edgar Degas: The Painter as Printmaker* (Boston: Museum of Fine Arts, 1984), pp. 170–73.

181 "that bored and respectfully crushed . . .": McMullen, *Degas*, p. 267.

181 ". . . friendship I am honored": Edgar Degas to Le Comte Lepic, undated, *Degas Letters*, Marcel Guerin, ed. (Oxford: Bruno Cassirer, 1947), p. 144.

185 The Renoir expert: Letter from François Daulte to the author, June 4, 1985.

185 But Adelyn Breeskin: Telephone conversation with author, late June 1985.

186 "We do not . . . in any way . . .": Robert Cassatt to Aleck Cassatt [1878], quoted in *HA*, p. 81.

187 "idea of an interesting picture . . .": *HA*, p. 132.

187 "You will see the day . . .": Robert Cassatt to Aleck Cassatt, April 18, 1881, PHIL.

187 "I feel it almost . . .": MC to Aleck Cassatt, November 18, [1880], PHIL.

187 "was very wrong . . .": Katharine Cassatt to Aleck Cassatt, September 19, [1881], PHIL.

188 "We have been trying . . .": Katharine Cassatt to Aleck Cassatt, December 10, [1880], PHIL.

188 "For several days . . .": Robert Cassatt to Aleck Cassatt, August 2, 1882, PHIL.

188 "after the most indulgent treatment . . .": Robert Cassatt to Aleck Cassatt, September 1, 1882, PHIL.

188 "Yesterday Mame and I . . .": Robert Cassatt to Aleck Cassatt, July 3, 1882, PHIL.

189 "she never mingled socially . . .": *HA*, p. 83.

189 Mathews believes that: Nancy Mowll Mathews, *Mary Cassatt* (New York: Harry N. Abrams, 1987), p. 45.

190 "If painting is no longer . . .": MC to Bertha Palmer, September 10, 1892, quoted in *CAR*, p. 79.

190 "I have been abandoning myself . . .": MC to Emily Sartain, May 22, [1871], *LET*, p. 70.

190 "I long to see you . . .": MC to Emily Sartain, June 7, [1871], ibid., p. 74.

190 "Oh how wild I am . . .": MC to Emily Sartain, October 27, [1871], ibid., p. 77.

190–91   "I got here this morning . . .": MC to Emily Sartain, October 5, [1872], ibid., p. 103.

191   But as Suzanne Lindsay points out . . . : Suzanne G. Lindsay, *Mary Cassatt and Philadelphia* exhibition catalog, Philadelphia Museum of Art, 1985, pp. 54–55.

193   "Mame is lamentably deficient . . .": *HA*, p. 118.

193   "Mame was very sick . . .": Robert Cassatt to Aleck Cassatt, August 20, 1883, PHIL.

194   ". . . good spirits . . .": Robert Cassatt to Aleck Cassatt, May 25, 1883, ibid.

194   "Do not forget . . .": Robert Cassatt to Aleck Cassatt, June 25, 1883, ibid.

194   "As the time approaches . . .": Robert Cassatt to Aleck Cassatt, July 16, 1883, ibid.

194–95   "I feel very badly . . .": *HA*, pp. 128–29.

195   "I am glad you wrote . . .": ibid., p. 129.

195   "The apartment in Paris . . .": ibid.

195–96   "had had a fall . . .": Guérin, *Degas Letters*, pp. 125–26.

196   "This is not a natural . . .": Robert Cassatt to Aleck Cassatt, January 30, [1891], PHIL.

196   "I didn't tell you . . .": Katharine Cassatt to Aleck Cassatt, July 23, 1891, ibid.

196–97   "That is as much . . .": Robert Cassatt to Aleck Cassatt, July 28, 1891, ibid.

197   "Neither Mother nor I . . .": MC to Aleck Cassatt, December 17, [1891], ibid.

197   "There are two ways . . .": *HA*, p. 151.

199   "So you think my models . . .": MC to Theodate Pope, February 19, 1911, *LET*, p. 306.

199   "but gradually I began . . .": *HA*, pp. 163–64.

199   "I am wholly . . .": *SW*, p. 133.

200–201   "I have tried to express . . .": MC to Bertha Palmer, November 11, [1882], ibid., pp. 130–31.

204   "All my childhood . . .": *ML*, pp. 16–17.

204   " . . . After that I always imagined . . .": ibid., p. 15.

204   "fourth fortune": ibid., p. 16.

204–205   "Before the collapse . . .": ibid.

205   "state of perfect ecstasy": ibid., p. 49.

205   For Macdougall's remarks about the Duncans' situation, see *RAL*, p. 52.

205 many invitations to dance: *ML*, p. 54.

205 "Even the British Museum . . .": ibid., p. 59. (I owe to writer Lawrence Stewart the connection to Ira Gershwin's line.)

206 "The most general appearance . . .": Henry James, *Critical Prefaces*, quoted in Henri Dorra, *The American Muse* (New York: Viking, 1961), p. 130.

206 ". . . awakened a frenzy of enthusiasm . . .": *ML*, p. 65.

206 "to reconstruct the movements . . .": *RAL*, p. 54.

207 "Dear Mr. Ainslie . . .": This and the following undated letters from ID to Douglas Ainslie in this chapter, including the sonnet of December 13, 1899, are located in the Douglas Ainslie Archive, HRC.

209 "what a mind!": *ML*, p. 71.

209 "will go down the centuries . . .": ibid., p. 72.

209 "I was always . . .": ibid., p. 71.

209 ". . . give it another expression": ibid., p. 73.

210 "terribly embarrassed . . . the strange land of Love": ibid., p. 74.

210 "to erect a temple . . .": *ISA*, p. 56.

210 "visiting goddess from . . .": *ML*, p. 106.

210 "This is, in fact . . .": *ISA*, p. 58.

210–11 "two large black eyes . . .": *ML*, p. 101.

211 "critic of the senses . . .": ibid., p. 105.

212 "where the audience . . .": ibid., p. 141.

212–13 "explaining to me all the words . . .": ibid.

213–14 "strange change". . . "knell of Love's funeral": ibid., pp. 106–107.

214 "Beregi and Isadora . . .": Gedeon P. Dienes, "Isadora Duncan in Hungary," *Proceedings of the Society of Dance History Scholars 1987*, p. 153.

215 "I am as it were . . .": *YI*, p. 108.

216 "I had lived chastely . . .": *ML*, p. 147.

216 "a nice Greekish lady . . .": *YI*, p. 22, from *Book Topsy*, Craig Archive, HRC.

217 "just moving . . . speaking . . .": *YI*, p. 23; BBC radio talk; partially printed in *The Listener*, June 5, 1952.

217 "The next thing she does is to . . .": *YI*, pp. 24–29; from *Book Topsy*, Craig Archive, HRC.

218 "Thank you Thank you . . .": ID to Gordon Craig, December 23, 1904, ibid., p. 30. All letters between ID

and Gordon Craig in *YI* are from PARC-CD unless otherwise noted.

218 "You dear—dearest . . .": ID to Gordon Craig, December 25, [1904], ibid., p. 35.

218 "All has been easy . . .": ibid., p. 36; from *Book Topsy*, Craig Archive, HRC.

218–19 "psychically aware". . . "fairy tale of Psyche": *ML*, pp. 180–82.

222 "The mark of . . .": ibid., p. 17.

222 "Dear—I feel . . .": ID to Gordon Craig, March 1905, *YI*, p. 83.

223 "Be Calm Big Clear & Cool": Gordon Craig to ID, quoted in ID to Gordon Craig, March 16, 1905, ibid.

223 "I'll put it down . . .": ID to Gordon Craig, March 16, 1905, ibid., p. 84.

223 "If there is anyone . . .": ID to Gordon Craig, July or August 1906, ibid., p. 142.

223–24 "I am in love . . .": Edward Craig, *Gordon Craig* (New York: Alfred A. Knopf, 1968), pp. 195–96.

224 "If you could see . . .": ibid., p. 197.

225 ". . . I'm dying for you . . .": ID to Gordon Craig, March 22 [or 23], 1905, *YI*, p. 87.

225 "that he had . . .": ibid., p. 83.

225–26 "so complete". . . "preferred to turn . . .": *ML*, p. 183.

226 "I loved her . . .": Edward Craig, *Gordon Craig*, p. 223.

226 "In her opinion . . .": *YI*, p. 47.

226–27 "Dearest Sweetest Spirit": ID to Gordon Craig, December 23, 1904, ibid., p. 30.

227 "Beauty—Inspiration Genius . . .": ID to Gordon Craig, December 1906, ibid., p. 167.

227 "O you you you . . .": ID to Gordon Craig, undated, ibid., pp. 79–80.

227 "How do you find *me* . . .": ID to Gordon Craig, December 27, 1904, ibid., p. 50.

228 "How can I? . . .": ID to Gordon Craig, February 24, 1905, ibid., p. 73.

230 "Only true loneliness . . .": Gordon Craig to ID (draft), September 15, 1907, ibid., p. 260.

230 "The feminine spirit . . .": ID to Gordon Craig, March 1907, ibid., p. 212.

230 "terrible days and nights . . .": *Self Portrait of an*

Artist, Lady Kennet (Kathleen Bruce), John Murray, London, 1949, p. 61.

231 "with a faint childlike smile . . .": ibid., p. 63.

231 "a strange illness". . . "Craig came flying . . .": *ML,* p. 206.

231 Francis Steegmuller notes: *YI,* p. 192.

231 "Silly me, to get so ill . . .": ID to Gordon Craig, [January 24, 1907], ibid., p. 191.

231 "Dr. says *perhaps* . . .": ID to Gordon Craig, February 7 [or 8], 1907, ibid., p. 194.

231–32 "I am getting ashamed . . .": ID to Gordon Craig, late February 1907, ibid., p. 203.

232 "It is true . . .": ID to Gordon Craig, February or March 1907, ibid., p. 204.

232 "Are you my pulses . . .": ID to Gordon Craig, [March 9, 1907], ibid., pp. 204–205.

232 "O I tell you . . .": ibid.

233 "Black Figures". . . "antithesis . . .": ibid., p. 229.

233 "My money is at an end": ID to Gordon Craig, July or August 1907, ibid., p. 253.

233 "going ahead with . . .": Gordon Craig to ID (draft), July or August 1907, ibid., p. 254.

233 ". . . Topsy to help you": ID to Gordon Craig, July or August 1907, ibid., p. 256.

233–34 "sufficiently supplied in funds . . .": ibid., p. 228.

234 "I think that I . . .": ibid., p. 264 n.

234 "I adored Craig . . .": *ML,* p. 208.

234 "Jealousy was, astonishingly . . .": *RI,* p. 107.

234 "in all his beauty . . .": *ML,* p. 208.

235 "The presence of Pim . . .": ibid., p. 211.

235 "pretty, blond, blue-eyed . . .": *RI,* p. 108.

235 "he was always . . .": *ML,* p. 184.

236 "An ordinary walk . . .": ibid.

236 "a great Egyptian Temple . . .": ibid., p. 199.

237 "reading daily about Egypt": *YI,* p. 137 n.

237 "I study each day . . .": ID to Gordon Craig, probably early July 1906, ibid., p. 137.

237 "I am becoming so learned . . .": ID to Gordon Craig, probably July or August 1906, ibid., p. 141.

237 "the new Egyp. book . . .": ID to Gordon Craig, probably September 1906, ibid., p. 152.

237 "Two nice Egyptian books . . .": ID to Gordon Craig, October 11, 1906, ibid., p. 153.

237–38 " 'Thy Name, thy true Name . . .' ": M. A. Murray, *Ancient Egyptian Legends* (London: John Murray, 1920), pp. 83–85.

238 "I have a wild . . .": ID to Gordon Craig, probably January or February 1908, *YI*, p. 287.

238 "I.D. is expecting me . . .": ibid., p. 287 n.

238 "Very far back . . .": Arnold Rood, ed., *Gordon Craig on Movement and Dance* (New York: Dance Horizons, 1977), pp. 62, 67.

PART FOUR

Page

241 "Oh the world Louie! . . .": MMA, May 9, 1918.

241 "Americans have the defense . . .": ibid., June 25, 1918.

241 "Everything is difficult . . .": ibid., July 19, 1918.

241–42 "I have given up the idea . . .": ibid., August 16, 1918.

242 "My sight is getting . . .": ibid., August 24, 1918.

242 "Everything will be . . .": ibid., September 22, 1918.

243–44 "Had bad luck . . .": ID to Mary Desti, undated, UCLA.

244 "How can I . . .": ID to Mary Desti, undated, ibid.

244–45 "Have sent you . . .": ID to Mary Desti, April 16, 1918, ibid.

245 "Still not a word . . .": ID to Mary Desti, April 26, 1918, ibid.

246 "I spent some terrible . . .": *ML*, p. 346.

247 "The operation was . . .": MMA, November 14, 1919.

247 "Those who have gone . . .": ibid., January 1, 1920.

247 "Oh Louie dear . . .": ibid., March 31, 1920.

247 "If only I could . . .": ibid., April 13, 1920.

247 "I am so tired . . .": ibid., April 30, 1920.

248 "It is too nice . . .": ibid., April 30, 1920.

248 "even the nurse . . .": ibid., February 7, 1920.

248 "People think I lived . . .": ibid., April 4, 1920.

249 "Do you wonder . . .": ibid., April 9, 1920.

249 ". . . no one who is coming here . . .": ibid., May 18, 1920.

249 "I wanted to tell you . . .": ibid., undated.

249 "When I think . . .": ibid., February 7, 1920.
250 "I sold to the DR's . . .": ibid., March 22, 1920.
250–51 "by far the best . . .": ibid., November 18, 1920.
251 "What an irony . . .": ibid., November 29, 1920.
251 "The Lost Bower" can be found in Elizabeth Barrett Browning, *The Complete Poetical Works* (Boston: Houghton Mifflin, 1900), pp. 149–55.
253–54 "who only cared for spiritual . . .": MMA, December 11, 1913.
255–56 "Please don't let anyone . . .": ID to Duncan Dancers, undated, *RAL*, pp. 173–74.
256–57 "Much as we loved Isadora . . .": *DD*, p. 163.
259 " 'grande dame' of the art world": *LET*, p. 269.
259 "Mary Cassatt, sister . . .": Suzanne A. Lindsay, *Mary Cassatt and Philadelphia*, exhibition catalog, Philadelphia Museum of Art, 1985, p. 9.
259 "an artist of . . .": ibid.
260 "I am glad the Veronese . . .": MC to Henry Havemeyer, MMA, [August 1901].
260 "Here is a letter . . .": ibid., November 20, 1903.
260–61 "the great need . . .": *HA*, p. 187.
261–62 "The pictures belong . . .": *HA*, p. 203.
262 "I was scared to death . . .": ibid., pp. 203–204.
262 " 'dressed elegantly, from Redfern . . .' ": ibid., pp. 183–84.
262–63 "You and I . . .": MMA, March 10, 1908.
263 "You may not . . .": MC to Emily Phillips Cassatt, August 25, 1902, PHIL.
263 "You're nasty to . . .": *HA*, p. 150.
264 "I instantly realized . . .": *DD*, p. 185.
264–65 "appeared to be . . . awfully jealous": ibid., p. 188.
265 "tells of a spirit . . .": *ML*, pp. 347–48.
265 " 'preferred to make . . .' ": *RI*, pp. 246–47.
265–66 "holy hours, our united souls . . .": *ML*, pp. 350–51.
266 "a spasm of rage . . .": ibid., pp. 353–55.
267 ". . . the highest expression of all . . .": *DD*, p. 194.
267 "the Greek goddess Demeter . . .": ibid., p. 196.
267–68 "What a strange . . .": *ML*, pp. 356–57.
269 "a large mama . . .": *RAL*, p. 46.
270 "agony of spirit": *ML*, pp. 9–10.
270 ". . . Beethoven, Schumann, Schubert . . .": ibid., p. 13.

270   "beautiful and restless spirit": ibid., p. 22.

270   "too busy to . . .": ibid., p. 11.

270   "quite forgot about us . . .": ibid., p. 18.

271   "We *must* leave . . .": ibid., p. 20.

271   "somewhat dazed, but . . .": ibid., p. 25.

271   "went around to . . .": ibid., p. 183.

271   "shortly afterwards": ibid., p. 188.

272   "Why wasn't my dear mother . . .": ibid., p. 193.

272   "I have been having . . .": ID to Gordon Craig, [October 1907], *YI*, p. 265.

272   "Mama insisted on . . .": ID to Gordon Craig, [November 1907], ibid., p. 272.

272–73 ". . . the times of privation . . .": *ML*, pp. 187–88.

273–74 "Art in its highest forms . . .": Robert Ingersoll, "Art and Morality," *Collected Works* (New York: C. P. Farrell, 1900) 11:206–11.

274–75 "Isadora's mother used . . .": oral history, Sulgwynn Boynton Quitzow, "Dance at the Temple of the Wings: The Boynton-Quitzow Family in Berkeley" [a typescript of an oral history conducted 1972 by Suzanne B. Riess], Regional Oral History Office, University of California at Berkeley, 1973, p. 45

276   "attended Madame Campan's . . .": *HA*, p. 5.

277   ". . . an unnecessary expense": MC to Emily Sartain, June 25, [1873], *LET*, p. 122.

277   ". . . acquaintances among the Americans . . .": Katharine Cassatt to Aleck Cassatt, December 23, 1881, *HA*, p. 86.

277–78 "This morning I . . .": Katharine Cassatt to Aleck Cassatt, [1878], ibid., p. 77.

278   "I didn't encourage her . . .": Katharine Cassatt to Aleck Cassatt, December 10, 1880, PHIL.

278   "I don't know . . .": Katharine Cassatt to Aleck Cassatt, December 10, 1886, ibid.

278–79 "Mary is at work . . .": Katharine Cassatt to Aleck Cassatt, July 23, 1891, ibid.

279   "Anyone who had the privilege . . .": *HA*, p. 175.

279   "Nothing that my mother . . .": MMA, August 24, 1920.

279   "My mistake was . . .": *HA*, p. 276.

283–84 "an embittered old woman . . .": Forbes Watson, *Mary*

Cassatt (New York: Whitney Museum, 1932), pp. 7, 13.

283 "Watson told a friend . . .": *HA*, p. 280.

285 "I had the detached feeling . . .": *ML*, pp. 358–59.

286 "I believe there is . . .": Ingersoll, *Collected Works*, 11:451–53.

286 "I am sick of . . .": *RI*, p. 266.

287 ". . . a 'Callot Soeurs' creation": ibid., p. 274.

288 "six-foot high pile . . .": ibid., p. 275.

288 "Isadora gathered the children . . .": *IDRD*, p. 52.

288 "strangely impressed": ibid., p. 55.

288 "the red flag waving . . .": ibid., p. 57.

289 "might if he wanted . . .": ibid., p. 61.

289 "The last few years . . .": Ilya Ilyich Schneider, *Isadora Duncan: The Russian Years* (New York: Da Capo, 1968), p. 40.

290 "If Freedom means . . .": *IDRD*, pp. 67–68.

290 "world-famous artist . . .": *RI*, p. 284.

291 "Isadora's interpretation . . .": ibid., p. 285.

292 "Heroism, Strength, and Light": *ISA*, p. 299, PARC-ID.

293 "last village poet": *RI*, p. 293.

293 "his modesty was a fine cover . . .": *ISA*, p. 302.

293 "Esenin became her master . . .": *IDRD*, p. 105.

294–95 "He said: . . .": ibid., pp. 114–15.

295 "brilliant festival" . . .". . . my vocabulary": *RI*, p. 305.

296 "they were very sorry . . .": Sol Hurok, *Impresario* (New York: Random House, 1946), p. 99.

297 "that she had been held . . .": ibid., p. 100.

297 "grandly gesturing the . . .": ibid., p. 101.

298 "I watched a . . .": Edwin Denby, *Dance Writings*, Robert Cornfield and William Mackay, eds. (New York: Alfred A. Knopf, 1986), pp. 88–89.

298 "exquisite innocence": H. T. Parker, *Motion Arrested: Dance Reviews of H. T. Parker*, Olive Holmes, ed. (Middletown, Conn.: Wesleyan University Press, 1982), p. 56.

298–99 "Quite as sedulously . . .": ibid., pp. 59–60.

299 "grown somewhat too stout . . .": ibid., p. 65.

299–301 "Miss Duncan, who . . .": ibid., pp. 68–69.

301–302   "minor excess". . . "It was also . . .": ibid., pp. 71–73.
302   "I thought she was awful . . .": George Balanchine, quoted in Walter Terry, *Isadora Duncan: Her Life, Her Art, Her Legacy* (New York: Dodd, Mead, 1963), pp. 160–61.
303   "the pig is a symbol . . .": Erich Neumann, *The Great Mother: An Analysis of the Archetype* (Princeton: Princeton University Press, 1963), p. 139.
304   "It is absolutely necessary . . .": Camille Pissarro, quoted in *SW*, p. 119.
304–305   "If you would like . . .": MC to Berthe Morisot, [April 1890], *LET*, p. 214.
305   "together with the sets . . .": Frank Getlein, *Mary Cassatt: Paintings and Prints* (New York: Abbeville, 1980), p. 88.
309   "It seems Mr. Ivins . . .": MC to Joseph Durand-Ruel, January 13, [1924], ibid., p. 337.
309   "I must at once . . .": MC to William Ivins, January 17, 1924, AAA, William Ivins papers.
309–10   "I must be boring you . . .": MC to Joseph Durand-Ruel, January 19, 1924, *LET*, p. 339.
310   "I have no respect . . .": MC to Harris Whittemore, May 12, 1924, ibid., p. 341.
310   "But I have a joy . . .": MC to William Ivins, January 17, 1924, AAA, William Ivins papers.
311   "She's become a viper": A. F. Jaccaci, quoted in *HA*, p. 150.
312–16   "Yes, I am leaving . . .": ID, "America Makes Me Sick," Hearst's *American Weekly*, January 1923.

PART FIVE

Page

319   "If you would save . . .": *US*, pp. 120–21.
319–20   "delicious little dinner . . .": ibid., pp. 122–23.
320   " 'Mary dear, I can't explain . . .' ": ibid., pp. 124–25.
320–21   "I hear him coming". . . "an old rogue": ibid., pp. 125–31.
322   "Now began one . . .": ibid., pp. 133–34.
323   "very sight of this obese . . .": *RI*, pp. 334–35.

323–24   "All through Germany . . .": *US*, pp. 134–37.

325   "What had come over . . .": ibid., p. 143.

325–26   "wild with excitement . . .": ibid., pp. 162–64.

326–27   "Place your hands . . .": *IDRD*, p. 177.

329   "like one demented . . .": ibid., p. 196.

329   "creations of love . . .": ibid., p. 211.

330   "he was 'a broken man' . . .": Gordon McVay, *Isadora and Esenin* (Ann Arbor, Mich.: Ardis, 1980), pp. 204–205.

330   " 'When I felt passion . . .' ": ibid., p. 216.

330   "Don't send any more letters . . .": ibid., p. 215.

331   "presumably deserves little credence": ibid., p. 219.

331   ". . . Isadora would sit for hours . . .": *US*, p. 170.

331   "You spend too much time . . .": *IDRD*, p. 133.

331–32   "a much discussed scene" . . ."Isadora was stunned . . .": *RI*, p. 354.

332–33   "Then I will come . . .": ibid., pp. 350–51.

335   "was hailed and cheered . . .": *IDRD*, p. 235.

335   "Anyone with even . . .": *RI*, p. 356.

335–36   "Here is more catastrophe . . .": *IDRD*, p. 245. (This and the following letters from Isadora to Irma Duncan are in PARC-ID.)

336   "We go from one catastrophe . . .": ibid., pp. 247–48.

336   "This tournée is . . .": ibid., pp. 249–51.

337   "In fifty degrees . . .": ibid., pp. 251–53.

337   "You have no idea . . .": ibid., pp. 254–55.

337   "I haven't a bottle . . .": ibid., pp. 256–57.

338   "But this is a primitive . . .": ibid., pp. 250–51.

339   "blended into a great spectrum . . .": John A. Wilson, *The Burden of Egypt* (Chicago: University of Chicago Press, 1951), p. 47.

341–42   "The gestures of mankind . . .": Rainer Maria Rilke, *Rodin* (Salt Lake City: Peregrine Smith, 1979), p. 42.

343   "I am here *stranded* . . .": ID to Mary Desti, December 7, 1924, UCLA.

343   *"You never answer* . . .": ID to Mary Desti, March 24, 1925, ibid.

344   "I am installed . . .": ID to Mary Desti, ibid.

344–46   "I was a precious, spoilt youth . . .": Sir Francis Rose, "Isadora Really," *Vogue* (July 1969), pp. 103–105, 161–63.

346   "Mary Cassatt's life . . .": *SW*, p. 207.

346   "Laurence Vail had an exhibition . . .": Kay Boyle and Robert McAlmon, *Being Geniuses Together* (Garden City, N.Y.: Doubleday, 1968), pp. 182–83.

346–49   "The night I returned . . .": Mercedes de Acosta, *Here Lies the Heart* (New York: Reynal, 1960), pp. 170–73.

349   "Isadora Duncan will not . . .": ibid., p. 173.

349   "One of Isadora's . . .": ibid., p. 175.

349–50   "I await your coming . . .": ID to Mercedes de Acosta, undated, ROSE.

350–51   "*Beneath a forehead . . .*": ID to Mercedes de Acosta, 1927, ibid.

351   "Adorée J'ai . . .": ID to Mercedes de Acosta, undated, ibid.

352   "lean, bent, over-worked . . .": Forbes Watson, *Mary Cassatt* (New York: Whitney Museum, 1932), p. 14.

352–53   "While I was playing . . .": M. R. Werner [Victor Seroff], *To Whom It May Concern* (New York: Jonathan Cape and Smith, 1931), pp. 245–48.

353   "No one but Mademoiselle Cassatt . . .": *HA*, p. 281.

353   "I remember her . . .": Rose, "Isadora Really," p. 162.

353–54   "Her art was seen . . .": Janet Flanner, *Paris Was Yesterday: 1925–1939* (New York: Viking, 1972), p. 32.

354   "Once McAlmon and I . . .": Boyle and McAlmon, *Being Geniuses Together*, pp. 334–35.

354   "I went to see Isadora . . .": Mary Desti to Preston Sturges, May 7, 1927, UCLA.

354   "Isadora is dancing . . .": Mary Desti to Preston Sturges, June 3, 1927, ibid.

354–55   "The amateurish management . . .": *RI*, p. 422.

355   "The theatre was packed . . .": *RAL*, p. 271.

355   "Her last dance program . . .": Boyle and McAlmon, *Being Geniuses Together*, p. 342.

356   "The room at the Negresco . . .": Sewell Stokes, *Isadora Duncan: An Intimate Portrait* (London: Brentano, 1928), pp. 96–97.

356–57   "She lay, quite blind . . .": George Biddle, *An American Artist's Story* (Boston: Little, Brown, 1939), pp. 218–20.

358–62   "I hated to . . .": *US*, pp. 250–81.

362–63   "For a long time . . .": *SW*, pp. 208–209.

ACKNOWLEDGMENTS

Among the many who have been helpful to me in my work on this book, I am particularly indebted to Terry Craig, John M. Dean, Trent Duffy, Mary Boyd Ellis, Margaretta Mitchell, Bill Reynolds, Edith Shoor, Peter Stansky, and Inga Weiss.

I have received invaluable help from the following institutions: The Archives of American Art, Smithsonian Institution; The Bancroft Library, University of California at Berkeley; The Beinecke Rare Book and Manuscript Library, Yale University Library; The Department of Special Collections, the University Library, University of California at Los Angeles; The Harry Ransom Humanities Research Center, University of Texas at Austin (and, in particular, Cathy Henderson); The Metropolitan Museum of Art (and, in particular, Archivist Jeanie M. James); The Performing Arts Research Center of The New York Public Library at Lincoln Center; The Philadelphia Museum of Art; The Rosenbach Museum and Library (and, in particular, Ellen Dunlap); The San Francisco Performing Arts Library and Museum (and, in particular, Steve Steinberg and Cliff Bodamer).

I wish to express my gratitude to the following for their generosity: to J. Robert Maguire for permission to quote from published and unpublished letters by Mary Cassatt; to Angus Duncan for permission to quote from unpublished letters by Isadora Duncan; to Sandy Sturges for permission to quote from unpublished letters by Mary Desti; to OEloel Q. Braun for permission to quote from the unpublished memoir of Florence Boynton; to the estate of John Cowper Powys for permission to quote from a letter from Powys to Isadora Duncan; and to Madame Rhodia Dufet Bourdelle for permission to include photographs of drawings by Antoine Bourdelle of Isadora Duncan.

I want to thank the Rockefeller Foundation for granting me a residency at the Bellagio Center at a crucial time in the creation of this work. I also wish to thank the National Endowment for the Humanities for a Travel to Collections grant in 1986 and the Djerassi Foundation (and, in particular, Sally Stillman).

I wish to acknowledge my debt to previously published work on Isadora Duncan and Mary Cassatt. I particularly wish to mention, among Cassatt scholars and biographers, Adelyn Breeskin, Nancy Hale, Suzanne G. Lindsay, Nancy Mowll Mathews, and Frederick Sweet; and, among Duncan scholars and biographers, Fredrika Blair, Irma Duncan, Mary Desti, Maurice Dumesnil, Allan Ross Macdougall, Victor Seroff, and Francis Steegmuller.

Finally, though he should come first of all in these acknowledgments, I thank my friend and editor William Abrahams.

INDEX